ALSO BY TATE JAMES

MADISON KATE
Hate
Liar
Fake
Kate

HADES
7th Circle
Anarchy
Club 22
Timber

LIAR

TATE JAMES

Bloom books

Published by Bloom Books, an imprint of Sourcebooks
P.O. Box 4410, Naperville, Illinois 60567-4410
(630) 961-3900
sourcebooks.com

Originally self-published in 2020 by Tate James.

Cataloging-in-Publication data is on file with the Library of Congress.

Printed and bound in Canada.
MBP 10 9 8 7 6 5 4 3 2 1

For Irene.
You would have loved Kody, I think.

CHAPTER 1

Kody

It'd been two full weeks since Halloween.

Two weeks since I'd finally kissed Madison Kate the way I'd been wanting to for an entire year.

Two weeks since she'd run from us, crashed my car, then suffered a brutal attack at The Laughing Clown.

Two weeks since she'd looked at me with such horror on her face while blood dripped from her fingers. Pure, undiluted terror in her gorgeous violet-blue eyes.

Two weeks since I'd almost lost her forever.

Then again, maybe I had...

"Why isn't she home yet?" I grumbled aloud, looking at the time on my watch for what seemed like the hundredth time in the space of an hour. "You said she was getting discharged at ten, right?" I looked over at Arch, and he just glared back at me. His face was still showing the splotchy purple and green bruises from the ass kicking he'd taken in the octagon last week. Served him fucking right for fighting while distracted.

"You know that's what the hospital said," he replied in a growly, irritated tone. Well, fuck him. It was his fault we weren't there to pick her up ourselves. We should be.

It'd been two weeks since Madison Kate had collapsed at Steele's feet, that gut-wrenching expression of fear on her face. Two weeks since we'd loaded her unconscious body into our stolen vehicle and rushed her to the hospital, covered in blood from her head wound and the deep stab in her abdomen.

It'd been one week since she'd woken up. Since she'd seen Archer sitting beside her bed and *screamed*.

That sound still chilled me when I heard it in my dreams. She'd been hysterical, and the nurses had ended up sedating her again. Arch had left the room and not returned once. Not that he could have... We'd all been stricken from her permitted visitors list and no number of bribes or threats had changed that.

Madison Kate had accused us of attacking her. When the sedatives had worn off, the police had spoken with her. She'd pointed the finger at the three of us. Except, we'd already been questioned and cleared. Par for the course when three guys turn up to a hospital in the middle of the night with a blood-soaked heiress.

The police in charge of her case had assured us that they'd communicated this to her. But as the days had ticked by and the silence stretched, our unease had built.

"She's not coming back here," Steele said in a quiet voice. His fingertips drummed on the arm of the sofa, and I could tell he was itching to play again. To compose. But in some fucked-up self-punishment, he was holding himself back.

"You don't know that," Archer snapped. He was pissed off, and I didn't blame him. "She's stubborn, like a splinter. She'll come back just to be an infuriating bitch and stand her ground here in *her* house."

Steele shook his head, giving Arch the kind of pitying look that was likely to get him punched. "You can only hope, bro. I'm going for a run. All this waiting around is getting me fucking anxious."

He left the room with a heavy, defeated sigh. Neither Arch nor I said anything to stop him either. What the fuck could we even say? Steele was hurting, that much was obvious. He'd given MK space after her stalker had threatened him, but now he was regretting all the unfinished business between them.

So was I, for that matter. I was regretting all kinds of unfinished business with MK, and it was driving me crazy.

Arch? Who the fuck knew what was going on inside his head. He still maintained his delusional opinion that MK was some kind of spoiled brat that deserved a few hard knocks in life. But then… why'd he sit beside her bed around the clock while she was unconscious? Why'd he lose his debut UFC fight after she'd woken up screaming that morning?

"Maybe we should call the hospital again," I suggested, feeling utterly hopeless. She should have been home by now.

Arch rolled his eyes and sighed, like I was being a pest, but he still pulled out his phone and hit redial. He placed the phone to his ear, and I tried really hard not to fidget while waiting. I knew the drill by now. He'd have to speak to the right person to get information, now that we'd been removed from her list. It could take a few moments.

Steele's feet thumped on the stairs as he jogged back down, and I went to intercept him before he left the house.

"Running isn't going to fix it," I told him, leaning on the wall as he sat on the stairs to pull on his sneakers. It'd turned freezing in the past week, so he was dressed for the cold in sweatpants, a hoodie, and a puffer vest.

"Fix what?" he replied, in total denial. His fingers trembled slightly as he tied his laces, and I sighed.

"That." I indicated to his shaking hands. "You need to go and fucking work on whatever tune is rattling around in your brain. I haven't seen you this bad since…" I trailed off because there was a *line* and I'd just come dangerously close to crossing it.

Steele's face hardened, his eyes tightening. "Thanks for the advice, Kody," he muttered, his voice betraying his anger and frustration at my blunder. "I'll be fine. I'm not... I can't..." He shook his head, his hand clenched. "I'll be fine."

I was inclined to disagree but also wasn't in the mood to argue with him.

"I'll spar with you later if you want," he offered, his hand resting on the door handle. "You don't exactly exude calm right now yourself."

I grimaced, but he was right. I was next-level wound up and anxious. Maybe kicking the shit out of one of my best friends would help. Fuck knows I'd stopped winning against Arch about seven years ago, when he started getting massive.

"Sure," I replied with a sigh. "Sounds good. Just keep your wits about you out there, okay?"

Steele flashed me a cocky grin, lifting his sweatshirt to show me his Glock 19 in a concealed holster. "Let them fucking try me, bro. I've got this."

I snorted a laugh, clapping him on the shoulder. He was probably more dangerous than both Arch and me combined. If MK's stalker really did want to follow through on their threats, they'd get a rude awakening.

"Guys," Archer called out, pausing Steele halfway through the front door. As much as he wanted to act unaffected by MK's silence, he cared. "She was discharged early."

Archer's words were like a blow. "What? Like, earlier this morning? Why isn't she home, then?"

He looked at me with a flat, don't-be-fucking-stupid expression. "No, like three days ago."

My heart pounded a bit too fast. "How? How could they discharge her? Was Samuel—"

"No." Archer shook his head. "No, Samuel and my mom are still in Italy on a yacht with their shitty friends. They're due to

4

return in a few days, but last I spoke to them, Sam had no plans to come back early."

"So how was she discharged early?" Steele demanded. "I thought you—"

"She discharged herself." Archer cut him off, his jaw clenched and the vein in his temple throbbing. "She's a legal adult, and there's no reason why she can't."

He was right. She didn't need a direct family member to discharge her if the doctors declared her well enough to make that choice for herself. Stubborn girl.

I asked the question we were all thinking. "Where is she, then?"

Archer's eyes hardened further. "I have no idea."

"How is *that* possible?" Steele challenged him, and Archer's fist clenched at his side. I'd bet money he was thinking about punching Steele right in the face.

Stepping between them, I tried to diffuse the tension. "Back down, dude," I told Steele, giving him a hard glare. He scowled back at me but folded his arms and took a step outside to create a bit of space.

I turned back to Archer. "What *do* we know?"

"Just that she discharged herself and was picked up by an Uber. I'll find her, though. Even if it just helps you two stop sulking around here like your puppy got run over." He cocked a brow at Steele and me like *we* were the ones sulking.

I scoffed a laugh, shaking my head. "Right. You're doing it for us."

Steele muttered something under his breath, then gave us a tight smile. "I'm out. Catch you losers later."

His breath fogged in front of him as he flipped his hood up, then jogged down the front steps and across the fresh dusting of snow on the driveway.

"We need to find MK before Steele slides back into that dark place again," I commented quietly as both Arch and I watched our friend jog down the long driveway.

Archer grunted a noise of agreement, his arms folded over his chest. "I'll find her," he said with total confidence, "but she's not going to willingly stay here."

He went back into the house, leaving me standing there shivering and mentally cursing the infuriating girl who'd walked into our lives a year ago and set off a fucking pipe bomb.

Archer was right. She wasn't coming home. Not if she had any choice in the matter.

So…we'd simply have to take her choice away.

After all, we could do that.

Or Archer could.

CHAPTER 2

Madison Kate

It'd been three days since I'd discharged myself from Shadow Grove General Hospital. Three days since I'd taken Bree's offer of help… and her credit card.

Now I was doing something that could possibly be my stupidest decision to date. Or hell, who knows? Maybe it'd be the best thing I'd ever done for myself.

My Uber pulled away from the curb, leaving me standing out in front of a rough kind of bar, deep within what used to be West Shadow Grove. It looked identical to how I'd seen it just a few weeks earlier, when some deeply repressed memories had resurfaced.

My new phone vibrated in the pocket of my jeans, and I pulled it out to answer, all while stalling what I'd been on my way to do.

"Hey, girl," I said, shivering despite the warmth of my leather jacket. "What's up?"

Bree was the *only* one with my new number. I'd have happily not had a phone at all, but she'd talked me into it from a safety perspective.

"Your boys were just over here," she replied, and my stomach lurched. I'd known they'd work it out sooner or later—that I'd discharged myself and wasn't coming home. But that'd been quicker than I'd given them credit for. "Don't worry," she continued in a rush. "I didn't tell them anything. I didn't even lie because I *don't* know where you are. Why won't you tell me, again?"

I snickered. "For that exact reason. They'd get it out of you somehow. Fuck, they've probably already worked out I'm using your credit card, and I'll find them on my doorstep when I get back."

Bree made a thoughtful sound. "So you have a doorstep, then? Interesting."

I laughed again. "Idiot. You know I'm staying in a hotel, and it wouldn't be hard for you to check your credit card statement."

"I know," she replied, "but I won't. You trusted me when you had no one else to ask, and I won't let you down again, MK. You're my bitch."

"Stop it," I muttered. "You're making me blush with all this emotional crap."

"Jesus, you've got the emotional range of a damn cucumber sometimes, girl. Anyway, I wanted to let you know that they're on your trail. Want me to throw down any false leads?" Bree sounded far too into that idea, and I didn't have the heart to tell her it was pointless.

"Go for it," I replied instead. "I've got to go; I'm about to meet with an old family friend. I'll call you later, okay?"

"You better," she grumbled, "and I want to know which of those three bastards you're fucking, because guys don't act all caveman possessive like they just did when there's no penetration involved. Fact."

I had nothing to say back to that, so I just ended the call and slipped the phone back into my pocket. Her words had stirred up a whole pile of conflicting emotions, though.

I'd slept with Steele, and it had been incredible.

I'd made out with both Kody *and* Archer...

But was that enough for them to go "caveman possessive" like Bree said? She was likely exaggerating.

Then again, why did I care? A week ago, I'd thought they'd tried to kill me.

I still kind of believed they had, despite the evidence to the contrary.

Shoving those thoughts aside, I focused on the task at hand. My freshly colored pink hair was up in a messy bun, but loose tendrils tickled my face as I made my way across the parking lot. Motorcycles dominated the lot, but there were plenty of old beaters there too. I was certainly a long way from home.

I pushed through the main door and hesitated only a second before making my way to the bar. Every damn eye in there seemed to follow me as I picked my way across the room, but I kept my shoulders back and my head high.

"You lost, girl?" the middle-aged woman behind the bar asked me. Her brow held a crease of concern, but I shook my head.

"I'm looking to speak with someone," I told her with iron threaded into my tone. "I was told I might find him here at this time of day."

The bartender cocked a brow at me, clearly curious. "Oh yeah? Who's that, then?"

"Zane D'Ath," I replied. "Tell him Deb's daughter is here."

I waited for only a few minutes before the bartender ushered me through the kitchen and into a large back room filled with rough, tattooed guys and a handful of girls. Apparently the public side of the bar was exactly that: public. This side was all Reapers.

"Your funeral, girlie," the bartender muttered, closing the door again once I was inside. Shutting me in with the hungry wolves.

Shit. Maybe this was dumb.

Still, I couldn't back out now. So I hardened my expression and crossed the room to where a familiar face stared back at me.

"Madison Kate Danvers," Zane purred, raking his gaze over me and making a sound of appreciation. "You grew up."

I tucked my hands into my back pockets and gave him an unimpressed stare. "No shit. That's what time generally does to a person. The last time you saw me when I *wasn't* running away would have been, what, eight years ago? Seven?"

A cold smile curved his lips, tugging at the tattoos below his right eye. "Something like that." He stared back at me for a long, tense moment. There wasn't a lot of familial resemblance between him and Archer. For one thing, Zane was a fraction of Archer's size and all slim, wiry muscles where his little brother was bulk and hardened brawn. But it was there in his eyes, those same ice-blue eyes that seemed to cut like daggers.

"Why'd you come here, Madison Kate?" he asked when it became clear I wasn't going to say anything first. It was his kingdom, after all. "Seems like a real stupid move for a girl with your…connections." His lips twitched over that last word, like he was making fun of something.

I scowled. "If you mean the fact that your brother is living in my house, I have no control over that matter. I tried to get rid of him; he wouldn't go."

"*Your* house?" Zane repeated, that mocking smile pulling at his lips.

My glare flattened. "My father's house. Whatever."

He said nothing, his cold blue eyes not leaving my face for even a second, but then he nodded. "Look, I'm going to cut you the benefit of the doubt here, kid—seeing as you're clearly so deep in the dark you couldn't find your own cunt. Ask whatever burning questions made you put your life on the line, then get the fuck out of my bar."

A vaguely familiar guy with neck tats made a sound of protest, pushing the girl in his lap to the floor and slamming his beer glass down on the table.

"Boss," he started, but Zane shut him up with a sharp look.

"Actually, Skunk," Zane said, and the pieces clicked into place. Skunk. This was the guy Kody and Steele had beaten the shit out of a month ago at Bree's party. "You can serve as a visual example to Madison Kate of what happens when we wander into territory uninvited." Zane got up from his chair, dropping his own beer onto a table, and slouched his way over to Skunk. He kicked the table in front of Skunk out of the way, revealing two long plaster casts covering his legs from knee to ankle.

I gasped. Not out of shock—I already knew what had happened to him—but because I'd somehow managed to forget about that night in all the madness that'd followed.

"Here, little girl. Take a look at this." Zane yanked Skunks T-shirt up, revealing angry, purple-red scarring across his chest. I stared hard at the letters that had been cut into his flesh and made a mental note to stop pissing Archer off.

Strike One.

"This is what happens when my guys accidentally wander into my little brother's territory. So what do you think might happen to you, strutting straight into the Reapers' headquarters?" Zane released Skunk and took a few menacing steps toward me. He casually flipped out a butterfly knife that looked so much like Archer's I did a double take.

"She already knows, boss," Skunk answered for me, his voice a sneering growl of anger and resentment. "She was there when they did this to me."

Zane's brows shot up. "Was she, now?"

"I forgot until just now. Head injuries will do that to ya."

He glared daggers at me, and I skipped my gaze back to Zane.

Archer's brother was much closer now, allowing me to study him better. There were more echoes of Archer in his handsome face, and I could kind of see what my mom had been attracted to, even if he was probably fifteen years older than me.

"Maybe you're made of tougher stuff than I gave you credit for," he murmured, gesturing with his blade. On closer examination, it wasn't the same as Archer's. Where his had a blood-red blade and charcoal handle, Zane's was mostly black with a shimmer of red in the handle. Still, the shape had to be identical. Surely. It was such a unique design... "Come with me," Zane said, jerking his head in the direction of a fire door. He led the way outside, and I followed, shadowed by one of his silent men.

Once we were outside in the dirty alleyway beside dumpsters overflowing with beer bottles, the other guy took up a post beside the door, and Zane lit up a cigarette.

"Talk," he told me, waving his hand impatiently.

I flicked a glance at the silent guy, but Zane was totally ignoring him and I assumed I could do the same. "Are you stalking me?"

Zane's cigarette paused halfway to his lips, and the look he shot me was pure acid.

"Excuse me?"

Titling my chin up, I met his cool blue eyes unflinchingly. "You heard me. Are you stalking me? Because you're right up there at the top of my list of suspects."

Zane barked a laugh, throwing his head back, but it was hollow and fake. "Why the fuck would I want to stalk you, little girl? I'm no idiot; I won't mess with my brother's business."

I prickled at being called Archer's *business*. "Not what I've heard," I said instead. "Why was Skunk at my friend's party if not to *mess* with Archer's business?"

A cruel but amused smile lit Zane's lips. They were Archer's lips, I'd just noticed, and it sent a weird pang of sadness through me. "Just testing the limits a little. But back to your question. Why would you think I was stalking you?"

My fingers curled into balls, my nails digging painfully into my palms. "You tell me, Zane. Were you stalking my mom?"

He stilled, violent energy sweeping over him as he dropped his cigarette and stomped it out. He took a step closer, and a spark of fear ignited inside me. But instead of hitting me like I'd anticipated, he sighed and swept a hand through his black hair.

"No," he replied after a long, tense silence. "No, I would never have done that shit."

"Then why the hell were you chasing me on Riot Night?" I demanded, pushing on through my fear.

Zane's lips curved up again in a smile. "I'm an opportunist, Madison Kate. The daughter of Shadow Grove's richest citizen waltzes into my lap, I'm not going to pass that up. Besides, any chance I get to hurt Samuel Danvers, I'll take." He spat my father's name with clear disdain, and it confirmed what I'd already suspected to be the truth. The guys hadn't lied to me.

"Did you kill my mom?" I had to ask. I had to get it off my chest.

I already knew what his answer would be. After I'd woken up in the hospital, after I'd accused Archer of being the one who'd stabbed me and heard from the police that he'd already been investigated and cleared, I'd done my research.

For years, I'd been confident in my own memories. I had no need to look at the police reports because I'd *witnessed* it. But Steele's calm logic the night of Halloween had shaken me and made me question my own mind.

Sure enough, there had been a six-hour gap between my mom's time of death and Zane releasing me from the closet. He hadn't killed her, but he *had* saved me.

"No," he replied, his voice hoarse. "I didn't kill your mom, Madison Kate."

Neither one of us spoke for a while, and Zane lit up another cigarette. I fidgeted, all the bluster deflated from my sails suddenly, and he sighed.

"Here." He held out his freshly lit cigarette to me, then produced another for himself. "Calm your fucking nerves. You're so tightly wound you're making my skin itch."

I couldn't argue with that assessment, so I took a drag on the cigarette and noted the familiar hint of weed laced into the tobacco.

"So what prompted this visit?" Zane asked after we'd smoked in silence for a few minutes. "I take it you didn't just wake up determined to track down Deb's murderer and start knocking on doors?"

I wrinkled my nose and exhaled the smoke. "Long story," I muttered, "but I'd…forgotten lots of things. Until recently, anyway."

He nodded, not pushing me for more information. "Pretty normal when you experience such extreme trauma as an adolescent. They diagnosed you with PTSD, didn't they?"

I frowned slightly, unsure how he'd know that. "Not formally, but my shrink alluded to it. The only thing on my record is claustrophobia."

He grunted. "I can see that. When I found you in that closet…" He broke off with a shudder, no doubt reliving that night like I'd been doing every damn night for a week.

"Anyway. I remembered some stuff. My mom was being stalked. Like I am now. I think it's the same person." I took another deep drag on my cigarette, finishing it off, then dropping it to the ground to stomp out. I was in my favorite over-the-knee, black leather boots with a flat sole. It put me at a significant height disadvantage around all these big guys, but at least I could run in them if I needed to.

"Tell me everything," Zane ordered, dropping his own butt and folding his leather jacket–clad arms. "Start from the beginning and don't leave shit out, understood?" His voice crackled with authority, and I shivered. That supreme alpha-male bullshit must have been a genetic trait.

I glanced over at our silent guard again, suddenly aware of his presence, and he stared back at me with expressionless eyes. He was a tall guy, taller than Zane, and from what I could see, he was *covered* in ink. All the way up his neck, his fingers—he even had a few small tattoos on his scary fucking face. This guy…he was one terrifying motherfucker.

"Don't worry about Cass," Zane told me, answering my unspoken concerns. "He's my second."

I arched a brow. I had no idea what that meant in gang terms, but apparently it was supposed to inspire confidence in me. Somehow. Also, why the fuck was such a scary-ass guy called *Cass*?

Whatever. I sucked in a deep breath and started giving Zane my story. It wasn't what I'd intended to do. My plan had been to burst into his clubhouse and demand answers from him. He was, after my father, the only lead I had. And that spoke to how I felt about Samuel Danvers, that I'd rather walk into this viper's nest than pick up the phone.

I kept it as brief as possible, just the facts. It helped me to stay detached from the emotions of the whole fucked-up mess, but when I finished, Zane's brow was furrowed in a deep frown. Hell, even the mysterious Cass looked disturbed.

"Something doesn't add up here, boss," the scary dude said, his voice like gravel.

Zane nodded, still scowling.

"I'm not fucking lying about any of it," I snapped, folding my arms defensively.

"We didn't say you were," Zane replied with a note of annoyance. "But Cass is right." He paced the alley a few moments, clearly thinking as he lit up yet another cigarette.

"There was definitely more than one person trying to kill you at the Clown?" His question caught me off guard. I'd thought he would be more interested in the similarities between my mom's stalker and mine...

"Yeah," I confirmed, shrugging. "There had to be. He couldn't have been in two places at once."

Zane nodded, seeming to agree with my assessment there. "So. You have a stalker that sounds disturbingly similar to Deb's. He could have been stalking you for years if your piece-of-shit father hasn't been reporting the incidents."

"He possibly transferred his obsession from Deb to her daughter after she died," Cass commented. "Standard stalker behavior."

Zane grunted a sound of agreement. "So then the question is, who is trying to kill you?" His cool blue eyes flashed with something, and I suspected he already had ideas.

"You don't think they're one and the same?" I asked, even though I was already thinking a similar thought. "You don't think that was my stalker at The Laughing Clown?"

"I don't," Zane replied. "Neither do you. Someone is trying to kill you, but it's totally unrelated to your stalker. So, why? What does someone gain if you're dead? Remembering, of course, they tried to kill you last year too."

My brows shot up. "That girl who died on Riot Night?" There had been lots of deaths that night, but I knew he was talking about the girl who'd initially been identified as me. "You think that really was an attempt to kill me?"

Zane gave me a look like I was being naïve, and Cass huffed a small laugh.

"Look, kid. I know you don't remember everything from before your mom died, and that's normal. But Deb meant a lot to me, and I'll do what I can to help you out on this." Zane sounded almost…normal. Why had I spent so many years terrified of him?

"But mark my words, Madison Kate. You step foot on my turf uninvited again? I'll send you back to my brother in worse condition than he left Skunk. We clear?"

Ah, yep. There it was.

"You got a ride home? Best you don't hang around here much longer." The leader of the Shadow Grove Reapers was back, and a deep shiver of fear passed through me.

I shook my head. "I'll grab an Uber."

Zane flicked his fingers. "Cass will drive you."

"You don't have to—" I started to protest, but Zane cut me off.

"Someone finds value in your death, Madison Kate, which

means there's money involved and probably a lot of it. Watch your fucking back, girl, and don't be an idiot. Stick close to my brother and his friends. They're fucking psychopaths, but they like you." He jerked his head to Cass, then disappeared back into the bar without a second glance my way.

"Come on," the big guy said, leading the way down the alleyway to the parking lot. His hair was jet-black, shaved on the sides and long on top, styled in a messy flop, while his beard was short and neat. Still scary as fuck, regardless of his grooming, and not someone I'd ever want to find myself on the bad side of.

He stopped beside a huge, black-and-chrome Harley and handed me a helmet from the handlebars. "Let's go," he ordered me. "Boss will want you out of here before Arch comes looking."

My palms were sweating with nervousness, but I took the helmet from him and buckled it on. Cass didn't seem like someone who'd stand for girly bullshit about getting on the back of a stranger's motorcycle.

"What about you?" I asked as he slung his leg over the bike and waited for me to climb on. "You don't have another helmet?"

He didn't reply, just kicked over the engine as I situated myself and placed my hands tentatively on his leather-clad waist.

"Hold on tighter than that, girl," he told me as he rolled slowly out of the parking lot.

I did as I was told, gripping his leather jacket just in time to avoid being thrown off as he gunned the accelerator.

I'd wanted to ask him more questions, but beyond telling him which hotel I was staying at—which I'd needed to yell—there wasn't really any opportunity to talk.

Some half hour later, he rolled to a stop outside the midrange hotel I'd been staying at on Bree's credit, and I slid off the back.

"Thanks for the ride," I told him, unbuckling the helmet and handing it back.

He gave me a short nod, his face an unreadable scowl. "Zane will be in touch if he digs anything up."

"Thank you," I said again, genuinely meaning it.

Something shifted in Cass's face, and his expression hardened further—if that was even possible. A second later, I heard footsteps behind me and *felt* his damn presence.

"Archer." Cass greeted my new shadow. "Just dropping your lost property home."

"I'm not his fucking property," I seethed.

"Appreciate it, Cass," Archer replied like I hadn't spoken. Fucking prick. "Now get the fuck out of here."

A small—and I mean *minute*—smile touched Cass's lips. "Gladly. Keep track of your toys, Arch. That one looks all too fun to lose." He revved the Harley's engine, peeled away from the curb without another word, and left me standing there with Archer fucking D'Ath.

His huge hand clamped down on the back of my neck, and I stifled a small scream.

"You're in big trouble, Princess Danvers."

CHAPTER 3

I put up a fight. There was no way I was just getting in his car like a good little girl, *especially* after being spoken about like a stray dog. But when it came down to it, my choice was the lesser of two evils: go home to my sparkly pink bedroom at Danvers Mansion or suffer Archer staying the night in my crappy hotel room. With one *small* double bed.

No thanks.

"Where are the other two stooges?" I asked, slouching in the passenger seat of his Corvette. I was sulking, big time, but I was also a bit confused why only Archer had been lurking at my hotel.

"Home," he replied. Succinct.

I had no idea when I'd stopped thinking of Danvers Mansion as my father's house and more as my home…but I had. And so had they, apparently.

When he said nothing more, I blew out a long breath of frustration. It was fucked up, but I was actually hurt that Kody and Steele hadn't been the ones to find me. Why had it been Archer, the one who barely tolerated my presence? And why the fuck did he even care?

I should have just voiced those questions out loud, but I wasn't in the mood to deal with his cagey bullshit. I'd rather the tense, angry silence.

"Why?" he snapped after a long silence.

I frowned, trying to follow his train of thought. Why was I asking about Kody and Steele? Ugh, good question, dude.

"Why'd you go to that shitty hotel instead of coming home?" he clarified. "I know what you thought, but the detective on your case said he cleared all that up. He told you we were investigated and cleared, didn't he?"

I nodded, my lips tight.

"So what's your fucking problem, Madison Kate? Are you still pissy about that argument? Is that why you went to Zane?" His hands tightened on the steering wheel, his knuckles turning white, but his eyes remained on the road.

I scoffed, a bitter laugh erupting from my mouth. Of course he'd make this about himself. "Our *argument* had nothing to do with this, D'Ath," I informed him in a scathing tone. "It may come as news to you, but you're not the center of everyone's universe. Certainly not mine."

But also, that so-called argument made me cringe when I thought about it. They'd been telling me the truth, and I'd been so firmly entrenched in my beliefs that I'd refused to listen.

"So why go to Zane?" he demanded, his voice full of cold fury. "You saw what happened to his guy. You're fucking lucky you made it out of there alive, you fucking airhead."

My own anger rose to the bait, scorching through me. "Because I'm fucking sick to death of being *lied* to, Archer. It's about damn time I started getting some answers, and your brother was actually quite accommodating."

He scoffed. "Oh yeah? What did he tell you? Or did he just spin the conversation to pump *you* for information and give you nothing in return?"

I started to protest, but... *fuck.*

20

"That's what I figured." Archer was pure fucking condescension. "Zane didn't get to where he is without learning a thing or two about how to manipulate people."

I huffed, not responding as I stared out of my window. But Archer was feeling chatty apparently.

"And what exactly have we been lying to you about, Madison Kate?" he continued.

Not: *We haven't been lying to you.* No, he was asking what *I thought* they'd been lying about. Sneaky bastard.

I rolled my eyes, not interested in playing his game. "Omission is still lying, Archer, and you damn well know it. Until you three start coming clean about what the fuck is going on, you're on my shit list."

He shrugged. "Maybe I like it there."

Dickhead.

"Good, then that's where you can stay."

The rest of the drive was in silence, but after Archer parked us inside the garage and hit his remote to close the garage doors, I had a moment of weakness.

"Where did you get your knife from?" I asked before either of us stepped out of the car. I watched him from the corner of my eye as he froze with his hand on the door handle. "The red butterfly blade you showed me after Bree's party."

"The one you accused me of stabbing you with?" he asked, an edge of bitter disappointment coloring his tone. "The police swabbed it, you know. There was no evidence of your DNA."

I bit my lip. I knew that...but it was hard to reconcile with what I'd seen. "They told me," I admitted. "But that guy, the one who stabbed me, he had the same knife. You have to admit that's more than a coincidence."

"No, he didn't," Archer disagreed. "Those blades are hand-made, each one unique. It may have looked similar to mine, but it wasn't the same."

"Oh." My heart sank. It was the one clue I had, the only thing that might point at who wanted me dead. But that made sense as to why Zane had a similar one too.

Archer sighed, scrubbing a hand over the thick stubble on his cheeks. He looked like he hadn't bothered to shave in weeks, and his face was discolored with healing bruises. He'd look like shit if I weren't still so inexplicably attracted to him.

"It's not a coincidence, though," he said eventually. "You're right on that part."

Hope flared. "So is it a clue?"

Archer's mouth twisted in a grimace. "Yes and no. The guy who made those knives, he only gave them away as gifts. They weren't for sale, and they had to be earned. But he's dead now, so he can't tell us who he gifted with a red blade similar to mine."

My shoulders sank with disappointment. "Who was he, then?"

It seemed like an odd thing to give to people as a gift, and what did Archer mean that they had to be *earned*?

Archer shot me a quick look. "My grandfather, Phillip D'Ath."

He pushed his door open while I sat there a bit shocked, so I scrambled to follow, slamming my door shut behind me.

"Wait up, Archer!" My voice echoed through the silent garage, and he paused. "See, this is exactly what I'm talking about! You drop little fucking crumbs of information like that and then clam up. It's goddamn infuriating, and I've had enough." He turned around to face me just in time to catch a shove from my open palms in the center of his chest.

The mocking tilt to his lips only stoked my anger hotter.

"Oh yeah? What are you going to do about that, Princess Danvers?" he challenged, taking a step farther into my personal space and forcing me to crane my neck to meet his gaze. Fucker had almost a foot on me when I was in flats. I'd need to start wearing heels again just to try and even the playing field a bit.

I narrowed my eyes, but really... what was I going to do? Torture him for information?

"I'm not telling you shit, Madison Kate," he continued in that low, menacing voice, "because I don't fucking *trust* you. You're not one of us; you're just a liability."

His words hurt. More than they should have.

But I'd walk over broken glass before I let him know he'd affected me, so I tightened my jaw and lifted my chin to meet his eyes with a little more confidence. Bravado. Whatever.

"Then why were you so fucking desperate to bring me back here, Archer?"

His lips hitched in a sneer. "Because I'm fucking sick of seeing Kody mope around like a kicked puppy. Do me a solid favor, Madison Kate, and go fuck him stupid. Then maybe he can get you out of his system and get back to business."

Ouch. Every word cut like a razor.

Still, I gave a throaty, mocking laugh. "You think it'd be that easy, Archer? You think one fuck and he'd be over me?" I snapped my fingers. "Just like that, huh?"

Archer's handsome face turned colder than I'd even thought possible, and his next words hung in the air long after he was gone.

"It sure worked for Steele."

After collecting all the splintered shards of my emotions from the garage floor, I silently made my way up to my bedroom. I didn't want to run into anyone. Not Kody, not goddamn fucking Archer, and most definitely not Steele.

Had Archer been full of shit? Or was Steele really over me already? I shouldn't care either way. In fact, it'd make my life a hell of a lot easier if he was no longer interested in exploring that crackling, electric attraction between us. It had just been a one-night stand. Cool. Happened all the time, right?

So why did my heart ache so much and my stomach tangle into knots?

I made it up to my room without seeing anyone and let myself quietly inside, closing the door softly behind me. Then did a double take.

Had I walked into the wrong room?

The walls were...normal. Just a plain, off-white, flat paint. Not a sparkle in sight. The soft furnishings had all been replaced too. Muted purples, grays, and blues but not a single speck of pink in sight.

I took a couple of steps into the room, looking around and noting a few of my things that confirmed this was, in fact, my room. Just...renovated.

Who would have done this?

I paused at the window, touching my fingertips to the mirrorlike film attached to the glass. I'd be willing to bet that blocked anyone seeing in from the outside, even with a telephoto lens.

Taking in all the changes to my bedroom, I stood there a moment feeling all kinds of conflicted. It was a sweet gesture... wasn't it?

There was no way it'd been Archer, though. No fucking way. Despite the fact that he'd tracked me down to the hotel and essentially given me no choice other than to return here, he didn't *actually* care about me. That brief moment at Bree's party when we'd given in to the intoxicating tension between us was just that: a moment, and a weak one at that. Archer was hot, no denying that. And he was probably dynamite in bed, but that didn't excuse his shitty attitude and prickly personality.

Even through that whole intense, heartbreaking "argument" we'd had—when I'd poured out all my pent-up resentment and frustration and hatred—he still hadn't apologized to me. He *still* had set me up on Riot Night, and he *still* hadn't learned any kind of remorse for that crappy decision.

My first thought was that Steele had done it. He had offered to get it repainted on my first day in that sparkly pink room, and it seemed like the sweet sort of gesture he'd make. But Archer's words echoed through my mind, filling me with doubt. Maybe he was over me already. One and done, just like that.

Which left Kody. I toyed with that option as I drew the heavy curtains, but at the end of the day, it didn't matter who'd done the remodel. One caring gesture didn't change the fucked-up situation we were all in, no matter how much I loved my new room.

With a sigh, I grabbed pajamas from my drawer—exactly where I'd left them—and got changed for bed. It'd already been late when I ventured into the shadows to find Zane, so it was well after midnight now.

Sitting cross-legged on my new purple-gray comforter, I sent a quick text to Bree so she wouldn't freak out in the morning.

Me: Hey girl, I'm still alive. Archer tracked me down and dragged me home. Pick me up for class in the morning?

I turned my phone to silent, not expecting a reply from her at such a late hour, then plugged it in to charge. I flipped my light off and crawled into bed, getting comfy under the inoffensive blankets before I noticed one last feature that'd been added to my room.

A star ceiling.

Tiny pinpricks of light filled the dark expanse of my ceiling, making me feel like I was sleeping outdoors under the star-filled sky.

It was utterly perfect.

CHAPTER 4

My dreams were tortured, full of blood and violence. Black-masked killers lurking in every shadow and my mom's dead eyes staring back at me constantly.

When I woke myself up for the third time, thrashing and drenched in cold sweat, I gave up on sleep. Who needed it, anyway?

Instead, I dragged my exhausted, sleep-deprived ass into the shower before the sun was even up. I took a moment after I stepped out of the steaming water to inspect my healing injuries. My stitches in both my stomach and in my hairline had been removed just before I left the hospital, so neither needed dressings. The one on my head was healing nicely, showing just a jagged, red-purple scar, but the slash on my stomach was taking a bit longer. It had been a miracle that the knife had missed anything too vital and hadn't dragged when my attacker removed it. As it was, the scar was only about two inches long to the right of my belly button, but it still ached when I sat up too quickly.

Drying off with my new lilac towel, I went about getting dressed for the day. I'd missed two weeks of lectures. Combined with the two weeks prior to Halloween that I'd stayed home out of fear of my stalker…it was a miracle I was still enrolled. Unless

I wanted to royally fuck my future—worse than it was already fucked—I needed to get my head on straight.

No more distractions. No more gorgeous, infuriating men playing with my emotions, and for the love of God, no more stalker mail.

Of course, that was just wishful thinking.

As I made my way downstairs for breakfast, the sound of Kody's voice echoed from the gym, and my stomach flipped.

Damn it.

Drawn like a magnet, I found myself drifting down the corridor to where the door to the gym stood open, allowing his voice to travel through the house like it had.

"Again!" he barked, and when I peered around the doorframe, I found Archer running through some kind of grueling work-out drill. "Pick up the pace, Archer," Kody ordered, his voice cracking like a whip. "Push yourself. You're slacking off."

My brows rose. Archer was drenched in sweat, his ink-covered arms and chest slick and his shorts hanging low on his hips. I was no expert, but I was pretty sure he was giving it his all.

"You lost that fight, Arch," Kody railed on his friend. He was standing over him wearing nothing but a pair of red basketball shorts himself, and the sweat coating his chiseled abs suggested he'd been pushing himself just as hard.

Archer didn't reply, seeming to be lost in the zone as he went through his drill almost on autopilot. It gave an explanation for the bruises on his face, though. He must have made it to his UFC debut after all. And lost, if I was to understand Kody's statement correctly.

Fuck. I'd underestimated their reach if they could erase such a damning drug test result so close to the event.

I'd just have to try harder next time.

Archer was still firmly on my list…I just needed to be more creative. Think outside the box.

"You lost your first ever title fight because you were sloppy and unprepared." Kody continued laying into his friend, a deep scowl

27

pulling his features in a way that totally erased his usual mischievous, easygoing expression.

"Fuck you," Archer spat back, finally snapping and jumping to his feet to get in Kody's face. "I lost because I was fucking distracted, and you know it."

Kody just smirked back at him, not intimidated by the lethal fighter staring him down. "Yeah, I do. I just wanted you to fucking admit it, you stubborn prick."

Archer's fists clenched and he opened his mouth to say something in return, but Kody's attention shifted past his friend and landed on me.

"Holy shit." Kody gaped. "You're back."

I gave him a tight smile, unsure how the hell I should handle this situation. Last time I'd seen Kody, I'd thought he was trying to kill me. I'd been *so* scared of him. Emotions that strong didn't just disappear instantly, no matter how misplaced.

"I fucking *told* you she'd be back," Kody said to Archer, punching him in the arm pretty hard before rushing across the gym to me. I hesitated as he drew closer, but he didn't notice. Or chose not to, at any rate. Instead he swept me up in his arms, hugging me tight to his sweat-drenched body and burying his face in my hair. "I knew you'd come back."

My whole body was tense, the fear in my memory coloring my interaction with Kody in person. I was about to peel myself out of his grip when I locked eyes with Archer.

His face was a mask of sheer fury and resentment. Maybe even jealousy? Probably jealous that I was taking his trainer away from their workout or some stupid, macho-man bullshit like that.

But it gave me an idea.

Curious, I looped my arms around Kody's neck and hugged him tighter to me. Archer's expression darkened further, and I bit back a smug smile. I'd just found one of Archer's real trigger buttons.

Kody.

Or more to the point, me and Kody together.

He'd told me to do him a favor and fuck his friend? Well, I'd go one better. I'd date him. Let's see what that did for Archer's level of distraction.

"Kody," Archer snapped when his friend didn't release me immediately, "we were in the middle of a session here."

"Fuck that," Kody replied. "Take a break."

He barely even glanced over his shoulder at Archer as he set me down and started out of the gym. I did, though. I met Archer's furious blue eyes and smiled.

Game on, motherfucker.

I followed Kody back out to the kitchen, where we found Steele—shirtless, of course, like it wasn't snowing outside—fussing over my espresso machine.

"Whoa," I blurted out. "What the hell are you doing?"

Steele spun around so fast the jug of milk—which he'd definitely been burning—flew out of his hand and splashed all over the marble floor.

"Madison Kate," he said, and I cringed inwardly. So much for "Hellcat."

"What are you doing to my coffee machine?" I demanded, covering up the flash of hurt at my name.

Steele's eyes went wide, and Kody snickered as he tossed a washcloth at his friend's chest. "Oh, uh, I was…" Steele caught the cloth and looked down at it like the answers he sought were in there.

"Steele decided he can't drink Archer's coffee anymore," Kody answered for him, "so he's been trying to teach himself how to use your fancy espresso machine."

I arched a brow at Kody, fully aware of how much he appreciated the good coffee at Nadia's Cakes.

"An endeavor I have been supportive of," Kody added with a sly grin. "But now you're back…" The hopeful expression on his face was too much. My lingering fear of him had all but faded away to nothing, so I just rolled my eyes and stepped over the spilled milk.

"Move aside, Max Steele," I told the wannabe barista. "You were torturing that poor milk."

He gave me a tight smile, getting down onto his hands and knees to clean the mess up while I started fresh.

I lost myself to the process for a few minutes, letting my body go through the motions on autopilot and letting my mind go blissfully blank. Only when four perfect flat whites sat on their saucers did I let all the noise of my inner thoughts come crashing back into my mind.

"Thanks," Steele muttered, not meeting my gaze as he took one of the coffees, then just…walked away. He left the kitchen without another word and left me a bit stunned as Archer walked in.

"See?" Archer smirked at me, looking after Steele's retreating back. "You're already out of his system. Based on the way Kody's eye fucking you right now, I expect everything will be back to normal in about twenty-four hours."

He swiped one of the coffees, gulping half of it before I could stop him.

"Hey!" I shouted. "That one was for Bree."

"She doesn't need one," he told me, downing the rest of the coffee in three quick gulps. "I told her we'd be driving you to SGU from now on."

"What? Why?" Anger was making me trip over my words and get tongue-tied, which Archer used to his advantage.

He dropped his empty cup in the sink and clapped Kody on the shoulder as he left the kitchen. "Use protection, bro. No one likes an STD."

I was fucking *fuming* by the time he was gone from the room, my hands balled into fists at my sides like I wanted to hit him. Again. My knee was feeling the itch of needing to nail some balls.

"What," Kody drawled, casually sipping his coffee and actually savoring it, "was that all about?"

I turned my scowl on him, then gave a defeated sigh. I wanted to maintain that anger, that burning hatred that had fueled me for the first six weeks I'd lived with the three of them. But all that was left was fumes. At least when it came to Kody, anyway.

"He told me that Steele…" I trailed off, feeling stupid as hell saying it out loud—especially to Kody, who I was still attracted to. I cleared my throat and took a sip of my coffee. "He said that I just need to fuck you once so you can get me out of your system…like Steele has."

Kody's brows rose, and I held my breath while waiting for his reaction.

Then he started laughing.

"I'm sorry, MK," he finally said when his laughter died down. "It's just funny 'cause Arch is a bigger moron than I'd given him credit for."

I frowned. "How so?"

Kody shook his head, still chuckling as he drank more coffee. "For one thing, Steele is nowhere near 'over' you. He's been a fucking mess since Halloween. He's blaming himself for not stopping you before you drove away that night."

I frowned harder.

"And for another…" Kody snickered again, giving me a broad smile. "Have I ever told you how much we love to play games around here?"

I nodded slowly, my eyes narrowed with suspicion. "It's been mentioned once or twice. Why?"

His smile turned evil. "What would you say to calling Archer's bluff?"

I froze. "Um. Is that how you proposition a girl for sex, Kody? I thought you had more game than that."

He sighed like I was being deliberately obtuse. "I wasn't asking you to fuck me, MK. I mean, I'm all for that, don't read me wrong. But I meant..." He trailed off, running a hand through that platinum hair of his. "Will you go out with me? On an actual date, not a forced one where you get slapped by my crazy ex?"

I smiled at the memory, then gave Kody a cautious look. "I know why it'll piss Archer off—he hates being proven wrong. But what's in this for you? Sex?"

Kody shrugged, rolling those hard muscles of his shoulders in the most delicious way. "Hopefully. But I'll also just do it to spend time with you, MK. In case you have missed all the really obvious signals, I *like* you. I *want* to date you." He came around the island to where I stood and placed his hands to either side of me on the countertop, boxing me in. "So, how about it? Wanna be my girlfriend?"

I was confused. No doubt about it. "Fake girlfriend?" I corrected...or queried.

He shrugged again. "Sure, if that's what you want to call it."

I bit my lip, thinking over his suggestion. Except, it was exactly what I'd planned to do anyway, wasn't it? So why was I suddenly flooded with nervous tension and excitement?

"All right," I replied, my voice a bit breathier than I'd intended. "Deal. But you're dealing with his shitty attitude when he realizes you're not dropping me like sour milk."

Kody grinned. "Fuck off, you love his shitty attitude."

Before I could protest, his lips were on mine.

Bang.

Sparks flew and light bulbs exploded all through the kitchen while every electrical appliance in the house short-circuited.

Or at least, that was how Kody kissing me made me feel. Every touch, every nip, and every sigh was pure electricity, and I was melting under his hands in the best possible way.

"You have no idea," he whispered to me in a husky, serious voice as our kiss ended, "how badly I needed that."

His hands had found my waist, his fingers digging into my flesh like he was reassuring himself that I was, in fact, physically there.

"So did I," I replied, my voice so soft I barely even heard my own words. I hadn't even known how badly I'd needed that kiss from him. He'd grounded me and reassured me that nothing had changed where he was concerned…like that whole grisly mess on Halloween hadn't happened. We were right back on that dance floor at the warehouse, ready to rip each other's clothes off.

Kody combed his fingers through my loose tresses, gripping tight to the lengths and tipping my head back for another searing kiss.

"As badly as I want to take this further," he told me in a low voice, kissing my jaw, then my neck, "I need a favor."

I snorted a laugh. "Kodiak Jones, we've only been fake dating for five minutes, and you're already asking favors? The audacity."

His smile curved against the skin of my throat, and I filed it away as one of my favorite sensations. "I know. But this is an important one, and I'll owe you."

"You already owe me," I reminded him, "for scaring off Drew at Bree's party."

He moved back a couple of inches, wrinkling his nose at the reminder. "I'll double owe you?"

I rolled my eyes. "What's the favor? The last one wasn't all so terrible." I dragged my tongue across my lower lip, remembering the way he'd used me to get rid of his ex-girlfriend. His gaze was glued on my mouth, but he wrenched it away and back to my eyes.

"I need you to go and talk with Steele," he said with a hopeful tilt to his brows. "He's… He needs you."

My eyes narrowed. "He didn't exactly seem overcome with joy to see me back just now." Yeah, I was bitter.

Kody's intuitive green eyes held me captive, peering way too deeply into my soul and stripping back the layers of my tough exterior. "Babe, come on. Steele just deals with his shit a bit differently. You know that." The pointed look he gave me reminded me of the night I'd fallen asleep to Steele's piano music. Was that how he dealt with his baggage? "Please?"

Ugh. Puppy dog eyes. How was such a pathetic facial expression so fucking effective on a gorgeous guy like Kody?

"Fine," I groaned. "So eager to throw your fake girlfriend into another man's arms already? This relationship is doomed."

A wide grin spread across Kody's lips, and he ducked down to kiss me again. "Or is it just about to get all kinds of interesting? It's just a matter of perspective, baby."

I'd be lying if I tried to tell anyone my internal voice didn't scream "reverse harem" at the top of its lungs. Except there were two problems there. One, my mental voice sounded a whole lot like Bree. And two, reverse harems required *three* or more love interests.

Archer was *not* an option.

CHAPTER 5

I checked the time on my phone as I headed up to Steele's room. If I wanted to make it to my first lecture of the day, I needed to leave the house in about half an hour. There was no way in hell I could drive myself—not after crashing so recently—but maybe Kody would drive me.

Or Steele, if he didn't hate me like it'd sort of seemed in that brief interaction in the kitchen. Worse, if he was indifferent.

But Kody was right; I did need to talk to Steele. Even if it was just to gain some closure about where the fuck we stood with each other. It'd been a month since we fucked, and we'd barely spoken. That shit wasn't healthy, especially when we literally lived under the same roof.

I pulled up my metaphorical big girl panties and knocked on his bedroom door.

There was only a moment's pause before he answered and stared at me with a small frown pulling his brow.

"Madison Kate," he said, his pretty lips turning down slightly, "what's up?"

I blinked at him a couple of times. "Uh, wow. Okay." I ruffled my loose, dusky-rose waves with my fingers and shoved aside the sharp knife of hurt at his nonchalance. "Last time I saw you, I'd just been stabbed and thought I was dying... Guess I expected more than 'what's up' when I reappeared." I frowned, but he just stared back at me, his face impassive. "You know what? This was a dumb idea. I guess Archer was right for once; you really did get me out of your system."

I turned to leave, not even remotely interested in putting myself out there for Steele to trample all over. Kody could keep his fucking favor.

Steele's hand shot out, though, grabbing my wrist and hauling me into his room. The door slammed behind me, and my stomach fluttered with nerves.

"What did you just say?" he demanded, his beautiful gray eyes narrowed in fury.

I glared back at him, my own anger freshened up. "You heard me, *Max*." I don't know why I insisted on using his first name like that. Probably because he clearly hated it more than I hated being called by my full name. What were we, if not antagonistic assholes, really? "Archer *bragged* that all it took was one night with me and you were over your infatuation. I thought he was just being a prick, but I guess not."

Steele's jaw unhinged slightly, and I couldn't stop my attention from wavering to his tongue piercing for a millisecond.

"Are you kidding me right now?" he asked with a bitter laugh. "You must be. You're smarter than that, Madison Kate."

I ground my teeth together at the way he said my name. Tit for tat, I supposed.

"What else am I supposed to think when all I get from you is 'what's up?' like that?"

His fingers still circled my wrist, his grip tight enough to hurt. I wasn't pulling away, though. Hell, I was lost in a hailstorm of emotions that his touch had ignited. I was fast coming to the realization that I not only wanted Archer to be wrong because he was

36

an insufferable asshole, but I wanted him to be wrong because I still *wanted* Steele. Badly. Way more than I'd thought. Denial and I were way too well acquainted with one another these days.

"You're unbelievable," he muttered, dropping my wrist and turning away from me.

I rubbed at the spot his hand had touched, feeling the ghost imprint of his grip as disappointment flooded through me.

"Me?" I replied, shoring up my crumbling defenses once more. "That's the pot calling the kettle black, Max."

He swung around once more, his eyes blazing. "Madison Kate, *you're* the one who ran away. Not me. You ran from me a month ago after we slept together—"

"I did not!" I exclaimed. "My stalker took pictures of us and *threatened you*. I stayed away to keep you safe, you dense, arrogant, pigheaded moron."

His eyes narrowed farther, and he advanced on me. The sheer anger radiating from him made me back up a few steps until my back pressed against the door.

"You *ran*. I'm more than capable of handling myself, and you know it. We all are. You used it as a convenient excuse to hide from the fact that you'd started letting us in. You'd started letting *me* in, and it terrified you. So you ran." His words were cold and biting, and it tore me up inside to hear. But…he wasn't wrong. That was the most painful part.

"Then on Halloween, when we tried to give you the truth about your mom and Zane, when we tried to show you the falsities within your own memories, you ran again." He sucked in a breath, his nostrils flaring and his mouth a tight slash across his face. "You ran and you nearly fucking died, Madison Kate." His voice cracked over that last part, and a gut-wrenching flash of vulnerability passed across his face.

Words failed me, and silence filled the room as he stared at me with his eyes like storm clouds, turbulent and mysterious.

"You checked yourself out of the hospital four days ago, and you didn't even try to call and tell us you were okay. The cops must have told you we weren't responsible for what happened, but you still ran. Again." His voice was softer now, lacking the heat of his initial anger, and instead soaked in hurt and bitter disappointment. "I'm hurt and angry and so incredibly frustrated," he continued, raising a hand to cup the back of my head. His fingers gripped my hair tight enough to turn it from a tender gesture into something dominant and controlling. "But one thing I'm not, Hellcat, is *over* you."

His lips came down on mine in a bruising, furious kiss that stripped my soul bare and flayed me from the inside. I whimpered into his mouth, parting my lips and begging for more as I clawed at his body. He was fully in control, though, holding my head still with that iron grip on my hair. Steele kissed me, his piercing teasing my tongue and echoing the hardness of his hands, and my walls all crumbled to dust.

He was right about all of it. I'd been so totally consumed in what I believed to be the truth, I'd totally lost sight of what was right in front of my face.

Fucking hell.

"I'm sorry," I whispered when his lips left mine. My cheeks were damp, but I didn't care. I'd hurt him so much more than I'd thought, and he wouldn't feel that kind of hurt and disappointment if there wasn't something a fuckload stronger than a one-night stand between us.

Steele's eyes were still hard and angry as hell, but now at least there was a flame of desire tempering that fury. "Yeah, Hellcat," he murmured back. "So am I. I thought I was doing the right thing, giving you space. But then…"

"Then I had a meltdown and crashed Kody's car and got stabbed by a crazy, masked lunatic who I thought was Archer?" I finished for him when he trailed off.

Steele grimaced. "Yeah. That."

I ducked my eyes away from his, sucking in a calming breath. "I thought it was you guys. I thought all of it...*us*...I thought it was all part of some fucked-up plan to terrorize and then murder me. The cops told me they tested Archer's knife for my DNA and it came back clean, but I didn't totally *believe* that until..." I bit my lip, facing my own traitorous emotions. "Until he showed up at my hotel last night, I guess."

Steele nodded, understanding. His thumb rubbed reassuring strokes on the back of my neck, and I never wanted him to stop.

"He's still a fucking asshole," I quickly added, "and I still want to push all his fucking buttons until his head explodes, but I don't think he wants me dead."

Steele gave a soft laugh, stroking my loose hair behind my ear with his free hand, then tilting my face back up to meet his gaze. "Good."

"So, are we okay?" I asked, grabbing on to the lifeline of hope dangling between us with a tentative grip. "You and me, I mean."

Steele stared back at me for a long moment, then kissed me again. This time it was gentler and almost sad, and it sent a ripple of dread through me.

"No," he whispered in a husky voice when we separated. "I'm sorry, but no. I need more time to be okay with you again."

My brows shot up in hurt surprise, and my stomach churned.

"Not..." Steele shook his head, clearly searching for the right words. He let go of my hair, taking several steps away, and I felt the divide between us like it'd been chiseled into my heart. "I'm going to explain this in as few words as possible because it fucking kills me to talk about. But I need you to understand so you don't fucking *run* again."

I had no clue what was going on, but a roller coaster of emotions held me locked in place. Then again, it was likely a ride I didn't ever want to get off.

Steele blew out a long breath, passing a hand over his face and sinking down onto the edge of his bed. "I don't think anyone would have mentioned to you that I had a twin sister, Rachel."

My brows raised, but I stopped myself before I said anything dumb. *Had*. He'd *had* a sister…past tense.

"She died three years ago," he continued, bracing his forearms on his knees and looking at the carpet while he spoke. "She was on her way to see me play with the Chicago Symphony Orchestra but was running late. She and her boyfriend had been arguing, and she got in the car upset and…" He shook his head, and I could see the lines of tension in his shoulders from where I stood. It was causing him so much pain to tell me, and I could already see where the story was going.

I crossed the room and sank to my knees on the carpet in front of him, wrapping my arms around his waist and tucking my face into his chest. He didn't move for a moment, but when his arms closed around me, I let out a long sigh.

"You don't have to open your wounds for me, Steele," I muttered, digging my fingers into his flesh to hold him closer. "I'm not running away. Not today."

Steele stroked his fingers through my hair, tugging my face back so he could meet my eyes. "But that's just it, Madison Kate. I've—*we've* been keeping too many secrets, and it's driving you to make stupid fucking choices like you did on Halloween. Because you don't trust us. When I saw you drive away, knowing how emotional you were, all I could see was the wreckage my sister was pulled out of." He swallowed heavily. "I *saw* the G-Wagen when it got towed, babe. All I've been able to think for two fucking weeks is how we almost lost you, just like Rachel."

I cupped his face, my heart breaking for his freshly uncovered pain. "I'm so fucking sorry, Steele," I told him with total sincerity.

This time, I kissed him, pouring my regret and apology into every slide of our tongues and every shared breath. I'd fucked up on Halloween. I'd reacted badly and made some dumb fucking mistakes that almost saw me dead on the end of some sicko's crimson blade. But worse than that, I'd ripped open those agonizing memories of Steele's sister—his *twin* sister—by echoing her actions. I felt like a total asshole, even though I hadn't known.

Steele's forehead rested on the bend of my neck, and I looped my arms around his to hold him close. The emotions between us were so raw, so exposed, I didn't want to move or speak and ruin it all.

After a while, though, my knees started to hurt from the position I was in, and I let go of him with a sigh, sitting back on my feet.

"Any chance you want to give me a lift to SGU today?" I asked him, gently shifting the subject to something safer. "Stupid Archer told Bree not to pick me up, and I don't want to suffer his company if I don't need to."

The corner of Steele's lips hitched in a smile. "I suppose I owe that bastard a thank-you," he muttered, standing up and offering me his hand to pull me to my feet.

I snorted a sound of disagreement as I followed him out of his room. "For fucking what?"

"Well," he replied, taking my hand in his as we made our way downstairs, "for one thing, he found you when I was too busy sulking to even think about tracing Bree's financial records."

I rolled my eyes. I'd known that would be my downfall, but I hadn't been thinking clearly the day I decided to check myself out of the hospital.

"And the other?" I prompted him. When he gave me a small frown, I explained. "You said 'for one thing,' which means there's another thing you want to thank him for."

A smile danced across Steele's lips, like he hadn't intended to say that out loud. Like he'd finished the statement inside his own head.

"Are we ready to go?" Kody asked, joining as we passed through the foyer and interrupting before Steele could answer my question.

"You driving?" This was directed to his friend, who gave a nod and snatched a car key from the numerous hooks near the garage door.

"Yep," Steele replied, clicking the fob and directing us over to his sleek, silver muscle car. Thank fuck it was one with a backseat so I wouldn't have to sit in Kody's lap the whole way to school. Once had been funny, twice somewhat less so, and by this point that trick was a bit tired, considering how many four- or five-seat vehicles were in the garage.

"Sweet." Kody slung his arm over my shoulders and pressed a kiss to my temple. "Babe, you tell him yet?"

I stiffened under his arm.

"Tell me what?" Steele asked, his sharp gaze taking in the casual way Kody touched me.

Kody's grin was pure evil. "That MK and I are dating."

Christ on a goddamn fucking cracker.

If I had ever wished for a time that the ground would open and swallow me up whole, that was it. Right fucking here.

CHAPTER 6

To my intense relief, on the way to SGU Kody explained the whole "MK and I are dating" bombshell he'd dropped on Steele in the garage.

By the time he was done telling his friend about our diabolical plan to piss off Archer, Steele's infectious grin was back on his face. It reminded me of that first day when I'd returned from Cambodia and he'd smiled so much I wanted to hit him.

"I know," Kody said when Steele barked a laugh. "I'm a genius."

Steele rolled his eyes and shot me a quick look from the driver's seat. "You are," he replied to Kody, "but not for the reason you think, dickhead."

I gave him a tight smile in response but couldn't shake the tension out of my body until we pulled into Steele's designated parking space outside the university entrance.

Archer's midnight-black Stingray was nowhere to be seen, but that was no great shock. He only had three lectures a week.

The three of us got out of the car, and I slung my bag over my shoulder. A dull ache tweaked as my stomach muscles shifted, and I cringed.

"Come on, babe," Kody called to me with a smug grin. "I'll walk you to class."

Steele whacked him in the stomach as he shifted past, making Kody groan. "Give us a second, you sneaky fuck," he growled, jerking his head to the building behind us.

Kody snickered but did as he was told, heading inside the university without us.

"Are you okay?" Steele asked when his friend was out of sight. He came around the car to me and hovered his hand over my waist like he wanted to grab me but didn't want to risk hurting me.

I nodded. "Totally fine," I assured him, lifting my shirt up slightly to show him the healing wound. "It was a clean cut, and the stitches came out days ago. It barely even hurts now, unless I move too quickly."

Steele's brow furrowed, and he traced his thumb gently along the raised scar, his touch featherlight. "You know we're going to find whoever did this, right?" His gaze met mine, but his fingertips still rested on the bare skin of my stomach. "We'll find him and show him the true meaning of agony for what he did to you."

The cold violence in his eyes sent a shiver of fear through me, balanced equally by arousal. A therapist would have a field day with my attraction to these three mysterious, dangerous guys, but I wasn't in the mood to psychoanalyze myself.

Instead, I just pulled him in with a handful of his shirt, crushing my lips and my body to him in a physical display of what I thought of his promise.

Steele ended our kiss way too soon, but I was mollified by his reasoning. "Dammit, Hellcat. You're going to make me suffer through my lectures with a hard-on."

I smirked but gave him a second to rearrange his dick before we headed into the building, where Kody waited for us. Not that he was lacking for company. A beautiful redheaded girl that I used

44

to go to Shadow Prep with was flipping her hair and batting her lashes at him like she was developing a tic.

"You done pawing at my girlfriend, bro?" the gigantic, blond flirt teased, grabbing my hand and pulling me into his embrace right there in front of his admirer. Beth, I think her name was. Bree and I had kept a pretty tight circle at Shadow Prep, and it'd been over a year since I'd seen most of my old classmates.

"Your girlfriend?" she squeaked, giving me huge eyes. They lacked the spiteful jealousy women often threw around when they spotted competition. Instead, she just looked sheepish. "Sorry, MK," she told me, "I didn't realize. Good to see you back in Shadow Grove." Her smile was tight, a little cool, but not malicious.

"Thanks, Beth," I replied. She didn't correct me or look confused, so I must have gotten her name right.

Her answering smile was a bit warmer, like she hadn't expected me to recognize her.

Score.

"Well, I'll see you around," she told me, then flickered an appreciative gaze over Steele before walking away with a sway in her step.

"Friend of yours?" Steele asked me with his pierced brow raised.

I shook my head. "Some girl from Shadow Prep. And apparently a big fan of yours, Kody."

He just grinned this broad, arrogant fucking smile that made me want to hit him and kiss him at the same damn time. "Good thing she now knows I have a *girlfriend*, then." He tightened his arm around me, kissing my hair.

"You're insufferable," Steele muttered. "Archer isn't even *here*."

Kody snickered. "Like I care."

Steele flipped him off and went in the opposite direction to get to his class, but Kody walked with me all the way to the door of my lecture. Like we were dating for real.

Were we?

I was woefully behind in my classes; that much became clear before the day was even halfway over. My head was pounding and my scar aching by the time I made my way into the cafeteria, but my mood lifted dramatically when I spotted Bree at the buffet.

"Hey, girl," she greeted me when I sidled up beside her. "You made it! Sorry for not texting back; you sent that message in, like, the dead of the night. I wouldn't have made it in time even if Archer hadn't told me not to worry."

I shrugged. "All good. He's ramped up the caveman routine, so I'm not even surprised. I think me checking myself out of the hospital threatened his whole control-freak thing he's got going on."

Bree snickered, giving me a wrinkled-nose look. "Uh, yeah. Something like that. Anyway, how did the meeting go?"

I blinked at her, confused. "What meeting?"

"With your 'family friend' yesterday? The one you were being super cagey about on the phone when you wouldn't tell me where you were?" She arched a brow at me, and I nodded. The meeting with Zane. Leader of the Shadow Grove Reapers. That one.

"Um, it was good," I responded with total vagueness. I loaded my tray up with all the deliciousness on offer—pizza, fries, chocolate brownies, basically anything I could see that might trigger Kody's health-and-fitness button. What could I say? I liked the conflict. And the carbs.

Bree and I made our way over to a vacant table, but she paused before we put our trays down. "Uh, MK? I think..." She indicated over my shoulder, and I turned to look.

The guys—all three of them—were at their usual table with their usual crew of adoring women crowded around them. Kody had stood up and was indicating that we join them, but...fuck that. The brunette bitch who'd dumped juice on me was literally sitting in Archer's lap, and I wasn't about to go making friends anytime soon.

Meeting Kody's eyes, I shook my head firmly and dropped my tray onto the table.

He rolled his in response and abandoned his table to saunter over to us.

"Babe, Archer went to all the effort of *actually* attending classes today. The least you can do is rub his fucking face in the fact that we're hopelessly in love and probably going to fuck loudly on the table right in front of him." His tone was dead serious, and Bree made a choking noise.

"Uh, what?"

I tried and failed to hold back my grin at Kody's antics. "Long story," I muttered back to Bree. "But I'm not sharing a table with your cheerleaders, Kodiak Jones. Come sit here with us if you're so eager for my attention."

His eyes narrowed, and I knew he wasn't letting me off so easily.

"Just a moment, babe," he said with sarcastic sweetness, and I groaned as he swaggered back over to his table and exchanged a few words with his friends. And by that, I meant he said something that was probably caustic and nasty, and all the girls stormed off with faces like acid rain.

He turned back to face me, spreading his hands wide as if to illustrate the lack of adoring females left at his table. Except...the juice-spilling bitch was still in Archer's lap. Stubborn.

I gave Kody a pointed look, shifting my eyes to her and back again. In reality, it didn't matter if she was there. It didn't matter if she was squirming all over Archer's lap like she was trying to get his dick hard, and it didn't fucking matter if he had his tattooed hands around her waist.

But I knew it'd piss him off. And I was starting to discover I was unnaturally addicted to stoking the flames of his anger and irritation.

Kody rolled his eyes and leaned over to say something to the girl. Archer's face hardened, his angry-eyed gaze finding me across the room, but his show was upstaged by his girl attempting to slap Kody.

I said *attempting* because he caught her wrist before her palm connected. Whatever he said next had her storming out of the cafeteria with her cheeks heated and her brow drawn in a deep scowl.

Kody looked back over at me, grinning as if to say, *See? All cleaned up.*

"Fuck's sake," I muttered, looking at Bree. "Do you mind? We sort of have this thing…"

I trailed off, feeling like a total moron for admitting to a fake-but-not-actually-fake relationship with Kody. Because my feelings toward him were *far* from fake.

Bree grinned broadly. "Uh-huh, I can see that. I want to hear *all* about it too." She picked up her tray and gave me a smug smile. "Come on, then. Let's go join the kings of campus."

She strutted her sassy butt over to their table and sat down between Archer and Steele like she belonged there, leaving a seat beside Kody on the other side of the table free.

I sighed and followed. After I placed my tray down on the table, Kody's arm snaked around my waist and dragged me into his lap, rather than the chair I'd intended to sit in.

"Seriously?" Archer demanded, slamming his fork down. "First you pull that shit with the girls and now *this*?"

"Now what?" Kody replied with total innocence as he dragged my tray closer for me. "Oh, good choices, babe."

I snickered but stayed where I was. If Archer was already acting like a bratty three-year-old, then that's exactly where I wanted to be. "Oh really? You're not going to berate me for my high-fat, high-sugar choices?"

"Fuck no," Kody replied, looking outraged. "Any sane man knows not to tell a woman how to eat. If pizza and chocolate gave you this banging body, I'm all fucking for it. Eat up."

I grinned because he'd just passed a test I wasn't even aware I was putting him through. Straight-up common sense.

"Didn't you know, Arch?" Steele commented, eating his sandwich with a barely disguised smile. "Madison Kate and Kody are *dating* now. I guess whatever you said to her must have struck a chord."

Damn, I wished I had a camera to photograph the look of disbelief on his face in that moment. It was perfect.

I must have made a sound of amusement out loud because Archer's furious gaze snapped to me like a homing beacon. He shoved back from the table with a sharp scrape of his chair legs, and I wobbled slightly on Kody's lap. My foot hooked my bag on the floor and jerked it, spilling the contents on the ground.

"Ugh, thanks a fucking lot, asshole," I snapped at Archer, because clearly all of life's problems were his fault. I slid off Kody's lap and knelt down to pick everything up, and Kody helped me a second later.

"Hey," he said with a frown while I stuffed books back into my bag, "what's this?"

He held up a sealed envelope with my name—my full name—scrawled on the front in sharp, black-inked letters.

I froze, my breath halting and my skin prickling. I knew that handwriting.

"That's…" I stared at the envelope in his hand like it was a poisonous snake. "How did that get into my bag?"

"What is it?" Archer asked, coming around the table with a sneer on his face like he expected some childish prank that he could laugh at. "Oh, let me guess, a love letter? Kody, your new girlfriend isn't amazing at the whole monogamy thing."

Kody sneered back at him as he stood up. "Who said she needs to be?" he replied. "But no, you insensitive ass, that's not what this is." He ripped the envelope open, not waiting for me to do it myself. Fair call too—I probably would have just trashed the whole thing.

I got up off the floor, as everything else was back in my bag, and peered over at the photo in Kody's hand. It was of me—obviously—but taken just that morning in the SGU parking lot. I was standing beside Steele's car, looking up at him with an expression I'd never seen on my own face. His hand was under my shirt, his palm on my stomach, and his eyes locked on mine... It was an intensely intimate shot, one I'd kind of love if it hadn't been taken by a creepy stalker and mysteriously delivered to my backpack.

Scrawled across the bottom of the image in those same spiky letters, this time with a red marker pen, was just one word.

MINE.

Wordlessly, Kody handed the picture to Steele, who stared down at it a moment.

"Shit." Steele summed up all of our thoughts in that one word.

"Uh, that's creepy as fuck," Bree announced, staring at the photo with wide eyes. "What do you think it means?"

Before we had a chance to answer her, an explosion rocked the building, and a hard body slammed into me, pinning me to the floor.

"What the fuck was that?" Bree shrieked, and I struggled to get up again.

I was facedown, but somehow I knew who had me pinned. "Get the fuck off me, D'Ath," I hissed. "It was outside."

He didn't move immediately, probably to be a contrary prick, but when I started wriggling, he finally let me free.

"Parking lot," Kody told us, his mouth set in a grim line and his brow furrowed. "That's my guess."

Steele groaned and rubbed his hands over his face. "No. Please don't be from the parking lot."

It took me a second to catch up, but the timing of us looking at that image of Steele and me in the parking lot…beside his car…

"Surely not," I muttered.

The five of us—Bree included—rushed toward the parking lot, along with crowds of other students and staff.

We didn't make it far past the front door of the university building, though. From there we could see the tall column of flames rising from the wreckage of Steele's pretty, silver car. Chunks of metal and other debris were scattered all over the grass, and several students were bleeding and screaming, probably having been too close when the explosion went off.

"Holy shit." Bree gaped.

I was fucking speechless. He'd exploded Steele's car with zero regard for collateral damage. Had anyone been seriously hurt? Killed? My stomach rolled as I stared at the mess, wide-eyed and horrified.

"Fuck!" Steele shouted, his fist balled as he tried to hit the brick facade of the building. Archer smoothly intercepted, though, taking the full force of Steele's punch in his chest.

"Cool it," Archer said to his friend, his tone not angry or condescending but carrying that strong thread of authority. "I'm not letting you break your fingers when you just started playing again."

Steele looked like he wanted to punch Archer again, deliberately this time, but after a few moments he shouted another curse and stalked away from us, disappearing around the corner of the building.

"This is my fault," I whispered, feeling like a total piece of shit. My stalker had blown up Steele's car—something he obviously cared a lot about—because I hadn't heeded that creepy motherfucker's first warning.

Archer grunted a disgusted sound. "Yeah, it is."

I reeled back like he'd slapped me. My own guilt was bad enough without him rubbing my face in it.

"Shut the fuck up, Arch," Kody snapped. "MK didn't exactly

ask to be stalked by a deranged psychopath. Quit being a salty bitch and try being supportive to her before you really fuck shit up."

My jaw unhinged a bit, and Archer's temple vein throbbed as he shot me a lightning-fast glance. Somehow, I didn't think I was the only one shocked by Kody's outburst.

"Okay then," Bree commented, grabbing my hand and tugging me away from the two guys radiating testosterone like a heavily applied cologne. "Not to pour fuel on the fire or anything, but is that a message on Archer's car?" She pointed with a slightly shaking finger. The black Corvette Stingray was parked in its usual spot—directly beside Steele's burning wreck—and had taken a huge amount of damage to the closest side. But incredibly, all the windows were unbroken, and across the windshield were four words in what looked sickeningly like blood.

Welcome home, Madison Kate.

CHAPTER 7

My day went from bad to worse. After the police finished interviewing, photographing, and documenting, we were finally allowed to go home. Bree drove us because Archer's Corvette was considered evidence, but my curiosity was pricking at me the whole way.

"How did your windows not break?" I asked him, shifting in my seat to meet his gaze. I'd been a bitch and taken the passenger seat, leaving the three massive dudes all squished up in the back seat like a sexy sardine can.

One brow rose, and he met my gaze with cool detachment. "Bulletproof glass, Princess Danvers. It's also bombproof when the bomb isn't placed directly on the car itself."

I frowned harder. "Why do you have bulletproof glass, Archer?"

His glare was totally deadpan in return. "In case some crazy fuck tries to blow up the car next to mine. Why else?"

Prick. I flipped him off and turned back around to stare out the window.

Bree hummed something under her breath as she keyed in our gate code and waited for them to open. She was probably stressing right the fuck out over the level of tension in the car, but...welcome to my life, babe.

"You coming in?" I asked her when she parked in front of the main entrance.

"Uh, of course. You still haven't given me the gossip on this"—she waved a hand at the backs of the three guys making their way into the house ahead of us—"situation. Besides, I'm freaked right the fuck out about today and don't really want to go home right now."

I nodded and gave her a sympathetic look. "Too true. Come on, let's grab snacks and hole up in my room away from all the big dick energy."

She grinned in response and followed me into the house. I'd made it as far as the first step when my father's voice stopped me in my tracks.

"Madison Kate," he called out from the formal dining room, a room we basically *never* used. "Come in here."

My gaze shot to Bree, and she gave me a wide-eyed panic stare.

"Now," Samuel Danvers barked, not ever being one to be kept waiting.

"You better go," I muttered to Bree. "Call me later?"

She grimaced and gave me a short nod. "Count on it. We can go get late-night milkshakes or something."

I sighed as she scurried back out of the house, and reluctantly made my way through to where my father waited for me.

He was sitting at the head of the long table, a gorgeous blond-haired, blue-eyed woman hovering at his shoulder as she refilled his whiskey. Archer sat in the next seat along the table, Kody and Steele opposite him.

"Take a seat, Madison Kate," my father ordered in a voice equally bored and pissed off at the same time.

I dragged my heels as I made my way across the room. He must have yanked the guys in there as soon as they entered the house too, seeing as they'd only been a few moments ahead of me.

"Thanks for the fucking warning, asshole," I muttered under

my breath as I slid into the seat beside Archer. I didn't believe for a second that he hadn't been fully aware of when my father and Cherise would be back from Italy…even if I'd had no clue myself.

The corner of Archer's mouth pulled up, and he looked at me from the corner of his eyes. "Anytime, Princess."

Ugh, I want to junk punch him so hard.

"Madison Kate," my father started, not even glancing at his girlfriend, who I hadn't even been introduced to, "I hear—"

"You must be Cherry," I interrupted, speaking directly to the beautiful woman. It was no wonder my father had gone for her; she looked vaguely similar to my mom but with a whole lot more plastic surgery. "It's nice to meet you…finally." I gave her a tight smile. It wasn't her fault my dad was turning out to be a complete and utter sack of shit. It also wasn't her fault that her son was an antagonistic bastard who made me want to turn to violence on a daily basis.

The pink bedroom, on the other hand…that *was* her fault.

"It's so nice to meet you too, Madison Kate," she replied in a breathy, hushed whisper. It was actually a bit disappointing. I'd sort of expected Archer's mother to be a strong-willed, ballsy woman. Apparently not.

My father cleared his throat in a pointed way, and I hid a smile. Samuel Danvers didn't take well to being talked over. Ever.

"As I was saying," he continued in an annoyed growl, "it's come to my attention that you've been causing a bit of trouble since you've been back, Madison Kate. That's not what we discussed when you asked to come home from Cambodia."

My jaw dropped. "Are you for fucking real right now?" I spluttered. My father's face darkened with fury at my disrespect, but *fuck that*. Respect was earned, not demanded, and he'd done nothing to earn mine.

"Antagonizing your stepbrother with fake porn images—"

"Whoa. What? Archer isn't my fucking stepbrother!" I was

halfway out of my seat, already sick to fucking death of the bullshit my father was peddling. "And he *started it.*"

My father gave me a withering look. "Listen to yourself, Madison Kate. You're eighteen—"

"Almost nineteen." I muttered, even though my birthday wasn't for another five months.

"—and I expect you to start behaving like a mature adult if you're to live under my roof." He continued on like I hadn't said anything, and I ground my teeth together in anger.

One of the boys—probably Kody—made a small scoffing sound at that, though, which sent a flicker of amusement through my fury.

"First of all," I snapped back, balling my hands into fists under the table, "I didn't *ask* to come home from Cambodia. Aunt Marie died and I had nowhere to live because I don't get access to my trust fund until I'm twenty-one."

"Believe me, Madison Kate, I'd change that if I could." My father's words sounded a hell of a lot more threatening than reassuring, and I suppressed a shiver of dread.

"And secondly," I carried on, ignoring the anxiety he'd just sparked in me, "maybe if you hadn't literally moved the pricks who framed me for Riot Night into the same house, I wouldn't feel the need to lash out. Furthermore"—I sucked in a quick breath—"the rest of the so-called *trouble* is thanks to the goddamn stalker that you never felt the need to inform me about. So the explosion on campus today? That's on you. My getting stabbed and almost dying two weeks ago? On. You. Mom's murder? You as well."

My father didn't even flinch. The only reaction he had was a twitch to his brow.

"If you're done with your tantrum, Madison Kate, we are going to discuss some new rules."

I was speechless. Had he heard a single word I'd just said?

"Archer, Kody, and Steele are very concerned that you're acting out and that this so-called stalker is just your newest cry for attention." His voice was so bland he might as well be talking about the damn weather. This got better and fucking better. "I personally would like to see you checked into Riverview Heights for a thorough medical assessment"—I gasped aloud at the mention of the psychiatric hospital—"but Archer seems to think that you simply require stricter rules and boundaries here at home."

I swung my furious gaze around to my *stepbrother* and glared absolute death at him. I was under no illusions that this wasn't his bullshit at play. Kody and Steele were just being dragged down with the sinking ship.

"How very altruistic of *Archer*," I snarled. He didn't look guilty or remorseful in the least. Standard fucking D'Ath.

"This is what's going to happen, Madison Kate," my father continued. "You're not to leave this house without one of the boys to accompany you. You will go to class and come straight home again. You won't be running around with Bree, getting up to god knows what mischief, and you *certainly* won't be seeing that predatory delinquent Dallas Moore."

"This must be a fucking joke," I whispered, horrified. "I must be imagining this. Maybe that concussion was worse than they told me."

"Sit down," Archer hissed at me, yanking sharply on my hand. I hadn't even noticed I'd stood up from my chair. As such, I dropped back into my seat like a sack of bricks.

My father gave me a cold, unkind smile. "Consider yourself under house arrest until these stupid pranks and fake stalker stunts stop happening."

I was stunned to the point of speechlessness. But then... Nope. No way. I was a grown-ass woman, whether I lived in my father's house or not. And no one was forcing me to stay.

Taking a calming breath, I shoved my anger and outrage and

sheer disbelief aside. My father didn't respond well to emotions, only facts and logic.

"I understand the rules you're laying out, Dad," I responded with my very best *calm* voice, given the circumstances. "And respectfully, go fuck yourself."

Whoops.

But the damage was done, so I backed myself. "If those are the rules to living under your roof, then it's an easy fix. I won't." I shoved my chair back from the table and yanked my fingers out of Archer's grip—not until then realizing he hadn't let go. "Cherise, it was lovely to meet you, but your taste in men is, frankly, appalling. I recommend making some life changes."

With a tight smile to my father's girlfriend, I spun on my heel and started out of the dining room. My spine was ramrod straight and my chin high. Fuck them all. I'd survive on my own.

"Madison Kate Danvers," my father's voice boomed, and I flinched. As badly as I wanted to stand on my own two feet and walk out of there with my head held high...old habits die hard. I paused. "If you walk out of this house right now, I'll have you declared medically unfit and committed to Riverview Heights against your will."

I turned around slowly, hardly believing what I was hearing. "You can't do that," I said, shaking my head. "I'm over eighteen; I'm not under your control anymore."

My father looked totally unperturbed, and the guys—all fucking three of them—were like damn statues. None of them looked at me as my father removed my freedoms.

"I can, and I will." Samuel Danvers reached for his phone, holding it up in a threatening way. "Try me, Daughter. A few doses of sedatives and mood stabilizers might do a world of good for that rebellious nature of yours."

Speechless. I was fucking speechless. This *had* to be some kind of head injury–related hallucination. Disbelief warred with outrage and fury as I shifted my gaze over everyone else in the room. Samuel Danvers was the one delivering my sentencing, but no one else was speaking up. No one was defending me. *No fucking one.*

"You're all just going to sit there and let him threaten me like this?" I demanded, my glare sweeping across the guys. I knew Cherry was a lost cause already; my father's casual comment about drugging me had given me a solid clue why she was so fucking docile. Archer had probably been in on this whole plan all along. But...Kody? Steele?

"Say something!" I shouted at them. They weren't avoiding my gaze anymore, but their eyes were hard and their postures stiff. I would get no help from them. Not today.

"It's for your own good, Madison Kate," Archer said, his voice like glacial ice.

I'd *never* wanted to kill someone as badly as I did right then.

"I'm not fucking standing here and taking this," I replied, my mind whirling so hard I was growing dizzy. I started for the door again, but of course my father had to have the last word.

"You leave this house without supervision, you force my hand." He didn't even sound like he *cared*. "I expect this hysteria and acting out to stop, Madison Kate. You're making this family look ridiculous, and I won't stand for it any longer."

I had no words. I just flipped him off and shoved my way out of the dining room, letting the door slam against the wall.

Tears burned my eyes, but instead of running for my bedroom like a sulking child, I paused a moment outside the dining room. Listening.

No one spoke for a moment, and then someone let out a heavy sigh.

"Was that all necessary?" Steele asked, and my heart squeezed painfully. How could he not have stood up for me? After everything he'd said to me, after all the raw emotions he'd poured out. I'd thought he cared. I'd thought...

"She's still better off in Riverview, if you ask me," my father snapped back, his voice carrying more feeling in that one sentence than the whole time he'd spoken to me, "safely medicated and out of the public eye."

"We didn't ask you, Sam," Archer replied with a thread of disgust in his tone. "You've done your part. I think your girlfriend would really enjoy a world cruise, wouldn't you, Mom?"

A delighted female gasp and then, "Oh, I've always wanted to do a cruise!" Her voice was dreamy and…drugged. She was drugged. How the hell was Archer okay with that? It was his *mom* for Christ's sake!

"Good," Archer replied. "There's one departing Seattle in two days. You'd better leave Shadow Grove in the morning to make it in time."

What the fuck?

The sound of chairs being pushed back spurred me into action, and I silently slipped away, racing up the stairs and into my room. My heart pounded against my ribs so hard it hurt as I leaned my back on the door and tried—desperately tried—to make sense of everything that'd just happened.

But I couldn't. Once again, I was fumbling around in the dark, trying to plug a lamp into a nonexistent wall socket. Totally hopeless and insanely frustrating.

My father throwing threats and power trips around was nothing new. He'd never taken it quite so far before, but as furious and disgusted as I was…I wasn't overly shocked. What gutted me to the core was that the guys just sat there and said nothing.

Worse, if I was to draw any conclusions from what I'd just overheard, they almost seemed to be the ones in charge. Pulling my father's strings like he was an expensively suited puppet.

What the *fuck* was going on in this damn house?

CHAPTER 8

I'd only been in my room a few minutes when a knock sounded on my door. I scoffed aloud and rolled my eyes. Whoever it was, I didn't want to see them. No one in this godforsaken house was on my side.

"Fuck off!" I yelled when they knocked again. I'd locked the door before sitting down at my computer desk, so they could knock all they wanted. I wasn't letting them in.

"Babe," Kody called back, "let me in. We need to talk."

Anger choked me, and I needed to swallow before I could form words. "You don't want to hear what I have to say, Kodiak Jones. Just *fuck off.*"

"MK, come on," he replied, sounding frustrated. "You know you don't have the whole story."

Pissed right the fuck off, I shoved back from my desk chair and over to my bedroom door. I flipped the lock and swung the door open to glare at the gorgeous shithead whom I'd happily stab in the eye.

"Oh yeah? You offering to fill me in on all your fucking secrets then, Kodiak?" I kept my hand on the door, blocking access to my room in a clear signal that I wasn't letting him inside.

His brow creased, and his mouth tightened with something all too much like guilt.

I let out a bitter laugh. "Yeah, that's what I thought." I shook my head, then dropped my voice to a low, cold tone. "Like I said, go *fuck* yourself."

I tried to slam the door in his face, but he caught it and pushed back, stepping forward into my personal space. "MK, don't be dense. We only want you to stay safe. Someone literally tried to kill you two weeks ago, and today someone blew up a car—injuring six random students—just because you kissed Steele."

I seethed, my glare like daggers. "Oh, so now my stalker is real again? I thought it was all just a figment of my imagination. A cry for attention." My voice was scathing in its sarcasm, and Kody's green eyes turned sad, like I was hurting him for no good reason.

"None of us believe that, babe. Your dad is just a manipulative fuck who thinks it's okay to gaslight people to get his way." His voice was so sincere I almost believed him. Except…that conversation I'd overheard certainly sounded like this wasn't my father's doing at all. It was theirs—Archer, Kody, and Steele's. I wasn't foolish enough to think Archer had acted alone, not when the three of them were thicker than thieves.

I just met his eyes and hardened my own. I was sick to damn death of being taken for a fool. Sick of all their mountains of secrets that they were so unwilling to share with me. Archer's words to me from the night before echoed through my brain and turned my insides to acid.

Because I don't trust you, Madison Kate.

Did that apply to Kody and Steele too? Were they maintaining their mystery because they didn't trust me as well? Or was it out of loyalty to Archer?

"MK," Kody said, softer this time. Pleading. "Babe, please… trust us to keep you safe?"

I scoffed. "You must honestly think I'm as stupid as my dad thinks I am. Go to fucking hell, Kodiak Jones. I hate you. *Again.*"

This time I shoved him hard in the chest, forcing his hand away from my door so I could slam it shut. I flicked the lock with shaking fingers, then backed away a few steps as tears streamed from my eyes. I was putting up a good front, maintaining my cold fury, but inside I was breaking down. My emotions were in shredded tatters, and my chest ached. I wanted to scream and lash out and hurt them all back, but my father's threat hung over me like a dark cloud.

It wasn't even the first time he'd controlled me with looming danger from a psychiatric assessment either, and I knew he had friends on the board of Riverview Heights. It was far from an empty threat, that was for sure, and nothing scared me more than becoming a prisoner within my own mind.

So I just crumpled to a ball on my new cream-colored carpet and cried.

I had no idea how long I stayed like that, but eventually I picked myself up and changed my clothes for bed. My eyes were puffy and my nose hurt as I crawled under the covers, and I was no better off than I had been when I slammed the door in Kody's face. As good as it sometimes felt to just cry it out, it had done little to solve my problems. But that was future MK's issue.

My dreams were haunted, as they had been every night since Halloween, but this time it was different. Worse. Instead of the blood and violence that I'd started to grow used to on a nightly basis, this time it was dreams of being trapped in a tiny white room with no door, no windows—no way out at all.

I woke screaming, covered in cold sweat, only to have my mattress dip beside me and a strong pair of arms drag me into a tight embrace.

"Go away," I mumbled with a grand total of *zero* conviction. "I don't fucking need you here." Lies.

Fingers stroked through my hair and down my back, kneading the tight muscles beside my spine, and I tucked myself tighter into his hard chest. He was so freaking warm, it was like hugging a giant hot water bottle.

"Yes, you do," Archer replied in a dark murmur.

Tears squeezed out from behind my closed lids, running down my face and onto his skin as my soul screamed in pain. "I hate you so fucking much," I whispered, yet still I threaded my arms around his body, holding him tighter than Rose on the damn door after the *Titanic* sank.

Archer breathed out a long sigh, his heartbeat thumping under my ear. "Not nearly as much as I hate you, Kate." His voice was so quiet, I doubted I was even meant to hear him, but my pulse raced nonetheless. He'd never called me that before. It was so…intimate. "Not as much as I hate myself."

I didn't react. I was certain he hadn't intended to say that out loud, and frankly, I didn't have the energy to fight with him in the middle of the damn night. Instead, I let his steady heartbeat and warm embrace lull me back into a deep, dreamless sleep.

When I woke again, I was alone.

For a moment I questioned my own memories, whether I'd dreamed the whole encounter. But my second pillow smelled of him, tough and manly, like cedarwood and oak but highlighted with delicate notes of lavender and geranium.

I…I had no idea how to feel about Archer's late-night visit. Confused as hell and with a hectic, post-crying headache, I dragged my ass out of bed and went to find something to wear for the day.

It wasn't until after I'd showered, done my hair and makeup, and gotten dressed that I spotted the undeniable proof that I hadn't imagined Archer sleeping here with me. My bedroom door sat weirdly, and on closer inspection I found the wood around the flimsy lock had splintered, meaning it wouldn't fully close properly.

I stared at the broken door for a long moment, desperately trying to reconcile this action with the overbearing prick who'd *somehow* manipulated my father into restricting all my freedom of movement. Eventually, though, I came up blank. Breaking my lock was something done in the heat of a moment, without any regard for consequences. Which said he'd been worried enough about my screaming nightmare, he'd literally broken down my door. But this was Archer, so the math didn't add up.

Shoving the whole weird incident aside, I made my way down to the kitchen for breakfast. As mad as I was, I wasn't missing my lectures, and I wasn't going to starve all the way until lunch.

In the kitchen, I found Cherry sitting at the counter reading a magazine and sipping on a glass of orange juice. And Archer. He was sweaty and still in gym clothes, clearly having just come from his early morning workout with Kody and Steele. I'd unexpectedly slept in later than I'd gotten into the habit of doing, so I wasn't getting the kitchen all to myself like I'd hoped.

"Oh, good morning, honey!" Cherry sang when she saw me standing there scowling at her son's sweaty back. "How did you sleep?"

I blinked at her a couple of times before I realized she was dead serious, like she hadn't even witnessed the disgusting scene with my father the evening before.

"Fine," I grunted back. I moved into the kitchen and reached past Archer to grab my favorite sugary cereal from the cupboard—seeing as he seemed to have no intention of moving out of my way. "You'd better fix my damn door," I muttered to him under my breath as I leaned close. "I won't be held prisoner here without at least an illusion of privacy."

Archer leaned his ass against the counter, drinking from his protein shaker—probably using fresh protein powder after my steroids prank. A tiny smile pulled the corner of his lips. "Glad you understand it's only an illusion, Princess."

Anger rippled through me, and I slammed my breakfast cereal down on the counter so hard little pieces flew out and scattered.

"Now, now," he chided me under his breath, "none of that feminine hysteria of yours."

I could have murdered him. Right then and there, cut his throat with my breakfast spoon and watched as his blood poured all over the white marble of the kitchen tiles.

But he was saved by the barely concealed laughter in his blue eyes. It was an expression I couldn't remember ever seeing on his ruggedly handsome face, and it was enough to temper my immediate anger. He was making fun of my father's misogynistic bullshit... but that still didn't make it okay. Just less murder-worthy.

"Madison Kate," Cherry spoke up, tearing my attention away from her son, "your father had to take some early morning calls, and I know you're leaving for class soon."

I arched a brow, wondering *how* she knew that. It wasn't like we'd ever exchanged more than five words.

Archer took that opportunity to swagger out of the kitchen, mumbling something to his mom about needing a shower. That left me alone with my father's new girlfriend, who I knew next to nothing about.

"Honey, I was really looking forward to getting to know you better," Cherry continued when I said nothing at all. I just went about making my breakfast. Not that she deserved me being a bitch to her, but if anyone was guilty by association...

"Was?" I repeated, not really caring but feeling all kinds of awkward with the one-sided conversation.

Cherry gave me a beaming smile. "Your father booked us on a world cruise!" She was legitimately excited, and I felt sorry for her. "We have to leave today. I'm so sorry, Madison Kate. I know it's not..." She trailed off as her smile slipped, and she twisted her necklace in a clear sign of nervousness. "I know the boys are a bit intense, but they'll do anything to keep you safe. You know that, right?" Her smile was shaky, and her eyes haunted with shadows of past trauma. Fuck, I pitied her.

I gave her a tight smile in return. "Sure."

But she wasn't done. She came around the counter to where I stood with my cereal, then gripped my forearms with her thin hands. "I mean it, Madison Kate. They went through a lot growing up, and it makes them a bit difficult to be around. But whoever is trying to hurt you...they'll take care of it." Her gaze was laser-focused on me now, seemingly clear of the drug haze I'd seen yesterday.

"Uh, okay," I replied, beyond creeped out. "Thanks?"

She seemed satisfied with my response because she let out a sigh and released my arms with a smile. "Well, I better go and pack my bags again! I can't wait to visit Tahiti; it's always been on my bucket list."

The way she waltzed out of the kitchen again, it was like a whole different woman from the scary intense one who'd just grabbed me hard enough to leave nail prints in my skin.

"That was fucking creepy," I muttered to myself as I doused my cereal in milk and dropped a spoon into the bowl.

"What was?" A voice came from behind me, and I startled.

Spinning around, I speared Steele with an acidic death glare. "Oh look, there goes my appetite." Holding his gaze, I dropped my full bowl of breakfast into the sink with a crash and wiped my hands off on my jeans. "Something about the stench of betrayal always turns my stomach."

It was dramatic as all hell, but I gave zero fucks. I could eat at SGU and not have to suffer through Steele's undoubtedly half-assed apologies.

He let out a heavy, disappointed sigh, and his gray eyes swam with guilt. But still, no excuses left his lips.

"Archer's driving you to class today," he said instead, opening the fridge and pulling out a bottle of that sickly sweet iced coffee shit. I used to love those drinks, but after I got food poisoning from one, the smell now triggered my gag reflex.

"Fuck that," I snapped back.

Steele just cracked his drink open and took a long sip. At least he wasn't trying to murder my espresso machine this morning. "Ride with Arch, or you don't go."

My fists clenched, and I tried those calming breaths that Aunt Marie had tried to teach me. "Why him?" I had my back to Steele and was halfway out of the kitchen when I stopped to ask that question.

He didn't answer immediately, and I could feel him moving closer.

"Because my car got blown up yesterday, Hellcat," he said softly from far too close behind me. My hair shifted, and I knew he'd touched one of the loose waves. "And Arch has bulletproof glass in all his cars."

Curiosity warred with anger, and I stiffened. "Why does Archer have bulletproof glass in his cars, Steele?"

I knew I wouldn't get the real reason, but I had to ask. After his whole spiel to me yesterday, going on about how there were too many secrets between us...fucking hypocrite.

"You'll have to ask him that," Steele responded, and my shoulders sagged with disappointment.

I heaved a sigh and shook my head. "Forget I asked. Tell Archer I'll be waiting in the garage. I don't intend to be late for class just because he needs to manscape in the shower."

"Madison Kate," Steele called after me as I left the kitchen, but I was in no mood. I flipped him off without a backward glance and went to find my shoes and bag.

I'd planned on wearing my usual flat-soled boots, but now that the guys had made an enemy of me again, I felt the need for a bit more height.

Tossing my boots back into my closet, I stuffed my feet into a pair of high-heeled Timberland boots. They were a gorgeous deep crimson with black fur around the ankle and boosted me a solid four inches without killing my feet, thanks to the small platform at the toe. As if by fate, they matched the sweater I was wearing perfectly, and my black skinny jeans went with everything anyway.

Satisfied, I snagged my bag and slipped it over my shoulder as I headed down to the enormous garage. I seriously doubted Archer would have the Corvette back yet, but I hadn't seen him drive anything else, so I had no clue which cars were his. All three of the boys seemed to have a suspicious amount of money at their disposal, and only Steele had given me any impression it might have come from family.

The simple fact that his parents had been grooming him as a concert pianist and wanted him to attend Juilliard...that just sort of reeked of an upper-class upbringing.

"Over here, Princess," Archer drawled from somewhere farther into the line of cars and bikes. I followed the sound of his voice and found him leaning on the side of a low-slung black sports car. I was by no means a car expert, but the vehicle oozed dollar signs.

"Of course all your cars are black," I commented when he popped the passenger-side door open for me. I waited until he came around and slid into the driver's seat before finishing my statement. "Matches your soul."

He fucking *laughed*, and I seethed. Clearly he hadn't learned from the steroid powder incident. I needed to come up with something better. After all, what else would I do with my time now that I was under house arrest?

We drove to Shadow Grove University in silence, but stupid fucking Archer D'Ath just couldn't resist the urge to take one last stab at my sanity as we drove into the student parking lot.

"You're actually kind of adorable when you're asleep, Princess

Danvers." He delivered it as such casual commentary, like we hadn't whispered our hatred of each other in the darkness of my bedroom.

I shot a glare at him, waiting for the punch line. He didn't look at me, though, as he maneuvered into a new parking space—his usual one, along with Steele's, was still taped off.

He stopped the car and killed the engine before turning to me with a sly smirk. "Mainly because you're silent."

I rolled my eyes and unbuckled my seat belt. "Weak, D'Ath. Try harder next time, and maybe one of your arrows will fly straight."

Stepping out of his car, I slammed the door harder than necessary and made my way into the campus without waiting around for him to join me. He probably didn't even have classes today, given how infrequently he'd attended prior to this.

Still, I couldn't help but let his words replay in my mind, filling me with an unwanted warmth. He thought I was adorable.

But why the fuck did I care?

CHAPTER 9

The rest of the week dragged. I'd taken to only speaking with the guys when I absolutely needed to; otherwise they may as well have been as invisible as my father's household staff. Not to say I didn't physically see them—they seemed to be around more than ever—but I simply pretended they weren't there. It was driving them insane, I was fairly certain, but they fucking deserved it.

I needed to work out what the fuck was going on, and as badly as I wanted some petty revenge in the form of cling wrap over their toilet or salt in their toothpaste or something equally amusing, it wouldn't get me out of my current predicament.

I mean, some of those things might have happened as well... but they weren't the main focus of my attention.

As expected, Cherry and my father had disappeared again by the time I got home from classes that day and hadn't even left so much as a note. I would have ripped it up even if they had, but still, it was odd. One of many odd things that just added to the mystery around the three boys acting as my jailers.

The one saving grace to the whole dirty situation was that I still had my phone—the new one Bree had gotten me and linked to her plan. I'd been texting her all week, and we'd taken to skipping lunch in the dining room to hang out in the library. It was a location I'd never seen any of the boys. Shocker.

"So, have you had any more ideas?" she asked me on Friday as we shared the takeout Chinese she'd had delivered to the librarian. "They can't honestly keep you locked up forever. Something's gotta give."

I wrinkled my nose, chewing a piece of pork. "I agree, in theory, but I also wouldn't have thought them capable of all this in the first place."

"So aside from making their lives a living hell by withholding your magical, coveted vagina—"

"Ha-ha," I said sarcastically, cutting her off.

She grinned wickedly. "What else have you been doing to make them break? Come on, MK, if anyone can drive them nuts enough to give up on this whole house-arrest bullshit, it's you."

I scowled. "Gee, thanks."

She snickered, stealing the last spring roll. "You know what I mean. Have you tried shifting gears? Getting one of them on your side?"

I sighed. "How? Those three are the walking dictionary definition of *bromance*, girl. They give all-new meaning to the phrase *bros before hos.*" I frowned. "Not that I'm a ho. But it rhymes."

Bree laughed harder. "Uh, well, I was going to suggest you use your magical vagina to sway them to your side, but now I feel like I'm calling you a whore."

"Thanks," I deadpanned. "Come on, I need to think bigger. Why are they doing this in the first place?"

Bree took a sip of her soda, thinking. "Are you totally sure it's them, not your dad? He tried this before, remember? Just after your mom died."

I shivered at the memory. I'd been a wreck and would have posed a much better case for committal then than I currently did. But my psychiatrist—knowing I didn't need to be drugged and locked up—had talked him out of it. When it came to Samuel Danvers, it didn't matter what the doctors said, if it went against what he wanted. But somehow my doctor had managed to convince him to put me into regular therapy until I showed "improvement" by his standards. I was lucky my father hadn't just paid off another crooked doctor to do what he wanted.

"I know," I said, feeling sick at the reminder, "but I also know what I heard after I left the room. He did it all on Archer's orders, then literally left the country after one suggestion from Archer about a cruise. Archer's up to something. They all are."

Bree let out a long sigh, ruffling her hair with a hand. We were sitting on top of a table in the middle of the dead-silent library, thanks to ninety-nine percent of students doing their research and homework online these days.

"Have you wondered if maybe they really are doing it to protect you?" she suggested in a gentle tone. "I know they picked a really fucked up way to do it—you'll hear no disagreement from me there. But...is it possible they're just crazy worried your stalker will succeed next time he tries to kill you?" She paused, her mouth twisted down. "I know I am. As shitty as this house arrest is for you, is it so bad that I'm relieved you're safe?" Her voice was quiet but sincere, and it made me pause.

Had I been so wrapped up in myself that I'd totally missed how my near death might affect my best friend? Shit. I sucked.

"Breezie," I said, shifting closer and taking her hand in mine, "babe. Come on. You know it's going to take more than a couple of deranged, knife-wielding maniacs to take me down."

She sniffed, not meeting my eyes. "But they almost did, MK. If Arch and the boys hadn't been there when they were...you would be dead now."

Fuck.

She had a point. One I'd been deliberately ignoring for the past three weeks because it didn't fit the narrative I was clinging to.

"Can't you maybe consider the possibility that they—like me—were totally shit-scared that you'd almost been murdered and just made a crappy decision on how to keep you safe?" Her voice was a bit broken, and I was horrified to see a tear roll down her cheek.

I shoved our half-eaten food aside and wrapped my arms around her, pulling her into me for a long hug. "Bree, babe. I'm so freaking sorry. I didn't even…" I sighed. I was an insensitive asshole.

"It's fine," she lied. "I know you're okay now. I just think maybe they panicked and acted without fully thinking shit through. Can you blame them? You're incredible. It's no wonder they're all hopelessly in love."

I laughed at how thick she was laying it on and released her to sit back. "Uh-huh. Right. They're acting like overbearing, misogynistic dickholes because they're all so madly in love with me that they're acting irrationally. Good theory, babe."

Bree didn't laugh back, just shrugged and watched me from under wet lashes. "I would do the same in their situation, MK."

I frowned slightly, something in her tone giving me an uneasy feeling, but brushed it aside. "Well, even if that outlandish and totally incorrect theory were true…it only brings up the bigger question in all of this."

"What's that?" she asked, swiping at her eyes with the back of her hand and leaving a smudge of mascara. "Why none of them have gotten sick of you acting like a brat and spanked you yet?" Her smile was teasing but also seemed a bit forced. Weird.

"Uh." I gave a small laugh. "No, I meant…how exactly are they getting my father to do what they want? My father, Bree. Samuel Danvers the fucking Fourth, biggest douche in all of Shadow Grove. No one tells him what to do. Certainly not three twenty-something, ex-gangster punks."

Bree snagged a cold spring roll and crunched on it thoughtfully before responding.

"Well, I don't have all the answers, MK," she finally said with a grin. "But considering they're all up in your business twenty-four-seven these days, you're in the best position to find out, aren't you?"

I drummed my fingertips on the table. "That's true."

Bree just gave me a sly smile and kept eating the last of our lunch. I lay back on the table and stared up at the fancy stained-glass skylight while I thought over what she'd just said. Could they be acting out of genuine concern? It was possible, I supposed, in Kody's or Steele's case. Not Archer's. He was almost certainly pulling one of his power-tripping bullshit moves...but to what end? And what the fuck did he have over my father?

"It doesn't matter anyway," I eventually sighed. "As shitty as it all is, I'd be a total, brain-dead moron to rebel just for the sake of pride. I'm still being stalked, and someone still tried to murder me a few weeks ago. The only thing I'd achieve by deliberately sneaking out or running away is..."

"Possibly becoming someone's super pretty, pink-haired skin suit?" Bree finished my sentence for me, and I snickered.

"Exactly."

"So...what are you going to do?"

I breathed out a long sigh, covering my face with my palms and groaning. "I have no idea, Bree. What would you do?"

My best friend gave an evil sort of laugh. "Uh, girl, you know exactly what I'd do if I were forced to be alone with those three all day and *all night*." Her tone was low and teasing. There was no mistaking what she was trying to imply. Sex. She meant sex. "Come on, MK, you can't seriously tell me you haven't dreamed about a reverse-harem relationship with them all. It's the perfect setup. Just you and them, all alone in that big old house..." She trailed off like she was imagining herself in that position, and I laughed.

"You're the worst," I told her with a grin, covering my eyes with my arm. I was so freaking tired. My sleep had been better—no screaming nightmares—but still disturbed and restless enough that

I never woke feeling fresh. The last time I'd managed a restful sleep was when Archer had broken my lock and held me all night.

Bree chuckled to herself. "I don't hear a denial there, babe."

I scoffed, still not looking at her. "Yeah, well, I'm trying to stop lying to myself."

She cackled like some kind of cartoon villain. "So you *have* thought about it. I knew it."

"I've thought about plenty of things, girl. Doesn't mean I'm going to act on *any* of them. Besides, could you imagine Archer actually trying to share a woman?" I laughed at my own mental image in an attempt to ignore what a turn-on that idea was. "Pretty sure he would struggle to share a burrito, let alone a taco…if you catch my drift."

Bree laughed so hard I worried she was going to choke on her food, so I sat up slightly and frowned at her. "Damn, dude, it wasn't that funny."

She couldn't reply, though. She was red-faced and laughing into her hand while looking…over my shoulder.

Ah *fuck*.

Tilting my head back, I met Kody's smiling green eyes. "Well. I should have seen that one coming," I muttered.

His grin was wide and his eyes full of amusement, as well as raw, hungry desire. "I dunno, MK; Arch is pretty good at sharing when the incentive is right."

My cheeks flamed, but I refused to rise to the bait. Steele stood slightly behind him with his phone in his hand and didn't seem to be paying attention. I could only hope.

"Pretty sure hanging out with Bree is in direct violation of your father's rules, babe," Kody commented, giving me a warning look. I just scowled back at him, letting all my annoyance seep into my gaze.

"Pretty sure you want to stop being such a prick unless you want to find your ass superglued to the toilet seat tomorrow morning," I replied with all the snark of a hormonal thirteen-year-old.

I pushed myself back up and swung my legs over the edge of the table. Bree and I had been doing a bit of studying while we ate and gossiped, seeing as exams were coming up, so I packed my books and notes away into my bag.

"Thanks, Bree. This was fun until my jailers gate-crashed." I shot a glare at Kody and Steele—who'd put his phone away and was paying attention. "I'll call you later, and we can make plans for Thanksgiving."

"Sounds good," Bree replied at the same time that Kody shook his head.

"Sorry, Bree," he said, sounding anything but apologetic, "we already have plans for Thanksgiving."

"No we don't," I snapped back, slinging my bag over my shoulder and grimacing at the weight of it. Reality was catching up with me, and I knew I needed to put some serious study hours in during the next week if I wanted any hope of passing my classes. Thankfully, I was an excellent crammer.

Kody just smiled back at me, all smug and shit. "Yes, we do, babe. That's what Steele and I were coming to tell you. Right, bro?" He whacked his gray-eyed friend, who just cocked a pierced brow in confusion.

I folded my arms and called Kody's bluff. "Oh yeah? What are we doing that can't involve Bree?"

"Arch is cooking for us," he replied with a smug grin. "Mexican."

My glare turned murderous as Kody grinned wider.

"Fuck that," Steele muttered, sweeping a tattooed hand over his hair, then coming over to me and dropping an arm over my shoulders. "Arch can fucking starve for all I care."

I tried to stomp away in a huff, but Steele wasn't letting me go so easily. He shifted my heavy bag to his own shoulder, then took my hand in his, weaving our fingers together as we left the library.

Nothing had changed. I was still *furious* at them all. But...I didn't pull away.

So maybe something had changed after all. Maybe Bree had a point.

Maybe, *maybe*, they really were just trying to keep me safe.

Yet I couldn't ignore the certainty that they knew more than they were letting on.

CHAPTER 10

Thick snow blanketed everything by Thanksgiving morning. I'd been cooped up in my bedroom all week, studying my ass off for exams and kicking myself for being so damn distracted all semester. Something about the snow, though, made everything so calm and peaceful.

I hadn't heard a single word from my father since he and Cherry had left on their cruise, and I didn't care to reach out. He'd shown his cards, and I was no longer interested in making an effort with our toxic relationship.

It was still more than two years until I'd be permitted access to my inheritance—from my mother—but I couldn't fathom the idea of remaining a prisoner so long. I needed my freedom, my independence. More than that, I needed to be rid of my stalker. *And* my attempted murderer…if they really were unconnected.

I'd woken early again and shivered as I padded around the kitchen in my socks. I needed coffee more than I needed a sweatshirt.

"Good morning, Miss Danvers," my father's elderly butler, Steinwick, greeted me in a quiet voice as he came into the room. "Would you like me to make that for you?"

I shook my head quickly, giving him an alarmed look. "Uh, no offense, but no. I remember the last time you tried to make me a coffee on this machine." It had probably been about three years ago but was bad enough to stick in my memory.

Steinwick gave me a watery smile and inclined his head. "Well, if you need anything…"

He looked a bit forlorn, and I smiled. He'd been in my father's employment for about five years, but I saw him so rarely I barely knew the man. "I know how to find you," I assured him, nodding to the intercom that we *never* used. "But maybe just enjoy the break while my father is away. I trust he's still paying your wages, even if none of us really need staff around?"

The older man hesitated a moment, then gave me a small nod. "Yes, miss. My employer is taking good care of things, even if we are a bit bored."

I gave a short laugh. "Well, enjoy it. I'm sure he'll make up for it by being a demanding fuck when he gets back from his cruise."

Steinwick murmured a bland agreement and shuffled silently out of the kitchen. Seriously, the household staff were like ghosts. That was the most I'd spoken to Steinwick in…forever.

Rubbing my arms, I clenched my jaw to stop my teeth from chattering as I waited for the espresso machine to warm up.

A warm hoodie draped over my shoulders a few moments later, though, and I shivered into the garment.

"Thanks," I murmured, threading my arms into the sleeves and hugging the body-warmed fabric around me. It smelled like Steele, all clean soap and car grease. "You want coffee?"

"God, yes," he mumbled back, his voice thick with sleep as his arms came around my middle and he zipped the hoodie up for me. But he didn't move away when he was done, instead resting his face on the bend of my neck a moment while his inked arms rested across my middle. "Why are you down here shivering your cute ass off at this time of morning, Hellcat?"

"Making coffee, obviously," I replied. I didn't move out of his embrace, leaning back into his chest as I went through the motions to make our coffees. "What are you doing down here pretending like we're okay again?"

Not that I was complaining.

Steele sucked in a deep breath, releasing it in a long sigh that ruffled my hair before he replied. "I want us to be okay again. I hate all the anger and resentment and silent treatment... It's fucking killing me."

Damn him for speaking the thoughts I was too stubborn to say out loud.

After we finished our coffees, I set them aside and turned around in his arms so I could face him. He'd taken his own hoodie off for me, leaving him in just a T-shirt and sweatpants. His skin was prickled with goose bumps and he was rumpled from sleep, but *damn* he was attractive.

Blame it on the snow for bringing me a weird sense of calm in the early, predawn light. But I was ready to let go of some of that crap. I looped my arms around Steele's neck, letting the long sleeves of his hoodie cover my hands.

"I miss you," I admitted in a soft whisper. "It seems silly, considering we never really...I dunno. I just thought we were starting something and then..."

Steele grimaced. "And then we went and fucked it all up. Your dad—"

"Is a prick," I cut him off, my eyes hardening, "but he wasn't acting out of his own concern for my mental health, was he?"

Steele's eyes turned sad. Regretful. "Hellcat..." He sounded pained, and I shook my head.

"It doesn't matter. I know you guys—or Archer—have been pulling his strings. But what I want to know is how?" I kept my tone calm and nonconfrontational because deep down I already knew I'd get nothing out of Steele. This was Archer's circus, and we were all his monkeys. "How did you make him threaten me like that? Why?"

Steele's brow furrowed, his mouth twisting down, and I sighed.

"Forget it," I muttered, shifting my gaze away and dropping my arms from around his neck. He caught my wrists, though, and placed my hands back on his shoulders.

"Don't do that, Hellcat," he told me in a soft, tortured voice. "I want to tell you everything so badly. You have *no* idea. But…" He trailed off with a frustrated sound.

I nodded. "But Archer, right?"

Steele gave a small nod, his frown deep. "It's his story and his secrets, babe. I can't betray his trust before he's ready."

A small stab of disappointment shot through me, even though logically I understood where he was coming from. "Right. But it's okay to stomp all over mine." It came out more bitter than I'd intended, and Steele flinched like I'd hit him.

I tried to pull away from him again, but he tightened his grip, crowding me against the counter with the coffee machine at my back.

"Madison Kate," he said with a thread of iron in his voice. "It's never okay to betray your trust. Ever. It's something I think the three of us will spend a *long* time making up to you…but I owe Archer my life. When he asks me to keep his confidence, I can't—"

"It's fine," I interrupted. I was being combative simply for the sake of it. I *knew* all of this. It was abundantly clear to anyone who paid attention; Archer, Kody, and Steele had a bond forged in fire. It ran deeper than blood, deeper than family. To expect *any* of them to prioritize me or my fragile feelings when they barely knew me from a bar of soap…it was preposterous and arrogant. "I don't want to argue, Steele. I just…" I sighed and rested my forehead on his chest. "I just want this to all be over, okay? I want my stalker to disappear. I want whoever tried to kill me to die in a plane crash. I want to walk away from Shadow Grove and everyone in it, and never look back." I was whispering the words, but I knew he heard me from the way his arms tightened around me. He pulled me in close until I was surrounded by his scent, his warmth.

"I don't want that," he murmured back, "because then I might never see you again."

Pulling back slightly, I tipped my head back to meet his gaze again. "Steele—"

Whatever I was going to say...who fucking cared? His lips met mine, and suddenly my mind was blank to whatever bullshit I'd been about to spin.

Flutters of desire lit me up from the inside, and I leaned into his kiss, meeting him eagerly and tangling with that delicious tongue stud in the way I'd been craving for weeks.

A small, insecure part of me had been hurt by the space he'd given me after that night we'd spent together...even though it'd been me pushing him away. Part of me had bought into Archer's crap that Steele was no longer interested, even after our "talk."

His kiss now, though, erased those last, lingering worries.

A deep shiver ran through me, and Steele broke his lips from mine with a small chuckle.

"Any chance we can take these coffees back up to my room?" he asked, his voice low and husky. My brows shot up, and his eyes widened. "Oh, no. I didn't mean..." He shook his head with a laugh. "I mean, sure, that too. But I meant where it's warmer, seeing as you have my hoodie. Also, I was working on something..." His gaze shifted away, and he twisted his lips in a nervous movement. "I thought maybe I could play it for you?"

"Oh." I blinked a couple of times. I'd thought he wanted to fuck—which I was totally on board with, I might add—but he wanted to play me something. Knowing now what I did about his reluctance to play the piano for anyone, it seemed like a deeply intimate gesture. "Sure. Okay, cool. Let's go."

I released him and reached for the two slightly cool coffees I'd left sitting on the counter beside the espresso machine. He took one from me and then joined our free hands as we made our way through the silent house and up to his bedroom.

"Damn, your room really is warmer," I commented as we stepped inside and Steele softly closed the door behind us. He grinned, placing his coffee on the bedside table and climbing back into his rumpled bed. He'd brought his keyboard over and had clearly been working on something while in bed because there were piles of ink-covered music sheets scattered on the cover.

"Come, sit." He indicated to the other side of the bed. "It was too cold to sit at my desk earlier before my heating kicked in, so I moved over here."

"This is next-level adorable," I murmured, climbing into his bed and tucking my toes under the covers. His wireless headphones were tossed aside, and he made no movement to put them back on. It was a small thing, but knowing he hadn't played for anyone since his sister died…it touched something inside me. It made the secrets and betrayals just a tiny bit less hurtful because he was showing his feelings in other ways.

With a short glance at me, he got comfortable sitting cross-legged with his keyboard on a lap desk in front of him. Then he began to play.

The familiar tune sparked my memory, and I made a small sound that caused Steele to look over and meet my eyes.

"Is this the song you were working on last time you played for me?" I asked in a hushed whisper, not wanting to interrupt the beautiful, haunting melody. He nodded, a small smile pulling at his lips as his fingers moved with fluid grace.

"It's the first thing I've written since Rachel died," he admitted, his voice just as soft. "But that night, while you were lying here in my bed…it just came to me. It's been tugging at my brain for weeks, but I couldn't…I couldn't work on it when you weren't here. It just wouldn't come to me."

I snuggled down into his pillows, getting comfortable as I sipped my coffee. "Are you trying to tell me that I'm your muse, Max Steele?"

He shot me another quick look, his eyes like mercury. "I guess so."

Neither of us spoke again, and the lilting tune from Steele's keyboard filled the room as he played. It was the kind of music that conveyed a myriad of emotions. Deep, raw feelings threaded into every note he played, and the melody somehow managed to rip open something inside me.

When he finished, the last note hung in the air for what seemed like ages, and we just sat in silence for a long, comfortable pause.

"So, what did you think?" he asked me after a while, lifting his keyboard and lap desk off the bed and placing it on the floor. Sheet music in his handwriting was scattered everywhere, but he paid it no mind as he shuffled down onto the pillows to face me.

I licked my lips, tasting the remnants of my coffee, which I'd finished some moments ago. "You wrote that?" I asked him, almost disbelieving. "It was incredible. You're…" I shook my head. "You're crazy talented, Max Steele. But you already know that."

He gave me one of those cocky smirks. "Yeah, but did *you* like it? I only wrote it for you."

My heart beat a little harder. "What?"

He gave a small, self-conscious shrug. "I don't find any inspiration in writing for myself anymore. Or writing for…any other reason. I think I'm pretty much done with this phase of my life, but then something about you inspired me so…yeah. I wrote that for you. And I'll probably write something else for you too. If you're cool with that?"

I blinked at him, stunned. "Um, yeah, dude. Pretty sure this is the most flattering thing anyone has ever done for me. Ever. I'm not going to lie, I'm all kinds of girly for you right now. Have I turned into one of those heart-eyes emojis? Because that's what I feel like."

I was also rambling like an idiot, but who the fuck cared? Steele composed a fucking song for me. *For me.*

Steele's lips curved in a smile. "So, you liked it, then?"

Leaning in, I cupped his face with both my hands and stared deep into his eyes. "Max Steele. Stop fishing for compliments. I fucking loved it."

"Are you sure?" he asked me with total seriousness. "Because I was kinda hoping for a more enthusiastic response. I just composed a classical piano piece for you, Hellcat. Damn."

I rolled my eyes but gave him what he was so clearly begging for. I kissed him with all the emotions that his music had filled me with, climbing into his lap as our kiss deepened.

His arms circled my waist, holding me tight against his body as I took my time playing with his tongue stud, then sucking on his lower lip.

"That's more like what I was aiming for," he murmured when I started trailing kisses along his jaw to his neck. I owed him some marks from the last time we'd been in bed together...

A knock on his door made me pause, and he groaned into my hair.

"Go away!" he called out to whoever was interrupting us. "I'm sleeping!"

"No you're not," Kody called back. "I just heard you playing." There was a pause and then... "Do you have a girl in there with you?"

I froze. Steele froze. The door handle started to turn.

"Fuck," Steele hissed, tossing me off his lap and bolting across the room just in time to slam into the door before it opened more than a crack. "Kody, fuck off!"

"What the hell?" Kody sounded like he was laughing. "Dude, you totally have a chick in there." There was a pause as Steele flipped his lock and leaned on the door. "Kind of a dick move, bro. I thought you were really into MK."

Steele shot me a pained look, then scowled at the door. "What? I am. Kody, seriously. Fuck off."

"Okay, geez. I'm just saying, if you really cared about MK, you wouldn't be messing around with another chick." Kody sounded all kinds of disapproving, and it made my heart all warm and fluttery. "You're going to have to tell her, you know."

Steele rolled his eyes like he was in pain but left the door—once he'd double-checked the lock—and came back over to join me in his bed. "Yep, I've got it handled, Kody. Thanks for your concern."

"I'm not concerned, you dick," Kody shot back. "I just want to watch her punch you in the fucking face for messing around on her. Violent MK turns me on."

I needed to clap a hand over my own mouth to stop from laughing out loud at that, and Steele gave me an incredulous look.

"You're an asshole, Kody," he shouted back to his friend. "Now fuck off unless you want to hear more than you bargained for at this time of the morning." He kept his gaze locked on mine as he said this, and his eyes sparkled with invitation.

I raised my brows, tilting my head to the side and silently accepting. I mean…a girl had needs after all. And Kody already thought Steele was with a girl, so I didn't even need to be quiet. Right?

Right. Flimsy logic was good enough for me.

CHAPTER 11

When no response came from the other side of Steele's bedroom door, I glanced over at it, then back to Steele.

"Do you think he's gone?" I whispered with a mischievous smirk.

Steele's brows raised, his piercing catching the light. "Do we care? Door's locked."

I grinned in response, and that was all the confirmation he needed. His lips met mine again in a heated, open-mouthed kiss that made me squirm with desire underneath him. I wriggled around until my legs were wrapped around his waist, crushing his hard length against my aching core so I could grind on him.

"We don't have long," he breathed in my ear, his warm hands slipping under his loose hoodie that I still wore and finding the hem of my sleeping tank.

I groaned as his palms found my breasts and thanked the stars I'd been too lazy to put a bra on before going downstairs this morning. "How come? It's not like we have a big family Thanksgiving dinner to prepare for."

Steele didn't reply immediately, and I arched under him, hungry for more of what he was doing to me. My fingers tangled in his T-shirt, then stripped it over his head and tossed it aside to

reveal his smooth, tattooed chest. All the boys had incredible ink…
something that drove me a bit weak with arousal.

"We have a trip today," Steele admitted, sitting back on his heels
to unzip his hoodie from me, and I shifted just long enough to take
it off, along with my tank top. That left me in just a small pair of
shorts and him in sweatpants.

He paused a moment, stroking his fingertips over the scar on
my abdomen before dipping his head to place a light kiss on the
raised flesh.

I wrinkled my nose, curious about this mysterious trip but not
enough to stop what we were doing. "A trip? Where to?"

But his attention had shifted to my breasts, and when his
tongue started toying with my hardened nipple, flicking it with
his piercing, then sucking and biting…yeah, fuck chatting. We
could discuss it *after* orgasms.

Clearly, he thought the same thing, shuffling back down the
bed and hooking his fingers into the waistband of my shorts. He
dragged them down my legs, then cocked that pierced brow at me.

"No underwear, Hellcat?"

I smirked. "You're a bad influence on me, Max Steele."

He grinned. "Some might say I'm the very best influence."
Then he settled back on the bed with his shoulders between my
spread thighs.

I sucked in a sharp breath as his fingers stroked down my pussy,
his warm breath feathering my sensitive flesh and teasing me. My
hands came to his head, encouraging as my nails scratched over his
buzzed-short brown hair.

"I've been dreaming about doing this for weeks," Steele
confessed, dipping his face down and licking me ever so lightly.
Fucking cunt tease. "I could have killed Arch for pulling me out
of your bed that night."

That night. The one that I'd made out with all three of them—
individually—then witnessed them beat the crap out of a gangster.

"Is it what you think about in the shower?" I teased him with a small bubble of amusement in my hushed, lust-filled voice.

Steele hummed a sound of agreement, licking me with more determination and using his fingers to spread me open for his mouth. The way he used his tongue stud over my clit...pure fucking heaven.

"I think about all kinds of things in the shower," he murmured after a long torture session that had me writhing and whimpering, grinding against his face and begging for more. "I've even thought about sneaking into your bathroom and stealing your body wash."

A laugh escaped me at that suggestion, but it quickly faded into panting moans when Steele slid two fingers into me and latched back on to my clit with his mouth. Shuddering waves of pleasure rolled through me, and my toes dug into his mattress as my hips moved and my orgasm built sharply.

He added a third finger and fucked me hard with his hand while he showed me *exactly* what that tongue piercing was good for. At the last second, I grabbed his pillow and crushed it to my own face, muffling my screams as I crashed through my climax and Steele continued eating me out like...well...like his favorite food on earth.

"Holy shit," I exclaimed when my orgasm started to fade and I could safely remove my self-imposed gag. "Fuck, Steele. Please tell me *you* have condoms? I need to feel you inside me."

He made a self-satisfied sound, leaving my cunt with one last kiss and rising up on his knees. Leaning over me, he reached for his bedside table, sweeping a stack of music sheets onto the floor, but I was impatient and greedy as fuck. I hooked my fingers in the waistband of his sweats and dragged them down, freeing his huge erection, slick with fluid already.

Excitement bubbled through me, and my hypersensitive cunt pulsed with need. That first orgasm had been great, no fucking questioning it. But I just knew the next one was going to be even more mind-blowing... I wrapped my hand around his length, giving him a few firm strokes as he located a condom and sat back on his heels to tear it open.

A knock sounded on his door as he rolled the condom down his shaft, and I gave him a small brow raise. He shook his head, though, and hooked his hands under my thighs, hauling me closer and lining himself up with my soaking core.

"Ignore him," he muttered, pushing inside me with a sharp exhale. I moaned at the sudden movement, arching my back and reveling in the delicious feeling of having him fully seated inside me. As wet as I was from him going down on me, there was no discomfort, just sheer, blinding satisfaction.

The knock came again, accompanied by Archer's voice. "Steele, get up. We leave in fifteen."

Steele breathed a curse, but he didn't make any moves to stop. Instead, he leaned forward, bracing his arms to either side of my head as his hips pumped, fucking me slowly but so fucking hard I was seeing stars.

"Steele," Archer barked. "You hear me?" The doorknob rattled, and I tensed before remembering it was locked.

"Seriously," Steele muttered, his voice husky and dripping with arousal. "Ignore him."

I grinned up at him. "Fine by me." I reached up, linking my arms around his neck and tilting my hips in a way that allowed him deeper access to my throbbing, needy cunt.

"Steele!" Archer snapped again.

"I heard you!" he shouted back. "Just give me a minute!"

That seemed to satisfy Archer because no more obnoxious knocking came, and I grinned into Steele's hot, desperate kiss.

"A minute, huh?" I teased him, even as I already sensed my climax creeping up.

He gave me a devilish grin back. "Or more..."

My hands on the back of his neck, I brought his face to mine.

I kissed him long and hard, tasting the residue of my own arousal on his lips and groaning when his pelvis ground down on my clit.

Another knock on the door, and Steele let out a frustrated sigh. "Are they fucking serious right now?"

I snickered. "They know you've got a girl in here, so yeah. Probably deliberately trying to mess up your game."

Steele grunted his agreement. "Too bad they're way off the mark, Hellcat."

"Steele, MK is missing," Kody yelled through the door. "Hurry up and blow your load; we need to look for her!"

Okay, that made me pause.

Steele breathed another curse, giving me a pained look.

I bit my lip, trying to decide what to do.

"How fast can you finish?" I whispered with an edge of evil in my tone. There was no way in hell I was leaving his room without finishing us *both* off. Even if that meant Kody worked out who Steele's mystery girl really was.

Steele grinned, then grabbed me by the waist and flipped me over with a swift, fluid movement. His cock was back inside me before I even got my hands and knees braced on the bed, and he was moving again before replying to Kody.

"Coming!" he shouted back to his friend, then tightened his grip on my hips. "But not before you do," he whispered to me with dark promise.

My pussy clenched around him, loving the new angle, and he started fucking me hard enough to slam the whole bed frame against the wall.

"Come for me, Hellcat," he grunted, his fingertips biting into the flesh of my ass.

Panting moans poured out of me, but I was so close. So fucking close. Steele's open palm cracked against my ass cheek, and that was it. I didn't even try to muffle my cries as I came hard, backing up on his cock to force him into joining me.

He slammed into me three or four times, hard, grunting his release as I clawed at the sheets and writhed under his possessive, dominating grip.

We both collapsed in a boneless heap, his solid weight on top of me, and I could have happily stayed exactly like that for *days*. Except for the annoying knocking on the goddamn door.

"Fuck, okay!" Steele shouted. "Calm your tits, Kody. I'm sure she's just downstairs getting coffee." He shot me a curious look as he rolled off me, and I propped my head up with my hand. "Unless she's in my room?" he whispered. "Naked and freshly fucked and looking more gorgeous than I've ever seen her?"

I smiled, blushing, but shook my head. I'd deal with Kody in my own time. I didn't need him knowing what Steele and I had spent our morning doing. I owed none of them any promises of monogamy, and I sure as shit didn't owe them honesty when they lied to me every damn day.

"She's not," Kody yelled back. "Can you just *hurry up*? I'm really worried. It's snowing and she hasn't taken her warm coat."

Steele ran a hand over his close-cropped hair and sighed before climbing out of bed. He disposed of the used condom in his trash can, overflowing with screwed-up paper, then went to the door fully naked.

Panicked, I threw the sheet over myself but couldn't help peeking. In fairness, Steele only opened the door an inch and, even then, blocked the room with his body. His gorgeous, naked body. Clearly the boys had no qualms about seeing each other naked. A fact I'd file away for later.

"Dude, seriously?" Kody sounded disgusted. Not about seeing his friend's dick—and there was no way he'd missed it—but more about the whole *just fucked someone* look Steele was rocking. Or so it seemed to me. "You're unbelievable. MK is never going to forgive you when she hears about this. What the fuck happened to all that shit you told me the other day?"

"Bro, let it drop," Steele snapped. "I'll be out in five minutes. Go and check the gym or something. She's started going down there to work out when she can't sleep." I tensed. How the fuck had he known that? Not that I'd been doing it a lot…but sometimes when the nightmares were particularly bad, I'd found it useful to just run it off.

"I know *that*," Kody growled, "but she does that way before dawn."

Steele gave a shrug. "It's the holidays. Maybe she slept in."

Kody made another angry sound but stomped away, and Steele carefully closed the door once more.

"Better be quick," he said when I tossed the sheet back once more. "Go jump in your shower or something before he comes back up."

There was no time to argue or question how the fuck they knew what I'd been doing in the middle of the night, so I quickly pulled my pajamas back on and dashed across the corridor to my own bedroom. Not before Steele grabbed me for one last lingering kiss, though.

Inside my own bathroom, I cranked the water and stripped down in front of the mirror. My lips were red and puffy from Steele's kisses, and there was a definite pinkness to my left butt cheek. I loved it.

Grinning to myself, I stepped under the spray and soaked my hair thoroughly. I'd just lathered shampoo into my long, pink tresses when I heard my bedroom door open and angry, arguing voices traveled through to me.

"…see?" I heard Steele say in a mocking way. "Did you even check her bathroom? Fucking hell, bro. Wake up."

"Wait, what?" Kody sounded next-level confused, and a stab of guilt hit me. Maybe I should have just come clean about the fact that I'd spent the morning in Steele's bed. But then…no. Kody needed to earn my trust back. Archer needed to earn it full

94

stop. Until they started sharing, I'd be keeping my cards close to my chest.

"I was *sure* she wasn't in there," I faintly heard Kody say. "Sorry, dude. I was just... I dunno. I came in to wake her up and she wasn't here and I freaked out. I thought she'd finally run away."

There was a pause, and I thought maybe they'd left my bedroom. But then...

"Even if she did, we'd find her," Archer remarked in a gruff voice. I startled; I hadn't known he was out there with the other guys. "I made sure of that."

Their voices grew quieter, and I was unable to make out Kody's and Steele's responses, but the damage was done. I finished my shower with a sick feeling in my stomach, turning Archer's words over in my mind.

By the time I stepped out of the bathroom, I'd only drawn one logical conclusion.

Those fuckers had planted a tracker on me somehow.

CHAPTER 12

Archer had told Steele they wanted to leave in fifteen…and it'd been way longer than that by the time I'd made it back to my room and finished my shower. Nonetheless, I made sure to take as long as possible getting myself dressed, even stopping every now and then to randomly scroll social media and watch stupid home-hairdressing videos.

By the time I emerged from my bedroom, I'd made up my mind. Archer D'Ath was full of shit.

He'd *known* I could hear them talking in my bedroom. He hadn't made any attempt to lower his voice. He'd *wanted* me to hear him, meaning there was a pretty good chance there was no tracking device at all and he just wanted me to be paranoid.

Sneaky motherfucker.

Coming into the kitchen, I found the three of them sitting around the island with the remains of a pancake breakfast on the plates in front of them. All three sets of eyes seemed to follow me like laser beams as I grabbed out a coffee mug and set about making coffee—again.

"I thought you were going somewhere today?" I asked, breaking the awkward-as-fuck silence that seemed to be clogging the air of the kitchen. "I was quite looking forward to a nice, peaceful Thanksgiving with just the staff."

"*We* are going somewhere today, yes," Archer replied, sipping his pitch-black coffee sludge like he actually enjoyed it. "But how did you know that?"

My shoulders tensed. "I heard Kody yelling about it outside my room earlier," I half lied. "It's what woke me up, you asshole." I glared at Kody, and he just stared back at me with narrowed eyes. He was far too intuitive for my liking.

"Here, I saved you some breakfast," Steele told me, pushing across a plate wrapped in foil. "Arch wants to hit the road ASAP, so eat fast."

"Hit the road to where?" I asked, peeling the foil back and finding a short stack of pancakes. My stomach rumbled as I grabbed the maple syrup and drowned the whole pile.

"It's a surprise," Archer replied in a dry tone. It sounded less like a surprise and more like a power trip. Well, lucky for him, two orgasms before breakfast put me in a pretty chilled mood, so I just shrugged and started on my food.

Kody cleared his throat, and I looked up at him. Except he was glaring at Steele.

"Steele," he muttered, and there was a solid sound like he'd just kicked him. "You got something to tell MK this morning?"

"Uh..." Steele shot a look to me, and I kept my face carefully blank. Archer, though? He looked all kinds of smug. Was he seriously entertained by the prospect of Steele...what, exactly? Telling me he'd fucked "another woman" this morning? Even if that was what'd happened, he shouldn't be so damn gleeful about it.

Or maybe he just wanted everyone to be as miserable as he was.

Too bad it was going to backfire on him.

"What did you need to tell me, Max Steele?" I placed a bite of maple-smothered pancake in my mouth and gave him my very best blank and innocent expression.

He narrowed his eyes back at me, a smile playing at his lips like he wanted to call me on my shit. He wouldn't, though. We'd definitely crossed into new territory since the time he'd bragged to his buddies about finger-fucking me in that dirty bathroom.

"Nothing," he muttered, shooting Kody a dark look. "Kody's stirring shit."

Archer sat back in his seat, folding his arms like he was thoroughly enjoying himself. All he needed was a box of popcorn, smug fuck.

"Kody's *not* stirring shit," Kody growled, talking about himself in third person in a bit of an adorable kind of way. The fact that he seemed to be looking out for *my* best interests was going a long way in his favor. "Tell her about the girl in your room this morning, Steele. How'd you sneak her out without anyone seeing her, anyway?"

Steele glared death at Kody, then shifted his gaze to me.

Archer was watching me with barely concealed glee, like he was waiting for my head to explode, and all I could think was... *damn, these two are dumb as fuck.*

"I didn't sneak anyone out," Steele said truthfully, then fought a grin. "I was just watching porn."

My brows shot up, and I filled my mouth with more pancake to stop from laughing out loud.

"Bullshit," Archer remarked, cool as ever. "No porn sounds like *that*."

Steele just shrugged, his eyes not leaving me as he replied. "Maybe you need to watch better porn, bro."

I choked on my mouthful.

After a minute of coughing while Kody patted me on the back, I took a long sip of coffee to try to clear my throat before wiping my streaming eyes on the hem of my shirt.

When I was done, everyone was staring at me again. Except this time they weren't staring like they were waiting for my head to pop off with outrage about Steele's "other woman." This time they were staring with an odd mixture of anger and worry, all underscored with a thread of heated desire.

It took me a minute, but the way Archer stared at my midsection clued me in. They'd just seen my scar when I raised my shirt to wipe my eyes. And probably my bra too, but fuck it. Bras weren't anything to be ashamed of, and mine were pretty enough to be seen.

I wasn't in the mood to discuss heavy topics like my stabbing, though, so I swapped back to something less intense: Steele's fake infidelity.

"So, was she a better lay than me?" I asked him, totally deadpan. His eyes flared with heat, and Kody's mouth dropped open slightly. Archer just scowled like he could kill us all with the force of his frown.

Steele gave me a lopsided smirk, meeting my gaze without hesitation. "No one is better than you, Hellcat."

Archer made a disgusted sound and scraped his chair back to stand up. "Fuck this," he grumbled. "I'm grabbing the truck. Better pack a bag, Princess Danvers; we won't be back here tonight."

He left the kitchen muttering something under his breath about anticlimaxes, and I couldn't stop the grin spreading across my face at his sour attitude. One day he'd learn that he couldn't mess with me.

Kody still watched me with his perceptive green eyes narrowed in suspicion.

"Suppose I'd better go pack a bag." I sighed and leaned a hip against the island beside Steele. "Any hints what I should pack for?"

"You're…being really chill this morning, MK," Kody observed.

"Cold," Steele answered my question. "Don't stress about anything fancy; I doubt we'll be leaving the estate."

My brows rose and questions burned on the tip of my tongue, but I didn't push it. Archer wanted to play dumb games, and I wasn't in the mood to take the bait. So instead I just nodded.

"All right, can do."

Kody stood up to take his own plate to the sink, turning his back on us. It was the opening Steele must have been waiting for, though, and he kissed me with lightning speed.

"Tease," I whispered when he released me. Kody's back was still to us, and Steele just grinned with pure satisfaction. I turned to leave, and he swatted me on the ass, reminding me all too vividly of how he'd spanked me in bed.

Of course *that* sound Kody heard.

He gasped as I disappeared into the hallway, but I was still close enough to hear him.

"You *motherfucker*," he exclaimed. "Seriously? Fuck! I knew I recognized those moans."

Steele just laughed. "I don't know what you're talking about, bro."

"Sure you fucking don't," Kody grumbled. "I hate you so much right now. Prick."

I laughed quietly to myself and made my way up to my bedroom to pack for this mysterious trip. I wasn't even mad that Kody had worked it out. It'd been fun to sneak around, but I wasn't one for hiding who I was having sex with. Especially when there was still the possibility of becoming involved with Kody again.

Post-sex euphoria was holding my good mood strong, so I packed an overnight bag without grumbling too much.

When I exited the house, Archer's massive, black—of course— F-150 Raptor was idling in front of the main entrance with Kody leaning on the open passenger side door, talking to Archer in the driver's seat. Steele was placing his own bag in the bed, so I handed him mine and he tossed it in.

"Thanks," I told him with a smile. I moved to get in the truck, but he caught me by the waist and pulled me back to the rear of the truck for a heated, lingering kiss out of sight of the other boys.

"Max Steele," I chastised him, "what would your *other* girl think if she saw that?"

He laughed evilly and kissed me again. "She'd be totally under-standing because I quite clearly can't keep my hands off you."

I grinned in response but slipped out of his embrace and took my seat in the back of the truck. I had less than zero desire to fight for the shotgun seat when Archer would be driving, and consider-ing Steele usually took the back, there was a good chance I could sneak some decent cuddles. Or at the very least a bit of clandestine hand holding.

Except as Steele slammed the tailgate into place and rolled the bed cover closed, Kody slipped into the back seat beside me with a wide grin, quickly shutting the door after him.

"Hey, babe," he said to me with a wink, "you don't mind if I hang back here with you, right?"

I rolled my eyes. I should be mad at him—at *all* of them. I should still be angry as hell. But...*fuck,* he was hard to hold a grudge against.

"Suit yourself," I told him, "but I hold no responsibility if I fall asleep on you and drool."

His smile grew wider, if that was even possible. "Aw, gorgeous, I love when you drool all over me."

Steele sat in the front passenger seat with a huff, slamming his own door and clicking his seat belt on before giving Kody a side-eye. "You're a shithead," he told his friend.

Archer just made an annoyed sound in his throat but met my gaze in the mirror. Surprisingly, he didn't look as pissed off as his whole body language was implying. Instead he looked...I didn't even know. Curious, maybe. Intrigued.

Regardless, it made me shiver.

"So, are we ready to tell poor, clueless Madison Kate where the fuck we're going today? I'm in the car now and have no intention of doing a tuck-and-roll out onto the highway just to save myself the boredom of your company." I was speaking to Archer, and he knew it. His lips curved up in the mirror, but his eyes remained on the road ahead.

Neither Kody nor Steele answered for him, though, and eventually his eyes flickered to mine for just a second. "We're visiting the D'Ath family estate," he finally told me.

I jolted, shocked by his response. Whatever I'd been expecting him to say...it wasn't that.

"Don't worry," he continued, clearly misreading my expression of surprise. "Zane was disowned years ago when he took over the Reapers from our father. He won't step foot anywhere within two hundred miles of D'Ath land."

I thought of my last conversation with Zane. He'd vaguely offered to help me but then not so vaguely threatened my life if I trespassed on Reaper grounds again. Apparently being contradictory and infuriating was a family trait.

"Well, that's something," I muttered under my breath. "So you're taking us home for Thanksgiving dinner? That's a bit cute." Except...Cherry was on a cruise with my father, Zane had been disowned, Damien had died years ago, and Archer had told me his grandfather was dead too.

"Something like that," Archer mumbled back and turned the stereo up in a clear end to any conversation. It was the same song from his fight at The Laughing Clown, "Paranoid" by I Prevail, and I couldn't help feeling like it was becoming my anthem. I was *constantly* paranoid these days.

"It's about a four-hour drive from here," Kody told me quietly, leaning across the middle seat to be heard over the thumping music. "In case you really did need to nap. I know you haven't been sleeping well since...you know. Halloween. Or since you've been home, anyway."

I shot him a lopsided smile. Was it really any wonder I'd been struggling to sleep since being run off the road, then stalked through an abandoned amusement park, and stabbed by—in my mind at the time—someone I had started to trust? Yeah. I was a bit fucked-up at the moment.

"You guys need to stop keeping such close tabs on me," I muttered back, staring out the window. "It's creepy."

It was one thing for them to insist on chaperoning me to and from the university, but knowing that I went to the gym at three in the morning to run? Maybe Archer hadn't been bullshitting about that tracking device after all.

"I'll take creepy over you being dead any day, MK," Kody told me, his voice low and serious. I didn't reply, but his words struck a chord with me. Maybe Bree had been right about their motivations after all.

I kept my gaze locked on the snowy scenery, but I reached out across the seat to take his hand in mine. All their secrets still hurt like crazy, and we were bound to have countless fights ahead of us. But damn, I loved the part where we got to make up.

It almost made all the fear and heartache and *paranoia* worthwhile.

CHAPTER 13

At some stage on the drive, I took Kody up on his offer. I woke again when the car was still and silent, my face buried in the denim crotch of Kody's jeans.

Blinking to clear the thick fog of sleep from my brain, I rolled slightly away from his...uh...zipper.

"Hey," he said, giving me a shit-eating grin. "How'd you sleep?"

Frowning, I sat up and stretched some of the kinks out of my spine. "Like the dead," I mumbled, rubbing a hand over my face and grimacing when I touched the grooves his seams had left in my skin. Such a good look for when I needed to meet Archer's... uh...whoever the hell lived here. I peered out the windows at the impressive, *old money* mansion we were parked in front of. The front of the car was empty, and I wondered how long we'd been there.

"You could have woken me up," I told Kody, feeling a bit embarrassed for sleeping on him so long.

He scoffed a laugh. "Uh, babe, you were sound asleep with your face in my crotch. I wasn't going fucking *anywhere* in a hurry." He shot me a wolfish grin. "Might I also point out the extreme restraint I displayed in *not* getting a boner under your cheek?"

I grinned. "Oh yeah? Was that…*hard* for you?"

He rolled his eyes skyward, searching for some divine assistance after my shitty pun, then gave me a flat look. "You have *no idea*, MK. I had to picture Steele's mom in her underwear at least sixteen times."

I laughed, then yawned heavily. I hadn't been joking when I said I'd slept like the dead on Kody. Sometimes it was hard to understand just how deep exhaustion ran until it slapped me in the face with the promise of true, restful sleep.

"So, this is D'Ath Estate, huh?" I peered out of the window again, and Kody hummed a sound of agreement. Neither of us was in any great hurry to get out of the truck, and I wondered if he was kind of enjoying the companionable peace between us as much as I was. "Not gonna lie, Kodiak Jones, I sort of had you guys all pegged as neglected, delinquent kids from broken, working-class homes. This…this is definitely not where I thought Archer came from."

Kody laughed lightly. "Yeah well, you'd be forgiven for thinking that. The only family you know of his are Zane, the gangster, and Cherry, the gold digger. Come on, let's go in before someone comes looking for us."

I shivered when we left the warmth of Archer's truck, remembering I'd tossed my coat into my overnight bag. Kody wrapped his arm around my shoulders, though, sharing his body heat until we made it inside the massive sandstone mansion.

As soon as the door closed behind us—I noted Kody hadn't knocked—a robust woman with a deeply lined face and silver-streaked black hair came to greet us. She was dressed in the classic black-and-white uniform of household staff, but the smile she gave Kody was all familial warmth.

"Kodiak," she crowed, reaching up to grab his face between her palms. "Oh, boy, you just get more handsome every time I see you. How is everything? You been looking good in those half-naked pictures you post online." She fanned herself dramatically, and Kody laughed. Her voice was heavily accented, but it wasn't one I was familiar with. Maybe from somewhere in Eastern Europe if I was to guess.

"It's good to see you too, Ana. You look like you're keeping well. Is the lady of the house treating you well?" He gave her a mock serious look, and she tittered a laugh.

"You know she is, Kodiak, my boy." Her dark gaze shifted to me, standing there like an awkward popsicle. "Ah, and you must be the *princeza*, yes?" I scowled, and she threw her head back, laughing. "I'm just teasing, girl," she assured me with a warm smile. "Come along; the other troublemakers are in the sitting room with her ladyship."

Ana led us through the marble-tiled floors, despite Kody clearly already knowing the way, and into an old-fashioned sitting room. It was complete with gold-framed paintings of straitlaced women; stern, mustached men; and their beagles.

"Madam Constance, I located the stragglers." There was an edge of teasing in the housekeeper's tone, and it surprised me. I certainly wasn't one for staff acting deferential because we paid them, but it *was* what I'd grown up around. Ana's level of familiarity with her employer—who looked very much like a prim and proper high-society woman—gave me pause.

"Thank you, Ana." The immaculately dressed and made-up woman perched on the chaise longue. Deep lines framed her eyes, and the skin of her hands and neck held a certain delicate frailness of advanced age, yet she was still gorgeous. A shock of white hair was swept up in a perfect french twist, and her designer skirt suit was pressed to perfection. She even wore pantyhose with her sensible, low-heeled pumps. "We will be ready for dinner in around an hour, I think. I'm sure Madison Kate would like to freshen up after the drive here." She cast her ice-blue eyes over me, but it wasn't an unkind gesture.

"Not a problem, madam." Ana gave a genuine smile, one that creased her eyes, before leaving the room again.

Archer cleared his throat, drawing my attention. He was sitting beside the old woman on the chaise longue, and the resemblance between them was clear. They shared the same eyes and the same perfectly formed lips.

"Madison Kate, this is my grandmother Constance D'Ath." There was an edge of uncomfortable formality to the way he phrased that, and I wondered if he was just weirding himself out by not including an insult in a sentence with my name attached.

His grandmother gave me a small smile, though, and I pushed aside the uneasy feeling Archer had just given me with that introduction.

"It's lovely to meet you, Madison Kate," she told me, and she seemed to be sincere with the sentiment. "Archie, be a dear and get your beautiful friend a drink from the bar."

She raised a penciled brow at her huge, tattoo-covered grandson.

He gave a small, apologetic smile back to her. "I would, Baka, but Madison Kate hates it when we do things for her. She's an independent woman like that, aren't you, Princess?"

I allowed my eyes to narrow at him ever so slightly before giving Constance a smile. "For sure." I started in the direction of the bar across the room, and I heard a distinctive whack followed by a protest from Archer.

Constance hissed something to him, and he sighed dramatically as he stood and followed me to the bar.

I smirked at him as he hunted a glass out of a cupboard and plonked it down on the bar top in front of me. "You got in trouble for being rude, didn't you?"

He just glared back at me. "You cool with champagne? I'm not mixing you a fucking cocktail."

I clicked my tongue, teasing. "Such terrible manners, Archer D'Ath."

He rolled his eyes and bent over to retrieve a chilled bottle of

Dom Pérignon. As he opened the bottle, I glanced over my shoulder to where Constance chatted to Kody and Steele like they were old friends.

"Your grandma seems lovely," I told Archer in all seriousness. "So does Ana. Has she worked here a long time?" I was fishing for information and didn't even try to pretend otherwise.

Archer gave me an exasperated glare while pouring my champagne, then sighed. His gaze shifted past me to his grandmother, and his eyes softened.

"Ana's worked for my family her whole adult life. She was *purchased* by my great-grandfather as a teenager." His mouth twisted in disgust at that word, and my jaw dropped in shock.

"Purchased?" I repeated, dumbstruck. "As in—"

"Sex trafficking?" he finished for me, cocking a brow. "Yep. Anyway, she and my baka have been lovers for as long as I can remember. They think we don't know, and we don't pressure them to act otherwise. They both lived the kind of lives where their relationship wasn't even a possibility, let alone accepted. Now they're just too stuck in their ways to change."

"That's...equally adorable and heartbreaking all at once," I murmured, looking back at Constance with new eyes. She had *such* a story behind her; I could almost see it written all over her skin. I was insanely curious but also cautious not to push Archer too far. When he was in a sharing mood, I needed to be sly.

"It's not so bad," he commented, refilling his own drink from a crystal decanter and dropping in a fresh ice cube. "I'm the only one who ever visits here, so the rest of the time they live their lives comfortably like a normal couple." He gave me a sharp look. "And before you get all snarky at me, Princess Danvers, yes I hate that they feel like they need to pretend while I'm here. Believe me, I've tried to tell them we support their relationship, but Baka won't hear a word of it. She's a stubborn old bat."

I grinned as I picked up my glass and followed him back to

the seating area. "Sounds like a family trait," I whispered as we sat down, and he shot me a quick, narrow-eyed glare.

"So, Madison Kate," Constance said, turning back to face me, "tell me about yourself. What are you studying?"

I blinked at her a second, feeling a bit under the microscope, but something about her set me at ease. Soon I found myself in a comfortable, engaging conversation like I'd known her for years.

I definitely knew where Archer got his charm from, that was for sure. What a shame he so rarely turned it on for me.

Then again...I think I preferred grouchy Archer D'Ath, anyway. He kept me on my toes.

Soon Ana returned to let us know that the meal was ready. It was an odd time of day, somewhere between lunch and dinner, but I was starving so it suited me fine.

Archer hung back, pausing me with a hand on my arm as everyone else made their way through to the elaborate formal dining room.

"What's up?" I asked him when he didn't immediately speak.

His brow was furrowed, and he was watching me with suspicion. "I know you're probably up to something, Princess Danvers," he started, his voice pitched low so there was no risk of being overheard. "But don't."

My brows shot up. "Don't what?"

"Don't do whatever the fuck you're building up for. All the smiles and chitchat and laughter? You might have everyone else fooled, but not me. I see that anger simmering under the surface of your violet eyes, Madison Kate. I recognize the burning need to get even for your dad's threats, but—"

I scoffed and glared at him with acid in my eyes. "Oh yeah, sure. My *dad* is the one who restricted my freedom and threatened me with fucking committal into a psychiatric hospital if I don't toe the line. Of course. Nothing to do with you."

He paused a moment, his blue eyes cold and emotionless as he stared down at me.

When he spoke again, all traces of that casual openness from earlier were totally gone from his voice. "Well, if anyone could pull Samuel Danvers's strings like that, I'd be pretty damn careful about retaliation. Wouldn't you?"

He left me there in the hallway outside the dining room with ice forming in my stomach. His smile was back in place as he took a seat to his grandmother's left, but my good mood was left shivering in the cold. Every time I started to think he wasn't as bad as I'd thought, he went and proved me wrong again.

Even more insulting was the fact that I'd had no intention to fuck with him today. I genuinely enjoyed his grandmother's company and had thought we were making progress in not constantly taking swipes at each other. Evidently not.

Archer had taken a swipe and drawn blood.

Slowly I made my way into the dining room and hesitated for a moment. There was a vacant seat left on Constance's other side—as she sat at the head of the table—and directly opposite Archer. I doubted it had been left vacant for Ana—she was bustling around, serving up food onto everyone's plates with silver servers—and it'd be too pointedly rude to sit farther down the table.

With a sigh, I took my seat and gave Ana a tight smile as she filled up my plate with delicious-smelling food. My champagne glass was already refilled, so I took a long sip and quite deliberately avoided looking across to Archer.

Not that he was paying me any attention, but still.

"Are you okay?" Steele murmured, leaning closer to me. He was sitting on my other side and reached for my hand under the table. I squeezed his fingers on reflex, soaking up some of his strength and letting it ground me. I needed to get back in control of my own emotions or Archer really would win this round.

Stupid me for not realizing the game was still being played.

"Yeah," I replied with a smile, "just tired."

He started to reply, but Constance cleared her throat and drew our attention.

"My dears," she said with a warm expression on her weathered face, "it's such a delight to have you here today. All of you." She met my eyes and smiled. "Madison Kate, I can see you fitting into our little family just perfectly. It's not every day Archer meets his match." She shot me a wink as her grandson choked on his sip of scotch.

Constance chuckled, and Ana—refilling Kody's glass of water—grinned a smug smile.

"Well, dig in, then," Constance continued, waving a hand at the impressive spread of food. "Ana didn't slave in the kitchen all day for it to sit here and go cold."

Despite what Archer said about Constance and Ana keeping their relationship on the down-low, I'd have to have been blind to miss the adoring look both women gave each other.

It gave me hope. Surely Archer couldn't be all malice and cruelty when he had such strong, confident women in his life. Surely.

But once again, why the fuck did I *care* so much?

CHAPTER 14

After hours of incredible food, sweets, drinks, and conversation, Constance pleaded old age and retired for the evening. As the echo of her footsteps died away, an uncomfortable silence fell over the four of us as we sat around in front of a huge, roaring fireplace.

"So, when are you going to tell me why we're really here?" I asked Archer directly when the tension grew too thick for my liking.

He curved a cold smile at me, his thumb rubbing lazily across his lower lip as he stared me down, unblinking. It shouldn't have been a sexy gesture. It shouldn't. But my body had grown a mind of her own and reacted like he'd just opened his pants and—

"What makes you think there's an ulterior motive, Princess Danvers?" he taunted me, interrupting my train of thought before I could do something embarrassing. Like drool.

I rolled my eyes and shifted in my seat, taking Archer out of my direct line of vision and replacing him with Kody. Much better.

"As if there's not," I muttered in reply. "If you wanted a nice visit with your grandmother, you wouldn't have brought me along. This is too *personal* for us."

Archer grunted a sound that seemed almost surprised. Or agreeing. But either way, he just sipped his drink and stared into the fireplace. I knew because, despite taking him out of my direct vision, he was still in the periphery. Always, permanently in my periphery like some kind of nasty addiction I couldn't seem to shake.

Kody arched a brow at me, though, and I tilted my head at him in question. I sucked at interpreting his silent speech.

He rolled his eyes with a small smile and reached over to whack Steele on the arm. "Hey, bro. Want to go see if Connie still has that '62 Ferrari GTO in her garage?"

Steele let out a panicked sound. "That's a fifty-million-dollar car. Connie would never get rid of it."

Kody just shrugged. "That's what you said about the '57 Spider too, but didn't she donate it to some charity auction?"

Steele paled to the point of ill and shot me a worried look. "You want to come check out some cars, Hellcat?"

I opened my mouth to accept, but Archer got there first.

"No," he snapped. "Madison Kate and I have business to discuss."

Steele blanched further—even Kody looked a bit uneasy—but Archer just gave them a flat stare back. "About Phillip's knives," he elaborated, and the tension dropping out of his two friends was unmistakable. Which made me wonder what *other* business they'd just panicked about.

"Okay, well…" Kody stood up and stretched his arms over his head. "Try not to kill each other while we're gone. And let's all keep our fingers crossed that Connie hasn't off-loaded Steele's dream car to a charitable cause again."

Steele scowled, following Kody out of the room and muttering about negative thoughts.

Archer made no move to get up after they were gone, still staring into the fire with his fingers linked under his chin, and I gave an exasperated sigh.

"Come on, D'Ath," I groaned. "I'm not in the mood for more bullshit. Did you actually have anything to show me? Or were you just worried I'd somehow talk Kody and Steele into a three-way in the back of your grandmother's Rolls-Royce?"

A short huff escaped Archer, like a laugh he was trying not to let out, and he slowly swung his gaze back to me. "I highly doubt it'd take much to talk them into *that*, Madison Kate."

I sighed and folded my arms under my breasts. "Okay, so, good to know you're a major cunt-blocker."

Archer's lips curled up in a smile, like he found me amusing. I liked that. Then I hated myself for liking it.

"What do you *want* from me, D'Ath?" I asked in an exhausted voice.

That was exactly the wrong phrasing to use, though. He slid out of his seat with fluid grace, and the next thing I knew, I was flat on my back against the velvet couch I'd been sitting on. His huge frame hovered over me, the hard planes of his body pressed along the length of my body and his lips a fraction above mine.

"I want all kinds of things from you, Kate. Ask me again, and I'll fucking *show* you." His voice was a husky promise of pure hedonism, and my body responded like a well-trained puppy. Thankfully, he stood up again before I could take him up on his vaguely threatening offer. "Don't say you weren't warned. Now, come on. I need to show you something."

He stalked out of the sitting room, but I didn't miss the way his hand dropped to his crotch to adjust his cock. Apparently my body wasn't the only one affected.

I took a second to suck in a couple of calming breaths, then hurried after him. As badly as I hated *chasing* him down, my curiosity was burning. I needed to know the mysterious reason for this whole Thanksgiving trip. What was so important here at D'Ath estate that he'd suffer through me meeting his grandmother?

"Wait up," I snapped when I needed to actually run a bit to catch up to him, and he gave me a side-eyed look. "I'm sure we're not in any great hurry, so quit walking at double my pace just to piss me off. It's childish."

Archer rolled his eyes, then stopped outside a closed wooden door. He pulled an old-fashioned key from the pocket of his jeans and inserted it into the lock. The tumblers clunked heavily as he turned the key; then the hinges squealed as he pushed the door open to reveal a dark room.

"After you, Princess Danvers," he told me, holding his hand out in challenge. The interior of the room was pitch-black and smelled musty, like it hadn't been opened in *years*. I hesitated. "Unless you're scared of the dark?"

I scowled at him. "Only if that darkness hides creepy look-alike dolls or masked men with pretty red knives." But because I could *never* freaking back down from a challenge, I stepped into the gloom without another pause.

My shoulders bunched, and I tensed myself for an attack. Not because I still suspected Archer of being the one who'd stabbed me—I was at least ninety-seven percent sure he had some interest in keeping me breathing—but because that would be the kind of school-bully bullshit that was right up his alley.

Nothing jumped out at me, though, and when Archer flipped on the light, I let out my held breath with a long exhale.

His quiet snicker said he hadn't missed it either, and I seethed that he'd gotten one up on me. This time.

"So brave, Madison Kate," he murmured, flipping a lock of my hair when he walked past me. "I wonder how long that will last."

I scowled. "What's that supposed to mean?"

He didn't answer me, instead walking around the enormous wooden desk of what was clearly an office. Certainly not Constance's office, though, and not of anyone who'd used it recently, if the thick layer of dust on all the surfaces was any clue.

"Was this your grandfather's office?" I asked, peering around

at the bookshelves, the ornate globe, the gold-framed paintings…
It was definitely a masculine workspace.

Archer grunted a sound that I assumed to be, *Yes, MK, it was.*

He stood in front of a huge portrait of a strikingly handsome
man with jet-black hair and dark eyes. The resemblance to Archer
was uncanny; they could have been brothers.

"Is that him?" I pushed, feeling the need to fill the silence. No
one had stepped foot in this room for a long time, and it made me
wonder why the staff hadn't cleaned at the very least.

"Phillip D'Ath," Archer announced. "Yep, that's him, all right."

I thought of Constance and Ana's relationship and wondered
how Phillip had factored into that. Had he known? And if so, had
he supported them?

"How long ago did he die?" I asked instead, coming to stand
beside Archer and peering up at his handsome ancestor.

"Six years," he replied, his voice rough. I got the feeling he
missed his grandfather but the emotions there were confused. Like
maybe his grandfather wasn't the nicest guy on earth. Archer let
out a long sigh, then reached for the edge of the frame. "This is
what we came to see, though." He curled his fingertips under the
frame and pulled it off the wall. It swung out easily, hinged on the
other side, and revealed a mechanical keypad with a blinking blue
light on the display.

"Uh…we came to break into his safe?" I asked, startled but not
disapproving. If there was some evidence that might help me locate
whoever tried to kill me, I'd do just about anything.

Archer's lips pulled up in a half smile. "Something like that. It's
also not breaking in when I own it."

He keyed in the passcode, not bothering to hide it from me,
and that made me suspicious. He sure as shit didn't trust me, so did
that mean he planned to kill me one day?

When the light turned green and the mechanical lock bleeped,
the entire wall panel clicked open to reveal a room beyond. Halogen

lights flickered to life as Archer pulled the hidden door open wider, and I stifled a gasp of shock.

"Yeah, Phillip was an interesting character, that's for fucking sure," Archer muttered.

Every available surface of the secret room was lined with weapons. Guns of every shape, size, and caliber. Knives in all kinds of shapes and curves. Even...

"Is that a rocket launcher?" I squeaked, pointing to a scary-looking weapon with a long-ass tube attached.

Archer huffed a short laugh. "Bazooka. Phillip was a bit of a collector."

"Oh-*kay*." I looked all around me with wide eyes. "Will you explain this, or am I wasting my breath?"

Archer leaned his shoulder on one of the racks of weapons, folding his thick arms and giving me a considering look.

"I mentioned to you that Ana was purchased by my great-grandfather, Phillip's father." It wasn't a question, merely a reminder. I nodded. "He was a revolting man, crooked as they come, with his fingers deep in every type of crime imaginable. Gunrunning, drugs, sex trafficking, murder...nothing was out of his wheelhouse. It's where the bulk of the D'Ath fortune came from."

I raised my brows, processing what he was saying. But that was his *great*-grandfather, who could have died before he was born. "So, Phillip carried on the family business?"

It made sense. It explained the abundant wealth evident at D'Ath estate, and certainly lined up with Damien D'Ath having founded the Shadow Grove Reapers. However, knowing how deep into the criminal world their ancestor was, the Reapers seemed almost small-time in comparison.

Archer shook his head, though. "No way. Phillip despised his father and everything he was involved in. Gregoric buying a kidnapped fourteen-year-old Croatian girl in a flesh auction was just the last straw for Phillip."

My stomach churned, thinking of Ana's kind warmth and how hard her life must have been. What horrors she must have endured. It gave some serious perspective to my own petty problems.

"He enlisted the second he was old enough to do so without parental consent," Archer continued, telling me his grandfather's story, his eyes locked on mine without blinking, "then quickly worked his way through the ranks. When he met Constance, he was working for some highly classified division of MI6." He gave a small, rueful smile. "We haven't decoded his files enough to work out what exactly his role was, but it isn't hard to guess." He gave a head tilt to the room full of weapons, and I nodded.

"Yup, this is sort of a big clue," I murmured, not finding the willpower to tear my eyes from Archer's. Not yet.

"Anyway. Long story short, Constance and Phillip married, and she got pregnant. Phillip had some...residual trauma from his time in the service and grew increasingly paranoid that his father would find out about his wife and baby. Possibly even do something to hurt them. Gregoric was a proud man and hadn't taken his son's abandonment of his birthright well." Archer was delivering the story in a soft, emotionless voice, but I was hanging on every word. I was fucking *invested* and needed to know how it ended... even though I knew half the characters were now dead.

"So what did he do?" I pushed, desperate to hear more.

Archer shifted his weight, giving me a humorless smile. "What any decent person should do," he told me. "He went home to his father's estate over Christmas and shot Gregoric in the head."

My lips parted in shock, but then...was I really so surprised?

"The rest, so to speak, is history." Archer broke eye contact with me, looking around the room with sad eyes. "Phillip's past haunted him. His upbringing under Gregoric had been cruel and sickening. It'd shaped his mind in a way that he could never have recovered from. Add into that all the horrors he must have seen—or *done*—while working in covert affairs for the British government?"

He shook his head and sighed. "He and Constance moved out here shortly after Gregoric's death—bringing Ana with them, obviously—and tried to start over."

"I take it that wasn't a happily ever after for them?" I asked tentatively. I *wanted* that story to end in a happily ever after, even though I already knew it didn't. Phillip was dead, and Constance and Ana were still hiding their relationship after fuck knows how many years.

Archer gave me a short laugh, turning to run his hands over some of the drawers set under the countertop. Popping one open with a flick of his fingers, he revealed a padded drawer full of gleaming, colorful butterfly knives.

"Phillip fancied himself a Good Samaritan," Archer told me, running his fingertips over the gleaming metal like he was lost in his own memories. "He made it his mission to *rescue* kids who were heading down a bad path. But his methods were…" He trailed off with a grimace. "A bit off the mark."

"What happened?"

He cocked a brow at me. "His sons both ran away from home and started their own gangs in a lame attempt to follow in their granddaddy's footsteps."

I sucked in a breath, the pieces clicking together in my brain. "Ferryman is your uncle?"

"Yep." He nodded. "He and Damien turned their backs on Phillip and Constance, for good enough reasons. Cut all ties until Zane was a fourteen-year-old punk and Phillip saw a chance to fix what he'd broken with Damien and Ferryman."

I scoffed. "So much for that."

Archer shrugged. "Phillip never took into consideration the weakness of human nature and the strength of pure greed."

He fell silent, and I chewed the edge of my lip while I processed his family history.

"Why did you tell me all of this?" I asked softly when he made no sign of continuing his story.

He shifted away from the drawer full of knives and crossed the tiny room to where I leaned on the opposite countertop. Bracing his hands to either side of me, he crowded my personal space, and I *let* him.

"I have no idea," he admitted in a rough, quiet voice. "Maybe it's a test. Will you use this information against me in your relentless quest for vengeance?"

I held his gaze from just inches away, my breathing too shallow, too quick. "Maybe," I replied honestly. "I guess it depends how badly you piss me off."

A micro-smile touched his lips. "Fair enough."

Yet he didn't move away from me. His broad, strong frame caged me in against the wall of weapons, and I made no attempt to free myself, even when a shiver of apprehension shuddered through me.

I suffered some kind of mental break, and my mouth moved without my permission, forming words that shouldn't have passed the mental filter. "What do you want from me, Archer?" It was a husky whisper, and I fucking well knew I'd just unchained the beast.

Archer's ice-blue eyes flared with heat just moments before his lips crashed into mine.

I gasped into his kiss, and he claimed my mouth with raw need and hungry desperation—then all of a sudden, he wrenched himself away. He took two steps across the room, his back to me and his shoulders heaving.

"What I want from you, Kate, is more than you'd be willing to give." He didn't look at me as he spoke, his voice harsh as he braced his hands on the countertop. His knuckles were white and the muscles in his forearms stood out prominently, displaying his tension.

Anger and frustration and…*hurt* rose up in me at his rejection.

"What the actual fuck is your problem, D'Ath?" I demanded, planting my hands on my hips and scowling at his broad back. "This mood swing crap is getting seriously old. Make up your fucking mind and stick with it; you either want me or you don't.

I don't have the emotional capacity to navigate the minefield of your fucked-up baggage."

He barked a sharp, bitter laugh. "Just go to bed, Madison Kate," he told me in a cruel tone. "I don't fuck desperate chicks."

Cold indignation and disappointment lanced through me, and I sucked in a breath. "Screw you, Archer D'Ath. You're a damaged piece of shit, and straight up, you don't deserve me."

I didn't hang around to hear his answer, leaving the secret weapons room and Phillip's dust-filled office with my head held high.

All until I hit the main staircase, then the tears started to roll, and I hugged my arms around myself. One of these days, I'd learn.

Sadly, today wasn't that day, and my heart was paying the price of my own stupidity.

CHAPTER 15

I gave up on sleep sometime before dawn and decided to wake Bree up with a phone call to bitch about Archer instead. I'd rejected Steele's suggestion of sharing my bed, preferring to lick my wounds alone. But alone, when my nightmares woke me up sweating and shaking, I had no hope of getting back to sleep.

Talking to Bree helped, though. Even if her best suggestion was to sneak into Archer's room and superglue his nuts to his leg.

We ended our call as the deep red sun rose over the snow-covered grounds, and Bree promised to do some research and come up with more creative payback for Archer's shitty attitude.

A soft knock on my door pulled my attention as I was finishing my makeup, and I unlocked it to answer.

"Hey," Steele greeted me with a relaxed smile. "I figured you'd be up. Want to come for a walk?" He was already dressed in dark jeans and a charcoal-gray woolen coat and held a pair of black leather gloves in his hand. He looked incredible, and I was sorely tempted to drag him into my bed.

"Sure," I replied instead, pulling my door open farther. "I'll just find my coat."

Steele stepped into my room, waiting while I grabbed my

warm winter jacket out of my overnight bag, then pulled on my over-the-knee flat boots. A little extra height would have been nice around the guys, but I was more concerned with not falling on my ass in the snow.

"Ready," I announced, tucking my hands into my pockets and turning back to Steele.

He was staring at me with a strange, confused sort of expression, his head tilted to the side and a small smile on his lips.

"What?" I asked, frowning.

His smile widened, and he shook his head. "Nothing," he lied. "Come here." He held out his hand, and I pulled one of mine from my warm pocket to take it. Steele pulled me closer to him, then threaded his long fingers into my hair. He tilted my head back and claimed my lips in a sensual kiss full of dark promises and desire.

"What was that for?" I whispered when he released me.

His pierced brow rose, and his smirk was all satisfaction. "Do I need a reason to kiss you, Hellcat?"

A pointed and very fake throat clearing interrupted our private moment, and my glare speared Kody to the spot.

"There's this thing called knocking," I told him in a growl, not bothering to pull away from Steele. Why bother? Kody already knew we'd fucked and he'd just seen us kissing. It'd seem a bit silly trying to cover it up at this late stage of the game.

Kody smirked back at me. "There's this thing called sharing, MK," he retorted, and I laughed despite myself. "You guys heading down for breakfast? I smell bacon."

"Uh, we were going to take a quick walk," Steele told him. He released his grip on my hair but wove our fingers together instead, making a clear point of who the *we* in that scenario was.

Kody screwed up his nose at us. "Before MK has coffee? Are you insane or just suicidal?" He shook his head, dismissing the idea. "Come on, you know Ana gets upset if her food gets cold."

Steele gave me an exasperated look, and I just smiled. "He's not wrong," I said in a quiet voice. "You probably want to feed and caffeinate me before I need to deal with Archer's hormonal bullshit."

He wrinkled his nose but sighed. "Yeah, fair point."

Kody took the opportunity to pull me out of Steele's grip and sling his arm over my shoulders as we headed down to the dining room.

"So, what happened to you and Arch last night?" Kody asked as the three of us took our seats at the table and started loading up our plates while Ana dropped off *more* food. It was already more impressive than a country club buffet, but she clucked something about waffles still to come.

The mood-swinging, douchebag prick was nowhere to be seen, nor was his grandmother, so I just shrugged.

"Usual Archer D'Ath mind games," I replied vaguely. "Making sure I didn't go forgetting how much I hate him, despite how things are changing with you two."

Kody grinned at me across the table. "So things *are* changing for us. Excellent."

I gave him a flat stare back. "I didn't say changing for the better, jerk."

He winked one of those flirtatious green eyes. "But you meant it."

Damn him. I did.

"So, he told you about Phillip's butterfly knives?" Steele asked, forking some fluffy pancakes onto his plate.

I cringed at the memory of the night before, how he'd kissed me and I'd kissed him back...then he'd blown it all up in my face. "Uh, not really. He showed me the secret weapons room and the drawer full of knives, but then..." I trailed off with a shrug. "You know how it is. He went all *Archer*, and I didn't stick around to put up with any more of it."

The surprised look that passed between Kody and Steele didn't go unnoticed by me, but I didn't push the issue.

Kody smoothly changed the subject to talk of exam prep, and I quietly learned that he was studying sports therapy at SGU. Which made sense considering his side business as a fitness trainer.

"How many clients do you have, anyway?" I asked when he complained about how busy his winter break was already lining up to be. "I never see you training anyone except Archer."

Kody flashed me a grin. "Well, you should watch me more often, babe. But also, I usually go to my clients' houses to train them. It's the kind of service big bucks demands."

Archer chose that moment to stomp into the dining room. His hair, longer on top than the shaved sides, was in disarray like he'd just woken up, and his scowl was like that of a bear with a sore head.

"Good morning, Sleeping Beauty," Steele drawled, eyeing his friend. "Sleep well?"

"Fuck off," Archer snapped. He held something in his hand and slammed it down onto the table in front of me before taking his own seat.

"Uh, what's this?" I asked, eyeing the black velvet pouch with extreme suspicion.

Archer just shot me a quick glare, then focused on filling his plate with more food than I could eat in an entire week. "Maybe open it and find out for your fucking self, Princess Danvers."

I scowled back at him, but he wasn't looking at me anymore. Kody and Steele were, though.

"What are my odds of losing a hand from opening this?" I muttered under my breath, mostly rhetorically, but Kody answered me anyway.

"Something that small, with how hard Arch put it down? Pretty low chance."

I shot him a flat glare. "Thanks, Kodiak."

He grinned back at me, licking some syrup off his fork. "You're welcome, babe."

Archer was ignoring all of us, eating his food like it held the answer to his crappy attitude. But when I opened the neck of the bag and upended it onto the table, I caught him watching me from under his dark lashes.

My breath caught and my heart stopped. I stared at his gift, then up at him with an accusing frown.

"What the fuck is this for?" I demanded, running my fingertips gently across the gleaming metal of the folded butterfly knife. It was predominantly purple, but as the light glinted off it, a holographic shine showed off blues, greens, and even some golden-yellow tones.

Kody let out a low whistle and Steele made a small grunt of surprise, but Archer just gave an infuriating half shrug. "It's a knife, Princess. What do you *think* it might be for? I'll give you a hint. It usually needs cleaning afterward." His tone was dry and snarky, and I wanted to put my new knife to good use already. Right in his fucking throat.

"I can see *that*, you juiced-up baboon; I meant *why* are you giving it to me?" I needed to growl the words through clenched teeth for fear of snapping and shedding blood all over Ana's perfectly starched tablecloth.

Archer just gave me a flat glare back, like he sensed my desire to hurt him and didn't give two shits. "Because you're the walking definition of *victim*, Princess Danvers. Maybe if you had some way to actually protect yourself, we wouldn't be forced to chaperone you all day, every day."

I scoffed. "Like you didn't bring that on yourself."

Archer didn't show any emotions, just kept eating his breakfast like he was starving. Steele shifted slightly in his seat beside me, though, and Kody murmured something under his breath too quietly for me to hear.

For several minutes, there was silence as everyone finished their food. I couldn't stop running my fingertip over the mesmerizing, holographic-purple metal, though.

When Archer scraped his chair back, standing up, I looked up at him.

"It'll take more than a pretty knife to apologize for your shitty behavior, D'Ath," I told him with a level stare. "But it's a start. I appreciate the gesture."

His expression didn't waver for even a second, and he shook his head. "I don't know what you're talking about, Princess Danvers. Just don't accidentally stab yourself before Kody can show you how to use it."

He stomped out of the dining room, and I shifted my gaze to the two boys, who stared after their friend with some degree of shock.

"Uh, I'm guessing Arch was more of a douche last night than usual?" Kody asked, turning back to me with raised brows. He scrubbed a hand over his short stubble and shook his head. "I'm kinda gutted I missed it. Care to fill us in?"

I scowled, the embarrassment and hurt from Archer's cruel rejection bubbling inside me once more. "No."

"That bad, huh?" Steele commented, wincing. "Still...Arch has never given out one of Phillip's knives before. He must be feeling pretty guilty this morning."

It shouldn't have, but that statement gave me warm fuzzies inside. "Good," I muttered, "maybe he'll lose the surly grouch bullshit."

Both Kody and Steele started laughing at that, and even I had to crack a smile. Yeah. Right.

"Come on, gorgeous," Kody said, pushing back his own chair. "Me and Steele will give you some training today."

I cocked a brow at him, and a lust-filled grin crept over his lips.

"On how to use your knife without cutting a finger off, *obviously*." He rolled his eyes, but that smile still played over his lips as Steele and I wandered out of the dining room with him. "Unless you were into whatever else you just thought of? I'm totally on board for that too." His wink said it all, and my cheeks heated.

Sex. He meant sex. With him *and* Steele.

Fuck me, that was tempting.

"Maybe later," I teased, giving him a grin. "I want to know how to safely carry this thing first. I've got enough scars to last me the rest of the year at least."

"Boom." Kody held his hand up to Steele for a high five. "*Maybe later* is as good as a yes, bro."

Steele snickered, threading his arm around my waist as we walked down the long corridor to a section of the mansion I hadn't seen yet. "I'm not high-fiving that, Kody. God damn, how do you *ever* get laid?"

Kody's grin was pure arrogance. "Dude, have you seen me? I'm like walking sex."

Steele laughed, and I groaned.

He wasn't wrong, though.

CHAPTER 16

We stayed at the D'Ath estate for the rest of the weekend, but as my exams were set to start bright and early Monday morning, we needed to drive back on Sunday. By the time we loaded our bags into Archer's truck, I felt like I was leaving my own extended family.

Ana hugged us all, as did Constance, but I hung back when the boys all climbed into the truck.

"Thank you for hosting us these last few days," I told the impeccably dressed D'Ath matriarch. "I wish I'd known in advance that I'd be meeting you so I could have brought a gift or something."

Constance—or Connie, as she'd encouraged me to call her like the boys did—laughed and waved my comment aside. "Nonsense, Madison Kate. Just meeting you and getting to know the woman in my boys' lives has been the best gift an old woman can get."

"Well then, I hope you'll forgive a moment of bluntness before we go?" I asked it tentatively, knowing I was overstepping. If Archer heard me…yeah. I'd make it quick. "Connie, your grandson loves you more than I actually believed he had the emotional capability to love. And he wants you to be happy and comfortable to be yourself with *whoever* you want to spend your life with." I shifted my gaze to Ana in a deliberate way. "You don't need to pretend. Archer loves you both."

Connie's face flushed red and her hand fluttered over her pearls, but Ana just started laughing and made her way back into the house while waving goodbye.

I pressed a quick kiss to Constance's cheek, then turned to get into the truck. But the back seat was already full.

"They were fighting over who sat beside you," Archer told me with a grunt when I peered through the open passenger-side window. "And I'm not in the fucking mood for bickering. Sit in the damn seat, Princess. You've got exams tomorrow, and I'll put money on it that you haven't prepared."

I scowled but climbed into the seat anyway, buckling my seat belt. It could always have been worse. At least I wasn't sitting in Archer's lap.

"Don't you guys have exams this week too?" I asked, shifting in my seat so I could look back at Kody and Steele. "Surely I'm not the only one who legitimately attends SGU. I'm starting to think you three are faking it."

Steele laughed, giving me that wide, secretive grin, and Kody acted offended.

"Babe, the fact that you think we'd lie about our status as students offends me." He blinked those clear green eyes at me in total innocence and I gave him a flat stare back. "And for the record," he continued, "I *do* have exams this week. I'm just confident enough in my subjects that I'm not stressing over them."

Typical Kodiak fucking Jones. Confidence should have been his middle name.

"What about you?" I asked Steele.

He gave me a vague shrug back. "I'm doing an arts degree and only because I didn't know what else to do. I'll actually graduate after these exams, if I don't pick up any other classes for the sake of it."

It sort of fit with his whole vibe of not knowing where his future was going. But his casual attitude made me curious about his family again. How had they shifted from trying to make him some kind of piano prodigy to no longer being involved in their son's life? Had that happened before Rachel's death or after?

I let it go, though, knowing he'd tell me his story when he was ready. Instead, I shifted my attention to the silent, brooding asshole in the driver's seat. "Archer?" I prompted.

"What?" he snapped back, barely even sparing me a quick glance.

"Any exams this week?"

His brow twitched. "Why do you care? Trying to figure out our movements so you can hatch some diabolical revenge plot while we're out of the house?"

My mood soured. "Or maybe I was just making conversation," I muttered back, folding my arms and sinking back into my seat.

"Well, don't," he growled, then turned the stereo on. Loud. "Shut Up" from New Year's Day pounded from the car speakers, and I glowered. It was probably a coincidence, but still…this was Archer we were talking about. He could have had that cued up in preparation.

It made me think I really did need to plan something, seeing as he was constantly accusing me of plotting. Besides, he still fucking deserved some payback after that bullshit he pulled in the weapons room behind Phillip's office.

The next couple of hours mostly consisted of music blasting through the truck, interspersed with the guys fighting over what track should be played next. I didn't bother trying to engage them in conversation again because my pride hadn't appreciated Archer's shutdown.

About an hour outside of Shadow Grove, Kody started loudly complaining about being hungry and was soon joined by Steele. I expected Archer to ignore them—seeing as we'd had a huge spread for breakfast again—but he surprised me by pulling off the highway and into a roadside diner's parking lot.

"What?" he demanded when I gave him a quizzical stare. "I need the calories."

Rolling my eyes, I gave myself a mental reminder that I now lived with three fully grown dudes who spent a hell of a lot of time in the gym. So yeah, they really did need to eat like the apocalypse was coming.

I followed the three of them into the diner and slid into the bench seat beside Steele. He snaked his arm around my waist and pulled me closer until our thighs touched, then left his hand on my hip as he browsed the menu, pretending not to notice Archer's pointed glare.

"Burger," Steele declared as a smiling waitress came over to take our orders. "I need a burger."

I hadn't even looked at the menu but was still full from breakfast anyway, so I just ordered a Coke. No way in hell was I trusting the coffee in a middle-of-nowhere diner with all of four customers.

"So I guess you two made up then," Archer commented with a sneer in his voice. His glare at Steele was disapproving and angry, but Steele's arm around me just tightened and he dropped a kiss to my shoulder.

"Don't know what you're talking about, Arch," he replied, sounding like he was trying hard not to laugh. It took me a minute, but I soon clicked that Archer had *no* idea Steele and I had worked through our issues already.

Archer's brow dropped farther, and the look he gave me was pure venom. "I had you pegged for a girl who didn't take kindly to being messed around on. Didn't you hear Steele getting his rocks off on Thanksgiving morning with some chick? She sounded like she was having fun too." A cruel smile touched his lips like he was enjoying hurting me. Or...trying to hurt me. Sucker. "I guess your standards are lower than I realized."

I gave him a fake apologetic shrug. "You're right. I mean, I let *you* kiss me after all. My standards are practically nonexistent." His smile slipped, and Kody started snickering behind his hands, which were covering his face. "Oh, and for the record? That girl with Steele was having a *lot* of fun." I leaned into Steele more, placing a kiss on his neck tattoo before meeting Archer's eyes again. "Double orgasm fun, some might say."

Archer's face drained of color as he processed what I was telling him, and his gaze shot to Steele accusingly.

"Fuck you, dude," Steele snapped at him instead. "I put up with your shit because I *know* everything. But don't try and cockblock me just because you've got the bluest balls in history."

Kody was quietly dying of laughter in the corner but sobered up enough to wipe his eyes and shoot me a dark look at that comment. "Nah, that's probably me. Right, babe?"

I rolled my eyes, fighting the triumphant grin that wanted to steal over my face. "I'm going to the restroom," I told them. "I need a moment of fresh air away from all this big dick energy."

Steele reluctantly released my waist, and I slid out of the booth again, heading in the direction of the restroom sign. Sure, my hips might have swayed a little more than usual as I walked away, but I didn't force Archer to watch. He did, though. I could feel those ice-blue eyes glued to my ass the whole way through the diner, and I didn't release my breath until I closed the restroom door behind me.

I ducked into one of the small cubicles and did my thing, hearing the door open and close while I was pulling my jeans back up. I paid it little mind, though, figuring it was another customer or maybe the waitress coming in to use the facilities.

I unlocked the cubicle door and stepped out, heading for the sinks to watch my hands. A flicker of movement in the mirror was the only warning I got before a black-masked man looped his forearm around my neck and *squeezed.*

My feet left the floor as I kicked out, my hands clawing at his black-clad arm, and pathetic little squeaks escaped my throat. I needed to think smarter and do it *fast*, or I'd soon find myself unconscious and being cut up for a skin suit.

Fuck. *Fuck.*

I bucked against my captor's grip, my toes catching the sink and giving me enough leverage to shove him back into the cubicle door, but it wasn't enough. He just carried me with him like a sack of groceries or some shit, patiently waiting me out until lack of oxygen rendered me useless.

Archer's words seemed to echo inside my head, taunting me that I was a *victim* and couldn't take care of myself. As mad as it'd made me at the time…it might just save my life. Because it reminded me that I wasn't totally without defenses.

Giving up on trying to peel his arm from my neck, I simply held my breath as best I could and fumbled in the pocket of my jeans for the beautiful, purple butterfly knife Archer had given me.

Kody and Steele had given me some basic instructions while we were staying at the D'Ath estate, but basic was all I needed. It was enough that I could flip the blade open one-handed and stab blindly behind me.

My vision had started to darken around the edges, but as my deadly sharp blade sunk into flesh, my captor let out a howl of pain and his arm across my throat loosened.

I dragged in a greedy lungful of air, then released an ear-piercing scream on my exhale. Fuck this shit. I was woefully underprepared to fight off a full-grown man trying to kidnap or kill me, and not even my feminist pride was strong enough to die over asking for help.

"Bitch," the masked guy snarled, but apparently he wasn't stupid—much to my disappointment. The second my scream rang out through the bathroom, he threw me across the room and jumped out of the window.

A split-second later the door crashed open, and my three shitty bodyguards came barreling in. I was in a tangle of limbs against the wall. My back ached where I'd hit the tiles, and my hands rubbed at my throat while I tried to get my breathing under control between coughing fits.

"What happened?" Archer roared, his gaze sweeping the vacant restroom. "You're bleeding!" He took two steps toward me, and I waved him off.

"It's not mine," I croaked, pointing to the window. "I stabbed the fucker."

A feral grin split Archer's face, and something flashed in his eyes like pride.

"Fucking good," Kody grunted, striding over to the window. "Alleyway. He might have had a getaway vehicle. Do we go after him?"

Archer looked indecisive, his brow furrowed in thought as he stared down at me. Steele sank down to the floor himself and helped me to sit up against the dirty, tiled wall.

"Archer," I said, finding enough strength in my voice to make it a command. "He's got my knife."

He scowled at me. "So? I'll get you a new one."

I glared back at him. "I don't want a fucking new one. You gave me *that* one, and I want it back." Bracing my hand in Steele's grip, I pulled myself up on shaking legs like I wanted to go after my attacker personally.

Archer gave me a conflicted look, then cursed and ran his hand over his short black hair. "Fine. Fucking hell." He stabbed a finger in Kody's direction. "You get her home safe and don't fucking let her out of your sight, clear?" Kody nodded, giving no arguments. "Come on." This was directed to Steele, who smacked a quick kiss on my lips, then handed me off to Kody.

Within seconds, they were gone. The faint rumble of Archer's truck faded out of the parking lot, and I frowned up at Kody.

"I don't think I was totally serious about chasing him down," I murmured, confused as fuck about what had just happened.

He snorted. "Yes, you were. You want your knife back, and I don't blame you. Those fuckers are one of a kind, and Arch hasn't given one to anyone. Ever."

"Well, yeah," I admitted, "but how the hell are they going to catch him if he's in a car that they haven't seen? He could literally be in any car on the road."

Kody gave me a broad grin, his warm palm rubbing my upper arm in soothing strokes. "Aw, MK, it's cute how you think we're not secretly superheroes in disguise. I mean, shit, Arch even *showed* you the Bat Cave."

Rolling my eyes at him, I pushed away and moved to the sink to wash my hands. Somehow I doubted we were going to report this to the local police and go through the whole DNA testing process. The guys may not be superheroes, but they sure as shit operated on their own set of rules.

"Well, how are we getting home, then?" I asked him, drying my hands off on a paper towel, then tucking them under my armpits to try to stop the trembles that had started up. "They just took the truck to go rescue Gotham City."

Kody grinned, pulling me back into his body for a tight hug. His palm rubbed circles on my back, and I shuddered in his embrace. The fear of what had just happened was creeping up on me, and I was terrified of breaking down.

"Babe, I'll get us an Uber. It'll all be okay. Okay? Let's go back out and get some cake and coffee while I check the diner security footage." He all but carried me back out to the main diner as shock started to set in for me.

The waitress—the only other person in the diner who could have heard me screaming—did a bit of fussing about if I needed to call the cops or an ambulance. Kody brushed her off, though, with some assurances all was okay.

Back at our table he politely ordered a slice of every cake and pie available, then pulled me into his lap.

"You don't need to baby me," I grumbled as he stroked his fingers through my hair and whispered reassurances.

He huffed a short laugh. "What if I like taking care of you, MK?" He shifted so he could meet my gaze, his green eyes serious. "So let me. It's the least you can do after making me think you'd just been shot or something." There was a teasing edge in his tone, and I rolled my eyes.

"Don't be dramatic, Kodiak Jones."

"I'm not, Madison Kate. Have you *heard* you scream? I feel like I had a heart attack and an aneurysm all at once. So sit here and eat some sugary desserts while I convince myself that you're okay. Again." His voice was gruff, and the way his fingers tightened on my shoulder made me understand he wasn't joking. He'd been genuinely scared for me, and that...that wasn't something I was used to.

He wasn't even subtle when he lifted my shirt and ran his thumb over my scar—like he could somehow feel if I'd hurt myself more than I let on.

I stayed there on his lap until at least a third of the plates of dessert were gone, and then he gently slid me onto the bench seat and gave me clear instructions not to move. Not that he was going terribly far. Only as far as the counter, where he sweet-talked the waitress into showing him the security footage from when I'd entered the restrooms.

When he returned to me, he didn't look pleased.

"No luck?" I asked, wrinkling my nose. Somehow, I'd figured that would be the case.

Kody shook his head. "No, he somehow avoided looking at the cameras. Come on; Uber will be here in two minutes."

He tossed a stack of bills down on the table and held his hand out to me, which I took without hesitation. It was an unfamiliar thing for me to know someone cared so much for my well-being.

Unfamiliar but incredibly welcome.

Warm feelings heated my stomach as we stepped out into the snow-covered parking lot and Kody tucked me under his arm protectively. I smiled up at him as we waited for our car to arrive, and he gave me a curious frown.

"What's that face for, MK?"

Reaching up, I pulled his face down to me and kissed him. It wasn't a frenzied, passionate, let's-fuck-right-here kind of kiss, but it was definitely one to bank in my mental memory box as one of the most *meaningful* kisses ever.

"You're kind of amazing, Kodiak Jones," I told him softly when we parted.

His lush lips curled in a grin as a black Escalade glided into the parking lot. "I thought you would never notice."

Laughing, I climbed into our hired car with him and snuggled under his strong arm the whole way home.

CHAPTER 17

No one was home when we got back to my father's house, and after some convincing, Kody left me alone long enough to take a shower. I'd washed my attacker's blood off my hands back at the diner, but I needed to wash the memory of his touch from my skin.

Under the hot spray, I used my loofah to scrub the ever-loving shit out of my skin until I was tender and pink all over. As I reached for my towel, my bathroom door swung open and Archer stomped into the steam-filled room.

He froze, his eyes raking down my naked, wet body and pausing briefly at my midsection—staring at the vivid red scar of my healing stab wound.

"Can I help you, sunshine?" I drawled. I made no attempts to cover up because fuck it. He wanted to be a ballsack and pretend he wasn't attracted to me? I'd make it as hard as humanly possible for him. I slowly unhooked my towel from the drying rack and grinned when Archer wrenched his gaze away from my tits.

"Here," he said, his voice gruff but husky. He slammed my purple butterfly knife—still covered in blood—down on the edge of the basin and glared at me accusingly. "Try not to lose it again." Despite the sneering reprimand, there was a noticeable thread of arousal in his voice, and his eyes drifted down my body again like they had a mind of their own.

"See something you like, big man?" I taunted him, popping a hip as I dabbed my chest dry. I had no reason to be ashamed of my nakedness. Not when he'd barged into my bathroom unannounced and I wasn't in the habit of showering fully clothed.

His brow furrowed, and his lips twisted in a sneer. "I don't do sloppy seconds, Madison Kate. Or thirds for that matter."

"Okay, sure, and denial is totally just a river in Egypt," I scoffed. "What happened with the guy? Did you kill him? Where's Steele?"

"He's busy," Archer replied with a deep scowl, his eyes tight with anger and frustration. "Cleaning up your mess."

I glared at him hard, tossing aside my towel and propping my hands on my naked hips. "Oh, of course, because I *asked* to be attacked and choked in some random fucking diner in the middle of nowhere. I guess I forgot placing an order for that."

His eyes narrowed and the vein over his temple throbbed, but he couldn't seem to help the way his gaze dipped to my breasts… then lower. I thought he was just being a perv, but the flash of guilt that passed over his face when his eyes found my scar made me reconsider.

"Are you okay?" he asked me in a quiet voice, his gaze shifting from my scar only enough to inspect my neck. He—as a pro-MMA fighter—already knew a rear naked chokehold didn't leave bruising.

Still, the genuine question threw me for a loop.

I bit my lip, feeling my pulse race. "I'm fine," I replied, dropping the snarky bullshit for a second. "Are you and Steele okay? Whose blood is that?" I nodded to the stained blade he'd dropped on my vanity. I don't know why those three simple words from him had suddenly triggered my concern, but they had.

Of course, as the silence stretched between us, I realized I must have imagined that moment of humanity. His eyes were still on me, but they'd turned heated. Instead of answering my question, his pale blue eyes dragged all down the length of me like a caress, and he scrubbed a hand over his dark stubble.

I snorted a sarcastic laugh. "Yeah, sunshine. You're not interested in sloppy seconds at *all*. Makes me wonder why you can't stop eye fucking me."

His gaze snapped back to my face faster than a broken elastic band, and then without a word he stomped out of my bathroom again. He slammed my bedroom door so hard it made a picture fall off the wall, and I just laughed to myself.

I was getting to him. Maybe torturing Archer with his own conflicted feelings would be more fun than supergluing his nuts to his leg after all. It was certainly a plan that deserved consideration, that was for sure.

After I dried off, I dressed in comfy sweats and parked on the middle of my bed with all my study notes scattered around me. My lingering feelings about all the attempts on my life would need to wait a week before I could curl up in a ball and sob. My intro to psychology exam was first thing Monday morning, and there was no way in hell I planned on failing any class at the university my own father had built and funded.

Kody came to check on me, bringing me a plate of freshly baked cookies. But he didn't hang around when I made it clear that I was actually studying, not pretending to study so I didn't need to deal with Archer downstairs.

It was well into the evening when I packed up my notes and closed my laptop, mentally declaring my brain as full as it could possibly get with study notes. I was confident that I had a good handle on the material for the exam in the morning; I'd always tested pretty well, even if I barely retained any information a week later. But still, there was a gnawing anxiety building inside me that seemed totally separate from my usual stress of stalkers and murderers.

Then it occurred to me. I hadn't seen Steele since he'd blown out of the diner with Archer.

I could be jumping to conclusions, but worry churned my stomach and I hurried down the hallway to his room. I knocked softly, but when he didn't answer, I tried the handle. Sure, he could be downstairs with Kody and Archer, but it was worth checking his room first...right?

Right.

I tentatively pushed his door open and frowned at the gloomy darkness inside. Was he already asleep? I guessed it was possible...

"Steele?" I whispered, feeling like a total creeper and already second-guessing myself. "Are you asleep?"

Obviously, the second I said that I did a mental facepalm. If he was asleep...he couldn't exactly reply yes, now, could he?

I was about to creep out again and go look for him downstairs, but a movement in his bed startled me.

"Steele," I hissed, leaving his door open for light as I padded across his plush gray carpet to the bed. I didn't want to wake him up, but my gut told me something was wrong. I reached out a hand to touch his shoulder, then hissed a gasp when my fingers touched bandages.

He shifted in his sleep, and I bit my lip to keep from waking him up. But *what the fuck had happened?*

Covering my own mouth so as not to make a sound, I hurried back out of his room and along to Kody's. It was empty. So was Archer's. But I had a fair idea where I might find them both.

I ran so fast down to the gym I almost tripped on the stairs, but somehow I made it there without breaking my neck. Sure enough, they were in the gym wearing nothing but small shorts and fingerless MMA gloves and...*wow*. The mental image of Kody and Archer grappling on the padded gym floor while sweaty and panting was *definitely* getting filed in my spank bank. I didn't care how much of an asshole Archer was to me, he and Kody were goddamn walking orgasms.

"Hey," I said sharply, grabbing their attention and—hopefully—dragging mine away from the way they were all twisted up like a sexy pretzel. "What happened to Steele?"

Kody looked over at me, but Archer just used that distraction to his advantage. He flipped Kody over, twisting his huge, tattoo-covered body around, snaring Kody's arm and bending it up the length of his own body, hyperextending the joints.

I winced and tried really, *really* hard not to notice how Kody's shoulder was all squashed up in Archer's crotch. Fucking hell, I needed to get laid. Again.

"Ah, you fuck!" Kody yelled, but didn't tap out. Archer just grinned and leaned back farther, to the point I thought for sure Kody's arm would break.

"Tap out, bro," Archer taunted him. "Madison Kate already knows you've lost this round."

I rolled my eyes but folded my arms under my breasts and glared.

"Someone answer my fucking question," I snapped at them both, ignoring their stupid pissing contest. "Why the hell has Steele got bandages all over him?"

Kody groaned in pain and *finally* tapped out. Archer released him, and the two of them rolled away from one another on the padded blue mats while Kody rubbed his shoulder.

"He's fine," Archer told me with one brow cocked. "He just needed a few painkillers, and they always knock him right the fuck out."

Fury and *fear* were building inside me to the point of painful, and my nails bit deeply into my palms. "Painkillers *for what*?" I demanded through clenched teeth.

Archer just stared back at me like he wasn't going to tell me simply to piss me off.

Thankfully, Kody had a few more brain cells to rub together and rolled to his feet.

"He just caught a bit of gravel rash," he told me, casual as all fuck. "It's really not much worse than a bad graze but needs bandaging and rest so he can heal without it scarring."

I blinked at him. "Bad grazes don't fucking *scar*, Kodiak!"

He grimaced. "Really bad ones do."

Archer scoffed. "Steele's fine, Princess. Quit your fretting. Besides, don't chicks dig scars or some shit?"

"Probably not that many scars, dude," Kody muttered under his breath, then turned back to me. "Look, he just didn't want to worry you until after our doc had cleaned it all up and bandaged his arm. But then we might have slipped a couple of sedatives into his scotch, and he passed out before he could come and explain to you himself."

I needed to blink a couple more times in sheer disbelief. "You… What the hell were you thinking? You don't mix sedatives with alcohol! Kody, what the *fuck*? You could have killed him!"

Furious and stunned at their stupidity, I threw my hands up and stalked out of the gym.

"Babe, wait up." Kody chased after me, catching my arm with one of his gloved hands. "It's not as bad as it sounds. Trust me. We would never put Steele in danger deliberately; he's more than a brother to both of us."

"He's right," Archer drawled, leaning one of his heavily muscled shoulders on the doorframe. "We only take risks with high-speed car chases and shootouts. Drugs and alcohol are strictly under doctor's orders." His voice was heavy with sarcasm and his glare accusing.

Mother*fucker*. He blamed me for whatever had happened to Steele, no question in my mind.

"What happened?" I asked, my voice catching on my own turbulent emotions. "You clearly found the guy." Otherwise how did he get my knife back?

Archer unstrapped his gloves, tossed them behind him into the gym, then ran a hand over his long, dark stubble. "We found him. And his backup."

My brows shot up. "And?"

Archer shook his head. "And nothing. They didn't last long enough to tell us anything useful."

My heart stopped. "You killed them?"

Archer tilted his head to the side, ignoring Kody's sound of protest.

"That a problem for you, Princess? Who knows what they had planned for you. Would you have liked being sold into the flesh market? Or kept in a cage for *months* until your father caved and paid some insane ransom? Or, hell, I dunno, maybe let loose in an abandoned amusement park and then hunted like a fucking *deer*?" He grew more and more incensed with every word until he was practically shouting them at me. "They're lucky they died the way they did and I didn't get my fucking hands on them. Believe me, it was more humane this way."

With a disgusted sneer at me, Archer stomped back into the gym, and seconds later the heavy thud of fists striking a sandbag reached us.

"Kody!" Archer shouted when his friend didn't immediately follow.

Kody gave me a pained frown, and I shook my head. "Don't stress," I told him softly. "Archer actually made a good point. Whatever happened to Steele is my fault."

"It definitely wasn't," he retorted quickly, firmly. "You didn't ask for any of this. If anyone is responsible here, it's—" He cut himself off with a grimace, then sighed heavily. "I'll come back upstairs with you. Just give me two seconds to pack up the gym."

"No," I replied, laying a hand on his arm. "No, it's fine. Seriously. I'm going to go and creep into Steele's bed and hope he doesn't freak the fuck out when he wakes up and finds me there."

A grin curved Kody's lips. "Damn, MK. If I'd known that was

how to get you into bed, I'd have rolled out of a speeding vehicle months ago."

I groaned but rose up on my toes to smack a quick kiss on his lips. "Good things come to those who wait, Kodiak Jones."

He kissed me back, a brief peck of lips against lips. "You're fucking killing me, Madison Kate Danvers."

With that warming sentiment, I made my way back upstairs and into Steele's room. I closed the door softly behind me this time, then made my way around his huge bed to the vacant side. Someone had cranked the heat up in Steele's room, so I slipped out of my thick sweatpants and climbed under his covers in just my T-shirt and panties.

He let out a sigh as the mattress shifted, and I tensed. The last thing I wanted to do was wake him up or cause him pain. I just... needed to be near him.

Steele mumbled something in his sleep as I slowly lowered my head onto the spare pillow and got comfortable. I held my breath, trying to hear him, and was instantly glad I did.

"Hellcat," he said on a sigh so soft I wouldn't have heard it if the room weren't totally silent. "Don't leave me."

My heart thudded heavily, and I shuffled closer to him in the bed, finding his hand and linking our fingers together.

"Shh," I breathed, pressing a gentle kiss to his bare shoulder. "I'm here, Steele. I'm sorry."

He mumbled something more, but I couldn't make it out. A moment later, his breathing slowed into the steady, even rhythm of deep sleep once more.

I didn't sleep. I couldn't. But a small piece of my scarred soul rested at ease just lying there beside Steele.

That was better than any night's restful sleep I'd had in a long time.

CHAPTER 18

By the time two thirty in the morning rolled around, my usual nightmares were nibbling at the edges of my consciousness, trying to drag me down into the savage depths of my own mind. The last thing I wanted to do, though, was thrash around in my sleep and end up hurting Steele more than he already was. Chances were the nightmares would be worse than ever, given the attack I'd suffered at the diner.

I placed a gentle kiss on his cheek, then slipped out of his bed as silent as the night itself. I needed to sleep, but it was already so late it'd be a pointless venture. I'd be better off just keeping myself awake and passing out after my exam.

I didn't bother stopping at my room to get changed, because it was two thirty in the damn morning. If anyone else was awake at such an ungodly hour, they deserved to see me wandering around in just a T-shirt and panties. The heating for the whole house had been turned up, anyway, so I wasn't exactly freezing my nipples off.

On silent feet I made my way downstairs and let myself into the dark gym, just like I had done countless times since returning home. With a yawn, I flipped the lights on and headed over to the treadmill. I'd decided weeks ago that it was too cold, the snow too thick, for me to run outside. Not to mention, too dangerous. But half an hour of hard-core sprinting on the treadmill usually did the trick of clearing my head and either waking me up fully for the day or putting me back to sleep for a couple of hours—not long enough for the nightmares to sink their claws in, but enough to keep me functioning.

I dialed in my usual settings, then started running. My bare feet slapped the rotating belt, and my breasts jumped uncomfortably in the unsupportive crop top I wore under my T-shirt, but I ignored it all. I just needed to—

A hand slapped down on the power button, and I jumped out of my fucking skin.

"Kody, what the fuck?" I exclaimed. "You could have killed me!"

He arched a brow over those bright green eyes and twitched a half smile. "Uh-huh. Shutting down the treadmill could kill you. Pretty sure you've survived worse, MK."

I glowered at him. "What are you doing awake, Kody? Do you know what time it is?"

"Do you?" he countered, cocking his head to the side. "I came to find you, obviously. This middle-of-the-freaking-night work-out seems to be a habit of yours now, and I'm starting to become offended."

Propping my hands on my hips, I scowled in confusion. "Why the fuck would my early morning exercise have anything to do with you? Let alone cause offense?"

His glare flattened. "Babe. Seriously? I'm literally a professional fitness trainer, and you've resorted to sneaking down here at three in the damn morning to avoid training with me?" He clicked his tongue in a disapproving way. "That's just hurtful, MK. I'll have you know, I'm very good at my job."

I grinned, glad for the extra height the treadmill was giving me. It almost put me level with Kody so I didn't need to crane my neck like usual. "I'm sure you are, Kodiak Jones." Unable to help myself, I let my gaze travel down his bare chest, admiring the swallows and roses inked over his pecks. Every single one of his abs was sharply defined, and that V at his waist...*groan.*

"So?" He wasn't going to be distracted by my lusty looks. Damn. I released a sigh, catching the edge of my lip between my teeth as I tried to think of a polite refusal.

"Look, I don't really give a shit about *training*, you know? I just run to clear my head and keep the cookies from showing on my ass. Trainers can be a bit..." I shrugged, knowing this was going to go badly. "You know. A bit *mean*."

Kody gasped in fake outrage. Or I was pretty sure it was fake. Not much fazed Kodiak Jones, that was for fucking sure.

"Babe, you say that like you don't *love* a bit of mean in your life." His lips curved into a darkly suggestive smile, and it did all kinds of delicious things to my insides.

I needed to duck my eyes away from his in order to stop the drool running down my chin at all the mental pictures he'd just sparked. "In the bedroom, sure," I replied, piling on the sass to cover how turned on I was. "But not in the sweaty gym with angry, 'roid-raging muscle men pumping iron in the mirror."

A frown ticked at Kody's brow causing his smile to slip slightly. "You know you could have royally fucked up *my* future with that steroid stunt too? I'm only just growing my business, which relies entirely on word of mouth, referrals, and reputation. Having my most high-profile client suspended for doping would have had me dead in the water as far as my training career went."

Unease settled in my belly, and I looked down at my bare toes on the treadmill belt, unable to meet his eyes because I already knew there wouldn't be any anger or resentment there for what I'd done...only hurt and disappointment. And I fucking hated myself for that.

"I know," I whispered, letting myself feel all that guilt. I deserved it. "I'm sorry, Kody. I can only say that I didn't really think about the consequences for you. Sometimes when I fixate on a revenge plot…" I trailed off, scuffing my toes against the exercise equipment.

"You lose sight of everything and anyone else who might get hurt along the way?" Kody asked, his tone harsh enough that I looked back up at him. But his green eyes were just resigned. "I know. You and Arch are more similar than you realize."

My lip curled in denial, and Kody just laughed.

"Whatever," he said, shaking his head. "Come on." He held his hand out to help me off the treadmill like it was twenty feet tall. "You're training with me, whether you like it or not."

I groaned, dragging my heels as he tugged me across the gym to the padded mats he usually sparred with Archer on. "Kody, I really don't want to. It's the middle of the night… I just wanted to clear my brain of all the shadows and shit."

He gave me a sharp look. "Maybe if you knew how to defend yourself, those shadows wouldn't seem so scary."

I had nothing to say to that. He was right, as usual. Maybe if I'd known how to fight off my attacker, he wouldn't have nearly choked me out in that public restroom. If I hadn't had my butterfly knife in my pocket…I shuddered to think how it all would have turned out.

"Fine," I agreed grudgingly. "But go easy on me, okay? I only appreciate the domineering bullshit if we're both naked and your back is bloody from my fingernails. Got it?" I was teasing, but the responding flare of heat in Kody's eyes made my heart race and my nipples harden.

"I mean, that can be arranged too," he practically purred, dragging his teeth over his lower lip while stripping me naked with his eyes, "but for now, I'd honestly feel better if I knew you had *some* basic self-defense skills."

Sometimes in life we made decisions and just had to roll with it. That was my excuse, and I was sticking with it.

"You sure?" I teased, playing with the hem of my T-shirt and raising it up enough that he could see the tiny panties I wore underneath.

Kody swiped a hand over his hair, making it stick up in all directions. "Damn, babe. You really don't want to train with me. My feelings are hard-core hurt over here."

I rolled my eyes. "No, they're not."

His responding grin was quick. "Well, luckily for you, I'm a have-my-cake-and-eat-it-too kinda guy. I *am* going to teach you a couple of basic self-defense moves, which we're going to build on every time you can't sleep and come creeping down here like a black cat." He prowled closer to me, stopping only when we were close enough that his sweatpants brushed my bare thighs. "And *then* I'm going to fuck you hard enough to wake this entire damn house up. Clear?"

I shivered with desire, letting the hungry grin curve my lips as I peered up into Kody's eyes. "Clear," I replied, my voice a husky groan of anticipation.

He held my gaze a long moment, then shook his head with an unsteady sort of laugh. "This was probably a terrible idea," he muttered to himself, putting a few feet of space between us. "How the fuck I'll make it through this without a raging hard-on, I have no idea."

Short answer? He didn't. But he also didn't let it distract him from his mission to teach me some basic self-defense skills. Ways to break free from a larger man's grip and what to do if I was attacked from behind—again. Over and over, he simulated the same way I'd been grabbed in the diner, using that as a real-life example of what might happen to teach me how to free myself.

It took more than a few tries before I stopped panicking on instinct as he grabbed me like that, but it was easy to relax when I reminded myself that it was Kody grabbing me. Kody…who I was more than comfortable being pinned down by.

"Come on, MK," he groaned after I found myself pinned to the mat for the hundredth time. I was facedown with him pasted to my back, his hard length crushed against my ass. "You're fucking killing me. Learn this damn move so we can call it quits for the night."

"We could just call it quits now," I suggested, wriggling under him in a way that was far from subtle. Whatever, tact wasn't my strong suit.

He made a growling, frustrated sound, then pushed up off me. "And risk some creeper ending up in the position I was just in? Not a chance in hell, baby. Come on, you've almost got this. You just need to want to do some damage, or your attacker will always have the upper hand."

I grumbled but got back to my feet. "You should probably just piss me off or something. Say something douchey like Archer, and I'll happily knee you in the balls and run like hell."

Kody cringed and adjusted his hard cock in his sweatpants. "No thanks," he replied with a nervous laugh. "I still remember the noise Arch made when you nailed his nuts. No one is going to volunteer for that."

I chuckled at the memory. "Good times."

He just shook his head and swiped a hand over his hair. "You're vicious. No wonder Steele calls you Hellcat. Never heard a more appropriate pet name in my life."

I scoffed, grinning. "Nonsense; you hear me call Archer 'asshole' all the freaking time."

He groaned, hiding his laugh behind his hands as he scrubbed at his face. "Okay, let's do this again. Those tiny panties are legitimately driving me insane, and if I don't rip them off you soon, I might actually die."

"Dramatic much?" I teased, cocking my hip in order to draw attention to the panties in question. "You're the one who wanted to do this in the middle of the night while we're both half-naked."

Kody leveled a flat glare at me. "No one ever accused me of being smart, babe."

I rolled my eyes, folding my arms under my breasts. "You don't

152

fool me, Kodiak Jones. Nothing seems to slip past you." I paused and pondered that. "Except last week when Steele made you think he was fucking around with another girl."

"That was just mean," he grumbled. "I was blinded by outrage on your behalf, babe. He'd been moping around like he was head over heels in love with you, and then all of a sudden he's banging some random chick? I was ready to break his fucking nose."

Nothing gave me more warm tingles than hearing a guy threaten violence to defend his girl's honor. Yeah, I was totally aware how fucked up that made me. I also didn't give two shits, so there was that.

Crossing the padded blue mats, I reached up and looped my arms around Kody's neck. "You'd hit your friend for ruining his chances with me? That's all kinds of sweet, Kodiak Jones, but shouldn't you be encouraging him to fuck it up?"

His hands gripped my waist, his palms warm on my bare skin where my T-shirt had risen up. "I'd happily make him bleed if he ever hurt you, gorgeous. And I don't need him to fuck it up just so you'll pay attention to me. Humans have infinite, untapped possibilities, and I fully believe we're capable of equally strong emotions for more than one person." He dipped his head, bringing his lips to mine for a teasing kiss. "I'm also not so insecure I need him out of the picture. I know full well you want me just as badly as I want you."

He pulled me closer, bringing our bodies flush together and showing me just how much he still wanted me, even after an hour of failing his self-defense tutorial. He must be in pain by this stage, and I was about three steps away from begging to take care of it.

"That's a very mature mindset," I murmured. "So, you're okay with—"

"What the fuck are you two doing?" Archer's grouchy voice cut me off, and my shoulders bunched with tension automatically. His heavy footsteps padded across the floor, and I didn't bother turning around to face him. Why bother, when I could see him in the full-length mirrors behind Kody?

"Arch." Kody greeted his friend on a sigh. "You're up early."

The surly shithead just grunted a noise and made his way over to the section of the gym set up with cardio equipment. "Couldn't sleep," he muttered, then scowled at my back. I was perfectly aware that my ass was on full display, but seriously, he could kiss it.

"Seems like that's a common problem around here," Kody commented, releasing my waist and taking a small step away. "I was just trying to teach MK some basic self-defense moves to help if she gets grabbed again."

Archer curled his lip in a sneer. "Fuck knows she needs it."

I glowered. "She is right fucking here, dickwad."

He swung those cool eyes my way, condescension dripping from his pores. "What a shame your pants aren't, though. Or were you about to learn some of Kody's special grappling moves that don't require clothes?"

My temper flared. "You'd know all about those, wouldn't you, big man?"

"Sounds like something you've been fantasizing about, Princess. You worried I'll upstage you?" Archer sneered, calling me on my bullshit insult.

I snorted a laugh, not willing to back down. "Hate to tell you, Sunshine, but this is a pants-less party you definitely *won't* be invited to. Ever. Not unless hell suddenly freezes over."

"All right, that's enough," Kody announced as Archer's glare narrowed and his lips parted for what was sure to be a cutting comeback. "Arch, just go and warm up. MK, fucking ignore him. I swear the two of you feed off each other's anger sometimes."

Archer and I shot each other dark glares before Kody tugged on my hand and pulled my attention back to what we'd been doing. Self-defense training. Well, if Kody wanted me to get angry and think violent thoughts, now was the fucking time.

"Let's do this again," Kody said to me, totally ignoring his friend across the gym. There was a faint beeping as Archer changed the settings on the treadmill I'd just been using, but I determinedly ignored him. I just wanted to get this fucking move right once so Kody would let me leave. Hopefully with him.

Gritting my teeth, I went through the same motions that we'd been repeating for over an hour, taking several long strides away from him, then turning my back and bracing myself for his attack. The whole idea he was trying to prepare me for was being taken by surprise, so he never attacked quickly. There was always a pause of a random amount of time—just long enough that I was permanently off-guard.

This time, though, when his arm banded around my neck, I was ready for him. Anger burned through my veins—thanks to Archer's early morning bad mood—and I moved with swift strength. My hands came up to his forearm, giving my neck that extra half inch of space while I ducked and twisted. His choke hold unraveled as I backed into the gap on his left, then I shoved him away from me hard enough that he landed on his ass.

"Yes!" Kody cried out, clapping his hands together sharply. "Yes! That was it! See, all you needed was to get a bit pissed off."

Archer's sarcastic laugh from across the gym was unmistakable.

"You got something to say, smartass?" I hissed over at him. The elation at finally nailing that move soured, and I was back to irritated and grouchy.

Archer shrugged, not even pausing in his light jog as he warmed up on the treadmill. He just met my gaze in the mirror and smirked. That was my only warning of the hand grenade he was about to pull the pin out of.

"If you needed to make her angry, bro, why didn't you just tell her how it was really you who took away all her freedoms? Not her shitty excuse of an absent father. Although, in fairness, it barely took any effort at all to make him dance to our tune." Archer hit the cool-down button on the machine and slowed his pace before turning and jumping off the end. He gave me a smug, patronizing smile as I just stood there in shock with my mouth ajar. "The whole forced committal thing, though? That was all Samuel. He sure does have a hard-on for having your legal rights stripped, Princess. Not that it'd benefit him even if they were." That last comment was thrown in as an offhand remark, like he'd already moved on from tormenting me and was now pondering my father's motives.

"What the fuck is he talking about, Kody?" I demanded in a deathly quiet voice. My gaze left Archer—he was nothing but a shit-stirring fuckboy—and landed on Kody, heavy with accusation. "Is that true?"

Kody's lips parted, but the panicked look in his eyes said it all. I shook my head in disbelief, turning my back on him and starting out of the gym.

"Wait, MK," he said as he grabbed at my arm, and I snatched it out of his grip when I whipped around to face him.

"Don't fucking touch me, Kody," I hissed, all venom and wrath. I wasn't going to break down and scream and rage...that was exactly what Archer wanted. But I was beyond furious, and I needed to haul ass out of the gym before my resolve crumbled and Archer got himself a front row seat to the Madison Kate inferno.

Kody withdrew his hand but took a step closer anyway, his brow creased imploringly. "MK, please, just let me explain—"

"Nope," I cut him off, slicing my hand through the air to end whatever bullshit he was about to spew. "No, I think I'm about fucking done with explanations. You two can go fuck yourselves. Oh, maybe that's what you were angling for all along, Arch? We all know how much you love being Kody's bottom."

The big guy just smirked back at me, totally unfazed, while Kody looked like he couldn't decide if he'd rather grab me or punch Archer. I made the choice easier for him and left the fucking room.

CHAPTER 19

"What the *fuck* is your problem, Archer?" Kody's enraged roar echoed through the house as I stomped down the corridor in bare feet. His words were closely followed by the distinctive sound of a fist hitting flesh, and I paused a moment.

A hiss of pain came from Archer, and then… "I deserved that."

"You're *fucking right*, you did!" Kody bellowed, angrier than I could ever remember hearing him. "I swear to fucking god, Archer D'Ath, you need to sort your shit out with her before Steele and I murder you ourselves. We've both had enough!"

I hurried away from the gym corridor but not fast enough. Kody caught up to me as I ducked into the kitchen and grabbed me by the wrist again.

"Stop it!" he snapped at me when I struggled and tried to wrench my arm away. This time, though, he was prepared and simply held on. I was no match for his strength, so it was entirely pointless trying to pull away when he'd made up his mind. "Just stop it, MK. You're seriously going to let Arch push your buttons like that? He knew exactly what to say to rile you up, and look!"

My eyes narrowed to a poisonous glare, and my heart frosted

over. "It doesn't matter if he was deliberately trying to set me off. Is it true or not, Kody? The look on your face kinda gives it away."

"Yes, it's true," Kody replied, and my frozen heart shattered into jagged shards. "I didn't know how he was going to do it, and fuck me, MK, if I'd known…" He shook his head, looking bitterly frustrated. "I swear to you, I never asked him to do that. To *threaten* you like that. I just wanted you *safe*. Is that honestly so hard for you to understand?"

Fucking Bree was in my brain, her voice echoing Kody's words almost exactly and tempering my blistering anger. Not enough to make me just forgive and forget but…enough. Enough that I didn't punch Kody in his beautiful face, and enough that I wavered. It was enough, and he pushed his advantage.

"Madison Kate, I promise you, I would never have let your father follow through on that shit. Never." His emerald eyes were dead serious, silently begging for my forgiveness or, at the very least, my understanding.

Bitterness welled up in my throat. "No, but you were happy to let me believe it. Anything to keep me in line, right?"

"Anything to keep you *alive*, yes!" He shouted his reply, and his fingers tightened on my wrist to the point of painful. "If it means keeping you breathing, then I'd do it again a hundred times over. I can live with you hating me, but I *can't* live knowing I failed to keep you safe."

"Well, that's lucky," I spat at him with venom, "because I *do* hate you. All of you."

Kody laughed an arrogant, humorless sound. "See, that's the real reason you're so pissed off right now, isn't it? Because you *don't* hate me. You haven't hated me for months now, and even when Arch tells you something like that, you still don't hate me."

I seethed with fury at his audacity. "You're telling me what I'm feeling now? I must have missed the memo where you became a psychic. Go on then, Kodiak. Tell me what I'm thinking now."

He gave an arrogant smirk. "You're *thinking* you want to punch me, but it's not what you actually want to do."

I rolled my eyes. "Oh, of course. Enlighten me, oh great and omnipotent Kodiak. What is it that I *actually* want to do?" My sarcasm was thicker than molasses and my glare like razor blades.

Kody's cocky smile spread wider. "This," he replied, giving my wrist a sharp yank that made me stumble and fall against his chest. His free hand cupped my face, and before I could even catch my balance, his lips were on mine in a crushing kiss.

I gasped, foolishly kissing him back for a moment of insanity before I wrenched myself free and took two steps away. Shaking my head, I wiped my mouth on the back of my hand like I could erase the searing heat of his lips so easily.

"No," I muttered, my conviction weaker than wet tissue paper. "No, you threw away your chances with me when you went behind my back to my father. You tried to have me shackled, Kody, and that's unforgivable."

"So don't forgive me," he declared, throwing his hands wide in a dramatic gesture that only seemed to give him a bigger presence in the kitchen. His sweatpants hung low on his hips, and his upper body was all muscles and ink. Bodies like his should be illegal because they made women like me lose all sense of sanity or self-preservation.

"Spend the rest of our lives making me pay for lying to you, if that's what will make you feel better. But I don't fucking regret it, and I won't fucking apologize for it. You know we've had four new deliveries from your stalker since you got out of the hospital? Not to mention what could have happened yesterday if we hadn't been there." His tone was aggressive and passionate, and I swallowed heavily with anxiety. Four new deliveries? Photos or dolls? Or something new? What about whoever had tried to kill me? Fucking hell…maybe he had a point.

I wrapped my arms around myself, ducking my gaze away

from his intuitive, soul-searching stare. I'd backed myself against the pantry door, so I couldn't even make an easy escape without pushing past him.

"Kody..." I started, then licked my lips as I searched for the words. I was so, *so* angry at him for what he'd done. For fucking lying to me and letting me think it was all on Archer and my father. But...

"Pretend to hate me all you fucking want, Madison Kate," he continued, stepping closer and crowding my personal space once more, "but don't even try to pretend you don't feel this magnetic pull between us. Don't fucking act like you're not basically crawling out of your own skin to fuck me right now."

His hands planted on the pantry door to either side of my head, and he leaned in, hovering his lips over mine just a fraction of an inch away from kissing me again. He wasn't going to, though. I knew it as certainly as I knew he was *right*. God damn him straight to hell, he was right.

"So what are you scared of, MK?" He taunted me, waving that red flag like he had a death wish. "Fuck me now to get it out of your system, and then plot your revenge tomorrow."

I wavered. I should say no. I should tell him to go fuck himself with all that arrogance.

"Come on, Princess," he purred, deliberately poking my feral anger with his use of Archer's nickname for me, "Fuck me like you actually hate me, because we both know you don't."

I planted my hands against his chest, ready to shove him away from me and storm out of the kitchen with my pride and fury firmly intact. But as they say, the road to hell is paved with good intentions. My fingers kissed the hot, hard muscles of his chest, and before I could follow through on my intention, my mouth found his.

Well, shit.

Kody didn't question me. He knew I was still riding the fury and was more than happy to let me fuck him angry. Which was good because angry was the only way he was getting me at all. His lips met mine kiss for kiss, his tongue sweeping into my mouth and swiftly turning the tables of power on me. Before I knew it, I was pinned to the pantry door with his huge body pressed to every damn inch of me while he kissed me with rage of his own, claiming my mouth in a way that promised he'd do the same to my body.

I groaned into his kiss, biting his lower lip and curling my fingertips into the hard flesh of his back. Suddenly I was more than willing to give him exactly what he'd been taunting me with. Kodiak Jones wanted hate sex? I'd fucking well show him the meaning of that.

My teeth sunk into his lip harder, drawing blood, and he pulled away with a hiss of pain. The look on his face wasn't indignation or disgust, though. Nope, that was pure, undiluted lust. Something he confirmed a second later when his mouth crashed back down on mine and his hands slid to the backs of my thighs. He hitched my legs up, and I happily wrapped them around his waist, clinging on as he ground against me and made me moan in encouragement.

"Fuck," Kody hissed against my lips as my fingernails tore down his bare back. He didn't stop, though. He just kissed me harder, letting the coppery tang of blood taint our kiss. My back left the pantry door as he stepped back, causing me to cling onto his body until he spun us around and deposited my mostly bare ass down on the marble island.

"Holy shit, that's cold," I protested, shivering as the stone met my warm skin.

Kody just smirked, then gave me another teasing kiss, all lips and no tongue. "Want me to turn up the heat?" His jade eyes danced with mischief, and I knew perfectly well he meant that in a metaphorical sense.

I arched a brow, challenging him. "You won't get another chance at this, Kodiak Jones; I suggest you bring I game."

He huffed a laugh, then stripped me of my shirt. Then my crop top.

His head dipped, his mouth sealing over one of my hard nipples, and I sucked in a sharp breath as heat zapped through my whole body. I leaned back on the counter, arching my back to give him better access to my breasts, even as my thighs tightened around his body. The movement of relocating us to the island had created a gap between us. A gap I badly needed to close because I was all but ready to come just from his shaft grinding me through his soft sweatpants and my thin panties.

One of Kody's hands paid attention to my other breast, rolling my nipple between his fingers in the most delicious way. His other hand skimmed over my bare stomach, then lower, stroking a teasing line under the band of my panties, making me whimper with frustration. For all my taunting him to bring his A game, I really just wanted his cock inside me. ASAP.

Except I couldn't shake a nagging feeling of urgency and paranoia. "Kody, wait," I breathed, then groaned when his fingers dipped lower between us, rubbing me through my damp panties. "We should… Shouldn't we go upstairs? Someone could walk in on us…" I raised my brows, nodding in the vague direction of the gym. If it'd just been the two of us awake, I wouldn't have even given it a second thought. But knowing Archer was awake and *just* down the hall…I'd like to say it made me worried, but if I was honest, it was just turning me on.

I fucking loved sneaking around.

"No," Kody replied, peering down at me with hungry eyes and lush, swollen lips that begged to be kissed. Or put to other good uses. "Fuck Archer. He won't come out until he's finished a full circuit of weights."

"And if he hears us?" I countered, and my traitorous stomach fluttered with excitement. I kinda hoped he did hear us. It'd serve him right.

Kody took a moment before responding, his palm cupping one of my breasts and his thumb circling my taut nipple. "He won't hear shit over that music," he replied in a murmur, and I cocked my head to listen. Sure enough, the thumping bass from some heavy rock song was reverberating from the gym. More was the shame.

"But even if he did," Kody continued, still locked in a staring competition with my tits, "he'd deserve it. I hope his balls are so blue they hurt right now. Asshole."

I laughed coldly and grabbed his face between my palms, kissing him hard. "Vicious."

"You love it," he growled as his lips came back to mine again, kissing me like he was claiming a piece of my soul. Like he was doing everything possible to leave a mark on my psyche that I'd never be able to remove.

My hands trailed down his chest, my nails biting into the hard flesh of his abs before hooking into the elastic waistband of his sweatpants. His cock was so hard and straining against the fabric, but I paused again with a groan of frustration.

"Condom?" I asked with an annoyed sigh. I loved a good, spontaneous hate fuck on the kitchen island as much as the next girl, but goddamn I did not want to risk an STD. Not when I had no idea where Kody'd been sticking his dick, and I seriously doubted he had a convenient copy of his clean records tucked into his pants. Pregnancy wasn't a concern, thanks to my IUD. Not to mention the damage done by my recent stabbing.

I expected Kody to suggest we relocate upstairs. Or even try to convince me that he was a squeaky clean choir boy. But nope.

"I got you, babe," he muttered, pulling back from me just long enough to pull open the drawer below the cutlery. Sure enough, he popped back up with a foil-wrapped condom between his fingers and a smug-as-shit grin on his face.

I stared at the condom in disbelief, then at the drawer he'd grabbed it from, then back at Kody. "You're disgusting," I told him.

He just shrugged. "So?" He pushed his sweatpants down, kicking them aside and leaving him in just boxer briefs. His hands came to the waistband of my panties, and then they were gone too. "Apparently disgusting and infuriating turns you on, MK." He demonstrated that observation by swiping his fingers down my pussy and sliding his index finger into my wet heat.

I wanted to shut him down and deny it, but my body was doing all the talking. I was powerless to do anything except moan and writhe on his fingers, silently begging for more. When he didn't immediately deliver, I got impatient.

"Kody," I growled, "seriously. The window of opportunity is closing. Fuck me now or never because I'm about three seconds away from remembering how furious I am at you and leaving you high and dry."

He scoffed but still pushed his boxers down and kicked them aside with his pants. I drooled a little at the sight of him fully erect; I wasn't even going to lie to myself and pretend I didn't. Holy hell. That tease I'd gotten the first day I got back, when I walked in on him naked, was nothing more than that. A tease. The real deal? Better than I'd imagined. Because I *had* imagined it, several times.

"Well," he murmured as he rolled the condom down his considerable length, and I tried to close my unhinged jaw, "that would only make one of us. Dry, I mean."

He teased me, rubbing his tip down the length of my decidedly *not dry* pussy until I growled with frustration and grabbed him.

"Kodiak, I'm not in the fucking mood for games. You're either sticking this in me, or I'm going back upstairs to finish myself off. Make a decision. Quickly."

He didn't need to be told again. In roughly a nanosecond, he thrust into me, and I gasped at the slight sting of his girth. I wanted to smack the cocky smirk off his face as he pulled out and pumped back in, hitting me deeper this time. But I also desperately wanted him to fuck the daylights out of me.

"Kody," I moaned, and he pushed into me for a third time, finally making it all the way inside and pausing a second.

He huffed a satisfied laugh against my neck as he trailed hot kisses along my skin. "Is that what you wanted, beautiful?"

"More," I moaned. "Fuck me hard, Kodiak Jones."

"As if I could deny you anything you wanted, Madison Kate," he murmured back, his voice dropping the arrogant amusement for a second. "Especially when you ask so nicely." There it was, back again.

I was past caring, though. All I wanted, all I could focus on, was chasing down that orgasm by way of Kody's huge, rock-hard cock buried inside my cunt.

He did as he was told, though, and braced his hands on my waist while he started to move, fucking me hard enough I had to hold on to his neck. Otherwise, I might have ended up halfway across the damn countertop.

"Holy shit, MK," he gasped against my lips after I kissed him again, all rough and savage. "Holy fucking shit. You feel so good. So damn tight." He thrust into me a couple more times, groaning as he demonstrated his own point.

I was past the point of coherent speech, though. The level of head-spinning, sweat-dripping arousal I was at, I feared all my words would come out in a slurred mess like I'd just downed a gallon of vodka. Instead, I just arched my back and bucked my hips into his, encouraging him to hit me at a different angle.

I was so close. So fucking close.

"Lean back," Kody told me, pushing a less-than-gentle hand in the center of my chest. I obliged, though, hissing when the cold marble touched my bare back. It was a necessary evil, and one I was quickly rewarded for. With my back flat on the countertop, Kody hooked his hands under my thighs, hauling me closer to him and slamming his dick even deeper than he'd been before.

I cried out, but he was just getting started. His strong grip spread me wide and held me firm as he pounded into my cunt exactly like I'd been wanting. Holy, ever-loving fuck, *yes!* His cock was hitting me in *exactly* the right spot, and my breathing spiked sharply as my orgasm built like a tsunami.

My back arched, and I rolled my head back on the counter, feeling my hair spilling around me like some kind of gloriously pornographic mermaid. Then something caught my eye.

A flicker of movement. A shadow out of place.

For a split second, my heart seized with panic, convinced it was my stalker watching from the darkness of the corridor. But then the figure shifted farther into the light of the kitchen, and my heart thumped back to life. Harder, even, than it had been before.

And so it should. The raw shock on Archer's handsome face was better than I could have hoped for.

I expected him to make a scene. To yell at us and get all fired up with piss and vinegar and ultimately cheat me of what was promising to be a glorious climax. But he surprised me for once.

He didn't shout and scream. He didn't throw insults. He just stood there, transfixed.

"Shit," Kody cursed, clearly seeing Archer as well. "Fuck *right off*, dude," he snapped with pure venom.

Archer's gaze snapped up from me to his friend, and his scowl darkened. But he didn't argue, just stalked across the kitchen to grab his protein powder and shaker.

Kody paused, looking down at me with a pained expression. He was balls deep in me, with his hands pinning my legs open and my breasts on full display, but the message in his eyes was clear.

Fuck that, though.

"Don't you dare stop," I ordered him with a clear threat in my tone.

Kody huffed a short laugh, almost disbelieving, but started moving again. He was going slower, though, grinding into me with torturous thrusts that scraped across my G-spot and left me whimpering for more.

Archer's eyes were on me. I could feel them like a physical touch as he raked his gaze all over my naked body, yet I wasn't running and hiding. Damn my messed-up, bad-boy complex, I *liked* him watching. Watching and knowing I was never, ever, not until hell froze over, going to ride his cock like this.

I turned my head slightly, meeting his eyes across the kitchen and licking my lips. Yep. I was *that* level of fucked up.

His ice-blue eyes flared with heat, then his brow creased with anger. Somehow, he knew exactly what message I was sending, and it pissed him right the fuck off.

He slammed his protein shaker back onto the counter and stalked out of the kitchen the way he'd come, fading back into the shadows of the corridor to the gym, and I couldn't help the laugh that escaped my throat.

"I don't know whether I'm more pissed off that I lost your undivided attention for a moment there," Kody commented in a husky, sex-filled voice as his hand shifted from my thigh to my cunt, found my clit, and circled it with his index finger, "or turned the fuck on that you like to be watched. Or both."

I gave him a small shrug, wetting my lips again. All the panting and moaning was drying my mouth out something fierce. "Dealer's choice," I replied, somewhat out of breath, "but if you settle on pissed off, can you do it after I come? 'Cause I'm *right* fucking there, Kody."

He let out a feral sort of growl and picked up his pace. "Well, then fucking hell, babe. Do it. I want to feel you coming on my cock so hard you see stars." To drive his point home, he flicked my clit and thrust deep inside me, and I was a goner.

Screaming my release, I tossed my head back and arched my spine, thrashing and writhing on his dick as my cunt pulsed with each wave of pleasure.

Kody cursed and leaned over me, his hand braced against the marble as he finished a few moments later, his dick twitching and pulsing inside me as I shuddered through the aftershocks of my own orgasm.

For a second, neither of us moved, and the only sound in the kitchen was the harmony of our ragged breathing. Then Kody raised his head and blinked at me a couple of times.

"You still angry at me, babe?"

I narrowed my eyes, which was the best I could do while all my bones were still jelly. "Furious," I replied honestly.

Kody's lips twitched in a smile. "Good." He stood up with a groan, stepping out from between my legs and deftly disposing of the used condom.

"Good?" I repeated as I sat up with maximum effort and eyed him suspiciously. "Why do I feel like you're up to something?"

"Because I am," he replied, then grabbed me by the waist and threw me over his shoulder. "I want to drag a few more orgasms out of you while that rage is still burning hot. After all, you did tell me to bring my A game."

I shrieked a half-assed protest, but he shut me up with a slap to my bare ass. And not a playful one either. A full-palmed, stinging slap that made me groan and squirm in his grip as he carried me upstairs. Something he didn't fail to notice either.

"Oh, babe. We need to fight more often," he commented with a snicker as he shoved his door open. After he entered the room with me still draped over his shoulder like a naked, soaking wet trophy, he toed the door closed and dropped me onto his bed. His mouth was on my cunt before the door even fully clicked shut.

This time when I came, my attention was all on Kody, rather than on the ice-blue eyes that had just watched me fall apart from the shadows.

CHAPTER 20

Somehow, I slept. It wasn't long, maybe only half an hour, but thanks to my utter, bone-shaking exhaustion—courtesy of Kody seriously bringing his A game—that short nap was more restful than a whole night of restlessness.

I wanted nothing more than to stay in bed, curled up in Kody's warmth while I ignored how badly he'd pissed me off. But I had exams to tank and reality to face.

Groaning and cursing, I dragged my ass out of Kody's bed and winced as I dragged one of his hoodies over my aching body. It was a delicious sort of ache, though, one that made me grin at the memory of how each pain had been earned. Angry fucking was a dangerous sport, but I'd happily wear the consequences.

Kody mumbled something into his pillow, then shifted his face slightly to the side and cracked an eyelid at me.

"What?" I asked, wrinkling my nose as I hunted for my panties, then remembered they were probably still in the kitchen.

"I said," he replied, his voice thick with sleep, "are you still mad at me?"

I released a long sigh. "Yes."

A sly grin spread across his lips, and he snaked a hand out of the covers, reaching for me.

I dodged out of the way, though, and scowled. "Nice try, Kodiak. I've got my psych exam this morning."

He lifted his head from the pillow just enough to give me a rumpled look of disbelief and confusion. "You're still going to your exam?"

I frowned back at him, folding my arms and tucking my hands into the long sleeves of his hoodie. "Uh, yeah. I don't intend to fail so soon, and I don't exactly have any good reason to ask for an exemption."

"But you were assaulted yesterday and you haven't slept. You can't seriously—"

"Don't underestimate me, Kodiak Jones," I replied with a confident grin. "I do some of my best work under pressure."

His brows hitched. "Don't I know it."

Rolling my eyes, I started to leave his room, then paused. He was lying flat on his stomach, his arm curled around the pillow and his lids slitted as he watched me like a hungry predator. There was a noticeable chill to the air again—someone must have turned the heating off—which gave me an idea.

I grabbed the corner of Kody's comforter and yanked it off him, chucking it across the room. His howl of protest followed me as I raced back to my own room, and I chuckled to myself as I turned on my shower. It took a few moments for the water to heat up, and then I quickly stripped Kody's hoodie off and jumped under the warm spray.

I'd caught sight of the time on Kody's bedside clock, so I knew I had a few minutes on my hands—enough for a proper shower, anyway, which was good. Early-morning-slash-middle-of-the-night self-defense training followed by several hours of sex didn't leave a girl at her freshest, that was for damn sure.

Humming under my breath, I went through the motions of

scrubbing, shaving, and shampooing. It was as I rinsed my color-depositing pink shampoo out that the shower door opened and an extra pair of hands slipped across my soapy midsection.

"What do you think you're doing, Kodiak?" I murmured, not bothering to open my eyes. I knew it was him. He had a certain presence about him, a confidence in the way he touched me. Also, Steele was covered in bandages, and I *seriously* doubted Archer would be slipping into the shower with me.

"Your shower looked warmer than ours," he replied with an amused edge to his voice. His palms caressed my slippery body, and I let him back me against the tiled wall of the shower. I shivered at the cold tiles touching my shower-warmed skin but didn't object. How could I when Kodiak freaking Jones in all his naked glory was pressed up against me with his hands on my tits?

His head dipped, his lips seeking mine, but I turned my face away and bit back a smile.

"I wasn't done," I told him, fighting to keep my tone from sounding too damn playful. I hadn't forgotten *or* forgiven Archer's little revelation…even if I did believe Bree's theory that they were just trying to keep me safe from stalkers and killers. Kody still needed to atone, and I had no intention of going easy on him.

Then again, I was quickly coming around to his offer of penance by orgasms.

"Good, let me help," he offered, skimming his hands down my sides and grabbing at my hips. His gaze was full to overflowing with raw, naked desire, and it made me want to jump him and tell my exams to go fuck themselves. But nope. My education wasn't going to take a backseat to dick. No matter how great the dick was.

Narrowing my eyes at him, I shook my head and reached for my conditioner. "If you think we're going to fuck right now, you're wrong. My exam starts in just over an hour, and I still need coffee. Lots of coffee."

He swiped the conditioner from my hand and squeezed out

a dollop into his palm. "Well, good thing I just heard that SGU campus is closed today due to snow and all exams have been postponed."

My brows shot up. "What?"

"Turn around," he told me, indicating for me to face the wall. I did as I was told and tried really hard to contain my groan as he worked the conditioner into my lengths. "Turns out the snow fell pretty thick overnight. The snow plows are all out across the city clearing streets, but unfortunately the area around SGU won't be touched until later this afternoon."

My back was to him, so I allowed myself a grin. "Kody, did you have anything to do with that?"

"Babe," he replied, sounding offended. Fake offended. "I'm flattered you think I have that kind of sway with people in positions of power." His fingers worked the conditioner into my hair, and I couldn't fight the breathy moan as he massaged my scalp. My knees wobbled, and I needed to brace my hands against the wall to keep from collapsing into a puddle and disappearing down the drain.

He tugged me back into the shower spray and ran his fingers through my hair until it was all rinsed out, then claimed my lips in a heated kiss that left my whole body quivering with need.

"Did you come here to shower or to fuck?" I taunted him when his lips left mine for a moment, and he let out a dark chuckle.

He smacked another quick kiss against my lips, then released me to reach for my shampoo. "Both," he replied with a cocky grin. "Can't I fuck you *while* I shower?"

I grinned, hoping he'd think the evil edge to my smile was all sexual. He held my gaze as he lathered up his hair, and I bit my lip. "I guess we'll soon find out." As soon as his hair was thick with suds, I reached for him.

"Fuck, MK," he hissed crowding me back against the wall and skimming his soapy hands over my body. "I think Steele was on to something when he used your shower. There must be something

172

in your water…" He trailed off with a groan as my hand pumped his hard shaft, working him over and grinning like a maniac.

"Shit," he cursed on an exhale, snatching my hands away and pinning my wrists to the shower wall above my head. "You're fucking trouble, babe."

I craned my neck up, rising on my toes so I could kiss him without needing my wrists freed. There was something disturbingly sexy about being at his mercy, so I wasn't demanding my freedom anytime soon. Instead, I just pulled him into a searing, soul-deep kiss. I arched my back, pushing my chest out so that my nipples grazed his skin, and he snapped.

A bare split second later, his hands were under my thighs. He hoisted me up against the shower wall, and his cock found my core with scary precision. I let out a gasp of surprise, but instead of stopping him, I grabbed his face between my palms and kissed him hard as he sunk into me.

I groaned into his mouth as his full length rested inside me, but he tensed and broke his lips from mine.

"Baby girl, I can't believe I'm even saying this, but…" His words trailed off as I nipped his earlobe between my teeth and ground my hips against him, silently pleading for him to move. To *fuck* me.

"Shit, MK," Kody exclaimed on a heavy exhale. "The condoms in the kitchen were a lucky fluke. I don't suppose you have any hiding behind the soap?"

I froze. Crap.

But then… "I've got an IUD," I told him, panting lightly and trying really, really hard not to squirm. But what's a girl to do when she's pinned to her shower wall with a gloriously large dick inside of her?

Kody's eyes flashed with excitement, and I narrowed my own at him.

"If you've given me a disease, though, there's going to be hell

173

to pay." I dug my nails into his neck a little, just to drive my point home, and he smirked.

He took his time kissing me, torturing me by not moving his dick, even when I whimpered a protest and bucked my hips in desperation.

"I promise, I'm totally clean," he murmured when he eventually released my lips, "and you have no fucking idea how good you feel right now." He sucked in a long breath through his teeth, his gaze dropping between us as he shifted his stance. Benefits to fucking such buff dudes? He held me there against the wall with seemingly little effort at all.

I licked my lips, my hands clinging onto his strong neck as he pressed me harder against the wall and withdrew from my cunt slightly. "Kody," I breathed, my voice dripping with desperation, "either make me come or get the fuck out. The water will run cold soon."

He huffed a laugh, then bit the bend of my neck with enough teeth to make it a threat but light enough not to break skin. Just. "I love when you get all sappy romantic like that, MK," he teased me. "It's easily one of my favorite things about you."

I growled low in my throat, pulling him tighter to me. "Kody…" It was a groan of pure frustration, and he snickered.

"Calm down, baby girl," he murmured. "I've got you."

He really fucking did.

When he quit with the teasing bullshit and actually went to town on me, I almost regretted taunting him. Almost. Mostly I was giving myself mental high fives for not icing him out just because I was pissed off. A little anger just flavored the sex to something crazy delicious.

At some stage—I'd lost all concept of time—Kody shifted his grip, holding me up with just one arm. His free hand snaked between us, finding my clit and tweaking it with utter perfection as he fucked me into the shower tiles.

When I came, it was the blissful, explosive sort of climax where my vision went spotty and my hearing dipped out for a second. I clawed at Kody's back as I rode out the aftershocks on his cock, grinding my pussy against him and urging him to come with me.

He grunted, bucking his hips hard enough to bruise, and came in three deep thrusts punctuated with whispered curses and kisses.

Points in Kody's favor: he didn't immediately drop me, despite the way his arm trembled where he held me. Instead he stayed like that for a minute or two, his forehead against the wall and his lips pressed to my neck like he was soaking in every inch of my skin or my scent.

"You okay, babe?" he asked in a rough, husky whisper when he gently set me back on my feet and pressed a tender kiss to my mouth.

I nodded, still dazed. "Yup," I replied, pressing my hands to my hot cheeks. "Just need a quick cleanup."

Kody's eyes immediately shot down, and he caught his lower lip between his teeth with a groan. "Fuck, that's hot," he muttered, looking pained. "I've never fucked without a condom before. That was...and this is..." He trailed off, talking to himself more than me.

I rolled my eyes and stepped under the somewhat cooler shower spray, washing away the object of his attention with a squirt of body wash. "You're kinda cute, Kody."

He scowled. "Shut up; I am not." He edged me out of the water but wrapped his arms around me in a tight embrace, like we were a couple who showered together all the time.

I laughed anyway, refusing to overthink my own actions. Kody was hot, I was insanely attracted to him, and the sentiment seemed to be mutual. And if I was being honest, ninety-nine percent of the time, I enjoyed being around him. So regardless of his bad decisions, why *shouldn't* I enjoy what he did to my body? Steele didn't seem to have any issues with it.

I didn't think.

Maybe that needed to be a conversation.

"I'm getting dressed before you get hard again, and then we'll never get out of this shower," I told him with a teasing smile. "If I really did get a bonus day on my exam, I need to use it for studying."

Kody pouted but released me in order to rinse the shampoo out of his hair. I bit back my grin and handed him the bottle of conditioner.

"Don't forget to condition, babe," I told him sweetly. "Stops your hair from drying out."

Before he could see the mischief all over my face, I got out and closed the glass door behind me. I dried off quickly, then wandered back into my bedroom to find some clothes while Kody finished his shower. I needed to check on Steele and find out how the hell he'd gotten so hurt.

The shower shut off and I heard Kody step out, so I moved back over to the bathroom and leaned on the doorframe with a broad grin on my face.

Except...this was Kody. Kodiak unflappable Jones. Damn him straight to hell. He just stared at his newly pink hair in the mirror with a considering look, then shrugged and grinned at me.

"Cute prank, babe, but now we just match. Like a *real* couple." His whole face lit up with mischief. "Aw, we're the cutest boyfriend and girlfriend ever. Wanna bet Archer gags on his coffee when he sees us all loved up and matching?"

I glowered. "We're not a fucking couple, Kody," I growled, folding my arms in a sulk. "And you're only making me want to hit you harder with this nonchalance."

He smirked, tucking my towel low around his waist and prowling toward me. I backed up, but he caught me around the waist and hauled me against him as he dropped his lips to my ear.

"Bring it on, babe. Your pranks turn me on." He pressed himself harder against me, showing me exactly what he was talking about and making my mouth water with desire. "And you can call

176

us whatever the fuck you want, so long as I get to make you scream like that again. Hottest fucking sound I've ever heard, MK."

I melted. I was a melted puddle of goo.

Kody grabbed my earlobe between his teeth and sucked it briefly before releasing me and sauntering his fine ass toward my door. "Quit stressing about Steele. He's fine."

I rolled my eyes and scowled after him. "Quit reading my mind, asshole!"

He threw a quick grin over his shoulder as he held my bedroom door open. "Quit being such an open book then, babe."

Lucky for him, he disappeared before I could find anything to throw. Smug fuck.

But still, he was right that I was worrying about Steele. Not just about his injuries, which I thoroughly needed to get more information about, but also about how he would react to me fucking around with Kody. It wasn't like we were dating, any of us. But they were closer than brothers, and I couldn't see things ending well if we ever went past what it currently was—mind-blowing casual sex with a side of animosity.

Sighing and mentally berating my own stupidity, I found my hairbrush and went to work on my tangles. I'd dry my hair, and then, hopefully, Steele might be awake.

Anything had to be better than facing Archer this morning, anyway.

CHAPTER 21

To my surprise, Steele wasn't in his room. His bedding was rumpled and thrown back like he'd just gotten up not long ago, though, so I went looking.

The kitchen was empty, except for Karen—our weekday chef who was in the middle of preparing our meals for the day. She tended to pre-prepare everything first thing in the morning and leave it all clearly labeled in the fridge, allowing us to just finish it all off whenever we wanted to eat. It was a good system, and I wasn't looking forward to my father returning and changing it all up.

"Good morning, Miss Danvers," Karen greeted me in a hushed voice. "Can I get you something to eat?"

She looked like she was halfway through making a lasagna for our dinner, so I shook my head. "No, thanks. I was just looking for Steele. Have you seen him?"

She smiled. "Yes, he came through here about half an hour ago. He should be in the workshop."

"Thanks," I replied. I continued through the house to the garage, then past all the expensive cars to the far side where Steele's workshop was set up. I found him standing beside Archer's Raptor with a deep scowl on his face and his black hoodie pulled up to cover his head. He looked all kinds of dark and dangerous and... *delicious.*

"What are you doing down here?" I asked him, coming around the truck to where he stood. Then I saw what he was frowning at and gasped. "Uh...wow."

Steele sighed and nodded. "Yep."

I took a step closer to the truck and reached out to touch one of the *many* bullet holes riddling the body of the vehicle. It looked like a giant cheese grater and totally unfixable.

"I hate writing off cars," Steele told me, his whole demeanor annoyed and disappointed. "But this would cost more to fix than to buy a new one."

"Wait." I frowned. "I thought Archer had bulletproof cars. Wasn't that his whole thing about why his cars were safer?"

Steele arched his pierced brow at me, his lips curving in a half smile. "Bulletproof *glass,* Hellcat." He untucked a hand from the pocket of his jeans and knocked on one of the perfectly intact windows. "Dumbass didn't consider bulletproof bodywork too— something we will rectify on the next one."

He winced as he moved his arm, and I frowned at him in concern. I couldn't see any bandages, but he was fully covered up in a hoodie. They were probably still there. "Steele, why are you down here and not resting?" I moved closer to him, tugging the zipper of his hoodie down and confirming my suspicions. Thick, white bandages covered his left shoulder and upper chest, and I scowled at him in reprimand.

He gently removed my hand and tugged the zipper back up again. "It's not as bad as it looks, gorgeous. Just a few scrapes, thanks to Archer's shitty driving while I was hanging out the door to shoot at your attacker." I gave him a small frown of confusion, and his smile grew wider, self-deprecating. "Arch turned sharply to avoid hitting something, and I sort of, uh, tumbled out of the car. At high speed. On gravel."

I winced just imagining that, and he laughed.

"Seriously, it's far from the worst I've ever suffered. The bandages are way overkill. But Arch got all fucking alpha about it, so I'm humoring him." He slipped a hand around my waist and tugged me closer to him, peering down at me from the shadows of his hood. "And as for why I'm down here and not still in my room? Because if I had to listen to Kody making you come one more time, I was going to break down the damn door and either punch him or demand to join in. Neither of which I'm in any state to do right now."

I wrinkled my nose but couldn't fight the grin on my face. "Can I be honest with you, Max Steele?"

He let out a small groan. "I swear, you're the only person who can ever make my full name sound sexy. Go on, then."

I stepped in closer, tentatively looping my arms around his neck and hoping I wasn't hurting him. He didn't flinch, though, so I relaxed a little. "Honestly? I'm not totally sure which of those options turns me on more."

Steele's grin was pure smug satisfaction, and his gray eyes flashed with desire. "I knew fighting got you hot, Hellcat, but I had no idea you were down for a three-way."

I snorted and rolled my eyes. "Yes, you did, you liar. You've seen my vibrator collection, *and* you deliberately dropped that into casual conversation specifically to see what my reaction would be."

His grin just spread wider, but he didn't deny it.

"Where is Kody, anyway? When I realized it was a snow day, I didn't think he'd let you out of his bed for *hours* yet." Steele's brow creased with a small frown. "Lucky prick."

I shook my head in a small amount of disbelief, biting the edge of my lip. "I think he knew I wanted to check on you," I admitted, "and...you know...talk about recent developments."

Steele made a noise in his throat but brushed the damp hair back from my face with his fingertips. "You mean the fact that

Kody *finally* talked his way into your pants? You know that has to be the longest any girl has made him work for it?"

I blushed. "There wasn't a huge amount of talking involved," I mumbled, remembering the angry way we'd hate fucked on the kitchen counter while Archer watched. Ugh. That was *another* complication that needed dealing with soon. "But yeah, that's what I meant."

Steele leaned down and kissed me softly, all lips and lingering touches, then sighed. "It's hardly a new development, gorgeous. Kody's had a hard-on for you since Riot Night. But I guess you're asking if I'm cut up about the fact that you guys fucked?"

I arched a brow and gave a small nod. Steele took me by the hand and started leading me back through the garage toward the house. I thought he was going to keep talking while we walked, but after a few moments it became clear he wasn't.

"Uh, are you going to answer that question?" I prompted him as we passed back through the foyer and started up the stairs. Not that I had any objection to following him back up to his room. Despite what he'd said, I had no doubt he was *supposed* to be resting.

He glanced at me over his shoulder, a small smile playing over his lips. "I am," he replied as he opened his bedroom door and stood aside for me to enter.

"And…we needed to relocate to your bedroom for that?" I raised my brows at him but sat down on his bed anyway while he closed the door and shrugged his hoodie off. Underneath he was shirtless, covered only in bandages and ink, and my breath caught.

He gave me a sly smile as he crossed the carpet and stopped directly in front of me. It put his chiseled abs directly in line with my face, and it took all kinds of willpower not to strip his jeans off and take him in my mouth.

"We relocated to my bedroom because I was cold as shit in the workshop, and I didn't want Archer crashing in on our conversation and killing the mood." He ran his fingers through my hair, then cupped my face to tilt it up. His gaze met mine, and my hands went to his waist on reflex.

"He does have a bad habit of doing that," I muttered in agreement. I licked my lips, wetting them and trying really hard to be less of the open book Kody accused me of being.

Apparently, I failed. Steele's gaze intensified, and he caught my chin in his fingers as he leaned down to me. "Stop looking at me like that, Hellcat. You're making me want to do things I shouldn't be doing right now."

I couldn't help myself. "Like what?"

His response was a frustrated growl and a hard kiss, claiming my mouth in a harsh and demanding way that promised far more than his injuries were likely to sustain. Damn. Then again, if he just lay back and let me do all the work…

Rein it in, MK. You're not a fucking succubus.

Clearing my throat, I shifted back on the bed to create a little physical space between us. Steele seemed to follow my train of thought and stretched out on the mattress with his head on the pillows. Now that he was lying down and shirtless, I could recognize the stiff way he was holding his left arm and the hard lines of pain in his tense neck.

"Okay, so I'm gathering you don't necessarily have a problem with me and Kody?" I shifted around until I was lying beside him, my head on his pillow despite the multiple other options. He was like a magnet, and I was made of metal. I just couldn't stay away, no matter how sensible the distance might be.

Steele released a long breath, his hooded eyes glued to me. "That's not a straightforward answer, Hellcat. Do I wish Kody had totally fucked things up with you and I had you all to myself? Absolutely. I'd love nothing more than to claim full ownership of your time…and your body…twenty-four-seven. But I'm not afraid of a little competition. So long as Kody doesn't break your heart…"

He gave a slight shrug, then winced. "I just hope you know what you're getting yourself into."

My eyes widened. "Uh, what does that mean?"

Steele's smile turned pure evil. "Let's just say it's a good thing we've got winter break coming up. Kody and I don't share our toys well…unless, of course, we're *sharing*."

Heat flooded through my body, and I clenched my thighs together at the mental images he'd conjured. There was no mistaking what he meant by that, and I was *all* for it.

But still…I held up my finger in a warning gesture. "For one thing, Max Steele," I chastised him, "I'm not your toy; you're mine."

His grin flashed wider, and he inclined his head. "Fair correction. And the other thing?"

I raised a second finger. "How long are these grazing wounds going to take to heal? Because I'm *very* interested in seeing how well you and Kody can share."

Steele's eyes lit up, but he rolled his eyes to the ceiling like he was praying for patience.

"As badly as I want to tell you a day," he groaned, "it's probably more like a week. At least."

I pouted a bit. In a perfect world I would have had a sassy, flirtatious comeback, but pouting was what I was feeling, so it's what I did.

"Well, then I need to get the fuck out of your bed before I'm tempted to test that timeline," I muttered, mostly to myself, but Steele laughed anyway. When I tried to get off the bed, he grabbed my hand and hauled me back to lie beside him.

"Just because my range of motion is limited," he told me in a conspiratorial whisper, "doesn't mean I'm totally broken." He demonstrated that point by grinding his erection into my thigh and catching my mouth in a determined, possessive kiss. His tongue stud teased me, and I groaned into his kiss like a horny teenager.

Goddamn. My hormones were all over the fucking place around these boys.

"Mmm, nope." I wrenched myself away with way more willpower that I even knew I possessed. "Nope, it's my fault you're even hurt in the first place. I'm not risking you ending up in more pain thanks to my impulsiveness. We can revisit this in a week."

The whimper of protest that left Steele as I pulled away and climbed out of his bed was adorable, and I bit back a laugh at his expense.

"Hellcat, you're killing me," he complained. "You have *no* idea how wound up I've been all morning after hearing you with Kody. Please don't make me wait a whole week." His puppy dog eyes were really playing dirty, and I groaned.

He had a point, though; that was a bit unfair. "Fine, he can wait too. That's fair, right?"

Crap, wait. This was a terrible idea; I was punishing myself.

Steele gave me a shrewd look. "One day. I heal amazingly fast."

I rolled my eyes at his bargaining. "Five days, and only if you really are healing up."

He stared back at me, but I just folded my arms and hardened my eyes. It was for his own damn good, something they pulled on me all the freaking time.

"Fine," he eventually agreed with a heavy sigh. "But if Kody convinces you otherwise, deal's off."

I shook my head with a smile. Fucking hell, here I was trying to save him further injuries, and he was acting like I'd just made him agree to run naked through the snow. "Fine. But he's not going to convince me. I don't want to be the reason you need a skin graft or something."

Steele tried to reply, but his words cut off with a heavy yawn.

"Just chill," I told him in my best stern voice. "Seriously. It's a snow day, so exams are all canceled. We don't need to go anywhere or do anything. Just sleep. I promise I won't wake you up with a screaming orgasm again."

Steele gave me a flirtatious grin, even as his lips drooped so heavily his eyes were almost closed. "Unless I'm the one giving it to you, right, Hellcat?"

I rolled my eyes. Of fucking course I'd gotten myself involved with two of the biggest Lotharios I'd ever met. "Go to sleep, Steele," I ordered him.

His flirty smile slipped, and he raised one eyelid enough to meet my gaze. "You're not leaving, though, right?"

Warmth flooded through me at the edge of vulnerability in his voice. It spoke to that damaged corner of my own dark soul, the part that gave me violent nightmares but calmed when I had company.

"Nope, I'm just going to hang out over here," I told him, sinking down into his desk chair, which was set up in front of his keyboard again.

He gave me a tired smile. "You don't trust me, Hellcat?"

I scoffed. "I don't trust *me*, Max Steele." I absentmindedly ran my fingers over the keys of his keyboard, not depressing any but just feeling them out.

He was silent for so long I thought he'd fallen asleep, but then he spoke again.

"Can you play?"

I looked back over to him and found him lying on his side with his drowsy eyes fixated on me. His voice was so thick with sleep I doubted it'd take long before he was asleep for real.

"I'm no concert pianist, that's for sure," I teased. "But my mom taught me to play when I was little. I don't totally suck."

Steele murmured a sound, his lids drooping shut. "Play me something," he mumbled.

My brows shot up, but his eyes were already closed. It'd been years since I'd played the piano, so I was bound to be rusty. I'd heard Steele play; he was like a fucking piano prodigy. How embarrassing to muddle my way through "Ode to Joy" while he was listening and cringing every time I hit the wrong key. I couldn't...

"Please, Hellcat?" he added in a sleepy whisper, and my heart melted. I couldn't fucking deny him. Taking a deep breath, I searched my brain for something to play. Of course, now that I needed to think of the notes, they were all gone from my brain. So I glanced at the handwritten sheets scattered on Steele's desk, and slowly, quietly, I started playing from that.

Soon I was able to shake off my awkwardness and lose myself in the melody that he'd written, appreciating the beauty of it even as my fingers created the sound. The steady rhythm of Steele's breathing acted as my metronome, and I kept playing long after he'd fallen asleep.

When I stopped, something had shifted inside me. Somehow, without even being awake, Steele had helped me find a small measure of closure with my deceased mother. Somehow, the dark streak across my soul had lightened a fraction, and my mind felt at ease for it.

CHAPTER 22

After I was certain Steele was fully asleep, I tiptoed out of his room and went in search of food. My stomach was grumbling with embarrassing volume, and my blood was screaming for coffee.

I passed Karen on her way out of the kitchen, and she gave me a kind smile.

"I left you some breakfast, just in case," she told me, placing a hand on my arm, "and James brought a package in for you. I left it on the counter."

I thanked her and wished her a good day, vaguely recalling James was the name of the new groundskeeper my father had hired while I was in Cambodia. I still hadn't met him personally, but given the immaculate condition of the grounds—when they weren't blanketed in snow—he must be hardworking. All the staff lived off-site, with the exception of Steinwick and Karen, who each had a room in the cottage at the back of the property.

To my disappointment, the kitchen wasn't unoccupied.

A surly, brooding bad boy covered in ink and sweat was draped all over one of the barstools, and I heaved a sigh. Briefly, I considered turning around and walking out again, but he'd seen me and I refused to back down to his superiority complex.

"Nice shiner," I sneered when his eyes met mine across the kitchen, one of which was surrounded by some heavy purple and blue bruising. Kody hadn't held back, that was for sure.

"Nice tits," he replied, his cold smile elaborating on that for me. He wasn't talking about right now, drowned in Steele's hoodie that I'd commandeered. He was referring to when I'd been spread out naked on the kitchen island with Kody's dick deep inside me.

I hadn't flinched away from his gaze then, and I didn't flinch now. Instead, I just leaned across the island, propped my face up on my hands, and batted my lashes at him.

"You know, you're really starting to reek of desperation and jealousy, Archer. If you want me so badly, maybe try a personality adjustment? Then maybe you'd stand a chance of getting what Kody got *all* morning…then again in the shower." I dragged my teeth over my lower lip, letting the pure lust of those memories show on my face. Archer—for all his stoic resolve to remain unaffected—couldn't stop the flash of desire from crossing his face. He wanted me, he just didn't want to want me, and *that* was what had me morbidly curious. "Then again, maybe not. Not all sins of the past can be forgiven with repentance."

Archer's glare flattened to something cold and dangerous. "You certainly seemed to *forgive* Kody easily this morning. Or were you just that eager for dick that you didn't care where it came from?"

I gave a cold laugh, moving around the island as I made my way over to the coffee machine.

"Don't be silly, Archer. Right now, I wouldn't touch your dick with someone *else's* pussy, let alone my own." I flipped the espresso machine on, letting it warm up as I drummed my fingertips on the counter. I didn't bother turning around to throw my insults at Archer because why the fuck should I waste the energy? But also, if I were to say that to his face, he'd likely see the lie written all over me.

A scraping of chair legs against tiles was the only warning I got before his huge frame bracketed me, his hands braced on the counter on either side of me and his hot breath on my neck. Suddenly I was cursing my decision to put my hair in a ponytail before coming downstairs. He wasn't touching me, not even a finger, but I could feel him over every fucking inch of me.

"Oh yeah?" he challenged me. "Do you make a habit of lying to yourself, Princess Danvers? Or is it just me that you lie to? Because we both know you were more than happy to touch my dick *all over* at Bree's party. And don't get me started on the way you threw yourself at me in the weapons room of Phillip's office."

"Excuse me?" I whirled around to face him in outrage, then immediately regretted that choice. He was bending down slightly, and suddenly I found my neck craning so that our eyes met—a foolish move on my part. "You fucking started that. Both times. And you also blew me off both times, so clearly you're either suffering some kind of split personality malfunction, or you choked under pressure. Either way, big man, you lost your chance. As someone told me recently, I don't fuck desperate."

His lips curved in a vicious smile and his ice-blue eyes flared with victory. "Liar," he breathed, then kissed me.

For a moment—okay, a few moments—my brain shut down, and I kissed him back. When his hands shifted from the countertop to my waist, I didn't push him away, I just pressed my body into his, shuddering at the hard planes of his muscles and the barely concealed danger lurking within him.

Then I snapped the fuck out of it and shoved him away from me.

The two of us just stood there a moment, staring at each other with hungry eyes, our chests heaving and our lips wet. It was scary how badly our bodies wanted one another while we also wanted to kill each other.

"How's that denial going for you, Princess?" Archer taunted me with an arrogant smirk.

I sneered back at him. "Pot calling the kettle black, dickhead. Or maybe all those steroids are making you delusional."

His pale blue eyes narrowed, but the tilt to his lips was still pure sex. "Madison Kate, it's adorable how you're pretending you're *not* currently ruining your panties just thinking about what I could do to you right here on the counter." He leaned back against the island, but his eyes didn't leave me for even a second. It was a deliberate move, reminding me of the fact that I'd fucked Kody right where he stood, and damn, it was working.

Someone cleared their throat in a pointed way, and I wrenched my eyes away from Archer's and over to Kody, who stood in the doorway looking both amused and annoyed all at the same time.

"What's going on in here?" he asked with an edge of suspicion. "I hope you found your manners this morning, Arch?"

The surly guy just glared at his friend—he made no reaction to Kody's pink hair, much to my disappointment—then shot me a warning look. The message was crystal clear: *This isn't over, Princess Danvers.*

"He's still hunting for them," I replied to Kody in a cool tone while sending a silent message back to Archer. *Bite me.*

"Shocking," Kody muttered with dripping sarcasm. "What's in the box?" He pointed to a package on the counter, which I'd totally overlooked thanks to Archer's oozing sexual frustration.

I shrugged and moved closer to it. "No idea. Karen said the groundskeeper brought it in this morning sometime."

The package was fairly nondescript, just a plain brown box with a printed label on it displaying my name and address. Except...

"Guys, there're no postage marks on this," I pointed out while a chill ran down my spine. The package was totally devoid of any postal stamps or barcodes. Like it'd been hand-delivered.

Kody swiped the package out of my hands without a word, then grabbed a knife from the cutlery drawer and sliced the packing tape open. He flipped the flaps open as Archer swooped in between us, blocking the contents from my view.

"Hey, what the—fucking move, ass pig!" I jabbed Archer in the ribs, but the glare he shot me froze any further protests from me. Whatever was in that box…it wasn't books from Amazon. Not with that reaction.

"Show me," I demanded.

Archer shook his head at the same time that Kody made a sound of disagreement.

"Show me!" I snapped, meeting Archer's glare head-on with one of my own. "It's addressed to me, so fucking show me what's in the box, you overbearing ape."

Archer's brow cocked, and he gave me one of those looks that suggested I was being an idiot but he wasn't going to stop me. Prick.

"Uh, I don't think—" Kody started to say, but Archer had already moved out of the way and I could see into the box in Kody's hands.

I sucked in a gasp, pressing my hands to my mouth as bile rose in my throat. Inside the nondescript box was another clear threat. This time it was against Kody; there was no doubt about that. The dead bird held the distinctive forked tail of a swallow, and the white rose was smeared in the bird's blood. Swallows and roses. Just like Kody's chest tattoos.

"Give it to me," I whispered, not trusting my full voice for fear of throwing up. Still, I was slowly becoming desensitized to these things, blood and threats. I wasn't sure if that was a good thing or not, but it was helping me keep my shit together on a daily basis.

Kody wanted to refuse, I could tell, but I snatched the box from him before he could do anything dumb. Like give it to Archer.

Holding my breath and praying for strength in my stomach, I reached in and carefully moved the bird aside so I could grab the blown-up photograph underneath it. The image was coated in blood and grainy like it'd been taken from a surveillance video, but it only took me a second to recognize the image.

Then I gagged for real. I flipped it over, and sure enough, there was my stalker's distinctive handwriting. LIAR, LIAR, PANTS ON FIRE.

My gaze shot up to Kody's, and he shook his head slowly. "I didn't know," he told me, his voice edging on panic. Except his fear didn't have anything to do with my stalker somehow catching us fucking on the kitchen island. No, his clear green eyes were locked on mine, pleading with me to believe him. He was worried that I would shut him out over this. That I might think he'd set me up somehow.

"Of course you fucking didn't," Archer growled, snatching the picture from my hand and scowling down at it. I didn't try to hide it because it wasn't anything he hadn't seen firsthand. Still, this was the second time my stalker had documented me having sex, and I was starting to feel decidedly paranoid.

Archer looked up from the picture and scanned the kitchen until he spotted what he was looking for. "Mother*fucker*," he spat, slapping the photo down on the counter and striding across the kitchen to the perimeter-alarm sensor. In a smooth motion he boosted himself up onto the counter, then ripped the sensor clean out of the wall—totally oblivious or uncaring of the electrical sparks that flew—then hurled it at the floor. Jumping back off the counter, he landed one sneaker clean on top of the sensor, crushing it into a useless pile of broken plastic, metal, and electrical wiring.

My jaw had fallen open in shock. "How...?"

Archer wasn't paying attention to me, though. His phone was already out in his hand, and he was searching for something. "I'm getting a security overhaul," he announced. "Go and get Steele, fill him in. We need to sweep the entire place for more cameras."

"Got it," Kody replied, starting to leave the kitchen.

"Wait!" I shouted, pausing Kody halfway to the door. "Stop. Steele needs to sleep; just leave him. This is nothing new. Let's just...handle it calmly, okay?" I shared my stern glare between the two of them, and they both frowned back at me, Kody with concern and Archer with confusion.

Keeping my breathing as calm and even as I could manage, I shoved my fear and anxiety aside in favor of a clear head.

"Archer, call your security people and get to the bottom of this. Kody..." I glanced down at the dead bird and grimaced. "Call the cops. We need to report this."

"Madison Kate—" Archer started to argue, but I cut him off with a sharp look.

"Do what I fucking tell you, D'Ath. I want to see those other deliveries too," I announced. "Kody said you'd received more mail that no one felt the need to share with me."

Archer shot a death glare at his friend, but Kody just met his stare and shrugged. "She should have known," Kody told him. "Keeping secrets is only going to bite us *all* in the ass later. Clearly, someone else agrees." He indicated to the bloody photograph, accusing him—or me—of being a liar.

I bit the inside of my cheek to keep from jumping all over them about what *other* secrets they were keeping from me. But it would get me exactly nowhere, especially given the way Archer's jaw clenched so hard he looked like he might crack a tooth. Better to keep the focus on task.

"Go," I snapped at the big guy. "You know what you need to do." Then I turned my attention back to Kody. "You too."

He frowned back at me, all concern. "What about you, MK?"

I sucked in a deep breath, then gagged slightly when the faint tang of dead animal touched my nostrils. "I'm going to wash my hands," I told him with a tight smile. "Then I'll meet you in my father's office. I need to catch up on all the other letters before the police get here."

Kody reached out for me, but I dodged out of his reach and hurried out of the kitchen. I needed to wash my hands more than I needed to breathe, and I couldn't stand the thought of him

193

touching me until that was done. I'd only touched the bird and the photo briefly, but it was like my stalker's taint was creeping over my skin. I needed it gone.

Sadly, though, no amount of soap and scrubbing could remove the marks left on my mind.

My stalker was escalating, and that fear, that constant feeling of eyes on me, was going to take something a whole lot stronger than soap to be washed clean.

CHAPTER 23

It was well into the evening when the cops and security company left the house, by which time I'd pretty much given up on any last-minute studying for my exams. How the fuck could I concentrate on my university work when I had a stalker delivering dead animals in boxes and taking pictures of me having sex inside my *private* residence?

As if that weren't bad enough, I'd had to deal with prudish, judgmental bullshit from the cop who interviewed me, like he was totally disgusted that I'd been fucking Kody in the kitchen. Because I totally asked for my stalker to take pictures? Asshole.

All the photographs the boys had hidden from me were nothing in comparison to the dead bird package. Just images of me coming and going from school with each of the guys, but every one of them had LIAR scrawled over the back of them. So either my stalker was accusing me of being a liar or saying all three of them were. I'd bet my entire trust fund on the latter.

I'd had a small spark of hope early on when someone had mentioned checking security feeds for whoever had delivered the packages—because of course there were cameras over the entrance gates. But it had been quickly squashed. My stalker was somehow smart enough to have ensured the camera angles had all been changed or the feeds wiped blank *exactly* at the right times to cover his gruesome delivery.

"You guys want pizzas or something?" Kody asked as the last cop car cruised out of our driveway and I collapsed onto the couch. I was a ball of anxiety and depression, a sick feeling curling in my stomach thanks to the cops' pointed questions and the way they'd implied it was my own fault I had a violent, sexual stalker. Because why? I had a vagina and didn't intend to let it grow cobwebs?

Sexist fucks.

"I want to just go to sleep and not wake up until this is all over," I muttered sullenly, hugging a pillow to my chest. "And I definitely don't want delivery dudes coming to the house right now."

Kody winced. "Yeah, fair point. I'll go and pick up, if you want."

I gave him a vague nod, and he disappeared out of the room. Steele had woken from his nap about an hour ago and was slouched in the recliner chair with a hoodie covering his bandages and his arm held cautiously across his middle to prevent anything touching it. My heart hurt to see him in pain, but he'd firmly shut me down when I tried to send him back to bed.

Archer came back into the room, having just finished learning everything there was to know about the *new* security system, and flopped down on the couch beside me. Closer than I would have expected, but I also wasn't moving away in a hurry. Goddamn magnetic attraction.

"You guys wanna play video games?" Steele suggested, and Archer shot him a dark look. Steele just glared back, though. "Seriously, bro? You gonna pull that shit right now?"

Archer just sighed and got up, grabbing the controllers from the entertainment unit and handing one to each of us—to my surprise.

"Jase is coming by the house tomorrow morning," he told Steele in a neutral voice. "He wants to chat about a fight offer that got submitted over the weekend."

Steele groaned, shifting in his chair. "I can't deal with his guilt trips about my music, dude. You're gonna have to run interference for me."

Archer just nodded, his eyes on the screen as he navigated through the start-up menus to select a game, then set all the parameters. I noticed he selected difficulty level Beginner. I didn't comment. They were far from beginners, but I appreciated the gesture.

"I've got it," he replied after a moment. "Just a heads-up to stay out of sight. I don't need him bitching me out for getting you hurt."

Steele nodded with a grunt. I watched their interaction with fascination. There was so much to them that I didn't know, like how the three of them had ended up with the same agent-slash-manager or how they all had even met in the first place. Questions burned on my tongue, but I didn't voice them.

My stalker was trying to tell me they were lying to me, and I doubted it was over where they'd grown up or what their first dog's name was. It had to be something big...something life-changing. Something they would rather risk me hating them over than just fessing up to, which led me to think it directly concerned me. But how? Was there something there surrounding my mom and Archer's brother? That seemed to be my only connection to the guys. Other than Cherry.

"You're awfully quiet, Princess," Archer commented in a low voice as we all selected our race cars on the screen. "Stalker got your tongue?"

I scowled. "You're a fucking prick, D'Ath."

An amused grin curled his lips as he slouched lower on the couch. The movement brought his shoulder closer to mine, but still, I didn't move away. Call me a masochist, I guess.

"Come on, Madison Kate, you know I'm just teasing," he replied, his voice a low purr and his eyes glued to the screen. He spoke quietly, making it clear he was speaking *only* to me. It was kinda sexy, if I were inclined to admit that kind of thing where Archer was concerned.

"Whatever," I muttered back, tearing my eyes away from his grin and back to the plasma. "I was just thinking about who might be behind all of this. Whoever it is, they're escalating, and that makes me somewhat concerned for my own safety. I don't want to end up like my mom."

Archer stiffened with tension. "That won't happen." His voice was hard and unwavering.

"Agreed," Steele added. He'd pulled his hood up again, and it was a ridiculously hot look on him as his gray eyes flashed in the low light of the room. The sun had gone down, and none of us had bothered turning lights on. It was just the blue glow of the TV lighting up the den, but that suited me just fine. It felt safer. Less exposed. Easier to hide...from everything.

I wanted to believe them *so* badly. I wanted to have that blind faith that they'd protect me and find this stalker before I turned into a skin suit hanging in someone's creepy skin closet. But the still-tender scar on my stomach suggested no one was infallible and no one was untouchable.

"Zane thinks whoever tried to kill me on Halloween is different from my stalker," I commented, curious to see what both Steele and Archer thought. "He thinks—"

"Zane doesn't know shit," Archer growled. "He made vague promises about helping you out, but I guarantee he is just buying time to work out how he can monetize your situation. Trust me, Princess, if he thought your stalker would pay good money to have you hand-delivered in a body bag, he'd have done it. Or tried to, at least. He wouldn't get far with us around."

My heart sank. Some small part of me—since believing Zane *hadn't* killed my mom—had started thinking he wasn't as bad as he'd been painted. If he'd loved my mom, then he couldn't be. Right?

Steele made a sound that caught Archer's attention. The big guy sighed and swung his gaze away from the TV to look at me with an edge of apology in his eyes. "I know you think he has some redeeming features that your mom fell for, but…he just doesn't. He was a piece of shit even while he was with Deb, and he's a hundred times worse now. You've probably blocked the memories out, but he was quickly dragging your mom down a dark and dangerous path. There's *no* silver lining to Zane D'Ath."

Disappointment burned through my veins like acid, and I bit my cheek to keep it from playing out across my face. Archer seemed sincere, for once, and I couldn't think of a reason for him to lie about that.

But where did that leave me?

"So you think it was my stalker at The Clown on Halloween?" I asked him with an arched brow. The TV screen showed our race cars all lined up at the start line, but Archer hadn't hit the button to start the game yet.

He looked back at me with one of those intense, guarded stares—the sort of stare that stripped me bare and made me shiver. "No, I think Zane's right on that. Your stalker, like Deb's stalker, is obsessed in a sexual way. He wouldn't kill you before…" He trailed off with a small cringe, and I could guess the rest.

Before he got a chance to play out all his twisted fantasies. It was probably why he'd shifted his fixation from my mom to me after she'd died. Unfulfilled desires and all that. It was sick, no doubt, but it definitely gave weight to the theory that it'd been someone else trying to kill me that night.

"Also, you said it was more than one person that night, didn't you?" Steele asked, thoughtfully tapping his controller against the arm of his chair. "I think they were after you for something else. The girl that died on Riot Night was an attack on you too. So this has been going on for a while."

I had nothing to say to that. He was right, of course. I'd convinced myself that the girl killed on Riot Night had just been a coincidence. An accident or something. But the second attempt to murder me suggested it'd been, in fact, a deliberate attempt on my life.

"But *why*?" I lamented aloud. "I don't get it. Why would anyone want to kill me?"

"That's what we want to work out," Archer murmured. He rubbed his thumb over his lower lip, lost in thought. "Does *anyone* spring to mind who might want to kill you? Or who might benefit from your death?"

I shook my head, chewing at the corner of my lip. "I've legitimately gone over this in my brain a thousand times, and I can't think of anything. My trust fund, maybe? But it's not even a million dollars. Hardly worth hiring someone to kill me for, considering how much paid killers probably get."

Steele shifted in his seat, and I looked over at him, worried he was uncomfortable or in pain. His eyes were locked on Archer, though, and his brow was deeply furrowed.

"I doubt that's it, then," Archer replied, his voice flat and emotionless. He was probably pitying me for my *small* inheritance when he had the entire D'Ath Estate up his sleeve. Prick.

Steele huffed an annoyed sigh. "Arch—" he started but broke off when the sound of a door slamming echoed through the house.

My shoulders bunched, my whole body tense with fear, but seconds later the mouthwatering aroma of pizza met my nose, and Kody appeared in the doorway.

"Pizza's here!" he announced. "What did I miss?" His eyes shot to the TV, then to the controller in Steele's hand, and he arched a brow.

"Oh, fuck off," Steele grumbled. "I think I've earned it."

Kody didn't argue but placed the pizza boxes down on the low coffee table in front of us and detoured back into the kitchen to grab drinks for everyone.

When he returned, after handing beers to each of his friends and offering me the options of beer or Coke—I took the Coke—he took a seat on the floor in front of the couch and opened the pizza boxes.

"So, are we playing or…" He shifted his position enough that he could look up at me with an arched brow. "I get the feeling I walked in on a particularly tense conversation."

"You did," Steele muttered, cracking his beer open and taking a sip. "We were discussing why someone would want to kill Madison Kate."

"And getting nowhere on it," Archer added in a sullen growl. He was still sitting so damn close to me, it was like I could feel his presence radiating off his skin. "That bastard who tried to jump Madison Kate at the diner was a hired goon. Cheap one too."

Kody took a slice of pizza, eating a bite while he seemed to be thinking. "Okay, well, what about the stalker, then? Any ideas on who that is?"

I reached out for the cheese pizza, and he handed me a slice. I gave him a smile of thanks. "Uh, I guess the suspect list is a whole lot longer on that one. It could be anyone that I've crossed paths with, right?"

"It could be Bree," Archer commented, and my gaze snapped to him with fury.

"It's not fucking Bree, you twat."

He cocked a brow at me, those ice-blue eyes curious. "Why not? She has the access—she knows the gate code—and she knows more about you than anyone else. It wouldn't be the first time a girl developed an infatuation with her attractive friend."

I carefully avoided the fact that he'd just called me attractive and addressed his blatantly incorrect theory. "Bree *couldn't* be my stalker, you idiot. She was eleven when my mom died…I hardly see her developing a sexual infatuation with her friend's mother at that age, let alone being devious enough to do all the shit this stalker is doing. No. Just, no."

Archer just gave a shrug that seemed to shift him closer to me. Or maybe that was my imagination. "Okay, what if it's her dad and he's somehow convinced her to do his dirty work? I'm just saying, she gives me some pretty intense vibes the way she looks at you."

I glowered. "Don't let jealousy cloud your judgment, Archer. It's not fucking Bree; let it go."

Bree was my best friend. One of my only friends, really, seeing as I couldn't exactly count the guys as my "friends" unless we added "with benefits." The idea that she could be putting up a front with me for some devious motive? Nope. I couldn't even entertain that possibility, and I wouldn't. She wasn't involved, and if Archer tried to suggest it again, he would find out just how hard I could junk punch.

"Okay, how about Dallas?" Steele offered up, and I scowled in his direction. "Hey, I didn't mean anything by that," he said, defending himself as he raised one hand—not disturbing his damaged arm—in surrender. "I just think we need to consider all the obvious options. Dallas would have been, what, sixteen when your mom died? Teenage boys are messed up, and Dallas came from a rough upbringing. He's clearly attracted to you too, *and* possessive. He fits the profile."

I was simmering with anger, but I had to appreciate what they were doing. They were trying to help, and they didn't know Bree and Dallas the way I did. Of course my friends looked like suspects to them.

"Your stalker clearly has a sexual interest in you, and you *have* had sex with Moore, haven't you?" Archer pointed out in a pissy sort of tone.

"It's not Dallas," I replied, trying to control the anger in my voice. I couldn't defend him any further than that because Steele's points were all valid. I was just running on gut feelings about my friend and onetime lover. Dallas wasn't evil. He wasn't the guy who killed a bird or blew up a car and injured innocent bystanders. "Next?"

Kody rested his head back on the couch beside my thigh, his pink hair brushing my skin. "Okay, how about Steinwick?"

"Ew," I replied, wrinkling my nose. "That's gross."

"So is a dead bird in the mail," Archer retorted.

I narrowed my eyes at him, then turned my attention back to Kody. "What's your reasoning?"

"Same as any of the staff, really. Access." His gaze was clear of accusation or maliciousness. He was simply spit-balling ideas, like we were brainstorming for a school project together. I kinda appreciated that level of detachment and latched on to it. "I mean, it's probably not. But I can't see any reason for him to *not* be on the list of suspects. Can you?"

I rolled my eyes. "By that same reasoning, everyone I've ever met should be on the list. You three included."

"Hmm, yeah, I could have planted a hidden camera then deliberately convinced you to fuck me in the kitchen and then sent a dead bird to myself as a threat. I mean, it's a bit fucking kinky, but anything is possible," Kody replied with a grin.

He had a point. And Archer had been watching from the hallway. Didn't totally clear them, but again, I'd have to trust my gut and scratch them from the list of suspects.

"What about the QB?" Steele pondered. "He would have been too young to stalk Deb, but what if it's a copycat stalker?"

I groaned, rubbing my eyes. "That just complicates it even more. If it is a copycat, then literally anyone could be responsible. The freaking gardener or my criminology professor or one of the cops or the security company or, fuck, one of those Madison Kate groupies that Bark told me about. You know his sister was one of them? Colored her hair and everything."

Kody scoffed a laugh. "So creepy."

"Seriously?" Archer snickered, reaching over and flicking Kody in the side of the head. Right on his *pink* hair.

Kody just looked up at Archer with a smug smile. "Big difference between some random chicks trying to look like MK and me accidentally dying my hair pink because she distracted me with sex while

I had color shampoo in." I rolled my eyes and smiled, but Kody just shifted closer and kissed the side of my thigh. "Totally worth it. And now we match like a super cutesy couple, so I think I might keep it."

"Don't," Steele commented. "It takes a rare breed to pull off that color, and you, my friend, aren't it."

"Asshole!" Kody reached up to the couch and grabbed a pillow, then chucked it at his smirking friend. Steele deflected it but groaned as he brought a protective hand to his injured arm. Meanwhile, the pillow Kody had chosen was one I had wedged slightly behind me, and without it I slipped down the couch and collided with Archer's shoulder.

He shot me a sharp look, and I quickly rearranged myself to *not* be touching him. But I already knew it was going to take a while for the warmth of his shoulder to fade from mine. Fucking mysterious bad boys were definitely proving to be my kryptonite based on these three bastards.

"All right, are we playing this game or not?" Steele asked, indicating the TV and chomping through a slice of pizza. He didn't even try to hide the eagerness in his voice; we all knew he was dying to do some gaming without the guilt.

I sighed. "I need to go and study. This whole stalker thing is going to see me dropping out of SGU soon, otherwise."

"You'll do fine," Archer commented in a quietly neutral tone.

Kody nodded, finishing his mouthful before speaking. "Also, we're snowed in for another day, so you may as well just relax tonight. I'll help you study tomorrow if you want."

"Really?" I gaped at him. I didn't even know where I'd left my phone earlier in the day so couldn't check for myself. But Kody passed me his, which showed the official message from the SGU administration. "Well, that's lucky. I should probably start tonight, though…" But I didn't want to. I wanted to stay on the cozy couch and play stupid video games with the boys. I wanted a moment of normalcy after such a crappy, fear-filled day.

"Just play the damn game, Princess," Archer growled. "You can't possibly get any worse, but maybe driving into a few walls will chill you out a bit."

I seethed. "I'm not *that* bad."

But I was. I really was.

"Prove it," Archer replied, turning his challenging gaze on me, "or are you scared?"

Kody snorted a laugh. "Weak effort, bro. It's a video game, not a real race car. MK isn't gonna—"

"Fine," I snapped, holding Archer's gaze with my own brimming full of defiance. "Let's play, then."

Yes, I was a giant sucker. Yes, I was well aware I'd played beautifully into his hands. But also? I didn't care. It suited my own desire to stay in the den with the three of them, so I let him think he'd won.

For the rest of the night, we sat around playing racing games—all of us getting our asses kicked by Steele—and indulging in playful banter. Like we were friends. It was...strangely nice. Of course, I lost every damn game, driving so badly that at some point Kody took pity on me and pulled me onto the floor with him so he could show me how to correctly use the controller.

His strong arms wrapped around me, his hands on my hands as he showed me which buttons did what I needed them to do and in what order to do shit. After a couple of races under his tutelage, I was driving a hell of a lot better. Still losing, but at least I was going the right direction.

"Somehow, I don't think I have any future as a professional gamer," I muttered as my race car hit the barrier and started rolling. On the upside, it hit Archer's car—lapping me again—and took him out in a ball of computer-generated flames.

"Hey!" he protested. "I was winning that one!"

Steele snorted. "No, you weren't, dickhead." His and Kody's cars both sailed across the finish line, confetti and streamers displaying on their quarters of the screen while mine and Archer's flashed with LOSER.

"I'm grabbing more drinks," Kody announced, getting up from his seat on the carpet. Without him sitting beside me, I climbed back up onto the couch and stretched out my back. As much as I loved having Kody's arms around me, the couch was a hell of a lot more comfortable.

Steele was eagerly queuing up a new game, and I noticed him flick the difficulty setting up to Expert. I groaned. "Come on, like I wasn't failing hard enough on beginner level?"

He just flashed me a wicked grin, the metal of his tongue stud catching the light between his teeth. "Yeah, so what difference does it make? Come on, let me thrash Arch on the hardest setting."

I laughed and tossed my controller onto the coffee table. "I'll sit this round out and just watch, then. Kick his ass, Max."

Archer just narrowed his eyes at me, but it lacked the heat our glares usually held. Steele whooped with excitement and switched the game to two-player, starting it before Kody even got back with their fresh beers.

Their race this time was all serious intensity, and I got the distinct impression they'd just been playing around while I was in the game with them. This time, though, it was an actual race.

"Fucking hell," I muttered when Steele won—of course—by a hair. "I guess I should be glad you don't drive like that in real life." Then I paused. "Do you?"

Steele grinned. "Nah, babe. I just like to fix cars and play video games. It's Arch that drives like a reckless fuckwit. He just can't beat me on consoles, and it drives him nuts."

I shot a look to the brooding bastard beside me on the couch. Had he gotten closer during that game? There was hardly an inch between our shoulders, and a long section of my rose-colored hair rested on his sleeve. When had that happened?

Archer just scowled at the TV screen, seeming not to notice our close proximity. So maybe I was reading too much into it.

"Rematch?" he suggested. He acknowledged, then dismissed my searching look with a quick flick of his blue eyes. "Best of three?"

Steele snorted. "Your funeral, bro."

Kody dropped cold beers down in front of everyone, and then instead of sitting back on the floor, he pulled me up from the couch and took my seat. Before I could protest, though, he tugged me back down into his lap and closed his arms around me in a warm embrace. It was...perfect.

I tucked my feet up on the couch and settled into his chest, getting comfortable to watch the boys battle it out with their CGI cars for bragging rights.

It was exactly what I needed to let go of all the fear and paranoia my stalker had sparked with his package. That feeling wasn't totally gone, but it had eased enough that I could relax, and for that I would be eternally grateful to the boys and their video games.

CHAPTER 24

The next day I forced myself to study all day. Kody was a shitty study buddy and proved to be way more distraction than help, so I ended up shutting myself in my bedroom to study with Bree on a Zoom call. Not that she was a lot of help, seeing as she was taking totally different classes, but it helped to have her company. Even if it was only on my computer screen.

Also, her steady stream of gossip and chatter was better than any studying soundtrack I'd ever tried, so by the time SGU campus opened the following day, I was confident in my course materials.

"Miss Danvers," someone called out as I climbed out of Kody's royal-blue Maserati before my first exam of the day. Thanks to the two snow days, I'd ended up with three back-to-back exams, and I'd just finished my third strong coffee of the morning.

I looked around and spotted my criminology professor heading in our direction, so I gave him a small wave. "Professor Barker, hi."

"I'm glad I caught you, Madison Kate," he replied, tucking his briefcase under his arm and peering at me with an intense gaze. "You missed a lot of lectures this semester; are you sure you're up for taking this exam?"

I gave a small, confused frown and laughed lightly. "Uh, I didn't know it was optional."

He nodded, seeming distracted. "Of course, no, it's not. But if you really weren't feeling up to it, I'm sure there is some arrangement we could come to. The dean has informed the faculty of your situation, and I'm more than willing to work with you to recover your grades."

Something about the tone of his voice made me uneasy, and I took a half step backward. "Um, that's really kind of you, Professor Barker—"

"Roy," he interrupted me. "You can call me Roy."

"Uh…" I narrowed my eyes, getting definitely creepy vibes from him. Thankfully, Kody had finished his phone call and came around the car to sling his arm over my shoulders.

"Sorry, babe; that was Jase rescheduling yesterday's meeting. Hi,. Professor Barker, right?" He held his hand out to *Roy* and pulled me in closer to his body, protectively.

My professor glowered at Kody, his eyes flicking to Kody's pink hair. But he shook his hand briefly—like it hurt him to do so—then turned his attention back to me. "Like I was saying, Madison Kate, we can come up with an extra-credit project that can help you out if this exam goes badly. Just come and see me in my office at the end of the day."

He gave me a smile that was all too friendly, then continued across the parking lot to the administration building without giving Kody another glance.

"Uh…is it just me, or was that a bit weird?" Kody asked me, wrinkling his nose. His arm was still around me, and I didn't shrug it off. The professor had given me some hard-core creeper vibes, so I reached up and tangled my fingers with Kody's and snaked my other arm around his waist.

"Majorly weird," I agreed. "I get the feeling Professor Barker has been abusing his position of power with the female students."

Kody gave a dramatic shudder, his breath fogging in the freezing air. "That's next-level gross. I'll get Arch to look into him."

I shook my head, walking with him toward the lecture hall where my first exam was to be held. Kody wasn't starting his until the afternoon but had offered to drive me so Archer didn't antagonize me right before my exam. It had been a fair point.

"All right, ignore that letch," Kody told me as we reached the door of my lecture room. "You got this, babe. I'll have coffee and food waiting when you get out."

He clamped his hand around the back of my neck, pulling me to him for a deep, heated kiss, then released me and smacked my ass. Fucker.

"Thanks, Kody," I muttered, feeling my cheeks heat as some other students filed into the room past us. "Check on Steele for me?"

He nodded, walking backward away from me. "I'm on it, babe. You go kill that stats exam!"

I snickered, rolling my eyes as I went into my *psych* exam. Kody was quickly working his way into my heart, and I already dreaded the day he was going to break it into pieces. Because that day was coming, as surely as the sun rose every day. Whatever they were lying to me about, it was undoubtedly going to ruin us all.

So for now, I'd close my eyes to all the hints and enjoy the bliss of ignorance.

———

The remainder of the week flew by in a haze of multiple-choice questions and essay answers, but by the time Friday evening rolled around, I was *done*.

"We need to celebrate," Bree announced as I collapsed in a heap in the vacant chair she'd held for me in the library. She'd finished her last exam a few hours earlier but texted to say she was waiting for me. "Let's go out."

I gave her a flat stare. "Uh...stalkers and hired killers hunting me, remember?" But I really did want to go out. I wanted to get dressed up and drink and dance and forget I was *Madison Kate Danvers* for the night. Still, I'd learned my lesson the hard way about making dumb-shit, girl-in-a-slasher decisions, so I shook my head. "Nope, I think my celebration is going to consist of watching Netflix in bed."

Bree's lips curled in a grin. "Oh yeah? Whose bed?"

I bit back a laugh. "Perv." But she wasn't wrong; my mind was already wandering to whose bed I could "Netflix and chill" in for the evening. Steele'd had his bandages removed during my morning exam—he'd sent me a thumbs-up picture, seeing as apparently none of us were adhering to the no-phones rule at SGU anymore. So depending on what his doctor had said...tonight could be all kinds of fun.

"Come *on*," Bree groaned with a pout. "I never get to see you anymore. Please, can we just have a fun night out? You worked so freaking hard on those exams; you deserve to cut loose."

I sighed. "You try convincing my jailers of that."

She scowled, and a pang of guilt hit me. I hadn't told her what I'd found out about who was really behind my loss of freedom, so she still believed it was all my father. There was no reason for me to keep Kody's involvement a secret, except for the fact that I didn't want her hating on one of the dudes I was falling for—despite my better judgment.

"All right, challenge accepted," she announced, standing up and grabbing her bag. "You coming?"

I blinked up at her a couple of times. "Uh, what?"

She shrugged and tossed me my bag. "You told me to convince your jailers to let you come party with me tonight. So that's exactly what I'm going to do. Kody drove you again today, didn't he?"

I nodded, still confused as fuck but willing to follow along. "Yeah. He should be getting out of his biology exam about now."

211

Bree grinned like she'd already won. Poor thing. I didn't want to dash her hopes when she looked so excited, but there was absolutely no way in hell Kody would agree to her idea. No freaking way. The guys hadn't said anything to me directly, but they'd been subtly ramping up the protectiveness since Monday's bird-in-a-box incident. Security guards in black uniforms now monitored the front gate and patrolled the property perimeter at nighttime. I hadn't mentioned it to the guys because I was quietly glad for the extra protection.

She had a bounce to her step as she headed back outside and over to Kody's Maserati parked outside the admin building. He'd probably just gotten out of his exam and was now leaning against the driver's side door while he texted someone with his head down.

"Kody, gorgeous!" Bree called out, skipping over to him. I tried to ignore the small tendril of jealous possessiveness that curled through me, but it was hard. Bree was a total babe and a huge flirt to boot.

He looked up from his phone, frowning when he saw Bree; then his gaze slipped past her to me. The smile that curved his lips was all mine, and it eradicated any anxiety I had around Bree being a flirt. Kody only had eyes for one girl right now, and that was me.

"Hey, Bree," he replied to my friend as he slipped his phone back into his pocket. "What's up?"

She turned up her megawatt smile, but Kody wasn't even looking at her. He faced her, sure, but his line of sight was locked on me. It was making me all kinds of warm and fuzzy inside, and I was already planning out that Netflix date for later.

"Kody, sweetheart, you know how hard MK has been studying for these exams, right?" she started, really amping up her car-salesman persona. It made me grin. "Don't you think she deserves a bit of a celebration tonight? A chance to let loose and forget about all that other...crap...going on?" She was batting her lashes, but Kody was still watching me. I just met his gaze and gave a small shrug and head shake as if to say, *It's Bree; go with it.*

"Um, yes?" he replied to my friend, and he clearly wasn't concentrating on what she was saying. Rookie error.

"Great!" Bree exclaimed. "So you have no objections to me taking her out dancing tonight. I'm so glad we're on the same page."

Kody's gaze snapped away from mine, and he frowned at Bree. "Wait, what?"

Bree sighed, and I could tell she was annoyed that she hadn't just slipped through as easily as she often got permission from her father on shit like that. "I'm taking MK out clubbing tonight," she told him, her tone losing a bit of the sugary sweetness. "And you're not going to be a dick about it and stop her, okay?"

Kody's sharp gaze turned amused, and his lips pulled in a sly half smile. "Okay, sure."

"Huh?" I blurted out, stunned at his response.

Clearly, so was Bree. "Say what?" she replied, frowning in confusion.

Kody just shrugged, pushing off the car and reaching out to pull me into a half hug. "I said sure. If MK wants to go out clubbing, then we can go."

"Really?" Bree exclaimed, then scowled. "Wait. *We?*"

Kody's grin spread wider. "Yeah, it's been ages since me and the boys have hit a real nightclub. I'm assuming you girls have fake IDs already? I'll call Arch now and let him know." He pulled his phone from his pocket, and Bree shot me a panicked look.

"Wait, wait, wait," she hurried to say, putting a hand out like she was physically stopping him from texting Archer. "I meant just MK and me. Girls' night, you know?"

Kody snorted a short laugh. "I know that's what you meant, Bree. But this is what you're getting. We all go or no one does. What's it to be?"

My friend made a pained noise, shooting me an apologetic look, but I just raised a brow back at her. If she wanted to go out that badly, then she'd have to put up with my shadows tagging

213

along. I actually preferred that they did too. I doubted my level of paranoia would have let me enjoy a night out while constantly watching my back. At least with Kody, Steele, and Archer glowering over me all night, I'd feel safe.

"Ugh, *fine.*" Bree relented, sounding annoyed as all hell. "But I'm driving MK there; you all can come in another car."

Kody just shook his head and tightened his possessive hold on my waist. "Nope. We'll meet you there. Club Twenty-Two around nine, sound good?"

Damn, he was speaking her language now. Bree's brows shot up. "You can get us into Club Twenty-Two?"

He smirked. "I can. Can't you?"

I bit back a laugh, covering my face with my hand like I was scratching an itch and Bree scowled.

"Fine. I'll meet you there," she relented with gritted teeth. "But you'd better dress to theme."

She'd lost me with that comment. Club Twenty-Two meant nothing to me, except that it was the hottest new nightclub in Shadow Grove and had opened in the months following Riot Night. I'd never been there and had no clue what "theme" Bree was talking about.

"Please, Bree," Kody scoffed, "don't underestimate us. See you at nine!"

Without waiting for her to reply, he escorted me around the car and held the door open for me to slide inside. Apparently, we had a themed nightclub to prepare for.

CHAPTER 25

Club Twenty-Two, it turned out, didn't require a genius to work out what the theme was. Seeing as I didn't have any flapper dresses in my closet, though, Kody made a call on our way home. Sure enough, two hours later I was trying on a gorgeous, deep red, glass-beaded dress with flirtatious fringing around the short hem.

"Wow," Steele remarked, leaning against my open doorframe and running his gaze all over me. "You look incredible, Hellcat. You sure you don't want to just stay home instead?" His heated gaze said it all, and I was sorely tempted to accept. But...it would be such a shame to waste all the time I'd put into my hair and makeup.

"Nice try, asshole," Kody remarked, whacking Steele playfully around the head as he pushed past him into my bedroom. "If anyone gets to take that dress off her tonight, it's me."

Steele glared at his friend, and there was an edge of danger in his eyes that made me suck in a sharp breath.

"Okay, cool it, both of you." I eyed them both with suspicion. "You guys are dressing up too, right?" Kody was shirtless—again— and in just an unbuttoned pair of gray slacks. Steele was still in a hoodie and jeans.

"Of course we are, MK," Kody replied with a grin. "I just came to see if you needed help zipping up or...something."

I shook my head at him, not believing his flimsy excuse for even a second. "Fuck off and get changed, both of you. I'll wait downstairs."

They disappeared back out of my room again, and I went into my huge closet to locate some shoes to match my dress. Once I was ready, I started down the hall toward the stairs, only to pause when I heard Steele call my name.

"What's up?" I asked, pushing his slightly ajar door open the rest of the way and raising a brow at him. He was still in his jeans but had a white T-shirt halfway on and had clearly just gotten stuck with his injured arm. I bit back a laugh at his tortured expression. "Need help?" I offered.

"Could you?" he replied with a grimace.

I crossed the room, carefully peeled the tangled fabric away from his raw, scabbed-over skin, and helped him thread his arm through the sleeve. Steele winced as his muscles shifted under all that healing skin, but that sound quickly shifted to a groan as I smoothed his T-shirt down his body.

"Hellcat," he growled with warning, "you're being a tease."

I smirked. "Yeah, so?"

"So," he replied, catching my fingers before they ventured to his open waistband, "don't make me call your bluff before the week is up. My doctor was very pleased with how well my road rash is healing, after all."

I bit back a smile and tried to fix him with a stern look. "Max Steele, you just got stuck halfway into your T-shirt." He pouted a bit, and I kissed him to soften the teasing. I'd intended it to be just a light peck, but his fingers flexed on my waist, pulling me in close as he took charge and deepened our kiss to a whole other realm— like he was trying to prove he was perfectly capable of fucking me without hurting himself.

"Steele," I groaned as I peeled myself away from him with *way* more effort than it should have taken. "Did you need help with anything else?" His gray eyes flashed, and my cheeks heated. "To get *dressed*," I clarified, determinedly prying my hands away from his body and taking a step back.

Steele's grin was all mischief, but he nodded. "Actually, yes. Hang on a sec; I need to change these pants." He started stripping his jeans off, and I had to turn my back on him with a tortured whimper.

"Now who's fucking teasing?" I muttered under my breath, and he gave a dark chuckle.

"Okay, I'm decent," he announced a second later. "You can turn around without jumping my bones now."

I folded my arms over my chest—for something to do—and turned slowly back to face him. "I wouldn't be so sure about that," I murmured, running my gaze over his body. He wore gray slacks similar to Kody's and that tight white T-shirt, with his right arm's tattoo sleeve showing in contrast to the fabric. In his hands, he held a jumble of black leather straps.

"Help me with this?" he asked, holding the straps out.

I took it curiously, thinking at first that it was some kind of bondage accessory. Maybe I'd totally misjudged Club Twenty-Two and it was really a BDSM bar?

Steele smothered a laugh. "Oh god, your face right now, Hellcat. It's not what you're thinking…but if you're into *that* I can definitely oblige." He turned around, presenting his back to me, so I only just caught his muttered addition. "Or Arch would."

I ignored the effect his words had on me and cleared my throat as I held up the straps to figure them out. But Steele was way ahead of me.

"Here." He separated out one loop and threaded his good arm through, showing me how it was supposed to sit. I was then able to help him secure the other half over his injured arm and shoulder, but I frowned when he grimaced as he buckled the strap across his chest.

"Steele," I said as he picked up a handgun from his bed—somehow I hadn't noticed it there—and secured it in the leather holster I'd just helped him into. "That looks like it's going to hurt you all night. Also, isn't it a bit obvious?"

I frowned at him as he turned back to face me with a wicked grin on his face. "Actually, gorgeous, this is an authentic 1922 gun holster, so *technically* it's part of my costume. Besides, you didn't think we were seriously all going to a nightclub with no weapons, did you? What if someone attacks you again?"

I bit the corner of my lip in concern. "Well, sure. But *you* probably shouldn't be leaping into another gunfight right now. You can't even move that arm without cringing."

Steele just gave me a flat stare, and I knew perfectly well I was fighting a losing battle.

"Max…" I groaned, knowing I'd already abandoned my argument. He looked…wow. "You look like a male stripper," I muttered, trying really hard not to sound like a jealous girlfriend.

His grin spread wide, and he took a couple of steps toward me with *way* too much swagger. *Fucking hell, my ovaries just exploded.*

"Are you telling me you want to rip my clothes off, Hellcat?" he teased, flicking a finger under my chin to raise my face up to his. "Because I could be on board for that." He winked one of those gorgeous eyes at me, and I almost came. Goddamn, apparently five days was too long for my libido to go without because I was damn near gasping for it.

"Yo, time to go," Kody announced, banging on Steele's open door. "I want to grab burgers on the way."

"Fuck off," Steele replied, not taking his eyes off my face for even a second. "We were in the middle of something."

My stomach flipped with excitement, and my mouth watered. Whatever thoughts were putting that intoxicated, hungry look in his eyes, I was totally on board.

"Well, finish it later," Kody replied, coming into the room and grabbing me by the hand. "You cockblocked me all week with your injuries, so you definitely don't get to cheat me of a night out with our girl. Come on, move your ass." He left the room again, pulling me along behind him, and I barely had enough time to shoot Steele a grin over my shoulder before we were around the corner. Except Kody didn't continue leading me all the way downstairs.

Instead, he spun around and pinned me to the wall right outside Steele's bedroom. His lips came down on mine in a hard, possessive kiss that left my knees weak and my fingernails digging into the back of his neck.

"Trust me, babe," he said in a husky whisper. "I want nothing more than to rip that dress off you and stay in tonight. But this club trip serves a double purpose."

My brows shot up. "It does?"

He nodded, swiping his rough thumb across my lower lip where my lipstick was probably all kinds of smeared. "Arch got in touch with someone from his grandfather's training camp. He might be able to shed some light on how your attacker had a D'Ath blade."

Shock made my jaw drop slightly. "Seriously?" Kody nodded. "And...this guy is at Club Twenty-Two?"

"Should be." Kody released me, holding out his hand this time instead of grabbing me. "Also, I can't wait to get my hands all over you on that dance floor."

I laughed, taking his hand and walking with him down the stairs. "You could put your hands all over me anywhere," I commented quietly, "with considerably less of an audience."

The smirk Kody shot me was drenched in sex, and my thighs clenched. "The audience is part of the fun, babe." His long lashes closed over one jade-green eye in a saucy wink, and my heart raced. I was in *so* far over my head with these boys, and I didn't even care. I'd happily sign up for all the impending heartbreak if it meant I could keep feeling like the center of their universe a little longer.

Steele caught up to us as we made our way into the garage, and

Archer was already waiting beside a black Range Rover looking... holy fucking shit, wow. Charcoal pinstriped suit pants, a black shirt with the sleeves rolled up to show off his inked forearms, and fucking *suspenders*. I was sorely tempted to throw down and declare suspenders illegal. They should be. The whole themed look on him, combined with the fedora? It was a hell of a look. A great one, at that.

"We ready to go?" he asked us with a faint scowl marking his brow. He seemed to be talking to the boys, but his eyes were on me, no matter how hard he tried to pretend they weren't.

Steele nodded his response, flipping open the leather jacket he'd put on and showing Archer his gun. I expected some kind of reaction from him, but he just gave Steele a short nod before shifting his attention to Kody.

"Ready, boss," Kody replied, turning around and flashing a gun secured in the small of his back. I just gaped at the three of them like they'd grown three heads.

"Since when did you guys start wearing concealed weapons for a night out on the town?" I asked, mostly not expecting an answer. I got one anyway. Of course.

"Since you started getting stabbed and choked and stalked every fucking time you step foot in public, Princess," Archer growled back with an edge of something raw in his tone. Resentment, I thought. "Trying to keep you alive is a full-time fucking job."

I scowled, but I didn't retort with anything dumb like telling him not to bother looking after me. I wasn't that stupid. I needed them, or I really would end up like my mom. Beaten, strangled, and shot in the head.

"Should I be armed too?" I asked as Kody and Steele both climbed into the back of the Range Rover. Apparently they were being gentlemen and letting me take the passenger seat. Dickheads.

Archer just looked me over and rubbed a hand over his dark stubble with a small groan. "No, you're fine. We don't actually expect any trouble." He popped the passenger door open and held it for me, indicating that I get in. I was torn between thinking it was a polite, kind gesture or just a passive-aggressive way to tell me to hurry the hell up. Whatever it was, I got in and buckled my seat belt while he circled around the front of the car to his side.

Steele and Kody chatted in the back seat as we left the garage and started down the driveway, but I wasn't focusing on their words. I was too conscious of the tense way Archer gripped the steering wheel and the lightning-fast glances he kept flicking at me. Or rather at my exposed thighs, thanks to the short dress riding up when I sat down. I wore sheer stockings held up by a black garter belt, but he couldn't see that much, giving him the illusion of bare legs.

When we paused at the gates, waiting for the security guard there to open them for us, Archer reached into his pocket with a frustrated sigh.

"Here," he muttered, holding out his crimson butterfly blade to me. "Take this. It matches your dress at least."

Shocked, I just stared at the knife for a moment, then took it when the gates opened fully and Archer needed to drive through.

"What about you?" I asked, holding the folded blade in my fist. It was warm from being in his pocket, and it was almost like touching an extension of him.

Archer just cocked a brow at me with a half smile. "I'll be fine, Kate. Just don't fucking stab yourself."

My heart stuttered at the rarely used name. Dallas was the *only* other person who called me Kate, and a cynical part of me couldn't help wondering if Archer did it as a dig toward my old friend and first love. Then...another part of me secretly loved it.

I didn't have any pockets in my dress, so for lack of any better ideas, I pulled the hem of my dress up, unhooked one of the suspenders from my stocking, and looped it through the blade handle before reattaching it. I tucked the bulk of the knife into the lace band at the top of my stocking, then gasped as the car swerved sharply.

"Whoa, what the fuck?" Kody asked from the back seat. "First time driving, bro?"

Archer's scowl was firmly fixed on the road, his knuckles white on the steering wheel. "Sorry," he muttered from behind clenched teeth. "Thought I hit a squirrel."

Kody and Steele made jokes about Archer's shitty driving, but I just side-eyed him.

Squirrel, my ass.

CHAPTER 26

I don't know why I was surprised—nothing about these boys should shock me anymore—but the bouncers on the door of Club Twenty-Two didn't even bat an eyelid at Steele's poorly concealed firearm. They just gave Archer and the boys a respectful nod, then waved us all through with Bree in tow. We bypassed the huge line of people waiting to get in and checked our coats in the entry hall.

The first thing I noticed when we passed through the heavy velvet curtains and into the main club was the undeniable party atmosphere. The music was loud, the chatter and laughter louder, and everyone was dressed in theme. It was like we'd just stepped straight into *The Great Gatsby*…except with strippers. Yep, two parallel runways jutted out from a stage, each with a gorgeous but scantily clad dancer working the pole. The left was a gorgeous blond girl with an incredible body, and the right was a guy in nothing but a tiny, sequined Speedo.

"Equal opportunity nudity," I commented with a grin. "I like it."

Archer rolled his eyes, then turned to speak with Steele too quietly for me to overhear—not that I was paying a lot of attention to him—when a familiar face appeared out of the crowd.

"Kate!" Dallas boomed, rushing forward and sweeping me up in a hug that took my feet off the ground. "I'm so glad you came. I didn't think Breezie could pull it off."

"She didn't even tell me you were coming," I replied, giving Bree a small frown of confusion over Dallas's shoulder. She just gave me a small smile back and shrugged.

"I'll get some drinks," she offered. "You can help me, Kody." She grabbed his arm and hauled him after her before he could fully protest, and I realized Archer had already disappeared.

Apparently whoever he'd come here to meet with, I wasn't invited into the conversation. It made me all kinds of irritated that he'd snuck off like that when it was *my* life in question. Then again, I knew nothing of the dark world they all lived in. It was all too likely I'd make some social blunder and get us all shot at. Again.

"You can probably put me down now," I told Dallas with a laugh, and he reluctantly set me back on my feet.

Steele moved closer, possessively placing his hand on my waist and shifting me a step away from Dallas. It was such a stupid, testosterone-filled move that I couldn't help rolling my eyes. Dallas wasn't a threat. Far from it. But I wasn't going to waste my breath trying to convince Steele of that when he was in full possessive mode. Besides, it was kinda hot.

"I'm surprised to see you here, Moore," Steele commented, his voice low and cold.

Dallas's easy smile faltered a second as his eyes flashed to Steele's face. "All of Hades's clubs are neutral zones," he replied in a careful, even tone. "I'm not breaking the rules by being here."

Steele gave a small incline of his head. "Make sure that doesn't change. I'm not in the mood to send Ferryman a reminder tonight."

Dallas's smile totally slipped from his face at that thinly veiled threat. "I think the reminder you all sent to Zane and the Reapers was enough, thanks." He shifted his gaze to me, his brow creasing with concern. "I'm worried about you, Katie. Maybe we can talk tonight…alone?"

Steele's hand tightened on my waist, and Dallas flicked a nervous glance at him before pasting an all too fake smile back on his face.

"Anyway, let's go see what Bree's ordered for us. I don't trust that girl's choices in liquor." Dallas laughed, but it was a forced sound as he headed in the direction Bree and Kody had gone.

I paused Steele before we followed, placing my flat palm against his hard stomach.

"I know you guys have a lot of secrets," I said, shifting so I could meet his eyes and show how serious I was, "and I've been all kinds of patient with you, regardless of everything else going on"—like my stalker mail reminding me that they're all *liars*—"but that patience is running out."

Steele sighed, but it wasn't a frustrated gesture. It was more a sigh of resignation. "I know, babe," he replied, meeting my eyes without flinching away. "Trust me, it's on my mind more than you realize. Kody's too."

I pursed my lips, unable to help asking, "But not Archer's?"

Steele's gaze shifted away from mine a moment, looking over my shoulder and across the club with a frown pulling his brow. "Arch…" He trailed off with a small grimace. "Come on, let's find the others. This is supposed to be a night out for *you*, Hellcat. Have fun with your friends; we're just here to make sure no one tries to kill you."

I scowled as he tried to herd me toward the bar. "Max Steele, don't brush me off. Sooner or later, I'm going to need to know what's going on."

He gave me a weak smile, linking his fingers together behind my back. "I know. But can it be later? I really like it when you don't hate me." He leaned down, bringing his lips to mine for a coaxing sort of kiss, and I melted into him.

I groaned slightly as the hardness of his piercing teased my tongue, and I tried to shove aside my anxiety about the immediate future. But nothing could shift the sinking feeling his words had given me—his total certainty that whenever I discovered all their secrets, I'd inevitably hate him once more.

"Fine," I murmured when he broke away from our kiss. "But we're revisiting this later."

He gave me a short nod. "But not tonight," he added, linking our fingers together as we walked over to the bar.

I wanted to push the issue further, but I also agreed. I didn't want to know all their secrets and lies tonight. I *wanted* to get naked and fucked six ways to Sunday with Steele…or Kody. Or both. A girl could dream, right?

"Hey, there you are!" Bree announced as Steele helped me navigate the crowd to reach her, Kody, and Dallas near the end of the long bar. "I thought you got lost or something."

Her smile was touched by a small frown as she looked down at my fingers interlocked with Steele's. I wasn't letting go of him in a hurry, though, so she could speculate all she wanted. Contrary to popular belief, we didn't *always* need to tell our girlfriends every aspect of our sex lives, and I'd been keeping my mouth shut on my involvement with Kody and Steele. But it didn't take a genius to work it out simply based on body language and familiar touches.

"What did you order?" I asked her, deflecting the question written all over her face. On the bar top was a tray holding a whole array of drinks, and I was eager to get the party started. Within reason, obviously, seeing as I had no interest in getting blackout drunk when people were trying to kill me.

Bree beamed, happy with the topic of discussion. "Come on, let's get somewhere to sit, and we can drink a few of these before we dance."

Dallas snorted a laugh, sipping whiskey from his cut-crystal glass. "I'm not fucking dancing."

My bubbly friend just glared at him, then indicated he carry the drinks tray as she led the way to a circle of chairs around a low table beside the dance floor. It was marked with a Reserved sign, but as we approached, a staff member nodded to Kody and removed the sign.

Fancy.

For a while, the five of us sat and chatted and drank like actual friends. Like people who didn't have shady, dangerous pasts or psychotic killers hunting them. Like none of us had ties to violent gangs or...whatever else was going on. It was nice. It was exactly what I needed after the stress of my exams and the paranoia of my stalker delivering dead animals and unwelcome sex pictures.

"Oh, I love this song!" Bree exclaimed when a new tune came on, and she started bopping her head. "Come on, we need to dance." She held her hand out to me, indicating that I get up with her.

I laughed but didn't object. I used to *love* going dancing with Bree, and I was just the perfect level of tipsy to let myself go on a crowded dance floor.

Bree led the way, shaking her ass to the catchy beat as she found a space on the dance floor somewhere between the two stripper runways. She grinned at me under the flashing lights, grabbing both my hands and urging me into a groove with her. Not that I needed a whole lot of encouragement in that department.

"Yes, girl," she cackled as I started my hips moving and became one with the music. "Aw, there's the MK I know! I missed you!" She was all emotional drunk, looping her arms around my neck and bringing her body close to mine while she danced.

Her words kind of pissed me off, but I chalked it up to the number of shots she'd downed before we came out to the dance floor. But seriously, given everything I was dealing with, I'd think the shift in my personality was to be expected.

Shaking my head to dismiss the negative thoughts, I wiggled my hips and danced with her like old times. We'd probably only danced for a couple of songs, though, when Dallas joined us and Bree all but climbed him like a horny monkey.

Snickering at the panicked look on Dallas's face, I turned to leave the dance floor and give them some privacy but found a dance partner of my own waiting behind me.

"Kodiak Jones," I purred with a wide grin as he reached out and grabbed my hips, tugging me closer to him as he moved to the music. "Trying to re-create the last time we danced together?"

His lips brushed my ear as he chuckled, his breath feathering my skin and sending shivers rolling through me. "Hopefully with a drastically better ending to the night this time."

I laughed, despite the weight of that night still weighing on my mind. But I was determined never to end up in that situation again. Even if all of Archer and the boys' dirty little secrets got spilled before the night was over, I wouldn't put myself in that broken, vulnerable position that had made me such easy prey.

So I let myself dance with Kody, grinding my hips against him and losing myself in the moment. We danced together until sweat slicked my skin, and eventually I twirled around in Kody's arms to clasp his face between my hands.

"I'm done," I announced, smacking a quick kiss on his lips. "Take me home?"

A wide, predatory grin spread across his face. "I thought you'd never ask, babe." His head dipped and his lips met my neck. Then his teeth, and I moaned low in my throat. Fucking tease.

I looked around for Bree and Dallas, then gasped when I saw them drunkenly making out in the shadows across the dance floor. But then that explained a lot of the cagey way Bree had been acting every time I mentioned Dallas.

"Uh, should we…" I indicated to my two friends but then realized Dallas was looking back at us anyway, despite the way Bree was sucking on his neck. So I did an awkward kind of gesture to tell him we were leaving, and his brow creased in a frown.

Kody wasn't hanging around for a silent conversation across the dance floor, though, so I blew a quick kiss toward Dallas and

Bree—giving them my support—then let Kody lead me back to the table where Steele and Archer sat. They each had a crystal tumbler in their hand, but as neither of them looked even remotely drunk, I guessed the drinks were just for show.

Seeing Archer reminded me of why they'd been so willing to let me have a night out on the town, though, and I propped my hands on my hips with a stern glare.

"Did you do what you needed to do?" I asked him with a pointed look.

His brows rose slightly, and he rubbed at his stubbled cheek with his knuckles. "Yep," he replied, and I just barely held back a hard eye roll.

"And?" I prompted, seething with annoyance that he couldn't just front up the information all at once.

He took a moment to gaze up at me before answering, and there was a strange look in his eyes. "And nothing. It was a dead-end lead."

I scowled, folding my arms and debating whether he was actually telling the truth or not. But then, as impeccable as his poker face was, I'd have no way of working it out unless he was willing to tell me.

"Don't pull that face, Princess Danvers," he drawled, sitting forward in his chair, which brought him a hell of a lot closer to me. "I said we'd keep you alive, and we will. Leave it at that."

My frown deepened as I opened my mouth to bite back, tell him what I thought of his attitude, but he shifted forward, his hands clasping my waist. I gasped as he stood up, lifted me off my feet, and physically moved me out of his way before setting me back down.

"If you're done dry fucking Kody on the dance floor, we should go." There was a sneering edge in his voice, and the way his hands lingered on my waist told me something all too clearly.

Archer was *jealous*.

"*Dry* fucking? Yeah, I'm done with that," I snarked back with a smirk. "All bets are off for straight up *fucking* when I get him home, though. Like our clothes."

Archer's face darkened like a thundercloud, and my grin spread wider. I pushed up on my toes to bring my lips closer to his ear. "Don't worry, big guy. I'll be loud, so you can pretend you didn't completely blow your chances while you fuck your hand tonight."

Dangerous anger flashed over his face, but I just laughed as Steele grabbed my hand and yanked me away from his friend. He ushered me ahead of him through the club, with Kody and Archer following.

"You just can't help yourself, can you?" Steele murmured to me as we wove between dancing patrons, and I chuckled again. "If you keep provoking him, shit is going to blow up soon."

I snorted, looking at Steele over my shoulder. "Like Archer's ego?"

He just rolled his eyes, and I grinned.

We collected our coats from the pretty girl working the coat check, and I quickly huddled into mine as we stepped out into the freezing night air. It'd started snowing again while we were in the club, and I was woefully underdressed for the temperature.

"Fucking hell," I moaned, my teeth chattering as I hurried to button my cashmere coat closed. "Why did we park so far away, again?"

It was a rhetorical question, considering Club Twenty-Two was located down an alleyway that didn't permit any vehicle access. But Kody took pity on me and tucked me under his arm, burying his own hand into the pocket of my coat while we walked in sync.

We only needed to walk a couple of minutes to get back to the Range Rover, and Archer opened the passenger door for me with a pointed look. Like an…*I'm not fucking driving while you blow one of my friends in the back seat* kind of a look. I rolled my eyes at him but slipped out of Kody's embrace anyway.

"Spoilsport," I muttered, ducking under Archer's arm and into the car. If I was being honest, it was a selfish move on my part. As soon as the boys piled in and Archer hit the ignition, I flipped my seat warmer on and sighed at the almost instant warmth on my ass.

"Uh, babe?" Kody said from the backseat. "What's this? It was in your pocket."

I glanced over at him and found him holding up a piece of folded notepaper.

"Beats me. Why'd you take it out of my pocket, creeper?" I was teasing, seeing as it was probably just a receipt or something. But the serious look on Kody's face hinted at something more sinister.

He flipped the paper open, showing me what was on the inside, and my blood ran cold.

I KNOW SOMETHING YOU DON'T KNOW. BUT DO YOU WANT TO KNOW TOO? I CAN TELL YOU EVERYTHING...I KNOW MORE THAN THEY DO.

CHAPTER 27

The note from my stalker—because it was almost definitely from my stalker—seriously put a damper on the night, and the drive home was full of tense silence. Once we got home, the silence continued as we all dropped our coats and headed upstairs.

Regardless of the creepy fucking message from my stalker, I hadn't forgotten the totally unsubtle promises Kody had been making to me all night, or the heated way Steele had watched us while we danced. I wasn't going to let my stalker ruin *another* great night.

"Kody," Archer said as we all reached the top of the stairs. "Can I have five minutes?"

I scowled. Apparently, it wasn't only my stalker who was cunt-blocking tonight.

Kody sighed and scrubbed his hand over his face, looking tortured, but he nodded. "Sure, bro. I'm sure it's something urgent that can't wait until the morning."

Archer just glared back at him, but Kody wasn't flinching. I bit back a laugh, thinking Archer might come out on the wrong end of Kody's fist again if he wasn't careful.

"It is," Archer growled in anger. "Urgent, that is." He nudged his own bedroom door open and indicated that Kody join him.

"Fucking cockblocker," Kody muttered under his breath, echoing my thoughts perfectly. He took a moment before following Archer, grabbing my face with one strong hand and kissing me hard and fast. When he broke away, I was panting, and Kody made a growl of frustration. "I'll try and keep this brief," he told me in a husky whisper before releasing me.

"Hey, can I get your help taking this T-shirt off, Hellcat?" Steele asked loudly, his voice heavy with suggestion and amusement.

Kody let out a loud curse as he stomped into Archer's room, slamming the door behind him, and Steele laughed a bit cruelly. I shook my head at him, but he just grinned and held his own bedroom door open farther along the corridor.

"Please?" he asked, his pleading look more sincere than the way he'd just taunted Kody. "I don't want to get stuck again. It was so much easier when I had the bandages on." His slight pout was too freaking much, and I passed through his doorway with an indulgent smile.

"Kody will kill you, you know that, right?" I told him as he kicked the door shut and prowled toward me while I kicked my heels off beside his bed. Thankfully, the curtains were already closed. The thick material was blackout, just like the ones in my room. He reached me and threaded his fingers into my hair, tilting my head back for a long, lingering kiss.

He gave a small, satisfied noise when our kiss ended, and his smile was pure mischief. "A little competition is good for his inflated ego, gorgeous. Besides, I really do need help with this shirt."

"Mm-hmm, sure." I replied with a sarcastic nod, but weak excuses aside, I still slid my hands under his tight, white T-shirt and peeled the fabric up his body. Except he still had the leather gun holster on, so I quickly unbuckled it and helped him ease it off his injured shoulder.

The groan he let out when he tossed it onto his dresser—gun and all—made me frown with concern, though. A feeling that was confirmed by the specks of blood marking his clothing.

"Dammit, Steele," I scolded him, pushing his T-shirt the rest of the way up and helping him to ease it over his still-healing left side. For the most part, the road rash all down his arm and shoulder was healing well, but where the leather straps of the holster had sat, the fresh skin was red and inflamed with small splits that'd caused the spotting on his shirt.

"It's not that bad," he commented, touching his fingers to the top of his shoulder where the worst scrapes were. "They'll heal up in no time."

I huffed, looking around his room for something to clean it up with. There was a box of tissues on his nightstand, so I grabbed one of those and dabbed at the blood. He was right; it really wasn't that bad, not even needing any dressing, but still.

"Maybe refrain from playing bodyguard until this heals up properly?" I suggested, annoyed, worried, and a bit sick with guilt. If not for me, would he be getting hurt like this? I guessed I didn't know. I knew nothing about what their lives had been like before me. They were clearly mixed up in some dangerous shit, that was for sure.

Steele gently took my wrist in his hand, removing the tissue from my fingers and tossing it into his wastebasket. "Stop fussing, Hellcat. I'm fine. A few superficial scrapes are hardly the worst I've dealt with."

That only made me frown harder. "So you've said before, which only makes me want to know who hurt you in the past."

He released my hand, then stroked my hair with his fingers, following it down my back until he found the zipper of my dress… which he dragged down. "Why would you want to know, gorgeous? The past is the past. I, personally, am living for the here and now." His palms smoothed over my shoulders, pushing the straps of my dress off and causing the heavy, beaded fabric to puddle at my feet.

"So I can hunt them down and stab them in the fucking eyes

for you," I replied with a ruthless smile. I was only half joking, but Steele gave a short laugh.

He gave me a gentle push, making me sit down on his bed, and then knelt in front of me, sliding his palms up my stocking-clad thighs. "Bloodthirsty is such a sexy look on you, Hellcat," he murmured, his fingers deftly unhooking my garters and freeing Archer's folded blade from where I'd stashed it. "But what makes you think I let them live?"

I sucked in a breath, the feral, dangerous look in his gray eyes making my heart rate spike. Max Steele was the biggest fucking contradiction, and I loved every damn element of his complicated personality.

"As sexy as the stockings are," he commented, rolling the silky fabric down my leg and tossing it aside, "I need to remind myself what every damn inch of you feels like."

My suspender belt, strapless bra, and panties all quickly followed the stockings, and I found myself stretched out naked on Steele's bed with his mouth—and that tongue stud—showing me exactly what I'd been missing out on in the past week.

I let out a needy whimper as his piercing flicked my clit, and the fucker laughed into my pussy. I shifted my hands to his head, silently cursing him for having such short hair that I couldn't yank on it, but dug my nails in enough to show him I meant business.

Not that he needed the extra encouragement. He was already working me up into a frenzy, so much so that when he slid his long index finger into my cunt, I almost didn't hear the door open.

Almost.

"You *asshole*," Kody declared, kicking the door shut again and leaning his back against it with his arms folded. I was directly facing the door, so it only took a slight head raise to meet his blazing green gaze across the room.

Steele barely paid him any attention, though. His lips left my pussy only for a second. "Fuck off, Kody," he replied, sliding a second finger into me and making my eyes roll back in my head for a moment. "We're busy."

"Total dick move, Steele," Kody growled. "I'm going to castrate Arch for this."

I got ahold of myself enough that I could meet Kody's gaze again, and a sly smile crept across my lips. What could I say? The idea of castrating Archer got me hot.

"Then again, maybe MK doesn't *want* me to fuck off," Kody added in a thoughtful voice, his eyes holding mine with both question and promise. I licked my lips, my breath short enough to make me dizzy.

Steele paused, peering up at me with curious eyes. *"Really?"* He smirked, his pierced brow twitching up in a question he already knew the answer to. "Lock the fucking door, Kody."

"Fuck, *yes!*" Kody grinned.

The lock on Steele's bedroom door clicked shut, and I bit my lip with excitement as Kody stripped his shirt off with one hand. No joke, I thought that was a move only strippers knew how to execute, but apparently Kody was multitalented.

He kicked his shoes off while Steele dove back between my legs, and by the time Kody crawled onto the bed in nothing but his black boxer briefs, I was a writhing mess, gripping onto Steele's head as he teased me on the edge of orgasm.

Kody lay on the bed beside me, stroking his fingers through my hair, then turned my face to his in a demanding gesture. His mouth claimed mine, kissing me harder than Steele was tonguing my cunt, and I was a fucking goner. I came, moaning into Kody's kiss as my thighs tightened around Steele's head, totally forgetting about the injuries on his shoulder for a second.

"Fuck, sorry," I gasped when my orgasm started to subside and I'd regained a fraction of my senses again. Steele kissed the inside of my thigh, subtly wiping his face off before making his way up my body to lie on my other side.

He smirked one of those satisfied, totally male kind of smiles as his fingers caressed my belly, stroking over my scar. "Don't apologize to me," he replied, licking his lips. "That was hot as fuck."

As evidenced by the way his pants were straining across the crotch.

"Max Steele," I murmured as Kody palmed my breasts and kissed the side of my neck, "you're awfully overdressed. If you want to play—"

"I wanna play," he quickly agreed, standing up from the bed and stripping his gray slacks off. Standard Steele, he wore nothing underneath. He was fully naked with his cock in hand by the time I scrambled farther up the bed and eyed Kody's underwear.

"Well shit," Kody commented with a smirk. "No messing around, huh? I like it."

I didn't reply because I was too busy watching him peel those black boxer briefs off and freeing his erection. Yep, sometimes dreams did come true.

"Have you ever had a threesome before, babe?" Kody asked me as he took himself in his own hand and gave a few teasing strokes. His tip glistened, and my mouth watered. "Just so we know what we're dealing with."

I shook my head. "No...but I'm a very quick study."

Kody gave a small groan, his gaze heated. "I fucking bet you are."

Steele propped his head up on his hand—his unharmed side—as he lay beside me with a sexy grin on his lips. "Have you ever done anal before, Hellcat?"

My jaw dropped slightly, but he grabbed my hip and rolled me toward him so I couldn't even deflect the question. I had to laugh at the intense, excited look on his face, though. "Yeah...once or twice."

It was Steele's turn to let his jaw drop in surprise, and Kody let out a low chuckle as he scooted in close behind me on the bed.

"Fuck yeah," Kody snickered, then the two of them fucking *high-fived* over me. They slapped hands like goddamn teenagers. It was so incredibly arrogant and...yeah, okay, it was hot as sin.

I groaned and rolled onto my back, covering my face with my hands. "I should say this is a bad idea and leave now..."

Kody laughed, smug fuck. "But you won't." He peeled my hands off my face and placed them on his chest.

"Because you know it's a fantastic idea," Steele finished for him, leaning in and kissing me.

I groaned into his kiss, my hands skating down Kody's body as his hands found my breasts and palmed them both. His fingers rolled my hard nipples; then his mouth closed over one, and I shivered hard with desire.

"Wait," I said on a sigh as Steele's lips trailed to my neck. "Steele, you only just got your dressing off this morning. This seems like a bad idea *for you*."

"Mmm, nah, I'm fine. Totally healed up." He bit down gently on the flesh of my neck, and my breathing spiked faster.

Fuck, I wanted to believe his bullshit. Especially when his hand was skating down my stomach, then lower, finding my wet heat and—

"Steele," I moaned, "come on..."

He ignored me, his finger delving deeper and making my hips buck from the bed, but Kody released my nipple from his mouth to give his friend a smug smile.

"Maybe you need to sit this one out, buddy. I don't mind taking one for the team." He shot me a cheeky wink. "You can just lie back and watch, nice and safe."

Steele growled an angry sound and bit my neck hard enough to make me gasp. "Fuck you, Kodiak," he replied, and I laughed. I wasn't serious about stopping, but it was fun to tease him. And we *did* need to be conscious of his injuries.

"Kody, quit it," I scolded him, then wriggled to sit up and give Steele my best stern glare. "You *should* just lie back and not move your arm...but I think we can work with that. Right, Kodiak?"

He gave me a shrug in response. "I'll work with anything you wanna do right now, babe. Just don't send me back to my room with blue balls."

Steele snorted a laugh, shifting onto his back against the pillows and tucking his good arm behind his head. "How bad do you reckon Arch's blue balls are gonna be tonight?"

I bit back a laugh of my own and shook my head at the two of them. Kody cracked up, and Steele grinned like a shithead. "I guess that all depends," I replied, resituating myself to straddle Steele's legs and skimming my hands down the hard planes of his abs until I took his cock in my grip. He let out a small gasp as I pumped him, and his smile slipped.

"Depends on what, baby girl?" Kody purred in my ear, sweeping my hair over my shoulder to expose my back for his fingertips to stroke down.

I met Steele's eyes as I stroked his dick, licking my lips. "On how hard you make me scream tonight."

Kody let out a turned-on sort of growl while kissing my neck, then nipped the flesh. It was perfect symmetry to the place Steele had already left teeth prints on the other side. "I'm game," he murmured.

"Same," Steele added, and the two of them slapped hands again. *Assholes.*

But I wasn't pausing to reprimand their childish behavior. I was too busy sliding down the bed and taking Steele's length in my mouth. My hand was still wrapped around his base, and I pumped him lazily as my tongue circled his tip while he cursed and dropped his head back into the pillows.

"Fucking hell, that's so hot," Kody commented. He kept one hand on my back, stroking his fingers down my spine as he climbed off the bed and circled around behind me. He hooked his fingers under my hips, encouraging me to rise up on my knees while I sucked Steele off, which left my cunt totally exposed.

Exactly what he intended, no doubt.

239

I gasped when he stroked his hand down the length of my pussy, but Steele was quick to tangle a hand in my hair and bring my mouth back to his cock. He bucked his hips up, filling my mouth at the same time as Kody sank two fingers into me, and I moaned around Steele's girth.

By the time Kody's mouth closed over my cunt, Steele had an iron grip on my head and gave me no choice to do anything except shudder and groan my approval as his friend ate me out. Even from his position of "lying back and taking it easy," Steele still dominated my mouth, forcing me to take him harder and deeper than I might have tried on my own. It was exactly how I liked it, though, and I loved that he instinctively knew that.

"Fuck," he groaned after a couple of minutes, releasing my hair and letting his dick leave my mouth with a wet pop. "Shit, Hellcat." His breathing was heavy and his jaw clenched tight, but I didn't want to move because Kody was right on the verge of making me come again.

Kody's mouth left my pussy, though, and I whimpered my protest. "Hush, babe," he scolded me. "I'll take care of you. Max just needs a sec, don't ya, bro?" His tone was all teasing, and Steele glared murder at him.

"I do," he ground out, "or I'm going to blow my load down MK's throat and be useless for the real fun."

I grinned, smug as fuck that I'd almost made him lose his control there, but he just narrowed his eyes at me in silent promise of retribution.

"Hey, no judgments here," Kody replied, his fingers pumping lazily inside me and making me wriggle in desperate need for more. "You don't mind if I play a bit while you get a grip, do you?" Without waiting for Steele's response, he dragged his wet fingers up my crack and circled my asshole, making me suck in a sharp gasp.

"Fuck," Steele breathed, biting his lip as his eyes locked on my face. He was lapping up my every reaction like it was a fine wine, and he was no doubt getting plenty to work with. Kody pushed a slick finger into my ass, and my jaw went slack, my eyes widening briefly before dropping almost closed. I moaned, arching my back and writhing under his hand while he let out a low, dark chuckle.

Kody groaned as I pushed back against him, and his other hand grasped a hard handful of my ass cheek. "Shit, MK, don't do that." But the edge to his tone quite clearly begged me *please keep doing that.* I wriggled my hips again, gasping as his finger pushed in deeper.

"All right, I want back in," Steele announced, grabbing my upper arms and hauling me up the bed—away from Kody—and into his lap.

Kody just laughed a dark sound, though, and clambered back onto the bed with us. "So impatient, Max."

"Quit calling me that," Steele growled back at him as he palmed my breasts and rolled my nipples, "and check the top drawer."

Kody did as he was told, fishing out a little bottle of lube and a couple of condoms. "Why? MK calls you Max."

"MK is about to let us double team her, dickhead; she can call me anything she damn wants. You can't." Steele's glare was totally serious, and I just shrugged.

"He's got a point. Maybe he'll let you if we switch places?"

Kody cringed. "Nah, I'm good where I am, thanks." He held up the two condoms between his fingers, showing me and cocking his head to the side in question. I only thought for a second before shaking my head. "I'll tell you the same thing I told Kody," I said to Steele as I reached down between us and found his hard shaft. "You give me an STD and I'll cut your dick off. Clear?"

Steele's eyes widened, but he nodded quickly, shifting his grip to my hips as I lined him up. "Crystal clear," he agreed, then groaned as I sank down, taking him in almost fully. "Holy *fuck*," he whispered as I braced my hands on his chest to lean forward and take him deeper on the next thrust. His hand came up, tangling in my hair again and bringing my lips to his for a deep kiss that echoed the way his cock was seated within me.

Kody shifted on the bed behind me, planting a hand on my back to push me flatter into Steele. Something Steele was all too happy to help with, wrapping his good arm around my back and pressing my breasts into his chest as he kissed me like I was the last woman on earth. Or better than that, like he was the last *man* on earth and still chose to kiss *me*.

I shivered as Kody slicked cold lube over my ass, but it was mostly from excited anticipation. When his fingers entered me again, I moaned into Steele's kiss. I knew what was coming, and I was almost at the edge of orgasm just waiting. Of course, already having Steele inside me giving shallow thrusts while Kody prepped my ass helped. Fucking hell, I was likely to spontaneously combust if they didn't get on with it soon.

"Quit wriggling around, babe," Kody laughed, grabbing my hip with his spare hand as his fingers withdrew. "Just stay fucking still a second." The hot, spongey tip of his dick pressed against my ass, and I had to pull my mouth away from Steele for fear of biting him. The pressure built as Kody pushed forward, aided by the slick lube, and I buried my face in Steele's neck as I forced my muscles to relax and let him in.

It felt like forever but was probably only a couple of seconds, before Kody grunted and flexed his fingers against my hips.

"You good, babe?" he asked in a strangled sort of voice, and I needed to suck in a few deep breaths before I could reply.

"No," I panted. "No, I'm so much better than good. Fucking hell, you two need to start fucking me *now*, or I'm going to end up a boneless heap after I come from sheer anticipation." My words were a desperate, gasping plea, but they both responded perfect-ly—by giving me exactly what I fucking wanted.

"Oh fuck," I cried out as they moved within me. I was help-less to do anything except moan and thrash and scream as Kody and Steele filled me up with their huge dicks, fucking me with scary synchronization until I howled my release. But they weren't finished with me yet. They just waited, their cocks buried deep inside me as I cried out, trembling and panting through my orgasm. When the stars started to clear from my vision, I was just whispering a string of curses as Steele smirked at me with pure satisfaction.

"I could get used to that," he commented, his hands reaching down to grip the backs of my thighs and abruptly spread me wider.

Kody grunted and shifted his position to match where Steele had moved me to, and all of a sudden it was like they'd both hit me even deeper.

"What the *fuck*?" I moaned, but both boys just chuckled and started fucking me again, striking all new locations. Places I didn't even know I had nerve endings were lighting up like fireworks, and I already knew they were going to make me come again. Greedy fucks.

One of Kody's hands left my hip, where I already knew I'd find his fingerprint bruises tomorrow, and smoothed over the curve of my ass. I knew what was coming a second before it happened, but it didn't stop me from jumping halfway out of my skin when his palm cracked down on my flesh. Everything tensed. Everything. And both Kody and Steele let out twin groans, and I let a devilish grin spread over my face, even as my butt cheek flooded with warmth and my pussy tingled.

"Fucking hell," Steele muttered, stroking my sweaty hair back from my face and bringing my lips to his for another searing kiss. "That gives me way too many ideas. I'd almost forgotten how beautifully you responded when I smacked your ass on Thanksgiving morning."

Kody snorted a laugh, rubbing soothing circles on my tender cheek as he fucked my ass more slowly. "How the fuck could you ever forget? I'd put money on it that MK likes getting tied up too." He slapped my butt again, and the moan I let out was probably loud enough to wake the neighbors—and they weren't even close. I fucking hoped Archer was enjoying his night in with his right hand while listening to us.

That was confirmation enough for Steele, who yanked my lips back to his. The two of them kept fucking me, dragging me out of the depths of post-orgasm haze, but this time when I came, Steele joined me. He cursed, his pace faltering as he thrust deeper than ever and emptied his hot load inside me with a tortured sound.

Kody only took a few moments longer, taking advantage of Steele having finished to hitch my hips up higher and slam into me with ferocity until he also climaxed. He filled me with his cum before slapping my ass halfheartedly, then collapsed onto the bed beside us.

I didn't want to hurt Steele—any more than he'd already hurt himself—so I shuffled around on weak, jelly muscles until I was snuggled between the two of them in a warm, if sticky, pile of limbs.

Everyone was breathing hard, but when Kody raised his hand, I growled. "If you two high-five again, I swear—"

Slap.

"You'll what?" Steele taunted me, retracting his hand from Kody's crisp high five. "You going to withhold sex, Hellcat? 'Cause you just had a whole lot of fun getting fucked by both of us." His voice was pure smug satisfaction, and I couldn't even deny it. That one was getting filed straight in my mental spank bank for when I inevitably kicked these lying boys to the curb and returned to my drawer full of battery-operated boyfriends.

"Fuck no," I replied, letting my voice carry the horror of his suggestion. "I can find ways to get even without denying myself my *own* needs, thanks."

Kody laughed into his pillow, then turned his head enough to crack an eyelid open at me. "Something tells me I need to carefully check the sugar before making my coffee in the morning. And prepare for a new hair color." His blazing green gaze held me, and I just gave a sly grin back. "Worth it," he added.

"Shit yes," Steele agreed, snaking a hand around my waist to tuck me in closer to him. Apparently we were all going to sleep together...and I was totally okay with that.

I had no idea how this new dynamic was going to play out in the morning, and that was okay. The one thing I knew without a doubt was that I would need a hell of a cleanup in the shower before entertaining a round two.

Fuck, I hoped there would be a round two.

CHAPTER 28

I woke up at some stage in the dead of the night, needing to pee. So I took the opportunity to clean up a bit while I was in there before slipping back in between the two hot bodies in Steele's bed.

Good thing I did too, because the next time I woke it was to Steele parting my legs and diving his face back into my core. I groaned, arching my back and waking Kody up in the process. He grumbled for a second, then realized what he was missing out on and a grin spread across his sleepy face.

He was already hard from whatever he'd been dreaming about—hopefully me—so all it took to get him where I wanted him was a suggestive lick of my lips and a pointed look at his dick.

Steele made me orgasm with just his sinful tongue while Kody fucked my mouth, grunting his own release as I swallowed greedily.

Then they switched.

By the time Kody's phone alarm went off, buzzing in the pocket of his pants on the floor, I was two orgasms down and loving life. Maybe Bree's reverse harem heroines were onto something because I could easily get used to that kind of wake up.

"Why do you even have an alarm set?" I asked Kody with a

yawn, propping my face on my folded arms and then sighing as Steele trailed light patterns over my bare back.

Kody groaned but made no move to get out of bed to turn the annoying sound off. "Because I have an early training session. Damn it."

Steele let out a soft laugh as he kissed my shoulder. "Suck it, bro. I'll keep MK entertained while you're gone."

Kody yawned, rolling out of the bed and finding his phone to stop the alarm. "Actually, you won't. My session is with Lorraine."

"No." Steele groaned and buried his face in the pillow beside my face. "I don't want to go. It's so warm in bed this morning." His arm curved around the small of my back, pulling me closer to demonstrate what he meant.

"Who's Lorraine?" I asked, curious. "And why does that mean Steele has to go with you?"

"She's one of my older clients," Kody replied, pulling his boxer briefs on and hunting for his shirt. "Her elderly mother, Greta, lives with her and has quite advanced-stage Alzheimer's. Steele came with me one day that we had a photo shoot straight after the session, and Greta thought he was her husband, who died about twenty years ago."

"So now Kody volunteers me to come along once a month to sit with Greta and pretend to be her dead husband for an hour." Steele grimaced but climbed out of bed anyway. "Do you want to come with us?"

I rolled over and pulled the sheets up over my body. "Nah, I'm good. I need to call Bree and Dallas anyway, make sure they got home okay."

Kody gave me a small, worried frown as Steele went to his dresser to find clothes. "Are you going to be okay here with Arch? He's gonna be in one hell of a mood this morning."

An evil grin pulled my lips. "I can handle Archer," I assured him. "In fact, it gives me a chance to fuck with his head a bit more. I owe him for trying to constantly cunt-block me with you guys."

Kody's brow arched, and Steele turned to face me with a thoughtful look on his face. "Actually, I think *we* owe him for that," Kody mused aloud. "You just relax today, babe; we'll handle the pranks this time." He and Steele did one of those bro nods, like they were totally on the same page, and my smile spread wider.

"Yep, we've got this, Hellcat," Steele agreed, tucking his pile of clean clothes under his arm and making no moves to cover his dick. Which, fair enough, after the night the three of us had just spent together. "You just rest up." His wink said it all. Rest up because they were going to want a repeat performance again when they got back.

Shit yeah.

"All right," I agreed with a shrug. "I don't know how you'll top my steroids in the protein powder trick, though."

Steele just laughed and left the bedroom, ducking across the hall to the bathroom before Kody could get there first.

"Uh, yeah, I don't think we'll try for anything so drastic," Kody replied with a short laugh, "because we still have to live with the prick and he doesn't want to fuck us, so forgiveness will be a whole lot harder to come by."

I rolled my eyes. "Archer doesn't want to fuck me," I muttered. "He just can't handle not having chicks fall at his feet with their legs spread. I'm threatening his ego, that's all."

Kody cracked up. "Uh-huh, sure, babe. And the sky isn't blue." He disappeared out of the room before I could deny it any more. Not that I had any strong arguments for the contrary...I was pretty sure Archer *did* want to fuck me. He just wouldn't for some reason. But even if he did, it'd be a one-and-done deal. Just getting me out of his system like he'd accused Steele of doing after our first time together.

I sighed and rolled back over in Steele's bed, burying my face in the pillows and inhaling the combined scents of both boys. My whole body ached with fingerprint bruises and stubble rash. Not to mention, my pussy was warm and swollen from the morning's activities and my ass tender from the double up last night. But it was that delicious sort of pain that made me smile into the pillows with satisfaction.

Given that I had nowhere to be and nothing to do, I let myself drift back to sleep in Steele's warm bed. When I woke again, the clock on his bedside table showed a few hours had passed, and chances were the guys would be back soon.

Stretching and yawning, I reluctantly climbed out of bed and returned to my own bedroom to shower and dress for what was left of the day.

I was just padding around the kitchen making my coffee in a pair of thigh-high woolen socks—teamed with a pair of comfy shorts and one of Kody's sweatshirts—when I heard the first signs of life of anyone else in the house.

A loud, enraged roar came from the direction of the gym, and I paused what I was doing. When no other sounds immediately came, I continued to place my cup on the drip tray of my machine and pressed the button to pour a double shot of espresso.

Heavy footsteps thumped down the corridor, though, and a second later Archer appeared in the kitchen with three distinctive splats of paint decorating the chest of his T-shirt and a look on his face that would have put Medusa to shame.

"Seriously, Madison Kate?" he demanded in a bearlike roar. "We're still playing these stupid fucking pranks?"

I cocked one brow at him, inspecting the paint and tilting my head to the side. "To answer your question, Archer, yes, we most certainly are still playing these stupid pranks because you're an arrogant son of a bitch who needs to learn some humility and quit being such an insufferable asshole. But this? Wasn't me."

His glare darkened, and that vein over his temple ticked like the clock of a time bomb. "Oh, so now we have invisible fairies waiting outside the gym with paintball guns, huh?"

I took my coffee and sipped the straight espresso, licking my lips to savor the taste before I replied. "Sounds like someone rigged up a booby trap," I commented, impressed. "Maybe you should ask yourself whether you've pissed anyone *else* off lately."

Archer glowered at me, but his eyes flashed with understanding as he got my meaning—that his bullshit was turning his own friends against him.

Yeah, bitch. Suck it. They're mine now.

I smiled, smug as fuck, and sipped my espresso again.

Archer took two steps toward me, forcing me to look up to meet his gaze as his freshly painted shirt brushed my knuckles.

"Stop pushing me, Madison Kate," he demanded in a low, danger-filled tone. "I have been all kinds of lenient with you, but my patience is fast running out."

Defiance flared up in me, and I tilted my chin, letting the challenge play out in my arrogant, fearless smirk. "Do your worst, D'Ath."

His blue eyes flared, and his lips parted to retort or...something. But the peal of our doorbell interrupted whatever his snappy comeback was going to be, and his brow dropped in an irritated frown.

"Fuck," he cursed, moving away from me a step, "that's Jase. Do me a favor and don't piss him off? I need to get changed." He swiped his paint-covered shirt over his head, showing me the red swelling on his chest where the paintballs had hit him at close range, then disappeared out of the kitchen.

Moments later, a guy in maybe his midthirties strolled into the kitchen like he owned the place and paused when he saw me standing there.

"Hi. You must be Jase," I greeted him with a smile, holding my hand out for him to shake.

He took it, clasping with a medium pressure and eyeing me

with curiosity. "And you must be Madison Kate, the girl who caused my best client to lose his first UFC title fight."

My brows shot up at the animosity in his tone. "Maybe he lost because he simply isn't as good as everyone tells him he is. Or maybe his manager pushed him into a fight he wasn't ready for? I heard there was a bit of a scandal with doping too. Was that your influence, *Jase*?"

His face clouded over to something angry and dark. It was pretty clear I'd made a new enemy without even trying very hard, but something told me he'd already formed plenty of opinions about me before we met. "Listen here, you little *whore*—" he started to say, his voice like acid.

"Jase," Archer's voice barked across the kitchen, and his manager jerked like he'd been electrocuted. "I know you're not the brightest crayon in the box, but I'd seriously warn against insulting Madison Kate in her own home. She's got claws and isn't afraid to use them."

Now it was my turn to jerk in shock. Had he just *defended* me?

"Besides," Archer continued, "Kody and Steele are both hitting that on a regular basis, so if you want to keep your job, I'd probably keep the name-calling to a minimum." He shot me a nasty smile. "No matter how accurate the names are."

And there it was. Fucker couldn't help himself.

"Whores get paid to fuck, Arch." I clapped back with a sarcastic smile. "And no amount of money on earth would make me fuck you. But hey, I bet your hand is feeling pretty used and abused today. Maybe you should chuck yourself a couple of bucks for all the wanking you must've done listening to us last night."

I downed the rest of my coffee in one sip and dropped my cup into the sink, then raised both my middle fingers to both Archer and Jase on my way out of the kitchen. Call me crazy, but I could think of about seventeen thousand better things to do with my day than stand around and be insulted by Archer and his shitty manager.

What a *prick* the mysterious Jase turned out to be.

I returned to my room and hunted out my phone to call Bree, except the fucker was out of battery. With a sigh, I plugged it into the wall and flopped back onto my bed. Trading verbal blows with Archer always seemed to take all the energy out of me, so I draped my arm over my eyes and decided to take a little nap while I waited for my phone to turn back on.

Five minutes, that'd do it.

Then I'd call Bree and demand to know how long this thing with Dallas had been going on and why they'd hidden it from me. Not that I'd been super forthcoming about my own love life, but hypocrisy was the spice of life, right?

CHAPTER 29

My five-minute nap turned into an hour, and then I spent another forty-five minutes on the phone with Bree, talking about her fling with Dallas. Apparently she'd had a crush on him for forever and had been acting weird with me because she was feeling guilty.

After I'd assured her that I had zero interest in rekindling my old romance with Dallas, then backed that information up by telling her about my ménage relationship with Kody and Steele, she finally seemed to get the message. I wasn't mad, and I wasn't even going to be weird about it.

I was happy for her and Dallas; they were kind of perfect for each other.

Wandering back downstairs, I crossed my fingers that Jase the epic douchecanoe would be gone. I was too tired and hungry to deal with more of his preconceived issues with me, but I'd hand him his ass if he called for it.

Voices came from the den, and I was pleased to see Kody and Steele had returned home. Jase, unfortunately, was still here. The four of them were sitting around playing video games and drinking beer, and I was a bit jealous to be left out. Or rather, three of them were playing and Steele was just watching and looking shitty as hell.

I hesitated a moment, not wanting to deal with Jase *and* Archer together, but Steele spotted me standing there and held out his hand, inviting me over to join them.

"Hey, Jase, this is MK," he said as I reluctantly came over and let him pull me into his lap. He was in his usual seat on the recliner, so I carefully avoided his left arm when he tucked me onto his lap.

Their manager flicked me a sneering look before focusing his gaze back on the TV. "We met earlier," he replied, and I made a scoffing sound in my throat.

Steele's fingers flexed on my waist, his brow twitching in silent question, and I just shook my head. Their manager was a total cunt-wanker, but he was *their* manager, not mine. So he could think whatever he wanted about me; I didn't have to work with him.

"Hey, MK," Kody said as his onscreen race car crashed and burst into flames, "Jase booked us in for a photo shoot tomorrow over in Rainybanks. You didn't have any other plans, did you?"

If it'd been a few months ago, I would have taken that as Kody being a fucker and demanding I change my plans to suit their schedule at the drop of a hat. But shit was different. We were different. I could appreciate the fact that he simply wasn't comfortable leaving me at the house alone and was genuinely asking if I had other plans that they needed to work around.

"Nope, I'm free," I replied, enjoying the warmth of Steele's body beneath me. "What's the shoot for?"

Jase grunted a sound, shooting me a venomous look. "It's a closed set. No groupies, sorry. I'm sure you can entertain yourself for a day."

Archer won the race and tossed his controller onto the table with a loud sound. "Princess Danvers is coming, or we cancel the shoot. Nonnegotiable." He leveled a flat glare at Jase, who balked a bit, clearly having thought Archer would back him up.

Obviously, the boys' manager had no idea how contradictory and unpredictable Archer D'Ath could be where I was concerned.

Jase cleared his throat, looking uncomfortable, but gave Archer a shot nod. "Fine, you want to go breaking closed-set rules, that's on you."

Archer just grunted. "Yeah. It is."

That was an *end of conversation* if I'd ever heard one, but Jase must have really gotten his panties in a twist about me for some reason because he just couldn't let it go.

"Damn, Arch, you got a hard-on for her too, huh? Been forever since I've had a slut up for a gang bang, but I'm game." The sneering disgust on his face as he leered at me sort of painted a different picture, though.

I was ready for him, but I didn't get a chance to put him in his place. Archer shot out of his seat and grabbed Jase by the collar of his shirt, dragging him out of the den with Kody tight on his heels.

I arched a brow at Steele, but he placed a finger against his lips. He tilted his head as if to indicate we listen, so I pinched my lips closed and strained my ears.

"Get the fuck out, Jase," Archer told him in a voice like ice and death. "Sort out that fucking attitude before the shoot tomorrow or don't come." He stomped back into the den and flopped his ass back down on the couch without even glancing at me.

Kody wasn't done with their manager yet, though.

"Talk about our girl—or *any* girl—like that again and you'll find yourself right back where we found you, a penniless con artist working the streets for scraps and charity. Now *fuck off.*"

The sound of the front door slamming echoed through the house, and Kody returned to us in the den with a deep scowl marring his handsome face. He didn't immediately sit back down, though, first coming over to me where I sat on Steele's lap and grabbing my face for a bruising kiss.

"Sorry about him, babe," he told me, brushing his thumb over my lower lip and staring into my eyes with sincerity. "He's always been a socially awkward son of a bitch, but that was way over the line."

I snorted a dry laugh. "Don't sweat it, Kodiak. I put up with bigger assholes on a daily basis. I've got a pretty good handle on not taking shit personally." I shot a pointed look past him to Archer, who just glared back at me with an unreadable expression.

"We know you're capable of handling yourself, gorgeous," Steele told me, stroking his fingers through my hair, "but you shouldn't have to. Not if we can take care of it."

Archer made an exaggerated gagging sound and stood up from the couch. "The air in here just got sickeningly sweet. Kody, I'll meet you in the gym." He clapped his friend on the shoulder, then exited the room, taking his thundercloud of shitty attitude with him.

Kody sighed and scrubbed his hands over his face. "So much for winter break. You guys coming? MK needs to keep working on her self-defense training, Steele. Maybe you can help while I train Arch?"

"You bet," Steele replied, even while I made a sound of protest. The last thing I wanted to do was share a gym with Archer. Actually...having met Jase I could think of worse things.

"But why?" I complained as Kody helped me up out of Steele's lap. "Didn't Archer spend *all* morning in the gym already? That boy needs a hobby."

Kody laughed, cleaning up the empty beer cans. Actually, I was wrong; only a few were beer cans and the rest were sparkling water. "Jase secured a comeback fight for him in a few weeks. The original fighter fell sick with a virus, and the other guy asked for a replacement instead of a forfeit. So now it's back into hard-core training mode again."

"Come on, Hellcat," Steele teased, looping his arm around my waist and directing me back upstairs. "Let's get changed, and you can show me these moves Kody taught you last week."

I gave him a sly smile and winked. "Oh yeah? We probably don't need clothes for that."

Steele laughed. "Funny girl, but you're not getting out of this so easily. We all agree you need to know how to fight, how to defend yourself in case anyone catches you off guard again." He paused, looking thoughtful. "Although I could probably be persuaded to go easy on you."

Grinning, I picked up my pace and tossed my borrowed hoodie off before my bedroom door was even fully open. If any persuading was going down, I was willing to bet it wouldn't need clothes.

Sadly, Steele's idea of "going easy" on me in the gym still left me bruised and grumpy as shit, but even I had to admit that I needed to learn these things. Some small tricks up my sleeve or correct techniques could mean the difference between life and death if my attackers stepped up their efforts again.

The next day we drove out to a warehouse studio in Rainybanks for the photo shoot, and I quickly worked out why it was a closed shoot.

"You guys are doing a *nude* photo shoot?" I gaped as I looked around the set and then at the robes the photographer's assistant had handed to them. A short laugh escaped me as Archer glared, but Kody and Steele just grinned.

"Good morning, boys!" Jase the ass-face called out, entering the studio with a blast of ice-cold wind. He quickly closed the heavy sliding door behind him. "Ready for a good shoot?"

I rolled my eyes at his false cheer but said nothing. I'd given myself a small talking-to before leaving my room this morning about how to ignore him completely. I didn't need to go causing drama in the guys' careers just because I disliked their manager.

Kody wasn't letting it go so easily, though.

"Jase, you got anything to say to MK?" His pointed glare and folded arms said there was only one correct response to his question.

His manager knew it too. "I'm sorry for my rude comments

yesterday, Madison Kate. I was out of line, and I apologize." His smile was like broken glass, and I bit the inside of my cheek to keep from telling him where to shove his insincere bullshit. Instead, I just gave him a tight smile and a nod back.

I'd leave it at that.

The boys all ducked behind a curtain set up on the side of the studio to strip down, and Jase took two steps closer to me.

"You know they're just going to use you up and throw you aside when they're bored? I've seen them do it *hundreds* of times, and trust me, sweetheart, you're no different from all those other used-up sluts they've left in their dust." He spoke softly in a harsh whisper, and his words cut me deeper than I was comfortable with.

Still, I just gave him a pitying look and shrugged. "Careful, Jase, you're starting to sound jealous. Maybe that's a bit of sexual frustration talking? A word of advice for you...they'd be way out of your league, even if they did swing that way."

Jase's eyes tightened with fury, but the way his eyes darted across the room to Archer emerging from the changing curtain said it all. Nailed it.

"Let's get on with this," Archer snapped, narrowing his eyes at me, then giving Jase a small frown of warning before crossing over to where the photographer and her assistant were checking lighting and adjusting props. Kody and Steele joined him a moment later, all standing around in their white robes and bare feet while they waited on directions.

I used Jase's distraction to move away from him, wandering over to sit on the vacant chair beside the photographer's assistant, an artsy-looking red-haired girl called Luna with glasses and a trendy, oversized sweater. She'd been welcoming when we arrived, introducing me to her boss—Nicky—and telling me where to find the bathroom and kitchenette.

"All right, let's get started," Nicky announced, holding her heavy black camera in one hand and indicating to the white, fur-draped chaise longue. "Steele, sweets, you're up first. Over there, hun."

She was familiar with the boys but not in a sleazy sort of way, and I kinda appreciated that. Not that I had a say, but it made me a hell of a lot more comfortable with the prospect of the guys lying around and posing naked when the photographer wasn't leering.

Steele flashed me a cocky grin before tossing his robe aside—aw, damn, not totally nude but close enough—and heading over to the chaise.

"Whoa, what the *fuck*?" Jase shouted, drawing every eye in the room as he stared at Steele. "What happened to your arm?"

Steele just shrugged, taking up a reclining pose on the lounge and looking totally at ease with his near nudity. All he wore was a pair of white Calvin Klein underwear. "Don't get pissy at me, dude; Arch was the one driving like an idiot."

Jase turned his outrage on Archer, who just shrugged. "Shit happens."

"Okay, enough," Nicky interrupted, bringing her camera to her face and clicking a few test shots. "Steele already called me yesterday to let me know. It's nothing a bit of retouching can't fix."

For the next little while, the camera was on Steele, so Kody hung out with me and Luna, watching as the shots appeared on the computer screen and commenting on any particularly awesome frames.

When Nicky called a break, she came over to the monitor and clicked through the images quickly, searching for the one she was looking for, then expanding it for us to see.

"That's easily my favorite image I've ever taken of this boy," she remarked quietly, shaking her head with a pleased grin. I could tell she was appreciating her own artwork, but I couldn't tear my eyes away from Steele's face in the picture.

He stepped up behind us, tying his robe back on and peering at the image himself, then pressed a kiss to my cheek. "I was thinking about you in that one," he whispered in my ear, his voice low and husky, making me blush violently. He'd said it quietly, but not *that* quietly as evidenced by the look both Luna and Nicky gave me.

Nicky just chuckled and patted me on the shoulder. "All right, Kody. Get oiled up."

My brows shot up, and Kody produced a bottle of baby oil from the pocket of his robe. "Help me out, babe? I'd rather your hands all over me than Archer's." He shot me a wink, and I died.

The brow raise from Nicky sealed the deal, and I violently prayed the ground would open up and swallow me whole.

I still took the oil from him, though.

It was sometime toward the end of Kody's solo session that Luna checked a message on her phone and announced she was going outside for a cigarette.

"Come with?" she asked me, pulling on her coat.

I glanced over to the guys, but Nicky was talking to the three of them about some group shots she wanted to arrange, so I shrugged and grabbed my coat.

"Hey, MK," Kody called out as Luna and I headed for the door, "where are you going?"

"Just keeping Luna company while she smokes," I told him with a wave of my hand. "We'll be right back." He looked like he wanted to argue, so I rolled my eyes and pointed to the huge windows beside the door. "I'll stand right there where you can see me the whole time, okay?"

"I'll keep an eye on her," Jase offered, absorbed in something on his phone. "Keep shooting."

I rolled my eyes at the empty offer and followed Luna out the door before the discussion could get any more ridiculous. I understood the guys were concerned for my safety, but I still needed to be able to leave a room without one of them shadowing my every move.

Still, I remained in front of the window like I'd said I would, and Luna leaned on a rail while she lit up her cigarette.

"Sorry," she said to me with a wry grin. "I didn't mean to cause drama by asking you to come outside."

I shook my head with a smile. "It's fine. They're just a bit... overprotective."

She snorted a laugh. "No shit. Understatement of the century. The way those three stare at you..." She trailed off with a low whistle. "Anyway, none of my business. I did ask you out here with an ulterior motive, though."

I raised my brows. "Oh yeah? What's that?"

She gave me a sheepish look and pulled out her phone, swiping her thumb over the screen to call someone. An uneasy feeling flickered through me as she put her cell phone to her ear, and I shot a glance back through the window at the boys. Kody had slung his robe back on and was speaking to Steele while watching me carefully.

"Here," Luna said, pulling my attention back from the window and holding her phone out to me.

I frowned at it in confusion and she rolled her eyes. "He wants to talk to you, dummy."

Curiosity got the better of me, even as waves of terror rolled through me at the prospect that it could be my stalker on the other end of the phone. But surely listening to what he had to say wouldn't hurt me? And his note had promised me answers...

I took the phone and brought it to my ear. Nervous, I let my gaze catch on Kody's again through the window. "Hello?"

"Little Princess." Zane's familiar voice greeted me, and a wave of relief and disappointment crashed over me. "You're a hard girl to get hold of."

I cleared my throat, ducking my eyes away from Kody's and turning my back on the window so I could concentrate. "I had no idea you were trying to reach me," I replied.

"I told you I'd look into things, didn't I?" His tone was casual and distracted, and the sound of chatter in the background told me he was somewhere public. Probably at his clubhouse.

"Well, yeah," I said, tucking my free arm around myself to keep warm, "but I sort of thought you were just saying that to get rid of me."

Zane huffed a laugh. "My little brother has always had such a high opinion of me. But I owed it to Deb, kid. So I've been doing some digging."

My heart leapt. "Have you found anything?"

Zane blew out a breath, like he was still deciding how much he wanted to tell me. "Yeah, or maybe. I found some interesting inconsistencies, but I hit a dead end when I tried to dig deeper."

The vagueness of that statement made me want to snap at him, but I bit my tongue. Zane was under no obligation to help me, and I didn't want to test how far his sense of duty to his dead girlfriend went. "What does that mean?" I asked, trying to maintain a calm tone of voice.

"It means someone has done a hell of a job covering up any trace of your mother's family line. I think whatever motivation there is to kill you, it has to do with Deb's family. Do you know anything about your grandparents that might help? All the government records have been doctored to look like Deb was an orphan, abandoned as a baby and raised in a group home. Everything has been tampered with. Birth records, so-called state documentation, all of it." Zane sounded pissed off by that, and I was inclined to agree. Because it wasn't true.

"Why?" I asked, confused as fuck. "Why would someone want to erase her family?"

Zane barked a laugh. "Money, kid. It's always about money. So? Can you give me anything that might help? Names or places?"

"Um, yeah." I frowned, searching my memory. "I met my grandmother once when I was really little. I don't remember much; I was probably only five or six."

"Sounds right," Zane muttered. "Deb mentioned her mother had died a few years before we met. Do you know her name or where she lived?"

I screwed my eyes shut, trying to remember. It was so fuzzy though, just flashes of music or glittering earrings or floral perfume. "I can't...I can't remember," I admitted, frustrated as hell. "I can't remember any of it. Why? Why would—" My stomach sank. "This is my father's doing, isn't it?"

"Probably," Zane agreed. "And my little brother just stuck him on a world cruise with Cherry for the next six months to keep him away from you, so I doubt you'll be able to confront him anytime soon."

"Fuck," I cursed, feeling the familiar burn of bitter resentment fill my veins. "Fuck!" I shouted the curse, kicking at a pile of snow and sending the dirty white slush flying.

"My sentiments exactly," Zane commented in my ear.

"Just give me a minute," I snapped. I squeezed my eyes shut again, pinching the bridge of my nose while I tried to force my brain to recall that brief meeting with my maternal grandmother some thirteen-odd years ago. Why had I never thought about her since? Why didn't I even know her name?

Strong fingers snatched the phone out of my hand, and I gasped, my eyes snapping open to meet Steele's angry gaze head on.

He had Luna's phone to his ear, his jaw tight and his brow creased in anger as he listened to whatever Zane was saying to "me" on the other end. Anger burned through me, and I snatched for the phone, only to have Steele twist out of my reach.

"Zane," he said in a voice of clear warning. "You broke the rules."

I tried to grab the phone again, and he held me away with a hand on my chest. The look in his eyes said it all, though. It was a deadly serious *don't fuck with me* expression, and I stopped trying to reach Luna's phone.

"Well," Steele replied to whatever Zane had said, "loopholes aside, Archer will have words for you. Expect his call later today." He then hung up the phone and tossed it back to Luna, who caught it with fumbling hands, her cigarette dropping to the snow.

"Inside," Steele ordered me. "Now."

I scowled in defiance, my lips parting to argue with him, but his expression shifted to something dangerous and somewhat frightening.

"Go!" he shouted, pointing at the door. "I need a word with Luna."

I hesitated a moment, glancing nervously at the red-haired photography assistant, but she gave me a small headshake of assurance.

"It's cool, MK," she told me. "Go back inside."

I still wanted to argue, but the way Steele was glaring at me was pissing me off and I wasn't in the mood for the drama. He was standing barefoot in the snow, for fuck's sake, wearing nothing but a robe and underpants. Whatever he needed to say to Luna must have been of great importance, so I threw my hands up and stomped back into the studio.

I'd barely made it two steps inside when Archer stormed over and grabbed me by the back of my coat.

"Who was on the fucking phone, Madison Kate?" he demanded.

His whole tone made me want to punch him in the face—or maybe in the dick, seeing as he was all but naked. But instead I just tried to twist out of his grip. It wasn't hard, considering he was holding my coat. I just slipped it off and left him holding the garment as I walked away from him.

Take that, prick.

"Madison Kate!" he roared, following me and grabbing my shoulder with a bruising grip. "Don't turn your fucking back on me."

Enraged, I spun around to break his grip on my shoulder and brought my hand up to crack across his face. "Don't fucking manhandle me, Archer," I spat back at him. "You don't fucking own me, so quit treating me like a damn possession."

A cruel, cold smile curled his lips, and I could see the venom rising in his eyes. Well, I was ready for a fight. *Bring it on, sunshine.*

"Arch," Kody barked, "stop it. Steele is handling Luna—just *let it go.*"

Archer's eyes flickered over to his friend, and I let a smug smirk play out over my face.

"Yeah, Arch," I sneered, "let it go. There's a good dog."

Oops, that might have pushed it a little too far. His lip curled in a snarl, and I took a couple of instinctive steps backward. He advanced on me, though, and soon I found the backs of my knees hitting the edge of the fur-covered chaise longue.

"Archer!" Kody snapped, but his friend wasn't listening to him. Archer raised his hand, and I flinched, losing my balance and flopping down on the chaise. Something hardened in his gaze as he peered down at me, and a shiver of fear rolled through me at the darkness within him.

"Did you think I was going to hit you back, Princess Danvers?" he asked me in a low, dangerous tone. He sank to his knees in front of the sofa, bringing our faces almost level as he reached out again. This time I didn't flinch, and he barely touched me. Just a soft brush of his fingertips across my cheekbone that made me suck in a gasp like I'd been hit with a jolt of electricity.

I didn't answer his question. He knew full fucking well that's exactly what I'd thought.

Archer leaned closer, his nearly naked, ink-covered body between my spread legs in some kind of cruel mockery of an intimate moment between lovers. His fingers looped gently through my hair and his eyelids drooped, but I held myself rigid and alert. I'd fallen for his shit too many times already.

"Do you want me to tell you a secret, Kate?" he asked me in a husky whisper, his hooded blue eyes holding mine like a bear trap.

Fuck. My iron core turned to liquid, and the tension flowed out of my muscles like the tide receding. He was going to hurt me again, I could already see it coming, but he was also pressing my buttons in just the right way so I'd let it happen.

"Yes," I replied, my voice barely more than an exhale. The promise of secrets was becoming an obsession for me, and I was powerless to walk away.

Archer moved again, bringing his lips just an inch from mine, and my whole body responded. The memory of kissing him was still so fresh, no matter how badly I tried to bury it.

"I don't hurt women," he told me in a secretive whisper, his blue eyes flashing with cruelty a second before his fingers twisted in my hair and yanked my head back sharply. A startled gasp escaped my throat at the sting of pain. But against all my better judgment, that gasp turned into a breathy moan when Archer's teeth brushed the flesh of my neck below my ear. "Unless they beg me for it." He finished his "secret" with a bite, hard enough to leave a mark, and it took everything in me not to tear his tiny underpants off.

"I'll never beg you," I replied with weak-level sass as warm arousal flooded through me and made me tremble.

Archer huffed a smug laugh. "Begging isn't reserved for verbal communication, Kate. Your body screams everything you're too stubborn to say out loud."

I scoffed, leaning far enough away from him to meet his eyes again. "In your fucking dreams, D'Ath."

His lush lips curled in a smirk. "Relentlessly."

I raised my hands between us to shove him away, but he was already moving. He swiped his robe and threw it on in a quick motion, but he wasn't fast enough to hide the way his Calvins were strained by his thick erection.

He stormed out of the studio in just his robe, heading outside to talk with Steele, who still stood out there with a phone to his ear. Meanwhile, inside the studio, it seemed like I was the center of attention. Kody stared at me with a deep frown pulling his brow, seeming worried. Nicky was holding her camera with a wide grin on her face, and Jase was scowling like he was plotting my death.

Luna, though, was nowhere to be seen—inside the studio or outside. She was just…gone.

CHAPTER 30

God forbid I ever catch a fucking break. The week after the photo shoot, Nicky started posting some of the images to her social media. Images that *included* me, something I was pretty sure wasn't allowed, considering I hadn't signed any release forms. But apparently Archer had *oh so helpfully* taken care of that formality for me.

Legal? Hell no. Worth fighting about in court? Not even close.

Besides, even I had to admit the photos were pretty incredible, even if they had been taken without my knowledge or consent. The expression on my face while Archer's huge, tattooed form hunched over me, his face hidden in my neck... *Ugh, fuck.*

Of course, the day after I was tagged in the first image with Archer looking all too naked between my legs, a little MK replica Barbie was found attached to the front gate with zip ties. She was wearing the same outfit I'd had on the day of the photo shoot—black woolen tights with a plaid skirt, chunky-heeled boots, and a low-cut gray top—but this time my stalker had scrawled a word across her forehead.

Whore.

"Great," I muttered, tossing the offensive doll back onto the kitchen counter after Kody showed me. I appreciated the fact that they weren't hiding my stalker mail, but also...fuck it all. I was so tired of the paranoia and feeling like we were making *no* progress.

The doll hit the pile of Christmas decorations that the staff had been hanging, knocking a few bells to the floor. I didn't pick them up because I was in a shitty mood and all the festive decorations going up around the house only served as a reminder that my father *never* spent the holidays with me. Not even before my mom had died.

"Are you okay?" Steele asked me cautiously, like he'd been expecting a different reaction.

"MK, we're—" Kody started to say, but I cut him off.

"Forget it," I snapped. "We're no closer to working out who this freak is, are we? So let's just fucking ignore these creepy fucking dolls. He wants to scare me, and I'm sick of it. I'm done. They're *just dolls.*" Dolls that still scared the crap out of me and featured way too frequently in my nightmares, but just dolls nonetheless.

We'd been on our way to the gym when Steinwick had given the doll to Kody, so I just shrugged and continued through to the gym, where Archer was already on the weight bench lifting a heavily loaded bar. He was in full training mode with his next fight only a week away. Given that he wasn't getting any sly assistance from steroid powder this time, he was pushing himself so much harder.

I almost felt bad. But then he'd deliver some snarky barb, and I'd consider sabotaging him again.

But Kody and Steele had stayed true to their offer to prank Archer for me, and in the past week there had been more than a few explosive arguments in the wake of a bucket of ice water positioned above a doorway or, my personal favorite, laxatives in the coffee.

Kody had been dedicating just as much time to the gym as Archer, taking his role as trainer seriously and providing a decent sparring opponent as they worked through techniques, holds, and takedowns. But that meant he'd passed my self-defense training over to Steele.

Not in entirety, though; he still demanded Steele and I train while he was there to keep an eye on us. Every now and then he'd correct something in my stance, or Steele's, or give pointers on what to teach me next.

By the time Archer's fight night rolled around, I was amazed he still had energy left. But I was feeling pretty proud of my own progress in the gym. I'd regained my lithe muscle tone and was feeling more confident to be out of the house. Less fragile and breakable.

The four of us ended up driving to the fight in Steele's vintage Impala. Archer was in the front passenger seat, a ball of nervous energy, while Kody kept creeping his hand up my skirt in the back seat. Not that I was complaining, much.

"Can you two fucking *quit it*?" Archer snapped as we neared the function center where his fight was being held. Kody had just managed to get his fingers under my panties, and I was making a piss-poor effort of getting him to stop. Okay, fine, I wasn't trying at all.

Kody just made a smug sound. "Don't be a hater just because you've got the bluest balls in the history of the world. When was the last time you got your fingers knuckle deep in a pussy, anyway?"

Archer's ice-blue eyes met mine in the mirror, and my mind slapped me with the memory of Bree's party. The way he'd torn my panties off and—

"None of your fucking business, Kody," Archer snapped back, ripping his eyes away from mine. "It's bad enough that you three seem intent on giving the entire household a front-row seat to your sexcapades. I don't fucking need it before my fight."

Steele snorted a laugh, his eyes on the road, and Archer shot him a scathing look.

"You got something to add, Steele?"

"Nah, bro." Steele just scrubbed a hand over his freshly shaved head before slapping his palm back down on the steering wheel. "Nothing at all." His eyes sparkled in the mirror, contradicting his statement, but I didn't call him on it. Archer was right, much as I hated to admit it. He really didn't need me and Kody fucking around in the back seat and getting him all worked up before his fight.

Especially after losing his televised debut.

I slapped Kody's hand away and gave him a glare to keep him on his side of the car, and he rolled his eyes. But still, he didn't push the issue, and no one spoke as Steele found us a parking spot and we all piled out to head inside.

Archer had gone through all the mandatory weigh-ins and press shit earlier in the day, but it had all been pretty minimal, as it was a minor fight for entertainment, not titles. Still, I was excited to see some real MMA again. The closest I'd come in the last few months had been Kody and Archer sparring in the gym at home, and while it was sexy as all hell—I was woman enough to admit that—it wasn't a real fight. Kody was training Archer, not actively trying to beat the shit out of him.

I wanted to see some blood fly.

Once inside, I hung back with Steele to let Kody and Archer do their thing. We still followed along and were given seats right beside the octagon, but for the most part, we just kept to the background and tried not to distract Archer. Easier said than done, though, when his tense stare kept drifting back to me. Or to the way Steele's hand rested on my hip or when he kissed my hair or how he whispered in my ear to explain who was who and what was what.

I was distracting him just by being there, and for once, I was annoyed at myself over it. I wanted to see a *good* fight, not a blood-bath because Archer was too distracted to focus on winning.

Kody seemed to be having an intense discussion with him, but Archer wasn't responding. His jaw was clenched tight, his shoulders bunched with tension under his thin hoodie, and his face tipped to the floor…but his eyes were still on me.

"Any chance you can have a chat with Arch?" Steele murmured in my ear, clearly noticing the same thing as I was. "He's been a bit off all week. Maybe you can help get his head back in the game."

I rolled my eyes and snorted a laugh. "You want me to piss him off, don't you?"

Steele gave me a shrug that said, *If the shoe fits…*

I sighed. "No guarantees. I might make things worse."

"Doubtful," Steele replied with a grimace.

"Fine," I grumbled, "but I accept no responsibility if this goes really wrong." Because I already had an idea about how to get his head straight, and I couldn't decide if I wanted it to work or not.

Steele kissed the side of my head with a quick side hug. "You're the best, Hellcat."

We'd see about that. Moving over to where Kody was speaking to Archer with all sorts of violent gestures, I slipped my arm around his back.

"Babe," he said, looking down at me with a tight, frustrated expression, "now isn't the best time."

I wrinkled my nose. "Clearly. Can I have a second with Archer?"

Kody's expression shifted from frustrated to confused and… concerned. "Why?"

I raised my brows and fixed him with a level stare. "Because I asked nicely, Kodiak Jones. Now fuck off. I need to speak with *The Archer* alone." I gave a sarcastic eye roll at his dumb fucking nickname that was really his real name. That level of hiding-in-plain-sight bullshit was so typically Archer, it hurt.

Kody's brow furrowed and he looked like he might argue. But Archer gave him one of those dude head nod things, silently indicating he do what I said, and Kody sighed.

"Fine, just hurry the fuck up. They're announcing you in one minute." He gave me and Archer both a hard glare, then tugged his ball cap back on and retreated to where Steele stood with his arms folded.

"I'll make this quick," I told Archer, cutting to the chase before I could lose my nerve. "You and Kody are having fighter-trainer issues because it's driving you completely insane that he's doing unspeakable things to me and rubbing it in your face. You're jealous as fuck, and it's consuming your brain when you should be focusing on this fight."

His brow twitched, and his eyes narrowed at me. "Is that a question or a statement, Princess?"

"Statement," I snapped back. "So here's how it's going to go. You lose this fight, and I'm going to force you to watch while I suck Kody's dick at the after-party."

Archer's brows shot right up, and he let out a small laugh. "How are you going to *force* me to do anything, Princess?"

I let a cruel smile pull my lips. "I have my ways, sunshine. Wanna test them?"

His eyes narrowed again, and he swiped his thumb over his lower lip. "All right, and what if I win?"

I shrugged. "Win the fight and find out." Over the speakers the commentator boomed out Archer's intro, and I gave him a challenging grin. "Sounds like you're up, big guy." I clapped him on the shoulder and gave his muscles a squeeze because I couldn't help myself. "I better go touch up my lipstick because it's probably going to end up smeared all around the base of Kody's cock later. Loser."

The vein over Archer's temple throbbed, and I turned away from him before I cracked up. Of course, Steele and Kody got the full force of my grin, and that only seemed to confuse the fuck out of them.

When Archer stepped up into the octagon, though, and Kody went over to take his hoodie and give him one last pep talk, Archer was all business. When the fight started, he was a lethal machine, and my heart leapt into my throat as I watched his fists fly.

"What the fuck did you say to him?" Steele asked in my ear as we watched Archer catch his opponent with a swift right hook, making blood spatter the floor of the cage.

I didn't bother holding back my feral smile. "I just offered some incentive not to fucking lose," I commented with a short laugh. I technically hadn't promised anything if he won, but I think we both understood there was an implied offer. Shit. Was I actually going to go through with that? More to the point… would he? After all, I wasn't the one who'd ended our last couple of hookups.

"Well, whatever you said, it worked," Steele replied with a laugh of his own. Kody was right up there beside the cage shouting his advice and encouragement, but he turned around at some point to shoot us a thumbs-up. Apparently he was also impressed at the turnaround in Archer's concentration.

Still, despite how good Archer was, his opponent had experience under his belt, and it showed in how evenly matched they were. It was hands down a much better fight than the one I'd seen on Riot Night. The night that had started all of this.

Somewhere in the third round, the other guy got the upper hand, taking Archer down to the mat with a heavy crash and grappling for a full mount. The crowd roared to deafening levels, and at some stage Archer caught my eye through the cage.

I licked my lips.

Fists flew, blood sprayed, the crowd went *mental*, and all of a sudden his opponent was tapping out from a vicious arm-triangle choke hold.

Just like that, Archer D'Ath won.

Steele and Kody whooped with excitement, Kody crashing into the cage to grab his friend in one of those manly bro hugs and slap him on the back repeatedly while the crowd went nuts cheering and screaming for their victor.

"Well, now you've got me curious," Steele yelled to me over all the noise.

I just shook my head. It had all been fun and games when I was just taunting him over his insane level of sexual frustration, but now? Now I was so screwed.

Maybe literally.

CHAPTER 31

After the fight was over, Archer—as the victor—was pulled into a series of interviews with sports reporters, so Steele and I sat on the hood of the Impala to wait for them to get out. The after-party was in a shitty sports bar across town, but after so long cooped up in the house with just the three guys, I was more than ready for any party.

Of course, this one would be celebrating Archer's win, so I'd have to suffer through his ginormous ego all night. But so long as there was booze, we should be good.

"Fucking finally," Steele shouted out, seeing Kody and Archer emerge from the sports center. "We thought you'd gotten lost or something." He hopped off the hood and popped his driver's side door open as the boys approached with wide grins pasted across their faces.

That in itself was enough to give me pause. Archer smiling... *genuinely* smiling...it wasn't something I saw often. Not when it was so free of malice and discontentment.

Kody went for the back seat, but Archer stopped directly in front of where I sat frozen on the hood of the car, his smile wide and his blue eyes dancing with excitement. Like he'd been fucking body-snatched or something.

"Congrats," I told him, sliding down the hood to get off, but he didn't move. Instead, his hands fell to my bare thighs—thanks to my short dress—and he pulled me an inch closer to him.

His head bent down, his lips brushing my ear as he spoke. "I won. So now what do I get, Kate?"

Fuck me. The husky way those words rolled off his tongue went straight to my pussy and exploded like fireworks.

I tilted my head back, meeting his eyes with a sassy challenge in mine. "How about the sense of achievement you're currently riding like a high? Nothing quite like the pride of showing the haters you're the best, right, sunshine?"

He laughed, a quick, surprised sound like he hadn't even expected that response from me. Then the humor faded back to dark mischief, and his lips brushed mine in a ghost of a kiss. "Try again, Kate. I believe there was mention of dick sucking earlier? Work along that train of thought." He slapped my bare thigh, making me squeak, then winked and left me to take his seat in the passenger side of Steele's car.

I slid the rest of the way off the hood and made my way back to my seat with shaking legs, and when both Kody and Steele shot me curious, *knowing* glances, I dodged their eyes. I was all too aware I was playing a dangerous fucking game with Archer—with *all* of them—but I couldn't seem to stop myself. The rush of adrenaline I got from those brief encounters was too addictive.

Archer leaned over and turned the stereo on *loud*, and I breathed a sigh of relief that there wouldn't be any awkward conversation or tense silence the whole way to the after-party. It was an official party, so it would be packed full of VIP ticket holders and any annual pass holders who were willing to travel to this corner of the country to attend. But I'd managed to get Bree and Dallas some passes, and I was looking forward to seeing them both.

When Steele parked in the jammed parking lot in front of the venue, I leapt out like my seat was on fire. I wasn't one to ever renege on a bet, but *damn*, I needed a few drinks in me first. And I needed to find my friends and reassure them that I was cool with them being…whatever the fuck they were. Friends with benefits, by the sound of things.

"Babe, wait up," Kody called out, hurrying to catch up with me and slinging his arm around my shoulders. "Everyone is riding the high of Arch's win, but please don't get complacent. Stick with one of us all night, okay?"

I glanced up at him as we walked, my heart warming that he was so constantly thinking of my safety, even while this was his celebration as much as Archer's. "Hey," I said, stopping and grabbing his face in my hands. "Congrats on *your* win, Kodiak Jones. You're a kick-ass trainer, you know that?"

A smile spread across his face, and he dipped his lips to mine, kissing me in a way that warmed me right through, despite my lack of clothing. "Thanks, MK," he said when our kiss ended. "Maybe you'll let me start training you for real? Girls that fight are *hot*." I cocked a brow at him, and his eyes widened. "Uh, I mean…that…"

"Walk it off, dickhead," Steele told him with a snicker, whacking Kody around the head and tugging me out of his embrace. "Hey, isn't that the punk-ass QB for the Ghosts?" He pointed across the parking lot to where two guys seemed to be locked in a heated argument.

"Uh." I wrinkled my nose, squinting. "Yeah, it is. And his dad, Professor Barker. I didn't know they were UFC fans." Then again, why would I know that? Bark hadn't spoken to me since our failed date that'd left him with a black eye, and all I knew about Professor Barker was that he was a bit of a sleaze.

I shivered, and Steele gave me a pointed look. "Let's get inside. I told you to wear a coat over that dress."

Smiling, I rolled my eyes. "I keep losing coats when we go out. Besides, it's only cold out here. I bet you fifty bucks it's sweaty as fuck inside."

"Probably," Steele agreed, wrapping his arms around me to share some body warmth as we walked. He'd offered me his hoodie earlier, but I'd declined on the basis of vanity. My short black dress was a killer, and if I really was going to make Archer my bitch tonight, I needed the aesthetic.

Bouncers at the door checked our passes before allowing us inside, and I spotted several uniformed police positioned around the room, watching the partying patrons with sharp eyes.

"Heavy security here," I commented, curious. "Are they expecting trouble?"

Kody laughed. "From a group of hard-core fight fans with alcohol involved?"

"Yeah, fair point." I nodded. Archer must have just come through the door behind me because the crowd started clapping and cheering, raising their glasses in congratulations. I didn't want to take away from Kody's moment of victory too, so I tugged on Steele's hand. "Come on, let's find Bree and Dallas while these two bask in all the glory."

We found my friends sitting at a high table near a little stage where a band was setting up their instruments. They were both holding drinks in disposable cups, and based on their tense body language, they were in the middle of an argument.

"Hey, guys," I greeted them awkwardly. "I hope we're not interrupting anything. Lovers' quarrel?" I couldn't help myself, and a teasing grin pulled at my lips.

Bree just scowled at me, but Dallas shot out of his seat with a panicked look on his face. "Katie, we can explain," he started to say even as I shook my head. "I've been trying to call you, but your number keeps ringing out. Are you avoiding me?"

I frowned in confusion and shot Steele a questioning look. He dodged my gaze, though, looking around the room like he was bored. "What? No, Dallas, I wasn't avoiding you," I assured my old friend. "I don't know what happened; I haven't been getting your calls. But I've been chatting with Bree every other day." I looked to my friend, and she just rolled her eyes. Whatever she and Dallas had been arguing about it, it had her in a hell of a mood.

"I'm getting another drink," she announced, sliding off her stool. "Hey, Dallas, why don't you tell MK who else you invited tonight, seeing as you see *nothing wrong with it?*" She flounced off to the bar with more than a little wobble in her stride. Something told me that hadn't been her first drink of the night, and suddenly I was concerned for my friend.

Folding my arms, I glared at Dallas. "What's going on?"

I kept one eye on Bree across the room while Dallas blew out a breath and rubbed his hand over his face. "She's being dramatic," he said with a groan. "I didn't *invite* him, but I also don't think it needs to be a big deal. This venue was just bought by Hades, so it's technically neutral ground now."

Steele tensed beside me like a bow string. "Who the fuck is here, Moore?"

Dallas cringed. "Ferryman wanted to congratulate his nephew on his win."

Steele exploded in a string of curses, and I actually thought he was going to punch Dallas out of sheer fury. But he restrained himself with his fists clenched at his sides and an expression of pure violence across his handsome face.

"Dude, I couldn't exactly tell him not to come." Dallas defended himself, holding his hands up. "Besides, he insisted it was just to see Archer. He's not here to cause trouble."

Steele rolled his eyes with a bitter laugh. "Don't be fucking dense, Moore. Ferryman is *only* here to cause trouble. Come on, MK, we need to warn the boys before shit goes down."

He grabbed my hand a bit tighter than necessary, but I shot Dallas a stern glare. "Look after Bree," I ordered him. "She's drunk as shit, and that's on you."

Dallas didn't get a chance to reply as Steele all but dragged me away, heading for the area near the doors where we'd left Archer and Kody only a few minutes ago. Except they were no longer there.

"Shit," Steele cursed, swiping his hand over his face and looking tortured. "This is bad."

"You're going to have to explain this to me, babe," I told him, frowning as his gaze searched the room for his friends. "I'm not getting the panic. Is it just about Ferryman being the leader of the Wraiths? Because I didn't think you three were involved with the Reapers anymore."

Steele grimaced, shaking his head. "We're not. And no, not... totally. Ferryman is a vindictive fuck and holds a stupidly huge grudge against Arch for being named as the sole heir in Phillip's will. Constance wasn't even left with anything, let alone Damien, Zane, or Ferryman."

My brows shot up. "Wow, that explains where all your cars are coming from, I guess."

Steele snorted a laugh. "Not exactly. But yeah, Ferryman is definitely not here to *congratulate his nephew* or whatever other bull-shit he spun to get through the doors. Come on, let's find them."

I bit back my burning need for more answers and let him clutch my hand as we wove between people to hunt for the guest of honor. Luckily, it was an easy case of following the crowds, and we found both Archer and Kody in an outdoor seating area surrounded by people all hanging off their every word.

Steele started toward them, but I jerked to a halt when the girl beside Kody flipped her hair over her shoulder, shifting enough to reveal her face.

"Is that fucking *Drew*?" I exclaimed, rapidly noting her position pasted to Kody's side with her hand wrapped around his leg like she owned him. To his credit, he looked supremely uncomfortable, and as I watched, he peeled her hand off and placed it back in her own lap. Not that she was deterred, though. Her sticky paw was right back on his leg again a second later.

Steele groaned and cursed, then shoved past a couple of people to cross over to the boys.

"Drusilla," he spat at the brunette Reaper pawing all over Kody, "are you lost? Get the fuck out of here."

Kody's ex-girlfriend just sneered up at us, but there was a flicker of unease in her eyes as she took in Steele's expression. "Or else what?" she *stupidly* argued back. "This is neutral territory; I can be here if I want. I'm not breaking any rules."

Kody met my eyes steadily but gave nothing away. Not that I was questioning him… He'd be a fucking idiot to mess around on me, and he damn well knew it.

Steele barked a quick laugh, but it was a cold, hard sound. "I wasn't talking about gang rules, you dumb bitch. You're touching MK's man, and if you don't quit it, she's probably going to break every one of your fingers in six places each. I've been teaching her how."

He wasn't lying. Earlier in the week when Kody was fully engrossed in Archer's training, Steele had deviated off self-defense and wandered into more aggressive skills, which I'd taken to like a duck to water.

Drew turned her sneer on me, but I wasn't in the damn mood. I pushed past Steele and grabbed the persistent bitch's hand off my man's leg, twisting her wrist around and pinning her thumb in a painful lock that allowed me to drag her out of her seat and onto the ground at my feet.

"Get the fuck out of here, you pathetic bitch," I snarled at her, releasing her thumb with a shove that sent her sprawling. It was a bit overkill, but based on the way Steele had reacted to the news of Ferryman being at the party, I was betting we didn't have time for pleasantries.

Drew let out a shriek of outrage, looking to Kody for support, but he just averted his eyes and sipped his drink. Cold as *fuck*.

"Leave," I snapped, letting all my pent-up rage shine through my eyes. "Now."

She wanted to argue, I could see it all over her face, but she was also scared. Not of me—I wasn't all that scary yet—but of Archer and the boys. I could see it in the nervous way her eyes flickered between the three of them and her face lost a bit of color. She'd be getting no backup from any of them. Not tonight, not ever again.

"Just go, Drew," Archer drawled. Every eye in the area was on her. On us. "Climb another social ladder; you've been permanently removed from this one."

It was bad enough that she was being so publicly rejected; I was actually starting to feel bad for her. But then she scrambled to her feet and spat in my face before stomping off into the crowd.

Who fucking *spits* at someone? Of all the revolting things.

"Here," someone said, handing me a legit cotton handkerchief to wipe Drew's nasty saliva from my face. I had screwed my eyes shut instinctively—because fuck getting an eye infection—so it wasn't until I wiped the *ew* off my skin that I saw who'd rescued me with their old-school hanky.

"Uh, thanks?" It was a question, because based on the expressions on the guys' faces—and how Archer and Kody were on their feet now—I was going to guess this wasn't a friend.

The guy smiled at me, and I recognized those eyes. *Ah shit.*

"I'm going to take a wild guess here and assume you're Ferryman?" It really wasn't a huge stretch, given how he looked like an older version of both Archer and Zane. Strong genes in the D'Ath family, apparently.

The older gang leader let his smile spread wider. He was dressed sharply in a white shirt, unbuttoned at the collar, and an expensive sport coat. But every inch of skin from jawline down—every inch visible—was inked, and his hair was slicked back in a short ponytail with the underside shaved.

"And you must be Madison Kate Danvers," he replied, all shiny white teeth and sparkling eyes. "I've heard *so* much about you."

CHAPTER 32

"What the fuck are you doing here, Charon?" Archer growled in a dangerously quiet voice. His strong fingers closed on my hip, tugging me away from his uncle, the Ferryman, leader of the Shadow Grove Wraiths. How the fuck my father had tried to sell the notion that Shadow Grove was now gang free was totally beyond me. In fact, I'd say things were worse than ever.

Ferryman turned that wide, totally fake smile on his nephew, effectively dismissing me from his attention. "I couldn't miss the opportunity to congratulate you on your big win, Archie. Your dad would have been so proud."

Fuck me. If sharks could wear suits…

Archer scoffed a bitter laugh. "My dad would have been a whole number of things, but pride wasn't an emotion he was familiar with. I'm going to ask you once more. What the fuck are you doing here?"

Ferryman cocked his head to the side, his cool eyes sweeping over his nephew, then giving a cursory but cautious glance to Steele and Kody before resting on Archer's hand still on my hip. "What an interesting bunch you four are," he murmured with amusement before snapping his gaze back to Archer's face. "I wanted to speak with you on a business matter, Nephew. A party on neutral ground sounded like the perfect opportunity. Shall we get a drink and move somewhere more private?"

"If you wanted to talk business, Charon, you should have used the correct protocols. This isn't the time or the place." Archer's voice was glacial cold, and I burned with questions. What fucking pull did Archer D'Ath hold over both the Reapers and the Wraiths? I doubted it was simply a blood-connection thing.

"I'm inclined to agree," a familiar voice added, and as if in a scene from a suspense thriller, Zane D'Ath emerged from the crowd of partygoers.

Kody released a long breath in a hiss, and Steele let out a small groan. Archer was like a block of ice, though.

"I guess I missed the memo that this would be a family reunion," Archer commented, his voice calm and emotionless. "Don't tell me you *also* came to congratulate me on my win?" He eyed his older brother with a sneer, but the leader of the Shadow Grove Reapers just smirked.

"Nope, you don't need a bigger ego than you've already got, Little Brother."

I snorted a laugh, then tried to cover it with my hand. At least Zane had that right. My snicker had pulled his attention, though, and he eyed me with an intense gaze.

"I actually didn't come here to see you at all, but I *am* glad I interrupted whatever was going on here." Zane indicated to Ferryman, then propped his hands in his denim pockets to not so subtly show off the gun tucked into his waistband. "What's this business proposition, Charon? I'm most intrigued now."

Ferryman slid his hand to his own waist, where I strongly suspected he had a gun of his own tucked away. The whole thing would turn into a replica of Riot Night in seconds if we didn't do something to diffuse the situation...or at least get it away from all the innocent bystanders.

"Maybe you should take this elsewhere," I murmured to anyone who wanted to listen. The last thing I wanted was to be involved in more collateral damage when the Reapers and Wraiths clashed.

Archer's fingers—still on my hip for some reason—flexed with acknowledgment, and he nodded to Steele in some silent bro language. Steele inclined his head back and disappeared into the venue.

"Like I said," Archer told his uncle and brother, "this isn't the time or the place. Steele will sort us out a meeting room where we can discuss this further, seeing as I doubt either of you will leave until you say what you came to say."

Kody cleared his throat. "I'll also remind you both that Hades's rules still apply, no matter how recently this property was acquired."

Ferryman and Zane both glared at Kody but didn't argue with him. Whoever the fuck this Hades was, he must be someone damn scary to demand that kind of obedience from literal gang leaders.

Steele reappeared near the door, giving the boys a head jerk to indicate he had a private space, and Archer gave me a nudge to walk with them. Except Cass—Zane's tattoo-covered second—put a hand out to stop me.

"Don't bring the girl," he told Archer. His voice was firm but not demanding. It was more like sage advice from a friend than an order. "You know how Charon reacts when he doesn't get his way."

The tension rolled off Archer in waves that I could *feel*, and his jaw clenched so hard I could hear his teeth grinding together.

"I'll stay with her," Kody said quickly. "You go and deal with this shit. We don't need them breaking the truce here of all places."

A quick series of silent communications later, the group of scary-ass gangsters—plus Archer and Steele—disappeared into the venue to discuss some vague "business" together in private.

Kody blew out a long breath, wrapping his arms around me and holding me tight enough to bruise my ribs.

"I should be angry as hell about being excluded from whatever is going on right now," I muttered in his ear as he buried his face in my hair. "But for once I'm kind of glad not to be included. I get the feeling tonight might end in bloodshed."

Kody's chest vibrated against mine as he growled a frustrated noise. "Fuck, I hope not," he replied, releasing me and weaving our fingers together to lead me inside. "We didn't bring anywhere near enough ammo for a fucking gang war tonight."

I raised my brows at him as we made our way over to the bar. "But you brought *some*? Who's armed?" My money was on Steele.

Kody wrinkled his nose at me, a bemused smile on his lips. "Seriously? All of us. Damn, babe, you need to start feeling us up a bit more when we're in public if you didn't know we basically *never* leave the house unarmed." He waved a bartender over and ordered us both nonalcoholic drinks, which told me everything I needed to know about how worried he was.

"Kody," I said, frowning, "you should go and keep an eye on things."

He shot me a quick look, then shook his head. "Nah, they'll be fine. Steele is worth about six dudes, and it looked like Zane only brought Cass with him. Charon probably has his second, Skate, lurking in the shadows somewhere too. But I don't think they came here with the intent to spill blood."

That only made me *more* concerned. "You don't think? Well, I don't think either Zane or Ferryman thought their rival gang would be here either. But they are, and I can't help feeling like we just tossed a bucket of liquid nitroglycerine into a room and are now crossing our fingers that it won't explode."

Kody grimaced, and I knew he agreed.

"Look," I continued, "I get that Cass thinks it's a bad idea to bring me in, and I'm inclined to agree. Archer needs you guys one hundred percent focused on keeping *him* alive, and I'd only be a distraction. But you're never going to forgive yourself if something happens because you were too busy babysitting me to watch his back." Not to mention the fact that I'd never forgive *myself*. The three of them had a bond unlike anything I'd experienced, and I couldn't be the weak link.

He wavered for a second, his gaze shifting in the direction of the back room where the boys had gone, and I knew he was tempted. "No," he replied, shaking his head. "I'm not leaving you alone out here. Did you forget that people are trying to kill you?"

I snorted. "Like I ever could. But also, what if Ferryman is behind all of that?" It wasn't something I'd considered before, but nothing was beyond the realm of possibility.

"Babe," Kody groaned, "please don't make this harder than it needs to be. Arch and Steele trust me to keep *you* safe, so that's what I'm going to do. End of discussion."

I rolled my eyes, but the stubborn set to his jaw told me he wasn't going to be easily persuaded otherwise. We took our drinks and wandered a bit until we spotted Bree and Dallas, who'd very much made up from their fight.

"Geez, guys," I teased as Kody and I joined them at a low table where Bree was straddling Dallas and trying to eat his face off, "get a room or something."

They both startled, Bree almost falling off Dallas's lap, but she quickly recovered to smooth her silky brown hair back and tug her short skirt back down to cover her panties.

"Oh, hey," she replied, acting like she *hadn't* been grinding all over Dallas a second ago. She casually slid into her own seat and sipped her drink. "Did, uh, are things all okay?" Her nervous gaze darted between Kody and me as we pulled up chairs of our own.

Dallas cleared his throat, leaning forward with a concerned frown. "Kody, man, I didn't know Ferryman was going to—"

"Forget it," Kody snapped, cutting him off. "It wouldn't have actually been so bad if Zane weren't here too."

Dallas's eyes widened and he whispered a curse.

"Well, that sounds like a bad time," Bree muttered, swiping a hand through her hair. She was still drunk as hell, her cheeks pink and her eyes glazed. "Let's just hope tonight doesn't end up with my bestie locked up in a cell again, huh?"

I scowled. "Gee, thanks, Bree."

She gave me a drunken shrug. "What? It's true."

Kody just let out a frustrated sigh and sat back in his chair, his hand resting on my bare thigh. This time, though, it was a gesture of protection and safety rather than a teasing touch that might turn into more if I let him.

Dallas let out a groaning sound of frustration, his eyes going to a table not far from us where a group of people played a game of pool. One of them was Drew, which gave me a solid clue Dallas was groaning at the fact that she was accompanied by several other tattooed Reapers. How the fuck all these punks had gotten into the party, I didn't know. Probably paid someone off.

Still, there were cops stationed near the exits—looking bored, but present nonetheless—so I didn't think anyone was going to be dumb enough to start shit.

A couple of the guys playing pool with Drew, guys with prominent Reaper tattoos on the sides of their necks, spotted Dallas sitting with us, and Kody let out a sigh.

"Great, here we fucking go," he muttered under his breath, his grip on my thigh tightening and his chair subtly shifting closer to me. Possessive fucker.

"Yo, Kody," one of the guys called out, swaggering over, his sagging jeans barely covering his ass, with one of his buddies close behind. "The fuck are you doing sitting here with a Wraith?" He spat the rival gang name out like it was a curse.

Kody slouched in his chair, his elbow crooked up on the back like he was totally relaxed. "I'll sit with whoever the fuck I want, Guard Rail. You gonna question me?" His brow arched at the punk-ass kid, who was rapidly second-guessing his decision to walk over here in the first place. His eyes darted between Kody and Dallas nervously, and his tongue flicked over his lips.

What kind of stupid-ass name was Guard Rail, anyway? Who named these idiots?

"Nah, bro, I was just joking around," he replied with a forced, terrified kind of laugh. "You guys wanna play a game of pool?" He jerked his thumb over his shoulder to the pool table where one of his other friends was racking up the balls.

Kody and Dallas exchanged a look. I knew neither of them cared for each other, but this seemed like one of those "the enemy of my enemy is my friend" sort of situations, and Kody gave the Reaper a nod. "Sure, why not."

We got up to relocate to the pool table, and Kody held me back with an arm around my waist, his face dipping to my ear. "Are you going to be okay with Drew around, or do you want me to toss her ass out of here?"

Knowing that he'd do that for me, I couldn't help the cruel smile pulling at my lips. "I'll be fine so long as she stops putting her dirty paws all over you. And if she spits at me again, I'm personally going to punch her so hard that her implants pop. Clear?"

Kody laughed, his breath feathering my skin. "Clear. But I kinda think you kicking her ass would be all kinds of sexy. I need to have a chat with Steele about that *self-defense* training, though."

I snickered an evil sort of sound and walked with him over to the pool table. The Reaper boys suggested we play teams, but Bree was swaying on her heels so I declined. I was happy to just watch until Archer and Steele returned from their top-secret meeting.

For the most part, I just ignored Drew and chatted with Bree while the boys started their game. But it didn't take long for her to slide around the pool table and give me a false-as-fuck smile.

"Maybe we got off on the wrong foot," she said to me in a sickly sweet voice. "We should start over."

I arched a brow at her, and Bree did a totally unsubtle

bitch-cough that almost made me crack up laughing. "I mean, should we, though?"

A familiar face caught my attention in the crowd, and I touched Kody on the elbow. "Hey, Jase just got here. Is it me, or was he supposed to be at the fight fucking hours ago?"

Kody glared in the direction I pointed. "Yeah. He should have been."

His manager was making his way over to us with a cagey, paranoid look on his face. What the fuck had he been up to that was more important than Archer's fight?

"I'll get us some drinks," Drew offered, her tone all kinds of fake bright. "It's the least I can do after what happened earlier."

I scowled after her as she sashayed off toward the bar, but she was the least of my concerns. Some desperate chick who couldn't take no for an answer? She wasn't even factoring into my top five problems.

"She seems like a fucking bitch," Bree slurred, leaning her ass against the pool table while one of the Reapers lined up his shot.

One of the other girls who had been hanging around sent Bree a poisonous glare, but we both ignored her. The Reaper girls and their jealousy were like getting mosquito bites while swimming in crocodile-infested waters.

"Fucking hell, he's drunk," Kody murmured as Jase reached us and the potent stench of alcohol rolled off him. "Are you okay a minute? I need to have words with him." He paused, frowning. "I'll be right there." He pointed to a free table just a short distance away. "Dallas, you'll keep an eye on her?"

Dallas jerked a nod. "Of course."

Kody handed me his pool cue and dragged his drunk manager away from us to exchange some words, leaving me to take the next shot for him.

"You're up, Danvers," one of the Reaper boys announced. "Show us what you've got." He was eyeing me with way too much interest, and I wasn't the only one who noticed.

"Pull your fucking eyes back in your head before Kody sees you checking out his girl," the other punk—the one with the stupid-ass fucking name—hissed at his friend, whacking him with the back of his hand. "Uh, he didn't mean anything by that," he assured me, nervous as fuck, and I rolled my eyes.

"Whatever," I muttered, and Dallas snickered. I checked out the spread of balls on the table and picked my shot. As I leaned over to take the shot, Drew returned with a drink in each hand. She scoffed a laugh, and I narrowed my eyes at her.

"You got something to say?" I asked her, my voice cold and threatening.

She just rolled her eyes, setting the two drinks down on the side of the pool table. "Uh, yeah, there's no way you're making that shot."

What a fucking walking cliché. I snapped my wrist forward, nailing the shot and sending my chosen ball careening into the pocket.

Drew rolled her eyes like she'd been taking lessons from Regina George her whole life. "Yeah, well, I bet you can't do it again," she declared with a sassy lip purse.

Bree laughed beside me, leaning her drunk ass on the side of the table. "Of course she can," she replied for me. "In fact, if she gets it, then you have to down that whole drink in one go." I shot Bree a sharp look, but she wasn't focused on me.

Drew was so supremely confident, though, and I wanted to see her taken down a peg. She brushed her hair back, flashing the Reaper mark on her wrist. "Okay then, but if she misses, then your *Princess* has to do the same. And with a real drink, not that soda water shit she's been sipping on."

I shrugged. One drink wasn't exactly going to get me drunk, so who the fuck cared? "Sure," I replied, already eyeing up my next shot. I'd grown up as a bored only child with a father who had more money than god. I'd had my own pool table and I knew how to play. This wasn't even a challenge.

Rolling my shoulders, I leaned over the table, my breasts brushing the green felt as I lined up with the white ball and...

Bang!

My shot went wide, but I didn't fucking care. That'd been from the "private room" where Archer and Steele had gone with the gang leaders. I didn't think it was a gunshot, but...

"Kody!" I shouted, but he was already rushing back over to me. "Go!" I ordered him, pointing in the direction of the sound. His expression was torn, but I shoved him in the chest. "Go *now*. I'm fine here with Dallas and Bree."

"And me," Jase slurred, clapping Kody on the shoulder. "We can handle looking after one spoiled-brat girl. Go keep the boys alive, yeah?"

But still, Kody looked conflicted.

"Kody, fucking *go*. If it's all okay, you can be back here in seconds, but if it's not..." I didn't need to convince him any further. He grabbed my face, kissing me quickly.

"Don't fucking move from this spot, babe. I'll be right back."

As he rushed in the direction of his friends, I couldn't fight the sick feeling of unease pooling in my belly. No one outside of our little group seemed to have even noticed the sound, though. Or maybe they had but paid it no mind as they didn't know *who* was in that room. Let alone how armed they all were.

Turning back to the pool table, I found Drew standing there with a wide grin and a drink in her hand.

"You missed," she informed me, like I fucking cared. "Drink up."

She held the cup out to me, and I scowled at her. I'd missed the shot because something was going wrong in this "civil business discussion," but apparently no one else seemed concerned.

I wanted to throw the drink all over her and tell her to go fuck herself, but I also hated people who backed out of bets simply because they lost. Especially when the punishment was something as pathetic as drinking a drink.

Still, I was no moron. I ignored the drink Drew was trying to hand me and took hers instead. Call me crazy, but the eager way she'd tried to get me to drink *that* drink? She'd almost certainly spat in it or something.

Holding her eyes, I tipped her drink to my lips—ugh, gross, gin and tonic—and drained the whole thing before slamming it back down on the edge of the pool table.

"Happy?" I asked her, licking my lips and cringing at the bitter taste her drink had left behind.

The dark scowl on her face confirmed my suspicions, and she hurled "my" drink on the ground in a bit of a diva tantrum before trying to get in my face. I was a few inches taller than her, though, and if intimidation was her aim, she was falling way short. Literally and figuratively.

"Watch your fucking back, bitch," she hissed at me, pointing with her sharp, little red fingernail. "I'm coming for you."

Drew stomped off and I sighed. So much for her weak effort at "starting over."

Fake bitch.

CHAPTER 33

Kody didn't immediately return from the back room, and after a couple of minutes, I started worrying. Big time. My palms were sweating and I couldn't stop staring at the door he'd disappeared through, even though I knew it hadn't been long.

"Maybe just have another drink and relax a bit," Jase suggested with a sneer, like he found me totally pathetic for being concerned. "You're so fucking uptight. Have the boys stopped fucking you or something?"

He was drunk as shit, but that was no excuse. I grabbed him by the collar and hauled his unkempt face to mine. "Insult me again, Jase. I fucking dare you."

But he just curled his lip at me, and I released him with a shove. Something was wrong, I could feel it. My stomach was churning with anxiety, and I could feel sweat rolling down my spine.

"Dallas, something isn't right," I declared, my worried gaze still on that back room doorway. "How long has he been gone?"

My friend shook his head. "Like, maybe two minutes? Don't stress, Katie. Kody wouldn't leave you out here with me for long." His smile was all arrogance, and I snorted a laugh.

"Uh-huh, 'cause he's so worried you'll put the moves on and

steal me away?" I grinned, trying desperately to shove aside the gnawing feeling of panic that had seemed to manifest in me as physical illness. "Remember the one and only time we slept together?" I wrinkled my nose, expecting him to laugh with me.

I'd been a fourteen-year-old virgin, woefully inexperienced in *anything* sexual, and he'd been one of my best friends. We'd also been crazy high from smoking joints in my bedroom. To say it'd been awkward was an understatement, and then we'd ended up in a huge argument because I saw Dallas's fresh Wraith's tattoo...

"I remember it," he replied, but his tone was so much more serious than mine. He stepped closer to me, crowding me against the edge of the pool table and reaching a finger up to stroke my hair. "I think about it all the time."

"Uh..." The room was starting to spin, and I second-guessed what I'd just heard. Had he just hit on me? What the...? "Dallas, I'm not—"

I didn't get any further before Bree appeared beside us with an expression of pure betrayal and horror on her face. "Are you fucking serious?" she shrieked. "This is so fucking *typical*." She spun on her heels and took off in the direction of the bathrooms, leaving me feeling like a total fucking shithead.

"What the fuck, Dallas?" I shouted, shoving him in the chest to move him away from me. "What is *wrong* with you?"

He shook his head, swiping his hands over his face. "That's not what I meant! Fuck, *fuck*, dammit, Kate, I wasn't hitting on you! Ugh, Bree thinks—"

"I know exactly what she thinks, you moron," I snapped, shoving him again for good measure. "I need to talk to her." I started to follow her, but Dallas caught my wrist with his hand.

"Wait, I should go," he told me, looking all kinds of tortured. "I need to explain. She'll be fine when I can explain."

I bit my lip, considering. As badly as I wanted to go and comfort my friend, I also cared about Dallas. He needed an opportunity to redeem himself. "Fine," I growled, "but you better grovel and kiss her shoes and, for the love of God, Dallas, make her understand that you're *not into me*."

He nodded frantically and took off after Bree, not even hesitating before barging into the women's bathroom after her.

I let out a shaky sigh, glancing around. Jase was nowhere to be seen, unsurprisingly, and the Reapers we'd been playing pool with seemed to have moved on to a game of flip cup with a bunch of older MMA fans.

My stomach rolled again, and I swiped my hand over my forehead. It came away damp with sweat, and I swallowed heavily. I'd been right before. Something was wrong, *really* wrong. But I hadn't realized it was *me* that was in trouble...until now.

Breathing in short, sharp gasps, I tried to make my way across to the bathrooms. I needed to find Bree and Dallas. I needed to alert them that I'd been drugged. I needed water. I needed to ride out whatever had been in Drew's drink. More than *anything* I needed my guys...but I couldn't go barging in there now. Not like this. I needed to just weather the storm and hope to fuck Drew had only spiked her gin with a recreational drug like MDMA or speed.

Halfway to the bathroom, my ankle rolled in my heels, and I started to crash to the floor—only to be caught by a strong arm around my waist.

"Whoa, Madison Kate," the vaguely familiar voice said with a laugh. "I think maybe you've had one too many?"

I blinked up at my rescuer a couple of times, trying to clear the double vision that had just started. "Bark? What are you..." I dimly remembered seeing him in the parking lot on my way in, arguing with his dad, Professor Barker. "I'm fine," I lied, swatting his hand away from me. "Seriously, I just need water."

He frowned like he didn't believe me or like he was going to argue, but another guy in an SGU Ghosts jacket grabbed him by the sleeve and dragged him away to the bar, where a bunch of other football players were hanging out with girls.

Bark turned once, shooting me a concerned look, but I waved him off while doing my very best sober face. The whole venue was spinning dangerously, though, and I was almost positive I'd vomit before I reached the exit. Fuck finding Bree and Dallas—I needed fresh air.

"Miss," someone asked me as I staggered my way to the front doors, "are you okay? Do you need help?"

I shook my head, waving them off. "I'm fine," I insisted, but it just came out as a slur. My tongue felt heavy in my mouth and my chest was tight, like I couldn't get enough air. I brushed the helpful person off and burst through the doors, desperately trying to suck in air as I stumbled down the steps.

My legs weren't obeying me, though, and my ankles rolled. Sharp pain seared through me as my knees scraped against the hard concrete, followed by my palms. My wrists gave out and my face smacked into the rough asphalt. The coppery taste of blood filled my mouth. I moaned in pain but I couldn't move. Everything was getting dark, my lungs screaming in pain as my gasping breaths pulled shorter and sharper with every inhale.

Whatever was in Drew's drink…it was a hell of a lot worse than Molly.

Rough hands grabbed me, lifting me up like a rag doll and manhandling me into a vaguely standing position. None of my limbs worked anymore, though, so it was as effective as making a wet noodle stand up. My vision was nothing but a swirling vortex of shadows and lights, so even when the person smacked my face several times and peeled my lids back, I saw no distinguishable faces.

A moment later, a sharp, biting pain struck my nose high up in my nasal passage like I'd just inhaled something toxic, and a strangled scream wrenched from my throat. The person holding

298

me shifted his grip—I was assuming it was a *he*—and threw me over his shoulder. Vomit rolled in my stomach, threatening to eject now that I was upside down, but surprisingly I could breathe a little easier.

Flashes of vision broke the shadows, and I blinked sluggishly as my face passed car tires and my abductor's boots crushed the gravel. A dim popping sound rattled through my brain, and I wondered if that was my brain cells exploding. Whether maybe whatever I'd been drugged with was causing massive brain aneurysms or maybe my eardrum had just burst.

The guy carrying me jerked to a stop, and my face smacked against the rough fabric of his pants. Voices. I could hear voices. Sort of. Everything was muffled and dull, like I was underwater. The voice crackled and broke, like the reception was bad, and shadows swirled once more. They sucked me under, luring me with a promise of no more pain. All I needed to do was…let go…

My body jolted, spasms jerking my muscles in weird, excruciating ways, and I moaned in agony. My abductor was saying something to me, but I couldn't make out the words. How could I when my ears no longer worked? It was just the beginning of the end, and I doubted that journey would be a long one. Sweet darkness beckoned me, and I was too weak to resist. Pain wracked my body and dampness coated my cheeks, and I simply didn't want to exist anymore.

Then I was falling. Tumbling endlessly like Alice down the rabbit hole, and when I hit the bottom, I'd never get out again.

Thump.

I hit the bottom with enough force to shatter every bone in my body. The only beacon of hope was the shadowy outline of a person outlined way, way above me. But then everything went black.

I was alone. Broken in the dark and unable to move.

This was the end.

CHAPTER 34

I'd never thought too carefully about my own death or mortality before. Which seemed odd, considering how many near-death experiences I'd had in my lifetime. But if forced to think on the notion of death, afterlife, or anything in between, I'd have said there would be *something*.

Nonetheless, even having never considered my own death in detail, I was still surprised. Or…confused. There was no bright light at the end of a hallway. No angels beckoning for me to join them. No sparkly, magical cloud overflowing with sexy, muscular men waiting on me hand and foot. There was just…

Darkness.

But then, was I really dead at all? I tried to move, but my body spasmed again, churning my stomach painfully and threatening to make me vomit into the darkness. If I were dead, would I feel the need to throw up? Probably not. Right?

My breathing wasn't as labored anymore, and even though one of my arms burned like I'd been struck with a hot poker, I no longer felt like I was drowning. So where the fuck was I? And why was it so dark?

I was far from okay—so freaking far from okay—but I gritted my teeth together hard and stretched out my hand. Slow and cautious, not making any sudden movements that might make my body revolt against me again. At first, I felt nothing. Nothing. Just the endless space of darkness, and my breath spiked in the panic of that. Of the idea that I was in some kind of dark abyss…but then my fingers touched something hard, physical, and I released a shaking sigh.

Groaning in pain, I stretched my arm out farther, exploring my surroundings. It only took a matter of moments for the panic to set back in again.

"Holy fuck," I squeaked as my lungs tightened up again. "Fuck, no. No, no, no." My frantic plea dissolved into sobs as the reality sunk into my drug-affected brain. I was in the trunk of someone's car, I was almost certain. My legs were cramped up to my chest and my back was pressed tight to the trunk lining. There was something so distinctive about the rough carpet that lined car trunks, and considering my last memory was in a parking lot? Yeah, it wasn't a huge stretch.

"Help!" I cried out, feeling the wetness on my cheeks as tears streamed from my eyes. I'd been so careful, so fucking careful to never end up in small, dark places. Ever since that night where I'd watched my mother's murder from the safety of her closet. Ever since my therapist had diagnosed my lingering claustrophobia. Ever since I'd discovered that one thing that filled me with total debilitating fear and blind panic, I'd stayed well clear of small, dark spaces.

That one time, on Riot Night, when Kody and Archer had dragged me into the supply closet of the fun house, that was as close as I'd come in *years*. The only reason my mind hadn't snapped into full-blown terror that night was Kody. His reassuring presence, the way he'd distracted me and pulled my mind away from my panic.

But he wasn't here now. I was alone. Completely alone and no one knew where I was.

No one…except whoever had dumped me here.

That thought alone helped me push through my terror, if only to replace it with new fears. He'd locked me in the trunk of a car, drugged and half-dead. What were his plans for me? Leave me here to die? Or come back and finish the job with his hands?

Frantic, I tried to shift my position, searching for a release handle on the inside. All modern cars had them; they were a standard safety feature in case someone accidentally became locked in the trunk. But…what if this wasn't a modern car? What if…

Even in the pitch-blackness, my head spun with dizziness, and I sucked in a shuddering sob as I tried to get myself under control. Everything hurt—my stomach was twisted in knots, my limbs all ached, and I was coated in a cold sheen of sweat. Most of all, my head was *pounding*.

I called out again, but my voice was weak and thready. Pathetic. No one was ever going to hear me. No one would find me until it was too late. Until my oxygen ran out and I suffocated in this metal coffin, and even then it wouldn't be until my body decayed that anyone would open the random, abandoned car trunk in the parking lot of some shitty reception hall in the middle of nowhere.

A panicked moan tore from my throat, and I thrashed around, striking out with my hands and feet, desperate for some way out of the trunk. It was totally futile, of course, and just left me bloody and bruised, gasping for air and positive my real death was on the horizon.

Something tickled my bare leg, and I froze. It happened again, and I looked down on reflex. There was still no light, but somehow now I could see my legs. I could see my legs *and* the hundreds of spiders suddenly crawling all over them, swarming my body like they planned to smother me.

I screamed, then. I screamed and screamed as their tiny legs crawled all over me, touching every inch of my body, burrowing under my clothes. And then they started to bite me. Over and over and over and all I could do was howl in agony and terror while their venom flooded my bloodstream and paralyzed me.

Light flared above me, burning my retinas. I was already screaming, though, and the pain of the light was nothing compared to the spiders all over me. There was another sound now, though, something more than just the hollow sound of my own terror. Something deeper. Something not coming from me.

Searing heat brushed my skin, and I shrieked, my voice cracking as I sobbed uncontrollably and moaned. "Please stop," I cried, praying to any and all deities ever created. Surely one of them would help me. Surely. "Please, please, please, make it stop," I sobbed. "Get them off, get them off me, get them off." My words were all slurring together as my mind slowly cracked and the dark void of insanity called to me.

"...she can't hear you," someone said, their words reaching my ears as I gasped for air and whimpered. A sharp, stinging pain jabbed my upper arm, and I moaned as heat burned through my muscle.

Somewhere in the back of my mind I recognized that I'd been found. Someone had found me...but they were too late.

My panicked words dissolved into mumbles as I pleaded for them to get the spiders off. Just *get them off me!*

Huge hands stroked my face over and over, brushing my hair back. Soft, low, *familiar* murmurs rumbled through my ear, grounding me and slowly, ever so fucking slowly, bringing my elevated heart rate down. I knew that voice. I knew it. I trusted it. That wasn't the voice of whoever had dumped me in that trunk.

"...need to get her to a hospital," someone was saying. Someone farther away. The murmuring in my ear didn't let up, though, and I clung on to it like a life raft. The crawling sensation of spiders was fading away, replaced with uncontrollable shivering.

"Hey, hey, hey, shhh, come on, baby girl, don't do this," the voice whispered in my ear, so close I wondered if I was imagining it. The voice was almost *inside* my head. "Kate, baby, come on, stay with me. We've got you. We've got you. We've got you."

I couldn't stop the trembling, though. Something was still so very wrong. Suddenly it was like my whole form lost all density. I was weightless, floating, incorporeal...my featherlight eyelids fluttered open, trying to fix on my surroundings. I hadn't even realized they were closed, but as I blinked the shadows and glowing orbs away, I found the face of my rescuer.

And *screamed*.

But the fear was only momentary as the macabre, decaying clown's face flickered before my eyes like an out-of-tune television set and reformed as a face I knew. A face I fucking *trusted* now, despite all the secrets.

I threw my arms around his neck and pulled my whole body tight to him, as much as I was capable of with my shaking, pain-filled limbs. My chest heaved and gut-wrenching sobs wracked through me as I buried my face in his skin, inhaling the heady scent of oaky wood and subtle florals with gasping breaths.

"Shhh, Kate, I've got you," he whispered in my ear, his huge hands stroking down my spine over and over, his arms holding me tight and totally erasing the crawling feeling of insects. "You're safe. I've got you," he whispered. "I'm never letting you go. Not ever."

Someone else was talking, but I wasn't listening. My head was still swimming, my balance completely shot and my skin hurting all over...I wasn't okay.

"...needs to be checked out," the other person was saying, and another pair of hands touched my shoulders. I howled at the touch and shrunk myself smaller in Archer's embrace, shuddering and crying. I didn't mean to, but I wasn't in full control of my own actions. He just held me tighter, though, quietly cursing out whoever had just touched me.

I don't know how long we stayed like that, sitting on the cold gravel of the parking lot, but after some time I heard another familiar voice.

"Hey, gorgeous," Steele murmured, crouching beside us and stroking my hair gently. I knew it was him, and I didn't freak out like before. He just had an unmistakable presence about him. "We need to get you to a hospital and get you checked out. Is that okay?"

I understood what he was saying, logically, but that sentient part of me was trapped in a cage of fear, hallucinations, nausea, and *pain*. Still, after a moment or two, I was able to force a tiny nod of acknowledgment, and Steele blew out a heavy sigh of relief.

"Okay, beautiful. Can you let go of Arch? The paramedics want to pop you in the ambulance."

This time I managed a headshake. Nope. I couldn't *physically* make myself release my death grip on Archer... If they tried to make me, then I was going to—

"Whoa, baby girl, calm down," Archer's voice rumbled in my ear. "Calm down; no one is going to force you to do *anything*." This seemed to be pointed at someone else, and I caught the low rumble of Kody's voice responding with some colorful cursing.

"Arch's right," Steele added, "but we need to get you to a hospital. Are you okay if he carries you?"

I didn't know. Was I? Or would the motion of being carried just remind me of whoever had grabbed me outside the bar and dumped me in that trunk? But then, I could feel the drugs still coursing through my veins, making me physically ill. I needed help, medical help, before I ended up with long-term side effects.

Or death.

The boys must have taken my lack of an answer as acceptance because the next thing I knew, both Archer and I were in the back of an ambulance. I still wouldn't let anyone else touch me, though, and for the duration of the drive, the paramedics were forced to check my vitals by giving Archer instructions for what to do.

Just as the ambulance slowed to a stop and one of the paramedics moved to open the doors, I started trembling uncontrollably. My teeth chattered and my spine went rigid in Archer's grip, and then...it all went black again.

CHAPTER 35

When I woke up again, I was lying in a hospital bed with an IV line attached and an oxygen mask over my face. All three boys sat by my bed, but this time I didn't start screaming and accuse Archer of trying to kill me. This time, he'd been the one who'd saved me.

My mouth was drier than a desert, but Kody quickly offered me a cup of ice chips, which I gratefully accepted after tugging the oxygen mask off my face.

"What happened?" I asked when my mouth had regained a bit of moisture, but my voice came out husky and raw, giving me vague flashbacks of screaming. Lots of screaming.

"How are you feeling?" Steele asked, taking my hand that wasn't attached to an IV line and linking our fingers together. "You gave us a pretty bad scare, gorgeous."

I frowned. My brain was like mashed potato, and all my thoughts scattered and spliced with scenes from some kind of horror movie. "I feel like decaying roadkill," I replied in that hoarse whisper. "What *happened* to me?"

Steele shot a look at the other boys, not answering me. "Maybe we should get the doctor in here now that she's awake?"

"No," Kody replied, folding his arms. His brow was drawn in

a deep scowl, and his green eyes swam with worry. "No, tell her everything we know. Secrets just keep biting us in the ass, and I'm fucking done. Tell her what happened, and then we'll let the doc know she's awake."

Steele let out a frustrated sigh, sweeping his hand over his face and fiddling with his eyebrow piercing. He looked to Archer, but the big guy just gave a stern nod.

"We don't fully understand how it happened," Steele said, his gray eyes holding mine as he spoke softly and carefully, "but your toxicology report showed fentanyl in your system. Based on how out of it you were, it's safe to say you'd had an overdose."

My brows shot up and my pulse raced. "Isn't that lethal?"

"Yes," Kody replied before Steele could sugarcoat it. Not that he would, but Kody was clearly at the end of his patience about something. "In large doses, like we suspect you were given, yeah, it's lethal. Fast too."

I swallowed, remembering how fast it'd acted after I drank Drew's drink. How my body had failed me on the way out to the parking lot…

"So why aren't I dead?" I asked.

The three of them exchanged a look—sounds hard to do, but they pulled it off—before Steele answered me. "We think someone gave you a dose of Narcan before you were locked in the trunk of my car. Your nose was bloody, and there was no way you wouldn't have been dead otherwise."

I frowned, reaching my hand up to touch my nose. There had been something…

"So someone tried to kill me, then changed their mind and gave me an opioid reversal, but then dumped me in the trunk of your car to…what?" It wasn't making sense. Why bother drugging me in the first place? "Wait," I said, closing my eyes and rubbing at them. I was still so dizzy and nauseous. "Wait, it wasn't my drink. It was Drew's."

Kody shouted a curse, scrubbing his hand over his face, and Archer just looked grim.

"That sort of makes more sense," Steele pondered aloud, tapping at his chin with his fingertips. "The fentanyl was meant for Drew—to kill her—but MK drank it instead, and whoever was responsible panicked and tried to reverse the dose with Narcan."

This was all making my head pound. "Why was someone trying to kill Drew?"

"Any one of probably a hundred reasons," Steele muttered, a bit snarky.

"None of which we can *ask* her," Kody added. He blew out a long breath, rubbing his tired eyes before meeting my gaze. "Drew was murdered tonight. Her throat was slit and her body left behind the dumpsters at the party venue."

My jaw dropped. "What?"

Kody grimaced, and now I understood why he was so worked up. His ex-girlfriend had been murdered and his current girlfriend almost murdered… Yeah, that was bound to wind the tension up pretty tight.

"I'm going to get the doctor," Steele announced, standing up from his chair. "MK needs to be checked over properly, now that she's awake."

Neither of the boys objected this time, so I got the feeling they'd told me everything important. Or anything directly relating to how I'd almost died in the trunk of a car, at any rate.

"Can I get you anything?" Kody offered when I remained silent after Steele left the room. "I don't know if food is allowed, but I can go and ask."

My stomach churned violently at the mention of food, and I groaned. "No food," I replied with a grimace. "I feel like I'm hovering on the edge of vomiting as it is."

Kody nodded, frowning. "That's the fentanyl, I think. The paramedics gave you a dose of Narcan when we found you and it's in your IV, but it'll take a few hours yet for the fentanyl to pass through your system."

"Kody," Archer said, speaking for the first time since I'd woken up, with his voice low and husky, "can you give us a second? Go and grab us all some coffees or some shit."

Kody scowled. "That takes longer than a *second*, dickhead."

Archer turned a scathing glare on his friend. "So?"

Kody glared back but crossed the small room and pressed a kiss on my forehead. "Press your nurse buzzer if he pisses you off, okay? I'll be quick."

"It's fine," I assured him, blinking my heavy lids as he frowned in concern, then shot Archer a warning glare on his way out of my room.

Silence fell over the room as the door clicked shut once more, but for once it wasn't an uncomfortable silence. Archer made no move to speak, staring off into the distance like he was totally lost in his own thoughts, so I let my eyes close. Just for a moment.

I didn't even realize I'd fallen asleep until a warm hand touched mine, threading our fingers together. I cracked my lids and found Archer had moved from his seat in the corner of the room and taken Steele's right beside my bed. It was his fingers laced with mine, and his head bent over our hands like he was praying.

"Hey," I croaked, and his face shot up with a slightly panicked expression.

"Shit, I'm sorry. I didn't mean to wake you up." He started to release my hand, but I tightened my fingers around his, indicating that I wanted him to stay.

I let out a yawn. "It's fine. I wasn't asleep. Just…"

He grimaced. "Out of it."

"Yup," I agreed.

We fell silent again, and my gaze dropped to our hands. His thumb was rubbing small circles on my skin, and that small gesture gave me so much comfort it was almost staggering.

"You saved me," I whispered after some time.

Archer shook his head, not meeting my eyes. "I never should have left you alone. That whole meeting with Zane and Charon… what if that'd been a diversion? A distraction to strip you of backup?"

I gave a soft snort. "But it wasn't. That drugged drink was meant for Drew. I was just a fucking moron for drinking it."

He let out a shaking sigh but still didn't look at me. He just lowered his head until his face touched our joined hands, his eyes shut tight, and stayed like that while I drifted back into a weird, scattered dream state that made my pulse race.

I was kept in the hospital overnight for observation while the fentanyl passed through my system. It was a long night of vomiting, nausea, headaches, and panic attacks, but I didn't spend even a second of it alone. The guys took it in shifts to stay with me, and I took a huge amount of strength from their continued presence in my room, despite all the drama they must have been dealing with outside.

The police came by twice to speak with me during the night. Once to question me about my "attack" and ask what—if anything—I remembered about the person who'd given me that first dose of Narcan and locked me in the trunk of Steele's car. The second time was to interview me about Drew's death.

I wasn't a suspect in any way—my alibi was pretty solid—but a whole heap of people had seen me argue with her earlier in the evening. It was hard to believe in coincidences when I was almost killed and she *was*.

One of the cops let it slip that Drew had been found with a bag of Rohypnol in her pocket and they speculated that it was a gang-related crime. But a sinking feeling in my gut told me why she'd been in possession of that particular drug.

She'd tried to roofie me.

I'd been right to avoid the drink she was offering me, but I'd been oh so wrong in taking hers instead.

It was midmorning by the time my doctor cleared me for discharge, on strict orders to rest and maintain fluids for the next few days. He reminded me no less than six times of the fact that I was lucky to be alive and—essentially—not to fuck up again.

The boys drove me home in silence, everyone exhausted from a long-ass night, and I let myself doze off a couple of times in the back seat with my head propped on Kody's shoulder.

It wasn't until Steele stopped the car in front of our decorative iron gates with that ostentatious monogrammed *D* that I yawned and sat up.

"Why are we stopped?" I asked, my voice thick with sleep as I blinked focus into my eyes. The gates had rolled open on their automatic motor, but our car wasn't moving. Steele and Archer just sat there staring ahead like they'd seen a ghost.

Neither of them replied, but Archer released a heavy sigh and got out of the car. He walked around in front of the hood and stooped to pick something up, making my stomach drop to my feet.

Fucking stalker mail.

Like *that* was what I needed after a night in the hospital recovering from a drug overdose.

He got back into the car without a word, the large box on his lap, and Steele continued up our long driveway to the house. We all made our way inside, taking seats in the den where the comfiest couches were located, and Archer set the box on the coffee table.

No one spoke. We all just stared at the fucking thing like we expected it to grow legs and start doing the moonwalk down the length of the table.

"You gonna open it?" Kody asked after a few minutes, raising a brow at Archer. I don't know why he was being nominated, but I was just glad it wasn't me.

Archer cocked a brow at me, but I just shrugged and snuggled closer into Kody's side as he wrapped his arm around me. The box was a lot bigger than my previous stalker mail, so I had to assume it contained more than just a Barbie doll and some photos. Hopefully it was nothing dead this time. I'd had enough death in the past twenty-four hours to last me a lifetime.

But Archer reached into the box, looking resigned, and pulled out a replica black '67 Impala…just like Steele's car that we'd driven to the fight and the party. Just like the one that I'd been stuffed into the trunk of when I was overdosing on a drug ten times more lethal than heroin.

"Let me guess," I drawled—or tried to because my voice was still all rough and painful, "there's something in the trunk, isn't there?"

Archer flicked the little latch and lifted the mini trunk lid, revealing another Barbie doll all squished up to fit in the small space. Shocker.

"Well, at least we know who was responsible for Drew's death," Steele commented, having reached into the box and pulled out the stack of photographs there. There was one of Drew and me standing near the pool table and seeming to talk in a friendly way while Kody and Dallas stared at the pool table. Then another of Drew at the bar, talking to a rough-looking guy with a Wraith's tattoo on his neck. Then another of her dropping something into one of the two drinks the bartender placed in front of her. The last two photos were what made bile rise in my throat and my hands start to tremble.

One was me—totally out of it with my eyes just narrow slits—curled up in Steele's trunk. The fucker must have taken it before locking me in there.

The other was of Drew, dead, lying in a pool of her own blood with a gaping wound across her throat. Her lifeless eyes stared up at me from the paper, accusing, and I knew it was an image I'd never be rid of.

Steele pulled out a small digital recorder from the box and clicked Play before I could even think of an objection. I braced myself, expecting to hear my stalker's voice. But then…that'd be stupid. One thing my stalker most definitely was *not* was stupid.

Instead it was Drew's voice that had been recorded—Drew and a guy I didn't recognize but had to assume was the Wraith in the photo. None of us reacted as Drew's conversation filled the room, laughing with the guy as she detailed her plan. She was so casual as she told him what to do to me after the roofies knocked me on my ass. She'd even arranged a distraction to separate me from Kody and Dallas, so it was going to be, in her words, *too easy*.

I shuddered as the recording ended, and Kody's arm tightened around me like an iron band.

On the back of the image of me—the one where I was drugged out of my fucking mind and half-dead with a bloody nose—my stalker's familiar handwriting delivered a message I'd never fucking forget.

BE. MORE. CAREFUL.

"This is…" I croaked, swallowing to try and clear my voice. "This is too much right now. I think I need to sleep or something."

Steele nodded, gathering all the creepy shit up and dumping it back into the box it'd come in. "We should get this all to the police anyway," he commented, giving Archer a pointed look.

The brooding asshole just gave a shrug. "For all the fucking help they've been, sure." He shifted his attention to Kody. "Take Princess Danvers up to her room and make sure she doesn't fucking faint or something. I'm going to run another security check and make sure none of our feeds have been hacked again."

"Yes, boss," Kody agreed, scooping me up in his arms as he stood, like I was his damsel in distress. As much as I hated feeling so helpless, this time I really had been. All the self-defense classes in the world couldn't protect me against my own stupidity.

Kody took his task seriously, helping me when I declared I needed to shower before I could get into bed. I was so weak with the aftereffects of all the drugs in my system that I couldn't do anything except lean against the vanity while he stripped me down and placed me in the shower.

He got in with me too, but he kept his boxers on and just gently washed me with my soap and shampooed my hair for me. I sighed under his caring touches, and by the time he'd bundled me up in towels and carried me to my bed, I was almost asleep.

"Babe, I need to get you dressed," he whispered to me, kissing my cheek sweetly and stroking his fingertips down my neck. "Can you sit up?"

"No," I mumbled. "I'm fine like this."

Like this was just wrapped in a damp towel with another around my hair. Oh well, that's what beds had blankets for, wasn't it?

Kody chuckled softly. "Okay, let me just take the wet towels, though." He rolled me over until he could whip the damp fabric out of my bed, then tucked my blankets in around me like I was a human burrito. I wasn't even objecting; I just let it happen without offering any assistance whatsoever.

"I'm going to grab your hairbrush," he informed me with a kiss to my forehead. "I'll be right back."

I mumbled an incoherent response, but he was back again before I knew it. He lay on the bed beside me, gently brushing my wet, tangled hair with slow strokes, and I let myself drift back into sleep.

I was home. I was safe. That was all that mattered.

Murdering stalkers could go fuck themselves.

CHAPTER 36

I don't know how long I slept for, but when I woke again, my whole room was dark and the warm place beside me where Kody had been lying was empty. Yawning, I sat up and pushed my hair off my face. It was dry, which told me it had to have been *hours* since I'd fallen asleep. My hair didn't dry quickly, that was for sure.

Something moved in the darkness of my room, and a small shriek escaped my throat before I could get a grip on myself. It was my fucking reflection. Just my reflection in the dark mirror above my dresser.

Fucking hell.

Footsteps thumped outside my room, and the door burst open, spilling warm, golden light into my bedroom along with a broad-shouldered man.

"What is it?" Archer demanded. "What happened? Are you okay?"

He kicked the door shut and crossed over to where I sat in a pile of blankets wearing nothing but my freshly washed and tangle-free hair to cover my nudity.

"I'm fine," I replied, feeling like a total fucking moron for screaming at my own goddamn reflection. "I just thought I saw something, but...I didn't."

Archer was barely listening to me, though, as he sat on the side of my bed and took my wrist in his hand to check my pulse. But I snatched my hand away and scowled at him.

"I'm *fine*, Archer. My pulse is racing because I just scared the shit out of myself when I saw my own reflection in the dark." It killed me to admit that to him, and the slow rise of his brow and twitch of his lips only made me scowl harder. "Yeah, fucking real funny. Asshole. What time is it anyway?"

"Uh, around two in the morning, I think," he replied in that low, husky voice of his. "Something like that."

I blinked a couple of times. I'd been asleep for almost fifteen hours.

"Kody needed to go and take care of something for me," he said, answering the needy question I hadn't wanted to actually ask out loud. "He should be back soon, though. Or I can go get Steele to stay with you?"

Sliding back down under my blankets and tucking them under my armpits, I sighed at the awkwardness in his voice. "Or you could just man up and stay with me yourself," I muttered, mostly under my breath.

He didn't reply for a moment, then shifted his position to peer down at me with a frown. "Would you want that?"

My voice dried up, and I felt like someone had just turned a spotlight on me. Crap. But still, it shouldn't have been a hard question. Not after everything we'd just gone through.

"Lie down or don't, D'Ath," I snapped instead. "Just quit hovering. You're making me anxious."

He huffed a short laugh, and I expected him to leave my room and get Steele to come in and cuddle me, holding me tight and reassuring me that I was safe with them.

But to my surprise, he just kicked off his jeans and crawled under my blankets in nothing but his boxer briefs and black T-shirt.

Oh shit. I'm naked under here!

He shifted around, beating one of my spare pillows into the shape he wanted, before eventually getting comfortable on his side facing me.

"Happy?" he asked, his voice a rough growl of frustration and amusement.

I couldn't help the smug-as-fuck smile spreading over my face. "Calm down, sunshine. You're just lying in bed with me. I'm not forcefully prying that bad-boy bullshit out of your personality with pliers."

"May as well be," he grumbled, but even in the darkness of my room, I could see the small smile playing across his lips. "Now shut up and sleep if that's what we're doing."

I let the subject drop, closing my eyes and trying *really* hard to let sleep reclaim me. But...it just wasn't so easy to fall back asleep after already sleeping for fifteen hours. Especially when there was someone else in the bed that I was all kinds of hyperaware of.

"Princess," Archer groaned when I shifted my position for about the thousandth time. "Stop fucking wriggling around." He reached out, hooking one of those big hands of his around my waist, and hauled me backward against his body.

We both fucking froze this time.

"Are you—"

"Yup," I replied, my voice a tense squeak. "Naked. Yep, sure am."

I expected him to drop his grip on me like I was made of liquid magma, but he didn't—and that in itself shocked me more than anything else he'd done so far. Instead, his fingers flexed against my bare stomach, and his leg shifted to cover mine.

"Well, still," he muttered, "go to sleep."

I bit my lip, staring into the darkness of my bedroom and trying not to shiver every time his breath exhaled over my bare shoulder. But fuck me, I was only human, and the sexual tension between us had been building for way too freaking long.

It sure as shit didn't help that my naked ass was pressed right

317

against his crotch, so there was no ignoring the way he was growing affected by my nakedness. I couldn't help myself; I wriggled my ass against his hardening cock.

"Kate," he growled in warning, "stop it. It's hard enough being in bed with you naked; don't start that shit."

I snickered briefly. "It sure is."

Archer released a sigh in a heavy exhale, his breath warming my skin just moments before his lips touched my neck. He kissed me once, gently, then gave me a sharp nip with his teeth. "Fucking behave, Kate. You just went through a majorly traumatic event, and you need to rest."

My breath caught in my throat and heat rushed to my pussy. "I rested all day," I replied, my voice just this side of a feline purr. "I don't want to behave anymore, and I don't think you want me to either." Reaching a hand behind me, I grabbed on to his hip, pulling him closer and clearing up any confusion over what I meant.

Archer let out a groan, then grabbed my hand and removed it from his hip. He placed it back in front of me, then used his arm to pin me tight to his body. "Go to fucking sleep, Kate."

I made a sound of frustration, turning my head just enough to see his face from the corner of my eye. "I can tell you one surefire way to get me sleepy," I told him in a breathy whisper. I was starting to feel all kinds of desperate due to the number of times I'd been rejected by him…but I *knew* he wanted me just as much. He was just caught up on some imagined drama and denying this thing between us as a result. Well, I was ready to push that resolve and see how long it'd take to crack.

"Fucking hell," he snapped, his hand coming up and grabbing my face in a tight hold. He turned my head enough that his lips could lock down on mine like he was drowning.

He dominated that kiss, like fucking *everything*, his lips claiming mine in a way that was leaving his mark all over my soul. I moaned into his kiss, trying to turn over to face him, but his arm held me tight, keeping my ass against his huge, hard length.

"Stop. Fucking. Wriggling," he commanded me when he released my mouth. His kisses trailed down the line of my neck, sucking and biting my skin in a savage way that was so distinctively *Archer* that it made my pussy clench with desire and intense arousal.

I bit my lip, not arguing back. Not yet, anyway. Not while his hand was stroking across my bare belly and creeping lower with every movement. My breath was coming in short, sharp gasps, but this time it was for a damn good reason. Maybe this wasn't exactly what the doctor meant when he'd told me to rest and *take it easy* for a few days, but fuck that dickhead. He wasn't living with three hotter than sin men who played my body like their own personal fuck toy. Or…two of them did. I was really, *really* hoping the third was about to join the party.

Archer's fingers brushed over my smooth mound, and the rumbling growl that came from his chest was almost enough to make me come. Almost. I was holding out for something more, though…

"Quit fucking teasing me, Sunshine," I told him with a frustrated moan. I bucked my hips against him, reminding him of just how hard his cock was against my ass. Only a thin layer of fabric separated us, and I was going out of my mind hoping it would just magically disappear.

Archer huffed a short laugh, his lips on the bend of my neck. "Be careful what you wish for, Princess." His fingers dipped lower, finding my wet heat and sinking inside me with one firm push.

A strangled cry left my throat, but before he could pull away, I clapped a hand over his, holding him there as I writhed on his fingers. "Fuck," I breathed as he pushed deeper, his palm flattening on my mound and grinding my clit.

"You like that, huh?" he whispered in my ear. As if he needed fucking confirmation.

"God yes," I groaned. "Fuck, I'm already so close."

My skin was sensitive all over, a remnant of the drugging, but that had manifested in something pretty epic when it came to Archer's hand on my pussy.

His fingers withdrew, but he wasn't going anywhere. His thumb found my clit and rubbed teasing circles around it until I was whimpering and squirming against him. When he finally decided he'd tortured me enough, he pushed two fingers back into me and gave my clit a firm rub in a way that made me cry out.

"Shh," he chuckled in my ear, wrapping his free hand, which had been under my pillow, over my mouth. "If you're too loud, Steele will think you're in trouble and come barging in here."

I whimpered but swallowed my words as he fucked me with his hand. I was tempted to tell him I was more than fine with Steele hearing us...even with him joining us. But something told me *Archer* wouldn't be okay with it, and right now? I needed him. Just him. I needed to break the glass cage he'd erected around me. Smash it to pieces and grind the shards to dust because I was done being kept at arm's length.

When he added a third finger, I was fucking done. I came hard, my screams muffled by his strong hand over my mouth while his soft kisses feathered over the skin of my throat.

When he peeled his hand off my face, my breath was coming in hard gasps and my whole body was jelly. Electric jelly.

Slowly the weak, boneless, post-orgasm feeling subsided, and I reached behind me, sliding my hand along Archer's hip to find his waistband. Because if he thought I was a one-and-done kinda girl, then he must have lost his sense of hearing over the last few weeks.

"Stop," he ordered me, grabbing my hand before I could make it under his waistband. His grip was tight enough to not be playful, and the cold, unpleasant sensation of rejection washed through me like a toxic spill.

I gritted my teeth to not snap back at him, but my anger was quickly washing away the delicious fuzziness of my arousal. I wrenched my wrist out of his grip and rolled over to face him.

"Don't fucking start, Madison Kate," he told me in a cold, emotionless voice. "I made you come, now you go the fuck to sleep."

My jaw fell open as I stared at him, but he just rolled onto his back to avoid my outraged glare.

Oh. Hell no.

"What is your fucking damage, D'Ath?" I snarled, sitting up and glaring down at him. Fuck he was so gorgeous, all scowling and broody, and it made my heart twist painfully. "Are you seriously going to pretend you aren't lying there harder than diamond right now?"

He cocked one brow at me with that insufferable asshole expression on his face. "Yes," he replied, cool as the Arctic. "Because I have something you seem to be so severely lacking in. Self-control."

Bang. Just like that. Shot straight through the fucking useless heart.

"Get out, Archer," I ordered him in a low, furious voice. "Just get the fuck out. I'm done with your stupid games."

His eyes narrowed at me like I was being unreasonable. Seriously? He was the one who just finger fucked me until I came and kissed me like I was the missing piece of his stained, broken soul. Then flipped the switch and decided I was nothing but a needy, desperate slut who was basically gagging for dick like an addict.

Yeah. I was the unreasonable one.

"Get. Out." I repeated the order, holding his eyes with my furious, hurt gaze. Fuck hiding from him; he deserved to see what he was doing to me. He needed to understand that every rejection, every backflip on those tender moments was breaking me down and soon I'd have nothing left to give.

Archer let out a frustrated sigh, sitting up and scrubbing a hand through his dark hair, ruffling it in a sexy kind of way that made me want to run my fingers through it. His face was pure frustration and irritation, though, and it only sparked my anger hotter.

"You're acting like a brat, Madison Kate," he told me in a voice dripping with condescension. "I'm not going to fuck you, so you're throwing a tantrum? Do you even hear yourself right now?"

Outrage rendered me speechless for a moment, and my mouth moved like a fish out of water. It only took a second to find my voice again, though.

"I'm throwing a so-called *tantrum* because you're giving me fucking whiplash with your split-personality bullshit. I'm fucking sick of it, Archer D'Ath. You clearly want me; you can't even hide it anymore, it's written all over your face every time you look at me. I think I've made it abundantly clear I want you too, despite the *thousands* of reasons why I shouldn't. So what's the fucking problem here? How is it okay to finger fuck me until I'm screaming, yet not okay to *actually* fuck me?"

"What's the problem?" he roared, leaping out of my bed in an explosion of rage. I'd finally cracked his bullshit exterior, and the raw, molten emotions were seeping out. "The *problem* is that you don't fucking know me, Kate! You don't know anything about me or what I've done. You have no fucking idea what you're dealing with."

My brows shot up, and surprise tempered my anger. "Maybe I don't need to know everything, Archer. Did you think about that? Maybe I'm a big girl who can make her own choices and have come to grips with the fact that I'm okay not knowing all your deep, dark secrets. Why the fuck should I need to know your worst sins if they don't involve me?"

Archer barked a cold and bitter laugh, shaking his head. My room was still so dark, and he wore the shadows like a cloak, a visual representation of his inner self. "Because they do." He stormed out of my room, slamming the door behind himself before I could formulate any kind of response.

I had nothing to say back, though, even if he had stayed. His words had frozen me in utter shock. What could he have possibly meant by that? Tears slid down my face unbidden, and my shoulders shook as the fight fled my body, leaving me hollow and alone.

I was only alone for a few minutes before Steele slipped into my room. He didn't speak as he climbed into my bed and wrapped his arms around me. Instead, he just held me and stroked my hair while I cried. Then I mentally berated myself for crying over a guy who didn't deserve my tears. Then eventually, I calmed down and relaxed in Steele's comforting hold.

I fell asleep again to his soft, comforting whisper in my ear, telling me all the creative ways we could hurt Archer for his bullshit. His suggestions ranged from amusing to downright scary, but just the fact that he was willing to suggest creative revenge on one of his best friends warmed me.

When I woke again, the sun was up and Steele was gone. The bed was still warm, though, and my second pillow dented from his head, so I doubted he'd been gone for long.

I stretched and yawned, climbing out of my cozy nest and making my way to the bathroom. The fentanyl overdose had still left me with a range of side effects, which the doctor had listed several times before I was discharged from the hospital.

Dizziness, tick. Tiredness, tick. Headaches, tick.

I groaned, rubbing my pounding head, and hunted in my vanity for some nice, safe nonprescription painkillers.

Nausea, tick. Feeling cold, tick.

Drug overdoses fucking sucked. It was safe to say I wasn't likely to experiment with anything much harder than weed or alcohol anytime soon. I washed my headache pills down with water from my tap, then cranked my shower. I'd just showered before going to bed, but sleeping for almost twenty-four hours took a toll and I was confident the hot steam would make me feel a million times more human.

After I finished showering, I dressed warmly to try and combat the light shivers running through my muscles. Black jeans, long sleeve T-shirt, and a hoodie that I'd stolen from one of the boys. I didn't even know whose it was anymore, but I wasn't fussy. All boy hoodies were good in my book.

Stuffing my feet into a pair of Ugg boots, I scuffed my way downstairs to find where Steele and Kody were. Archer could go take a flying leap off a mountaintop for all I cared. The kitchen was empty, but my espresso machine was on and the intoxicating scent of freshly ground beans filled the air.

I shuffled over to it, but the faint sound of raised voices caught my attention before I could start making my coffee. Probably for the best, as coffee on a seriously empty stomach wasn't going to go down amazingly well.

As I moved closer to the window, the voices became louder, so I peered out to see what was going on. All I could see was the back of Steele's hoodie and fragments of Archer, but they were clearly arguing with someone in a seriously heated way. With Kody? Surely not.

Abandoning my search for food and caffeine, I headed back through the house and out the front door, pausing when I took in the scene before me. Kody was there, but it wasn't him that they'd been arguing with. And all of them fell silent when they saw me standing there. No points for guessing who they'd been talking about, I guessed.

"What's going on?" I asked, sliding my gaze over Steele, who wore his hood up and a cold, deadly expression on his face. Archer, I didn't bother looking at. He was already dead to me. But Kody had his gun out, aimed at Zane. The gang leader was the only one of the group of five—Cass was slouched against his motorbike with his hand loosely resting on a gun of his own—meeting my eyes.

On the white marble steps of the house, just two steps lower than where I stood, a bloody lump of meat sat. It took me a hot second to recognize it for what it was…a heart. Probably human.

"What…the fuck…is going on?" I repeated, staring at the blood-covered organ in horror.

"A gift," Zane replied when my boys all remained silent and stoic. "From your stalker. One of Charon's boys was found last night dumped outside The Laughing Clown and missing his heart…but I guess now we know where that went."

My already-nauseated stomach roiled, and I swallowed the rapidly increasing saliva in my mouth. This wasn't the fucking time to vomit.

"Was this the Wraith from the recording?" I directed my question to Steele—the most levelheaded of my boys—and he jerked a short nod. Apparently my stalker hadn't been satisfied with just taking out Drew for her premeditated drugged rape attempt.

I took a couple of steadying breaths, fighting back the looming panic clawing at my mind. But seriously, was it too much to ask for just one day of normalcy?

"So why are you here?" I asked Zane directly. "I get the feeling this violates whatever bullshit *agreement* you all have."

He gave me a tight smile and a head dip of acknowledgment. "It does," he replied, "but some things are too important to sit on for long. Especially when the correct channels of communication are being ignored." He shot this last part to his brother, who just scowled and folded his thickly muscled arms over his chest.

"This has nothing to do with you, Zane," Archer snapped, his voice like a thunder crack. "I won't tell you again. Get off my fucking property before you give Cass an instant promotion."

The Reapers' second-in-command raised his hands in a mockery of surrender and barked a harsh laugh. "I'm good with my current position, thanks. Besides, I'm with Zane on this one. She deserves to know." He jerked his head toward me, and my brows shot up.

"Deserves to know *what*?" I demanded, parking my hands on

my hips and doing everything possible to ignore the heart two steps below me.

Archer was ignoring me, though. So were Kody and Steele. That in itself filled me with near suffocating dread.

"Leave now," Archer ordered Zane. "This is between Madison Kate and me. No one else."

Zane's lips twisted in a cruel smile. "If that were the truth, I'd happily give my apologies and leave. But it's not. It *can't* be between the two of you when *she* knows nothing about it. 'Cause she doesn't, does she? It's so fucking obvious it'd almost be funny—if it wasn't Deb's daughter you were hurting."

"Someone tell me what the fuck you're all talking about before I start shooting people myself," I snapped, glaring at anyone who'd look at me. Spoiler alert—none of them would, except Zane.

"Don't fucking do this, Zane," Archer warned his brother. "You *really* don't want to make us your enemies, and you know it."

The Reapers' leader hesitated. For whatever reason, he was afraid of his little brother.

"Zane," I barked. "Start fucking talking."

"Do it, boss," Cass added in that rough, broken-gravel voice of his. "She's gotta know."

Zane shot Archer another look, but this time it was full of regret and resignation. "Sorry, Brother. You brought this mess on yourself. Maybe you'll think twice next time an in-debt businessman offers to sell his daughter."

Time. Fucking. Stopped.

Steele's shoulders slumped and his face dropped, his hood hiding his real reaction.

Kody breathed a curse, his hand tightening on his gun but not letting his aim leave Zane for even a second. Not even while his panicked gaze shot to me.

But Archer? He may as well have been made from stone for all the emotion he showed.

Zane pulled a stack of folded papers from his jacket pocket and tossed them toward me, letting them hit the steps right beside the bloody heart.

"It's all there if you want to fact-check it. Your father sold you—and your trust fund—just a week after you were arrested." He paused, looking disgusted. It was his next words that rocked me to my core, though. Words that would become printed across my mind like a cattle brand.

"Congratulations, *Mrs. D'Ath*. Welcome to the family."

BONUS SCENE
THE NIGHT MK WAS DRUGGED

Archer

Bang!

The chair Zane had thrown hit the wall, splintering into dozens of pieces. At least it was just a chair, though, and my brother was still respecting the rules of neutral territory. For now, anyway. The sooner we broke up this party, the better.

"Okay, I think this was too ambitious," I interjected before anyone could pull a gun and get us *all* killed. "Charon, you've said what you came to say. Perhaps it's best you leave Zane to think it over?"

Swear to fucking god, the only time I ever felt the need to play the impartial mediator was when I was stuck between the two of them. Biggest mistake of my life was becoming involved in my father's gang and dragging my best friends along with me. Despite everything we'd done to cut ties, we couldn't seem to escape.

A tense moment hung in the air, both gang leaders glaring death at one another. Then Charon gave a cold smile and nodded my way. "Archer. I've said it once and I'll say it again: the Reapers should have been yours."

With that uncalled-for and unwanted opinion, he gave my brother a sarcastic salute, then nodded to his second to follow him out of the meeting room. Shit-stirring prick.

Kody burst through the door right on Charon's departure, concern etched all over his face. No doubt he'd heard the chair hit the wall and came to make sure blood hadn't been shed.

"We good?" he asked, squinting with suspicion at Zane.

"Yeah, all good," I replied before my older brother could spark a fight with Kody while he was already on edge. "Just more of the same." Charon and Zane were permanently trying to push their agendas on me, since I held the keys to their illegal activity successes.

Steele pushed off the wall, where he'd been casually slouched for the duration of the meeting. "Where's Hellcat?"

Kody tipped his head toward the door. "Playing pool with Dallas and Bree. She was worried..." He gave me a pointed look, as if to say she'd been worried about *me*. Yeah right. More like she'd sent him to check on Steele, since even a blind man could see how fast they were falling in love.

Gritting my teeth against the sourness of that thought, I scrubbed a hand over my short beard. "Right, well. We're done here, so we should—"

"Hold up, Little Brother," Zane interjected with a pensive look on his face. Shrewd fuck that he was, he clearly had something up his sleeve. "Now that we have privacy, I'd like to discuss this little arrangement you have with Danvers."

My spine stiffened and ice formed in my gut. That was the *last* thing I wanted to discuss with him. "None of your business. Stay the fuck out of it."

Kody and Steele stayed silent, but the mood shifted. I was well aware of their feelings regarding my contract with Danvers, but I'd also made it perfectly clear that it was *my* contract and *my* problem to solve. No one else's.

Zane snapped his fingers, shaking his head. "See, that's where we disagree, Little Brother. I think it *is* very much my business... Deb would have wanted me to look out for her little princess, don't you think? It would be remiss of me not to tell the girl that she's been *sold*. Like a prize goat. She ought to know that the devil down the hall is holding her invisible leash."

I swallowed hard. Yes, she ought to know... but was I going to tell her? Hell no. Not now, not *ever*. I hadn't taken that contract with Samuel for a sex slave; I'd done it to save her. Okay, sure, maybe I'd also wanted to piss her off a little too, but that paled in comparison to the consequences *now*. Everything had gone too far for me to come clean.

"You have no idea what you're talking about, Zane," I growled, holding on to my emotions with an iron grip. He was fishing. He was trying to get under my skin. If he had any kind of concrete proof, I'd have heard about it by now... or he would have used it as blackmail.

Cass, Zane's six-foot-five powerhouse of a second in charge, gave a tiny head shake of warning. Meanwhile, Zane responded to me with a cruel smile. "You sure about that?"

Was I? No. But no way could I show him even a fraction of weakness. I knew what he wanted already. The same thing he and Charon had just been arguing over. I'd refused to choose sides. It wasn't a subject I could afford to flex on—my agreement with Hades trumped both Reapers' and Wraiths' aspirations.

Folding my arms over my chest, I leveled a hard glare at my brother. "Do I need to remind you what a bad idea it would be to threaten me, Zane?" In the blink of an eye, both Steele and Kody had their guns drawn on Zane, illustrating my point. We'd freed ourselves from his gang with *force*. If necessary, we would turn that force on him.

Cass didn't reach for his gun, confident that we were bluffing. He was right, but the flicker of doubt in Zane's face said he wasn't so sure.

"I think it's time you left the party, don't you?" Kody suggested, his gun hand steady and his expression flat. "Cass can stay to keep your crew on their best behavior." Because he was sane. Reasonable. A much better leader than Zane ever would be... largely because he had no desire to lead.

Zane spat an insult under his breath, shooting death glares at both Kody and Steele before sneering my way. "You'll live to regret this, Little Brother. That's not a threat—it's a promise."

He stomped out, Cass following silently behind him, and my friends put their weapons away. Was it technically a rule-break to pull them in the first place? Yes. But they hadn't *fired* any shots, so I was confident Hades would let it slide.

My breath rushed out of my lungs, my shoulders sagging. I was so fucking tired.

"Arch, you need to—" Kody started, but I cut him off with a sharp look.

"He won't leave it alone," Steele agreed, ignoring my mood. "Zane is like a shark who smells blood in the water. Maybe he doesn't have anything more than speculation right now, but how long will that last? He's not as stupid as you like to think."

He was right. I just didn't want to admit it.

"I'll handle it," I muttered. "It's my mess." And no one else's... except *hers*. My wife. She had no idea, and every minute that passed with her ignorance only dug my grave deeper. Fuck. "I need a drink. Kody, make sure your girl is still alive."

Your girl. Those words tasted like poison on my tongue.

The three of us left the meeting room, making our way over to the bar. Try as I might, I couldn't stop scanning the room, searching for her. She was a cursed addiction for me. I hated it so fucking much, yet I did nothing to stop it.

"MK!" a girl shouted from somewhere near the bathrooms, and my attention shifted her way without even a conscious thought. It was Bree, and she looked like she'd been crying.

"MK? Where are you?" Her puffy, red eyes scanned the crowd with an edge of panic.

Wait.

"Where is she?" I barked, storming over to the sniffling girl. "Where's Kate?"

"I-I don't know," Bree whimpered, trying and failing to jerk her arm free of my grip. I didn't even remember grabbing her. "I don't know. Help me find her?"

"What happened?" Kody demanded at my shoulder. "I left her playing pool with you and Dallas."

Bree nodded, her eyes watery again. "There was... Shit happened, okay? I got jealous and thought... It doesn't matter. Dallas came after me, and then by the time I realized I was over-reacting, she was just *gone*. Help me find her? Please? I have a bad feeling..."

That was all I needed to hear. I blazed through the room, des-perately searching for that pink-haired pain in my ass. Several times I thought I'd spotted her, only to discover it was a blond under colored lights. *Fuck.*

Furious and *scared*, I whirled around and ran straight into that dick from SGU. The one who'd tried to take my wife on a date.

"Whoa, bro, watch where you're going," he sneered as I shoulder-checked him.

My hand tightened into a fist at my side, the urge to vent my emotions on his face palpable, but I restrained myself as I went out on a limb. "Sorry," I gritted, insincere at best. "I'm looking for Madison Kate. Have you seen her?"

The football jerk eyed me like he was considering lying, then sighed. "Yeah, maybe five minutes ago? She's pretty wasted, so you should make sure she's okay."

Wasted? She had been dead sober and not drinking when I'd left her. There was no way she'd gone from zero to a hundred *that* fast. "Where?" I demanded. "Where did you see her?"

He gestured toward the exit. "She was heading that way. Getting some air, probably."

Panic rippled through me. "And you just *let her go alone*?" I practically bellowed the question, grabbing the front of his shirt.

"She's hardly alone, dickhead! Look how many cops and private security there are around this place. One of them would have had eyes on her. Check with them." He shoved me away and I let him. I couldn't waste time grinding him into the carpet when Kate was out there alone...*wasted*.

He was right about the cops stationed at all exits, but that didn't mean any of them cared enough to keep her safe. With that thought screaming through my head, I rushed out into the parking lot.

"Kate?" I called out, my voice rough with fear. "Madison Kate, are you out here?"

The parking lot wasn't empty, but I ignored the couple making out against a car as I strode through. Was she out here somewhere? Vulnerable and alone? I could fucking *kill* Dallas and Bree for leaving her.

"Madison Kate!" I yelled again, flinching when my own voice echoed back at me.

Crunching boots on gravel made me whip around, but it was Kody running toward me with a frown etched on his face. "She's out here somewhere," he called out. "Cops on the door reckon she was drunk, but that isn't—"

"I know!" I snapped. "She wasn't fucking drinking. She's not that stupid."

"Madison Kate!" Kody bellowed, his head tipped as he listened for a response. I strained my own ears, desperate to hear *something* in response. Right when I was about to lose my shit...I heard something.

A muffled scream.

Fuck.

"Did you hear that?" I whacked Kody's arm, already moving in the direction that scream had come from. "Madison Kate! Where are you?"

For a moment, I thought I'd imagined it. Then she screamed again, and my gaze zeroed in on a familiar car at the end of the row. Steele's car. Why the fuck would she be in his car? And screaming? It didn't make sense, but I was already pounding gravel as I closed the distance.

"Kate?" I exclaimed, frantically searching through the windows. Her screams were louder now, more definite. It was her; I was certain of it. But where the fuck was she? I couldn't see her in—

Oh shit.

"The trunk," I gasped aloud. Not thinking, I tried to open it to release her only to realize it was locked and I didn't have the keys. "Steele! Keys!"

But Steele wasn't out here with us. Kody sprinted back toward the bar, but that left me alone with the car...*and her screams.* Fucking hell, I had to get her out. I couldn't just stand there and wait. I needed to save her.

Frantic, I yanked on the trunk, trying to force it open, but when that didn't work, I went for the driver's side door and pulled my gun. One bullet through the window shattered the glass, and I reached inside to pop the trunk lock.

Madison Kate's screams doubled in volume as I lifted the trunk, and cold sweat ran down my spine. How long had she been in there? And why? Kody told me after Riot Night that she was claustrophobic, so I could only imagine...

"Princess, Kate, it's me." I tried to reassure her as I lifted her from the trunk. She seemed totally out of her mind with terror, though, thrashing and howling like her skin was on fire. Her nose was bloody and sweat coated every inch of her skin, and I collapsed onto the ground with her trembling body in my arms.

"Please stop," she moaned, shaking her head in panic. "Please,

please, please, make it stop. Get them off, get them off me, get them *off*."

Confusion gripped me as I ran my hands over her, searching for whatever she wanted *off*, but it wasn't until her cries turned to mumbles that I realized what was going on. She was delusional, her eyes rolling back to the whites as she continued moaning and begging.

"Princess, hang in there. We've got you, baby," I implored, then looked around when I heard Kody approaching once more with Steele tight on his heels. "She's been drugged, maybe overdosing, I don't know."

"Paramedic is right behind me," he replied in a gruff, worried voice.

"Good thinking," I replied, swallowing hard. I'd totally forgotten there was a pair of paramedics inside the bar. Technically they were off duty, but they had come straight from the fight and likely had all their gear.

"Spiders," Madison Kate whimpered. "Get the spiders off me. Hurts so much. Please, get them off. Please!" A gut-wrenching sob tore from her chest and tears streamed from her sightless eyes, absolutely killing me.

"You're okay, Princess, I swear. They're not real. You're imagining them."

"It's no use, bro, she can't hear you." Kody moved aside as the elderly paramedic—Joseph, I think his name was—knelt down with a syringe ready.

I hesitated, my grip around Madison Kate tightening. "Narcan?"

The guy nodded, paying me little attention as he swiped my wife's arm with an alcohol swab, then jabbed her with the anti-opioid drug. "That will help, but she might need more depending on how big of a dose she took. Is she a regular user?"

That question rocked me. "What? No. She didn't do this to herself!"

The guy just shrugged. "If you say so. We see this a lot, so forgive me for assuming. I'll call an ambulance." He straightened up, handing the empty syringe to his partner, who just scowled down at the fragile woman in my lap. Judgmental prick probably thought she was a junkie too.

"So many legs," she mumbled, tremors wracking through her body. "They keep biting me. Make them stop, make the spiders stop."

My heart in my throat, I smoothed her hair back, whispering reassurances. Ever so slightly, she started to relax under my touch. It gave me a glimmer of hope.

"You need to get her to the hospital," the second paramedic said. I totally ignored him, though, continuing to whisper to Madison Kate, trying with all my might to calm her from whatever horrors the drugs were inflicting on her mind.

Her sobbing ebbed, but in its place came totally uncontrollable—almost seizure-like—tremors. Enough that her teeth chattered and I feared she might swallow her tongue.

"Hey, hey, hey, shhh, come on, baby girl, don't do this," I whispered in her ear, then pressed a desperate kiss to her cheek. "Kate, baby, come on, stay with me. We've got you. We've got you. We've got you." *And I am never letting go...*

I had to tell her the truth. When she recovered from this—and she would, because my princess was strong—I would tell her the truth. I'd tell her everything and accept the consequences, because fuck me...she deserved better.

Better than this.

Better than me.

But still, I could never let her go...even if she hated me for it.

READ ON FOR A PEEK AT THE NEXT BOOK
IN THE WORLD OF MADISON KATE

CHAPTER 1

Archer

"Congratulations, *Mrs. D'Ath*. Welcome to the family."

My brother's words hung in the air like a death knell. Damn, they were exactly that because there was no way in hell she would forgive me for this.

I couldn't look at her. My head refused to turn and see what was sure to be horror and betrayal passing over her beautiful face. I didn't need to. Not when Kody's tortured expression said it all as his gun arm lowered and his eyes pleaded with her.

She wasn't looking back at him, though. I knew her better than I knew myself some days. The staggering silence that followed Zane's words told me how she would react to this new development. She wouldn't yell or scream or punch me…no matter how much I hoped she would.

From the corner of my eye, I caught her stooping to swipe the folded papers off the step. She didn't look at them, just stuffed them into her back pocket and gave a short nod.

"Thank you for letting me know," she told my brother, and the ice in her voice was like a jagged blade straight through my heart.

Zane's brows shot up in surprise, his eyes shifting to meet mine once more. He didn't know her, though. He couldn't sense the cold, acidic fury coursing faster through her veins with every passing second. He hadn't witnessed her highs and lows, and he had no idea that this was worse than all of those lows combined.

I was fucked. Totally, completely, utterly fucked.

But I would still do it again. Given the same choice, offered the same opportunity to buy her, to own her and all her assets? Yeah, I'd do it again. In a fucking heartbeat.

"MK, it's not what it sounds like," Kody started to say, his voice threaded with panic and his gun at his side, forgotten, as he implored the girl he'd fallen in love with.

She wasn't listening. The second Zane had dropped his truth bomb, she'd shut us out. All of us... Because regardless of the fact that it was me who'd purchased her like a fucking prize cow at market, both Kody and Steele were complicit. They'd known all about it, about how deeply intertwined our lives now were, and they'd kept my secret.

In that light, their betrayal had to be so much more cutting. They'd made her care for them... They'd fallen for her in return. That, surely, was a bigger crime than what I'd done.

At least I've never fucked her.

Anger burned through me as I eyed my brother, ignoring everyone else for a minute. They'd directly violated the rules of our agreement, and crimes like that couldn't go unpunished. I'd proven my point to Zane over and over, but apparently all it took for him to forget those bloody lessons was a pair of great tits and some silken pink hair.

"Boss," Cass said quietly in his damaged voice, "we should go."

Smart move. Cass had known me since I was a kid; he'd been there as my grandfather put me through training. Hell, he'd been through it himself. He—even more so than Zane—understood what I was capable of. He'd sensed the shift in my mood and recognized the impending danger.

Zane gave me a small, cruel smirk, and a growl of anger burned through me. He claimed he was doing this for some debt he owed Kate's dead mother? I called bullshit. He was doing this to hurt me, and it was working. That motherfucker.

Cass and Zane climbed back onto their motorcycles, kicking the engines over. Kody shot me a confused look, and I knew exactly what he was asking me. Was I going to let them leave unharmed? Probably not. But it was more fun to leave the illusion of freedom, only to shoot out their tires right before they exited the property. Then? Well...then I daresay my big brother was well overdue for a lesson on exactly why I was a bigger, badder wolf in Shadow Grove than anyone else.

"Wait," Madison Kate shouted, her voice like a bucket of ice water over my bloodthirsty plans. She stepped over the bloody heart—the one stalker gift I was glad to see—and approached the two Reaper leaders. "I'm coming with you."

She didn't wait for permission, just climbed onto the back of Cass's bike like she fucking belonged there, linking her hands around his waist in a way that sparked my anger to murderous levels.

Cass was a fucking dead man.

"Hellcat, don't do this," Steele pleaded, his silent resolve cracking. "Don't fucking run from us. Please, baby, you need to hear us out."

For a moment, I thought he'd got through to her. Those violet-blue eyes of hers flickered with pain—and any emotion was better than the cool mask shuttering her true feelings away. But as quickly as it came, it shut back down. Her eyes flicked away from Steele like he no longer existed in her world.

"Go," she ordered Cass in a whip-crack voice. "There's nothing left for me here."

He was smarter than that, though—certainly smart enough that he hesitated and his brow creased ever so slightly with indecision.

"Boss?" he asked Zane, seeking direction.

"You can't be fucking serious!" Kody exploded, shaking his head in disbelief. "Arch, do something. You know you can."

Zane met my gaze, his lips curled in a smug grin of victory, and sour hatred filled my body. I wanted to kill him so fucking bad. The only reason he was still breathing was that he served a purpose in running the Reapers. That usefulness was fast running out.

"MK, come on," Steele tried again, taking two steps closer to where she perched on the back of Cass's motorcycle. "*Please*, trust us. Don't run."

"Archer!" Kody snapped. "Say something. Fucking anything."

But what the fuck could I say? Zane hadn't lied. He hadn't even misled her, although I had no idea what was in those papers, what proof he'd provided. But it didn't matter, did it? Money had changed hands, her piece-of-shit father had had his bad debts cleared and his life saved. All it'd cost him was his only child.

What a bargain.

When I said nothing, Kate's curiosity won out. I'd known it would. Her eyes met mine for one tense, soul-destroying moment. Her expression was shuttered, her pain and fury tucked carefully away behind a mask of indifference, but I knew it was there. She couldn't hide from me.

"Let her go," I finally said, holding her gaze and giving away nothing in my own. Two peas in a pod, we were. A match forged in the blood-drenched bowels of hell.

"What?" Kody exclaimed at the same time that Steele shouted a curse.

I let a small smile touch my lips because if there was one thing I was good at, it was getting under my wife's skin. All the better now that she knew the truth. We were married and had been for over a year.

Happy belated anniversary, babe.

"Let her go," I repeated, bleeding smug satisfaction into my smile and locking down all the howling pain inside me. "She knows she can't escape me forever."

This provoked a reaction from her, just as I'd expected. It was small, just a fractional lift of her brows, but the message she conveyed was clear.

Bring it on, motherfucker.

The roar of motorcycle engines filled the air as Zane and Cass took off, carrying my wife with them, and I did nothing to stop them. My vicious plans were abandoned as quickly as they'd been formed because there was no way I'd shoot out their tires when she was involved.

They knew it too, those bastards. Kate was their shield, and they'd keep her close to save themselves from my retaliation. That knowledge both infuriated me and eased my mind. As badly as I wanted to tear carnage through the Reapers for this breach of the rules, for this literal act of war against me...I couldn't. They'd keep her safe, guarded, protected, and that was something I'd failed miserably at recently.

Maybe she would be better off with Zane and his gang of criminal misfits, at least until we could neutralize the threats against her.

The three of us stood there in silence as the two bikes disappeared through the main gates of our estate; then Kody turned to me with an accusation clearly written all over his face.

I closed my eyes but didn't flinch. I knew what was coming well before his fist met my cheek, snapping my head back and making my ears ring.

I deserved that. And more.

"This is on you, Arch," he seethed, glaring daggers as I squinted back at him and dabbed my lip. He'd split it open, but I'd wager he wanted to do a whole lot worse. "This whole fucking mess could have been avoided if you'd been honest with her from day fucking one!"

I gave him a casual shrug, totally at odds with the screaming turmoil inside me. "Well, you know what they say about crying over spilled milk. She'll get over it."

This time I didn't see the punch coming—despite how badly I deserved it—because it came from Steele and was delivered solidly to my kidneys. He may not have any interest in fighting competitively, but he'd trained with Kody and me for years. That fucker could make a punch hurt.

"You fucked up, and you dragged us down with you," Steele growled, his fists clenched like he wanted to keep hitting me. "And you're not fooling fucking anyone with this blasé attitude, Arch. Just because you refused to fuck her doesn't mean you haven't fallen just as hard."

I grunted but couldn't force the denial past my lips. He was wrong, though. I'd kept her at arm's length because I'd known this day was coming. They should have done the same.

The two of them gave me disgusted, disappointed looks and stalked back into the mansion—my mansion—without another word. Understandable, considering there was literally nothing else to say. Nothing could take back what I'd done over a year earlier, and nothing could fix the betrayal and heartbreak Kate must be feeling now.

I sank down on the front steps, sitting my ass right beside the bloody lump of meat which had once sustained a rapist Wraith. Her stalker and I seemed to be more alike than I'd originally realized, considering I'd sent Kody out during the night to kill that piece of shit Wraith himself.

Scrubbing a hand over my scruffy stubble, I released a heavy sigh.

The cat was out of the bag, and now I needed to figure out where we went from here. Did I even really want to bring her home?

AUTHOR'S NOTE

Hey, you! How are you? Your Kindle still alive? I hope so. They're valuable things and not to be thrown across the room lightly. Besides…if you've been reading me for a while, you know I've done waaaaay worse before! But seriously, though. How badly do you wanna junk punch Archer right now? Don't worry, MK feels the same way!

I know lately my author's notes have had a little of the thunder-cloud sort of vibe, so I'll keep this one a little more upbeat.

This book has been one of my absolute favorites to write yet. The story just flowed out so easily, even though it went a solid 20,000 words over my "goal" word count. I love all of these characters so freaking hard; it's seriously just so enjoyable to write them!

A serious shout-out this time, though, to John Snow. No…not Jon Snow. JoHn Snow…the multitalented other half to Kaydence Snow (author extraordinaire), who created a brand-spanking-new writing program for us to use. John, dude bro, you killed it. If not for you, this book would have taken double the amount of time to write!

I don't think I'll find many people to disagree when I say that 2020 fucking sucked. Like…seriously fucking sucked. But (so far) we're still here, and we're still standing. What doesn't kill us makes us stronger.

In the meantime, I'm doing my best to push out some awesome stories for you to escape the bullshit of the world. I'm challenging myself with every paragraph, every dialogue, and every chapter to step it up and improve my craft, and I really hope you agree after reading *Liar*.

So stay tuned... *Fake* will (hopefully) blow your fucking socks off. Or maybe just your knickers... ★shrug★. Thanks for sticking with me! You, my readers, make this life so rewarding for a pink-haired weirdo talking to the voices in her head all day long.

XXX

ABOUT THE AUTHOR

Tate James is a *USA Today* bestselling author of contemporary romance and romantic suspense, with occasional forays into fantasy, paranormal romance, and urban fantasy. She was born and raised in Aotearoa (New Zealand) but now lives in Australia with her husband and their adorable crotchfruit.

She is a lover of books, booze, cats, and coffee and is most definitely not a morning person. Tate is a bit too sarcastic, swears far too much for polite society, and definitely tells too many dirty jokes.